The Urbana Free Library

To renew materials call
217-367-4057

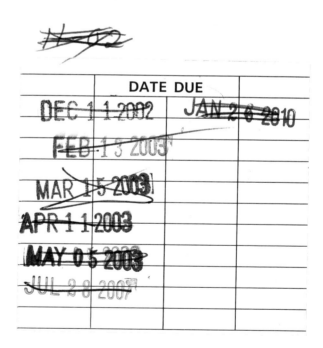

	DATE DUE	
DEC 1 1 2002	JAN 2 6 2010	
FEB 1 3 2003		
MAR 1 5 2003		
APR 1 1 2003		
MAY 0 5 2003		
JUL 2 8 2007		

EDITED AND WITH AN INTRODUCTION
BY LENA LENČEK AND GIDEON BOSKER

PHOTOGRAPHS BY
MITTIE HELLMICH

escape
STORIES OF GETTING AWAY

MARLOWE & COMPANY
NEW YORK

Published by
Marlowe & Company
An Imprint of Avalon Publishing Group Incorporated
161 William Street, 16th Floor
New York, NY 10038

Library of Congress Cataloging-in-Publication Data
Escape : stories of getting away /
edited by Lena Lenček and Gideon Bosker.
p. cm.
ISBN 1-56924-526-6
1. Adventure stories.   2. Escapes—
Literary collections.   I. Lenček, Lena
II. Bosker, Gideon.
PN6071.A38 E83 2002
808.88'8—dc21
2002019027

9 8 7 6 5 4 3 2 1
DESIGNED BY PAULINE NEUWIRTH, NEUWIRTH & ASSOCIATES

Printed in the United States of America
Distributed by Publishers Group West

To our families . . . and all the
other survivors of narrow escapes

Escape

It comes to me,

On the highway late at night,

When only lovers and loners,

Dare to peregrinate—

Lonely as falcons,

Content in motion

Commotion at a minimum,

Pursuing the dream.

BY CHRISTOPHER DILASCIA

contents

INTRODUCTION: Escaping and Entering   xi

awakening   1
    ISAAC BABEL

verona: a young woman speaks   9
    HAROLD BRODKEY

the nightingales sing   18
    ELIZABETH PARSONS

from *the amazing adventures of kavalier & clay*   33
    MICHAEL CHABON

from *young winston's wars*   61
    WINSTON S. CHURCHILL

from *passing*   73
    NELLA LARSEN

desperate passage   93
    MICHAEL FINKEL

the man who loved islands   115
    D. H. LAWRENCE

from *journey into the whirlwind*   141
    EUGENIA SEMYONOVNA GINZBURG

the things they carried   159
TIM O'BRIEN

the barber's unhappiness   179
GEORGE SAUNDERS

baby's first step   201
JOHN UPDIKE

the son   211
IVAN BUNIN

jamaica   225
DAVID SCHICKLER

escape   241
GROVER AMEN

from *too late to turn back*   257
BARBARA GREENE

from *speak, memory*   273
VLADIMIR NABOKOV

the first time i saw paris   291
JOSEPH WECHSBERG

a view of exmoor   307
SYLVIA TOWNSEND WARNER

the key   315
ISAAC BASHEVIS SINGER

the zulu and the zeide   327
DAN JACOBSON

from *voices of marrakesh*   341
ELIAS CANETTI

BIBLIOGRAPHY   347
PERMISSIONS   349
ACKNOWLEDGMENTS   351
ABOUT THE CONTRIBUTORS AND EDITORS   352

To escape is human. We enter the world wet, salty, slicked with a coat of hemoglobin, kicking, screaming into life with the urgency of one kept too long from a feast which everyone else has long since joined. And yet, once there, we spend so much of life running off, figuratively and literally, to anywhere but here: to other places, other loves, other states of mind. Escape is not a place, but a border between the real and the imaginary, the fated and the invented, the routine and the fantastic. It hangs suspended, always, between two prepositions, "from" and "to," from something that imprisons, blunts opportunity, oppresses the will, suffocates the spirit; to the promise of redemption, the crackle of ecstatic engagement, intensity of feeling, pleasure, and the grace of reciprocal love. The yearning for silk, music, Eros, and all the bonbons of civilization is as primal as the urge to flee abuse, hunger, privation, and the claws of evil that threaten to snuff out the pilot light of human will. Paul Theroux, one of the great escape artists of our time, writes in *Sunrise with Seamonsters,* "We are born with the impulse to wonder and, eventually, to yearn for the world before the Fall."

Some of our oldest memories play on the theme of escape. No sooner do we learn to walk, then we're off shrieking "Chase me!" in a breathless game of tag that previews the full chromatic scale of emotions life's escapes will offer. Nightmares feature plots of heart-stopping pursuits that, in the morning, leave you wondering what terrified you more: the miscreant breathing down your neck, or your own legs, heavy, super-glued, and refusing to move? Remember the Spaghetti Westerns you used to watch? The hero's thumping flight over hill and dale, a posse of villains giving chase, the wind roaring, the wild tattoo of hoofbeats—and you, holding your breath, until, with a whoop of relief and glee, you see the hero duck into a narrow canyon as the heavies gallop past in a cloud of dust. (Substitute, as needed, in future variations on the theme, real and imaginary: cars, spaceships, psychopaths, killers, stalkers, taxmen, estranged spouses, and deadlines.)

Our entire lives can be written as chronicles of escapes: from parental supervision to the chaos and abandon of drugs, sex, and rock 'n' roll; from bourgeois self-control into the swirl of the Seven Deadly Sins; from the city to the country, and back again. Sometimes, the transition itself can provide that needed morphine for the imagination, chamomile and honey for the heart. Sometimes you need to lose yourself in a place beyond the reach of language and cultural landmarks, in religious transport, in the silent contemplation of art, in quiet reverie at some remote outpost of humanity, so that you can connect the indecipherable threads of consciousness that bind you to the past.

There are times, however, when life itself hangs in the balance—when escape is no longer a matter of elective evasion, but a brutal, emergency procedure that does not ask for a signature of consent on the bottom line. Our own parents—survivors of wars, revolutions, holocaust—spent the biologically best years of their lives in zones of escape. Their stories are of bombs dropping in the dead of night; fists hammering on the door; flight, in high-heeled pumps across snow-bound Alps; soldiers pulling refugees from train cars; shootings, corpses scattered under silent pines; children cowering behind a barred door as a doorbell rings suddenly at dusk.

Their narratives remind us that all "voluntary" forms of escape are just substitutes—delusional at that—for that one great escape we'll never be able to pull off. And yet, in the face of the inevitable, why not delude ourselves with the fiction of our own power to shape our destinies and mold the stream of life to fit the contours of our souls? Escape, at heart, is the prerequisite for entering alternative states of mind and heart, for occupying alien physical or emotional places that permit reflections that might not otherwise be possible. Although limited and contained by the perceptual thresholds that life makes possible, escaping and entering appear to offer that binary experiential optic that permits us to distinguish good from evil, light from dark, pleasure from pain. In the transition from one state, one frame of mind, or one place to another, escape offers the opportunity to compare and contrast what lies on either side of the gap. In between what has been left behind and what has been entered, the gristle and ambiguities of life lie exposed. That, in essence, is the "mission statement" of this collection of stories.

Among the varieties of escape, however, reading reigns supreme. No other activity is as accessible or as efficient in conducting us to other worlds, other selves. After all, the world's literature, great and small, is monomaniacally obsessed with exploring, reproducing, and serving up, in endlessly enticing and hypnotizing iterations, the invariant plot of escape. The literature of escape—*The Odyssey, The Decameron, Tom Jones,* and *The Adventures of Huck Finn*—only proves that literature itself is an escape.

As Marcel Proust, for whom book and life were functional synonyms, wrote, "There are perhaps no days of our childhood we lived so fully as those we believe we left without having lived them, those we spent with a favorite book." The collection of stories in this book tells us that escape is as much a part of the infrastructure of human behavior and the imagination as language itself. Because if the drive to escape is a testimonial for anything, it is a confirmation of our willfulness, of our deep urge to survive, and of our capacity for exiting the negative and entering the positive.

The stories we have collected here are intended to tell a sort of story of escape. Read in sequence, they progress from stories about escapes into life, escapes that are experimental or dry runs of the future; to stories of escape from a set of restrictive conditions into seemingly more liberating ones. These segue into what might properly be called "escapist" narratives that explore the powerful impulses to leave behind a hostile reality in the save haven of the imagination. From here we move into the terrain of love, lust, and longing, where the centripetal force of desire to rediscover the self alternates with the centrifugal impulse to burst into the unfamiliar territory of paramourous sex, adventures in the skin trade, and absorption in alien customs, cuisines, and costumes. Finally, there are narratives of escape as transcendence, that tell of some moment of "apocalypse now" when we are suddenly launched into a new vantage point and, looking back on where we started, we find ourselves transfigured and transformed.

It has oftentimes been said that there is sweetness in sorrow, and to a great degree, that sweetness derives from our hardwired ability to escape what sometimes seems like an immutable state of despair. Sorrow, after all, is not easily counterfeited. Like a cheese grater, it scrapes up against the skin, delivering that cosmic sting that says we are among the feeling and living, and not the dead. To quote Lena's aphorism-loving father, "As long as you hurt, you know you are alive." And as poet Mary Oliver might suggest, an escape to nature will convince you that "the petals pooled with nectar, and the polished thorns are a single thing . . . that love itself, without its pain, would be no more than a shruggable comfort." In this sense, escape can help bring us to an understanding deeper than anything we've ever known—in a burst of unexpected clarity that one calls "grace"—that every living and not living thing around you strives unquestioningly, joyously, to be what it was meant to be.

Finally, there is the ultimate escape: the transformation to another state of existence altogether. We have stood on the weathering planks of our house on the Oregon coast overlooking the pugilistic Pacific, watching the wild pink roses that slather the cedar deck, opening their factories of sweetness, giving back to the world, and wondered: If we could escape to another life, would we spend it all on some state that offered no opportunities for escape? Perhaps we would stand as two sea pines clinging to a sand dune on the edge of the sea. Fear has not yet occurred to them, nor has destruction. Manipulation, betrayal, rationalization, denial, and domination they have not yet thought of. Neither do they ask how long they must be trees, and then what. Or any other silly questions. Their existence is an escape accompli.

—Gideon Bosker and Lena Lenček

Set in Odessa—that sub-tropical mecca of the
Diaspora beyond the Pale, nursery of gangsters,
geniuses, dreamers, rabbis, and madmen—
"Awakening" explores the escape hatches from the
"smell of onions and Jewish destiny" that marked the
horizon of the shtetl. In a separate unfinished story
about his feelings after a day spent with his
grandmother, Babel wrote, "I felt like running away
from it all and like staying there forever." This dual,
antipodal pull—between the security and warmth of
the family and the alarming, yet mysterious allure
of the world beyond—forms the warp and the woof of
this autobiographical piece. To the relentless rigors of
the domestic, achievement-oriented routine, Babel
counterposes the liberating "out there" of the world of
the senses: irresistible, primal, unstructured, and
endlessly beautiful.

awakening

ISAAC BABEL

all the people of our circle—brokers, shopkeepers, bank and steamship office employees—taught their children music. Our fathers, seeing no chance of success for themselves, devised a lottery. They established it on the bones of little children. Odessa was seized by this madness worse than other towns. For decades our town put *Wunderkinder* on the concert platforms of the world. From Odessa came Mischa Elman, Zimbalist, Gabrilowich; Jascha Heifetz began among us.

When a boy was four or five, his mother took the tiny, puny creature to Mr. Zagursky. Zagursky ran a *Wunderkind* factory, a factory of Jewish dwarfs in lace collars and patent-leather shoes. He sought them out in the slums of the Moldavanka, in the evil-smelling courtyards of the Old Market. Zagursky gave them a first push in the right direction, and then the children were sent to Professor Auer in St. Petersburg.

In the souls of these starvelings with blue, swollen heads dwelt the mighty power of harmony. They became renowned virtuosi. And so my father decided to hold his own with Heifetz and Mischa Elman. Though I had passed *Wunderkind* age—I was in my fourteenth year—my short stature and puny physique made it possible for me to be mistaken for an eight-year-old. In this lay all their hopes.

I was taken to see Zagursky. Out of respect for my grandfather he agreed to charge a rouble a lesson—a low fee. My grandfather Levi-Itskhok was the laughing-stock of the town, and its adornment. He stalked about the streets in his top hat and ragged boots resolving doubts on the obscurest of matters. He was asked what a Gobelin was, why the Jacobins betrayed Robespierre, how artificial silk was made, what a Caesarean section was. My grandfather was able to answer these questions. Out of respect for his learning and madness Zagursky charged us a rouble a lesson. Also, he spent time on me because he feared Grandfather, for there was no point in spending time on me. The sounds crawled out of my violin like iron filings. I myself was cut to the heart by those sounds, but Father kept up the pace. At home there was no talk of anything but Mischa Elman, who had been exempted from military service by the tsar himself; Zimbalist, according to my father's information, had been presented to the king of England and had played at Buckingham Palace; Gabrilowich's parents bought two houses in St. Petersburg. *Wunderkinder* brought their parents wealth. My father could have reconciled himself to poverty, but he needed fame.

"It's impossible," people who had dined at our expense said, to stir up gossip, "it's impossible that the grandson of such a man..."

But my thoughts were elsewhere. During my violin practice I placed on my music stand books by Turgenev or Dumas and, scraping out heaven only knows what, devoured page after page. By day I told tall stories to the neighbours' urchins, by night I transferred them on to paper. Writing was a hereditary occupation in our family. Levi-Itskhok, whose mind became touched as he approached old age, had spent the whole of his life writing "Man with No Head." I took after him.

Three times a week, laden with violin-case and music, I trailed off to Witte Street, formerly Dvoryanskaya Street, to Zagursky's. There, along the walls, waiting their turn, sat Jewish girls, hysterically aflame. They pressed to their weak knees violins that were larger than those who were to play at Buckingham Palace.

The door of the inner sanctum would open. From Zagursky's study, reeling, emerged large-headed, freckled children with thin necks like the stalks of flowers, and a paroxysmic flush upon their cheeks. The door would bang shut, having swallowed the next dwarf. On the other side of the wall the teacher in bow-tie and red curls, with weedy legs, exerted himself to the utmost, sang, conducted. The director of a monstrous lottery, he was inspired, peopling the Moldavanka and the black cul-de-sacs of the Old Market with the ghosts of pizzicato and cantilena. This chant was later brought to a devilish height of brilliance by old Professor Auer...

In this sect I had no place. A dwarf, as they were, I discerned a different kind of inspiration in the voices of my ancestors.

I found the first step difficult. One day I left the house loaded up with case, violin, music and twelve roubles in cash—payment for a month's tuition. I walked along Nezhinskaya Street. In order to reach Zagursky's I should have turned into Dvoryanskaya, but instead I went up Tiraspolskaya and found myself at the port. The time of my lesson flew by in Prakticheskaya Harbour. Thus did my liberation begin. Zagursky's waiting-room saw me no more. My schoolmate Nemanov and I got into the habit of going aboard the steamship *Kensington* to see a certain old seaman, Mr. Trottyburn by name. Nemanov was a year younger than I, but had since the age of eight engaged in the most intricate commerce one could imagine. He was a genius at commercial deals and always delivered what he promised. Now he is a millionaire in New York, the director of General Motors, a company as powerful as Ford. Nemanov dragged me along with him because I obeyed him without a word. From Mr. Trottyburn he bought smuggled tobacco-pipes. These pipes were carved in Lincoln by the old seaman's brother.

"Gentlemen," Mr. Trottyburn would say to us, "mark my words, children must be made by one's own hand...To smoke a factory-made pipe is like putting an enema tube in your mouth. Do you know who Benvenuto Cellini was?...He was a master. My brother in Lincoln could tell you a thing or two about him. My brother doesn't get in anybody's way. He's just convinced that children must be made by one's own hand, and not by somebody else's...We cannot but agree with him, gentlemen..."

Nemanov sold Trottyburn's pipes to bank managers, foreign consuls, wealthy Greeks. He made a 100 per cent profit.

The pipes of the Lincoln master breathed poetry. Into each one of them had been inserted an idea, a drop of eternity. In their mouthpieces gleamed a yellow eye, their cases were lined with satin. I tried to imagine the life in Old England of Matthew Trottyburn, the last master of the pipe, resisting change.

"We cannot but agree with him, gentlemen, that children must be made by one's own hand..."

The heavy waves by the sea wall distanced me further and further from our house, which was steeped in the smell of onions and Jewish destiny. From Prakticheskaya Harbour I moved on to the breakwater. There, on a stretch of the sand bar, the boys from Primorskaya Street spent their days. From morning to night they did not pull on their trousers; they dived under the barges, stole coconuts for dinner and awaited the time when the steamerfuls of water-melon would drift slowly in from Kherson and Kamenka, and those watermelons could be split open on the moorings of the port.

It became my dream to learn to swim. I was ashamed to confess to these bronzed boys that, born in Odessa, I had not seen the sea until the age of ten, and at fourteen did not know how to swim.

How late I had to learn the essential things! In my childhood, nailed to the Gemara, I led the life of a sage, and when I was grown older began to climb trees.

The ability to swim proved to be beyond my reach. The fear of water that had haunted all my ancestors—Spanish rabbis and Frankfurt money-changers—pulled me to the bottom. The water would not support me. Exhausted, saturated with salt water, I would return shoreward to my violin and music. I was attached to the instruments of my crime and dragged them about with me. The struggle of the rabbis with the sea continued until pity was shown me by the water god of those parts, the proofreader of the *Odessa News*, Yefim Nikitich Smolich. Within this man's athletic breast dwelt compassion for Jewish children. He lorded it over throngs of rachitic starvelings. Nikitich gathered them in the bedbug-infested rooms of the Moldavanka, took them to the sea, dug in the sand with them, did gymnastics with them, dived with them, taught them songs and, getting thoroughly fried in the vertical rays of the sun, told them stories about fish and animals. To grown-ups Nikitich would explain that he was a natural philosopher. Nikitich's stories made the Jewish children die with laughter; they squealed and fawned upon him like puppies. The sun besprinkled them with creeping freckles, freckles the colour of lizards.

The old man had watched my single-handed combat with the waves out of the corner of his eye without saying anything. Having seen that there was no hope and that I was never going to learn to swim, he included me among the tenants of his heart. It was always with us here, his merry heart, it never put on any airs, was never mean, never troubled. With his copper shoulders, with his head of a gladiator grown old, with his bandy, bronzed legs he lay among us behind the breakwater, among the last dregs of a tribe that did not know how to die, like the ruler of these water-meloned, kerosened waters. I loved that man as only a boy who is sick with hysteria and headaches can love an athlete. I never left his side and tried to oblige him.

He said to me:

"Don't you worry...Strengthen your nerves. The swimming will come by itself...What do you mean, the water won't support you?...Why shouldn't it?"

When he saw how I was reaching out to him, Nikitich made an exception for me alone of all his disciples, invited me as a guest to his clean, spacious attic covered in mats, showed me his dogs, hedgehog, tortoise and pigeons. In exchange for these riches I brought him a tragedy of my own composition.

"I *thought* you scribbled," said Nikitich, "you have that kind of a look...You no longer look anywhere else..."

He read my writings through, shrugged one shoulder, ran his hand through his abrupt grey curls, walked to and fro about the attic.

"I suppose," he articulated in a drawl, falling silent after each word, "that within you there is a spark of the divine..."

We went down to the street. The old man stopped, banged his stick forcefully against the pavement and fixed his eyes on me.

"What is it you lack?...Your youth is no problem, it will pass with the years...What you lack is a feeling for nature."

With his stick he pointed out to me a tree that had a reddish trunk and a low crown.

"What kind of tree is that?"

I did not know.

"What's growing on this bush?"

I did not know that, either. He and I walked through the small square on Aleksandrovsky Prospect. The old man poked his stick at every tree, he clutched me by the shoulder whenever a bird flew past and made me listen to the different calls.

"What kind of bird is that singing?"

I was unable to reply. The names of trees and birds, their division into species, the places birds fly to, which direction the sun rises in, when the dew is heaviest—all that was unknown to me.

"And you presume to write?...A man who does not live in nature as a bird or an animal lives in it will never write two worthwhile lines in all his life...Your landscapes are like descriptions of stage scenery. The devil take me, what have your parents been thinking of for fourteen years?"

"What have they been thinking of? Protested promissory notes, the private residences of Mischa Elman." I said nothing of this to Nikitich, I kept quiet.

Back home, at dinner, I did not touch my food. It would not go down.

"A feeling for nature," I thought. "My God, why did I never think of that before? Where am I going to find someone who can explain the calls of the birds and the names of the trees to me? What do I know about them? I might be able to recognize lilacs, when they're in bloom, anyway, lilacs and acacias. There are lilacs and acacias on Deribasovskaya and Grecheskaya Streets."

While we were having dinner Father told a new story about Jascha Heifetz. Near Robin's he had encountered Mendelssohn, Jascha's uncle. The boy, it turned out, was getting eight hundred roubles a performance. Work out how much that made at a rate of fifteen concerts a month.

I worked it out, it came to twelve thousand a month. Doing the multiplication and carrying four in my head, I looked out of the window. Across the cement yard, in a gently billowing cloak and cape, with reddish ringlets showing from under his soft hat, leaning on his cane, stalked Mr. Zagursky, my music teacher. It could not be said that he had noted my absence before time. More than three months had already passed since my violin had sunk down to the sand off the breakwater.

Zagursky was coming up to the front door. I rushed to the back door—it had been boarded up the day before to keep out thieves. There was no salvation. I locked myself in the lavatory. Half an hour later the family had gathered outside the door. The women were crying. Bobka, my aunt, was rubbing a fat shoulder against the door and going off into fits of sobs. Father said nothing. Then he began to speak more quietly and distinctly than he had ever spoken in his life.

"I am an officer," said my father. "I have an estate. I ride out hunting. The muzhiks pay me rent. I have put my son in the Cadet Corps. I have no reason to worry about my son..."

He fell silent. The women breathed heavily through their noses. Then a terrible blow fell upon the lavatory door, Father was beating against it with his whole body, he was hurling himself against it at a run.

"I am an officer," he howled, "I ride out hunting...I'll kill him...His number's up..."

The hook sprang off the door, but there was still the bolt, held by a single nail. The women, squealing, rushed across the floor and seized Father by the legs; out of his mind, he tore himself loose. In the nick of time father's old mother arrived.

"My child," she said to him in Yiddish, "our grief is great. It is has no bounds. Only blood was lacking in our house. I do not want to see blood in our house..."

Father began to groan. I heard his shuffling, retreating footsteps. The bolt hung by a final nail.

I sat in my fortress until night-time. When everyone had gone to bed, Aunt Bobka took me a Grandmother's. We had a long way to go. The moonlight froze on unknown bushes, on trees that had no name. An invisible bird gave a peep and was silent—perhaps it had fallen asleep. What kind of bird was it? What was its name? Is there dew in the evening? Where is the constellation of Great Bear situated? In what direction does the sun rise?

We walked along Pochtovaya Street. Bobka held me tightly by the hand, so that I should not run away. She was right. I was thinking of escape.

Like a snowdome with a swirl of snow, Brodkey's
"Verona: A Young Woman Speaks" is a souvenir from
the never-never-land of childhood happiness. Set in an
elegiac Verona—stern and sad with evocations of
Shakespeare's lovers and the noble heroics of
Pisanello's Saint George—the story probes the
currents of emotion that run from parent to child. Part
ode to the supreme tenderness of motherly love, and
part diatribe against the disconnection of men, this
story chronicles the defenses that mother and
daughter galvanize against a father–husband who is
always hovering around the perimeters of familial love
but, in the end, lacks the emotional intelligence to
penetrate its inner sanctum. Told in a breathy, run-on
style, the narrative mimics the sweep of the road, the
family's giddy dance from city to city, the mad rush
to keep one step ahead of disenchantment. Here,
the memory of that dizzying happiness, when all
three—husband, wife, and child—are yoked in the
tense and finely balanced reciprocity of love, becomes
its own escape.

verona:
a young woman speaks
HAROLD BRODKEY

i know a lot! I know about happiness! I don't mean the love of God, either: I mean I know the human happiness with the crimes in it. Even the happiness of childhood.

I think of it now as a cruel, middle-class happiness.

Let me describe one time—one day, one night.

I was quite young, and my parents and I—there were just the three of us—were traveling from Rome to Salzburg, journeying across a quarter of Europe to be in Salzburg for Christmas, for the music and the snow. We went by train because planes were erratic, and my father wanted us to stop in half a dozen Italian towns and see paintings and buy things. It was absurd, but we were all three drunk with this; it was very strange; we woke every morning in a strange hotel, in a strange city. I would be the first one to wake; and I would go to the window and see some tower or palace; and then I would wake my mother and be justified in my sense of wildness and belief and adventure by the way she acted, her sense of romance at being in a city as strange as I had thought it was when I had looked out the window and seen the palace or the tower.

We had to change trains in Verona, a darkish, smallish city at the edge of the Alps. By the time we got there, we'd bought and bought our way up the Italian peninsula: I was dizzy with shopping and new possessions: I hardly knew who I was, I owned so many new things: my reflection in any mirror or shopwindow was resplendently fresh and new, disguised even, glittering, I thought. I was seven or eight years old. It seemed to me we were almost in a movie or in the pages of a book: only the simplest and most light-filled words and images can suggest what I thought we were then. We went around shiningly: we shone everywhere. *Those clothes.* It's easy to buy a child. I had a new dress, knitted, blue and red, expensive as hell, I think; leggings, also red; a red loden-cloth coat with a hood and a knitted cap for under the hood; marvelous lined gloves; fur-lined boots and a fur purse or carryall, and a tartan skirt—and shirts and a scarf, and there was even more: a watch, a bracelet: more and more.

On the trains we had private rooms, and Momma carried games in her purse and things to eat, and Daddy sang carols off-key to me; and sometimes I became so intent on my happiness I would suddenly be in real danger of wetting myself; and Momma, who understood such emergencies, would catch the urgency in my voice and see my twisted face; and she—a large, good-looking woman— would whisk me to a toilet with amazing competence and unstoppability, murmuring to me, "Just hold on for a while," and she would hold my hand while I did it.

So we came to Verona, where it was snowing, and the people had stern, sad faces, beautiful, unlaughing faces. But if they looked at me, those serious faces would lighten, they would smile at me in my splendor. Strangers offered me candy, sometimes with the most excruciating sadness, kneeling or stopping to look directly into my face, into my eyes; and Momma or Papa would judge them, the people, and say in Italian we were late, we had to hurry, or pause and let the stranger touch me, talk to me, look into my face for a while. I would see myself in the eyes of some strange man or woman; sometimes they stared so gently I would want to touch their eyelashes, stroke those strange, large, glistening eyes. I knew I decorated life. I took my duties with great seriousness. An Italian count in Siena said I had the manners of an English princess—at times—and then he laughed because it was true I would be quite lurid: I ran shouting in his *galleria*, a long room, hung with pictures, and with a frescoed ceiling: and I sat on his lap and wriggled: I was a wicked child, and I liked myself very much; and almost everywhere, almost every day, there was someone new to love me, briefly, while we traveled.

I understood I was special. I understood it *then.*

I knew that what we were doing, everything we did, involved money. I did not know if it involved mind or not, or style. But I knew about money somehow, checks and traveler's checks and the clink of coins. Daddy was a fountain of money: he said it was a spree; he meant for us to be amazed; he had saved money—we weren't really rich but we were to be for this trip. I remember a conservatory in a large house outside Florence and orange trees in tubs; and I ran there, too. A servant, a man dressed in black, a very old man, mean-faced—he did not like being a servant anymore after the days of servants were over—and he scowled—but he smiled at me, and at my mother, and even once at my father: we were clearly so separate from the griefs and weariness and cruelties of the world. We were at play, we were at our joys, and Momma was glad, with a terrible and naive inner gladness, and she relied on Daddy to make it work: oh, she worked, too, but she didn't know the secret of such—unreality: is that what I want to say? Of such a game, of such an extraordinary game.

There was a picture in Verona Daddy wanted to see: a painting; I remember the painter because the name Pisanello reminded me I had to go to the bathroom when we were in the museum, which was an old castle, Guelph or Ghibelline, I don't remember which; and I also remember the painting because it showed the hind end of the horse, and I thought that was not nice and rather funny, but Daddy was admiring; and so I said nothing.

He held my hand and told me a story so I wouldn't be bored as we walked from room to room in the museum/castle, and then we went outside into the snow, into the soft light when it snows, light coming through snow; and I was dressed in red and had on boots, and my parents were young and pretty and had on boots, too; and we could stay out in the snow if we wanted; and we did. We went to a square, a piazza—the Scaligera, I think; I don't remember—and just as we got there, the snowing began to bellow and then subside, to fall heavily and then sparsely, and then it stopped: and it was very cold, and there were pigeons everywhere in the piazza, on every cornice and roof, and all over the snow on the ground, leaving little tracks as they walked, while the air trembled in its just-after-snow and just-before-snow weight and thickness and gray seriousness of purpose. I had never seen so many pigeons or such a private and haunted place as that piazza, me in my new coat at the far rim of the world, the far rim of who knew what story, the rim of foreign beauty and Daddy's games, the edge, the white border of a season.

I was half mad with pleasure anyway, and now Daddy brought five or six cones made of newspaper, wrapped, twisted; and they held grains of something like corn, yellow and white kernels of something; and he poured some on my hand and told me to hold my hand out; and then he backed away.

At first, there was nothing, but I trusted him and I waited; and then the pigeons came. On heavy wings. Clumsy pigeony bodies. And red, unreal birds' feet. They flew at me, slowing at the last minute; they lit on my arm and fed from my hand. I wanted to flinch, but I didn't. I closed my eyes and held my arm stiffly; and felt them peck and eat—from my hand, these free creatures, these flying things. I liked that moment. I liked my happiness. If I was mistaken about life and pigeons and my own nature, it didn't matter *then*.

The piazza was very silent, with snow; and Daddy poured grains on both my hands and then on the sleeves of my coat and on the shoulders of the coat, and I was entranced with yet more stillness, with this idea of his. The pigeons fluttered heavily in the heavy air, more and more of them, and sat on my arms and on my shoulders; and I looked at Momma and then at my father and then at the birds on me.

Oh, I'm sick of everything as I talk. There is happiness. It always makes me slightly ill. I lose my balance because of it.

The heavy birds, and the strange buildings, and Momma near, and Daddy, too: Momma is pleased that I am happy and she is a little jealous; she is jealous of everything Daddy does; she is a woman of enormous spirit; life is hardly big enough for her; she is drenched in wastefulness and prettiness. She knows things. She gets inflexible, though, and foolish at times, and temperamental; but she is a somebody, and she gets away with a lot, and if she is near, you can feel her, you can't escape her, she's that important, that echoing, her spirit is that powerful in the space around her.

If she weren't restrained by Daddy, if she weren't in love with him, there is no knowing what she might do: she does not know. But she manages almost to be gentle because of him; he is incredibly watchful and changeable and he gets tired; he talks and charms people; sometimes, then, Momma and I stand nearby, like moons; we brighten and wane; and after a while, he comes to us, to the moons, the big one and the little one, and we welcome him, and he is always, to my surprise, he is always surprised, as if he didn't deserve to be loved, as if it were time he was found out.

Daddy is very tall, and Momma is watching us, and Daddy

anoints me again and again with the grain. I cannot bear it much longer. I feel joy or amusement or I don't know what; it is all through me, like a nausea—I am ready to scream and laugh, that laughter that comes out like magical, drunken, awful, and yet pure spit or vomit or God knows what, makes me a child mad with laughter. I become brilliant, gleaming, soft: an angel, a great bird-child of laughter.

I am ready to be like that, but I hold myself back.

There are more and more birds near me. They march around my feet and peck at falling and fallen grains. One is on my head. Of those on my arms, some move their wings, fluff those frail, feather-loaded wings, stretch them. I cannot bear it, they are so frail, and I am, at the moment, the kindness of the world that feeds them in the snow.

All at once, I let out a splurt of laughter: I can't stop myself and the birds fly away but not far; they circle around me, above me; some wheel high in the air and drop as they return; they all returned, some in clouds and clusters driftingly, some alone and angry, pecking at others; some with a blind, animal-strutting abruptness. They gripped my coat and fed themselves. It started to snow again.

I was there in my kindness, in that piazza, within reach of my mother and father.

Oh, how will the world continue? Daddy suddenly understood I'd had enough, I was at the end of my strength—Christ, he was alert—and he picked me up, and I went limp, my arm around his neck, and the snow fell. Momma came near and pulled the hood lower and said there were snowflakes in my eyelashes. She knew he had understood, and she wasn't sure she had; she wasn't sure he ever watched her so carefully. She became slightly unhappy, and so she walked like a clumsy boy beside us, but she was so pretty: she had powers anyway.

We went to a restaurant, and I behaved very well, but I couldn't eat, and then we went to the train and people looked at us, but I couldn't smile; I was too dignified, too sated; some leftover—pleasure, let's call it—made my dignity very deep; I could not stop remembering the pigeons, or that Daddy loved me in a way he did not love Momma; and Daddy was alert, watching the luggage, watching strangers for assassination attempts or whatever; he was on duty; and Momma was pretty and alone and *happy*, defiant in that way.

And then, you see, what she did was wake me in the middle of the night when the train was chugging up a very steep mountain-side; and outside the window, visible because our compartment was dark and the sky was clear and there was a full moon, were mountains, a landscape of mountains everywhere, big mountains, huge ones, impossible, all slanted and pointed and white with snow, and absurd, sticking up into an ink-blue sky and down into blue, blue shadows, miraculously deep. I don't know how to say what it was like: they were not like anything I knew: they were high things: and we were up high in the train and we were climbing higher, and it was not at all true, but it was, you see. I put my hands on the window and stared at the wild, slanting, unlikely marvels, whiteness and dizziness and moonlight and shadows cast by moonlight, not real, not familiar, not pigeons, but a clean world.

We sat a long time, Momma and I, and stared, and then Daddy woke up and came and looked, too. "It's pretty," he said, but he didn't really understand. Only Momma and I did. She said to him, "When I was a child, I was bored all the time, my love—I thought nothing would ever happen to me—and now these things are happening—and you have happened." I think he was flabbergasted by her love in the middle of the night; he smiled at her, oh, so swiftly that I was jealous, but I stayed quiet, and after a while, in his silence and amazement at her, at us, he began to seem different from us, from Momma and me; and then he fell asleep again; Momma and I didn't; we sat at the window and watched all night, watched the mountains and the moon, the clean world. We watched together.

Momma was the winner.

We were silent, and in silence we spoke of how we loved men and how dangerous men were and how they stole everything from you no matter how much you gave—but we didn't say it aloud.

We looked at mountains until dawn, and then when dawn came, it was too pretty for me—there was pink and blue and gold in the sky, and on icy places, brilliant pink and gold flashes, and the snow was colored, too, and I said, "Oh," and sighed; and each moment was more beautiful than the one before; and I said, "I love you, Momma." Then I fell asleep in her arms.

That was happiness then.

There is a sweet, teetering moment of "in-between"
that happens at the ripening of adolescence into
maturity, when the future looks like a glamorous
escape from the mousy, rule-bound present.
Shortly, of course, that same future will morph into
the prison of routine, responsibility, and inextricable
complications, and the adolescence that just moments
ago seemed a suffocating dungeon turns into a vista
of limitless freedom. Elizabeth Parsons' exquisitely
written story takes us into that charmed gap between
two states of mind to expose for us the double optical
illusion that is the essence of every flight.

the nightingales sing

ELIZABETH PARSONS

through the fog the car went up the hill, whining in second gear, up the sandy road that ran between the highest and broadest stone walls that Joanna had ever seen. There were no trees at all, only the bright green, cattle-cropped pastures sometimes visible above the walls, and sweet-fern and juniper bushes, all dim in the opaque air and the wan light of a May evening. Phil, driving the creaking station wagon with dexterous recklessness, said to her, "I hope it's the right road. Nothing looks familiar in this fog and I've only been here once before."

"It was nice of him to ask us—me, especially," said Joanna, who was young and shy and grateful for favors.

"Oh, he loves company," Phil said. "I wish we could have got away sooner, to be here to help him unload the horses, though. Still, Chris will be there."

"Is Chris the girl who got thrown today?" Joanna asked, remembering the slight figure in the black coat going down in a spectacular fall with a big bay horse. Phil nodded and brought the car so smartly around a bend that the two tack boxes in the back of it skidded across the floor. Then he stopped, at last on the level, at a five-barred gate that suddenly appeared out of the mist.

"I'll do the gate," Joanna said, and jumped out. It opened easily and she swung it back against the fence and held it while Phil drove through; then the engine stalled, and in the silence she stood for a moment, her head raised, sniffing the damp, clean air. There was no sound—not the sound of a bird, or a lamb, or the running of water over stones, or wind in leaves; there was only a great stillness, and a sense of height and strangeness, and the smell of grass and dried dung. This was the top of the world, this lost hillside, green and bare, ruled across by enormous old walls—the work, so it seemed, of giants. In the air there was a faint movement as of a great wind far away, breathing through the fog. Joanna pulled the gate shut and got in again with Phil, and they drove on along the smooth crest of the hill, the windshield wipers swinging slowly to and fro and Phil's sharp, redheaded profile drawn clearly against the gray background. She was grateful to him for taking her to the horse show that afternoon, but she was timid about the invitation to supper that it had led to. Still, there was no getting out of it now. Phil was the elder brother of a school friend of hers, Carol Watson; he was so old he might as well have been of another generation, and there was about him, still incredibly unmarried at the age of thirty-one, the mysterious aura that bachelor elder brothers always possess. Carol was supposed to have come with them, but she had developed chicken pox the day before. However, Phil had kindly offered to take Joanna just the same, since he had had to ride, and he had kept a fatherly eye on her whenever he could. Then a friend of his named Sandy Sheldon, a breeder of polo ponies, had asked him to stop at his farm for supper on the way home. Phil had asked Joanna if she wanted to go, and she had said yes, knowing that he wanted to.

Being a good child, she had telephoned her family to tell them she would not be home until late, because she was going to Sandy Sheldon's place with Phil.

"*Whose* place?" her mother's faraway voice had asked, doubtfully. "Well, don't be too late, will you, dear. And call me up when you're leaving, won't you. It's a miserable night to be driving."

"I can't call you," Joanna had said. "There's no telephone."

"Couldn't you call up from somewhere after you've left?" the faint voice had said. "You know how Father worries, and Phil's such a fast driver."

"I'll try to." Exasperation had made Joanna's voice stiff. What earthly good was *telephoning*? She hung up the receiver with a bang, showing a temper she would not have dared display in the presence of her parents.

Now suddenly out of the fog great buildings loomed close, and they drove through an open gate into a farmyard with gray wooden barns on two sides of it and stone walls on the other two sides. A few white hens rushed away across the dusty ground, and a gray cat sitting on the pole of a blue dump cart stared coldly at the car as Phil stopped it beside a battered horse van. The instant he stopped, a springer ran barking out of one of the barn doors and a man appeared behind him and came quickly out to them, up to Joanna's side of the car, where he put both hands on the door and bent his head a little to look in at them.

"Sandy, this is Joanna Gibbs," Phil said.

Sandy looked at her without smiling but not at all with unfriendliness, only with calm consideration. "Hello, Joanna," he said, and opened the door for her.

"Hello," she said, and forgot to be shy, for, instead of uttering the kind of asinine polite remark she was accustomed to hearing from strangers, he did not treat her as a stranger at all, but said immediately, "You're just in time to help put the horses away. Chris keeled over the minute we got here and I had to send her to bed, and Jake's gone after one of the cows that's strayed off." He spoke in a light, slow, Western voice. He was a small man about Phil's age, with a flat, freckled face, light brown, intelligent eyes, and faded brown hair cut short all over his round head. He looked very sturdy and stocky, walking toward the van beside Phil's thin, New England elegance, and he had a self-confidence that seemed to spring simply from his own good nature.

"Quite a fog you greet us with," Phil said, taking off his coat and hanging it on the latch of the open door of the van. Inside, in the gloom, four long, shining heads were turned toward them, and one of the horses gave a gentle, anxious whinny.

"Yes, we get them once in a while," said Sandy. "I like 'em."

"So do I," Joanna said.

He turned to her and said, "Look, there's really no need in your staying out here. Run in the house, where it's warm, and see if the invalid's all right. You go through that gate." He pointed to a small, sagging gate in one wall.

"All right, I will," she answered, and she started off across the yard toward the end gable of a house she could see rising dimly above some apple trees, the spaniel with her.

"Joanna!" Sandy called after her, just as she reached the gate.

"Yes?" She turned back. The two men were standing by the runway of the van. They both looked at her, seeing a tall young girl in a blue dress and sweater, with her hair drawn straight back over her head and tied at the back of her neck in a chignon with a black bow, and made more beautiful and airy than she actually was by the watery air.

"Put some wood on the kitchen fire as you go in, will you?" Sandy shouted to her. "The woodbox is right by the stove."

"All right," she answered again, and she and the spaniel went through the little gate in the wall.

A path led from the gate under the apple trees, where the grass was cut short and neat, to a door in the ell of the house. The house itself was big and old and plain, almost square, with a great chimney settled firmly across the ridgepole, and presumably it faced down the hill toward the sea. It was conventional and unimposing, with white-painted trim and covered with gray old shingles. There was a lilac bush by the front door and a bed of unbudded red lilies around one of the apple trees, but except for these there was neither shrubbery nor flowers. It looked austere and pleasing to Joanna, and she went in through the door in the ell and saw the woodbox beside the black stove. As she poked some pieces of birchwood down into the snapping fire, a girl's voice called from upstairs, "Sandy?"

Joanna put the lid on the stove and went through a tiny hallway into a living room. An enclosed staircase went up out of one corner, and she went to it and called up it, "Sandy's in the barn. Are you all right?"

"Oh, I'm fine," the voice answered, hard and clear. "Just a little shaky when I move around. Come on up."

Immediately at the top of the stairs was a big, square bedroom, papered in a beautiful, faded paper with scrolls and wheat sheaves. On a four-posted bed lay a girl not many years older than Joanna, covered to the chin with a dark patchwork quilt. Her short black hair stood out against the pillow, and her face was colorless and expressionless and at the same time likable and amusing. She did not sit up when Joanna came in; she clasped her hands behind her head and looked at her with blue eyes under lowered black lashes.

"You came with Phil, didn't you?" she asked.

"Yes," Joanna said, moving hesitantly up to the bed and leaning against one of the footposts. "They're putting the horses away and they thought I'd better come in and see how you were."

"Oh, I'm fine," Chris said again. "I'll be O.K. in a few minutes. I lit on my head, I guess, by the way it feels, but I don't remember a thing."

Joanna remembered. It had not seemed possible that that black figure could emerge, apparently from directly underneath the bay horse, and, after sitting a minute on the grass with hanging head, get up and walk grimly away, ignoring the animal that had made such a clumsy error and was being led out by an attendant in a long tan coat.

Joanna also remembered that when people were ill or in pain you brought them weak tea and aspirin and hot-water bottles, and that they were usually in bed, wishing to suffer behind partly lowered shades, not just lying under a quilt with the fog pressing against darkening windows. But there was something here that did not belong in the land of tea and hot-water bottles—a land that, indeed, now seemed on another planet. Joanna made no suggestions but just stood there, looking with shy politeness around the room. It was a cold, sparsely furnished place, and it looked very bare to Joanna, most of whose life so far had been spent in comfortable, chintz-warmed interiors, with carpets that went from wall to wall. In this room, so obviously untouched for the past hundred years or more, was only the bed, a tall chest of drawers, a washstand with a gold-and-white bowl and pitcher, two plain, painted chairs, and a thread-bare, oval, braided rug beside the bed. There were no curtains or shades at the four windows, and practically no paint left on the uneven old floor. There was dust over everything. The fireplace was black and damp-smelling and filled with ashes and charred paper that rose high about the feet of the andirons. Joanna could not make out whether it was a guest room or whose room it was; here and there were scattered possessions that might have been male or female—a bootjack, some framed snapshots, a comb, a dirty towel, some socks, a magazine on the floor. Chris's black coat was lying on a chair, and her bowler stood on the bureau. It was a blank room, bleak in the failing light.

Chris watched her from under her half-closed lids, waiting for her to speak, and presently Joanna said, "That was really an awful spill you had."

Chris moved her head on the pillow and said, "He's a brute of a horse. He'll never be fit to ride. I've schooled him for Mrs. Whittaker for a year now and ridden him in three shows and I thought he was pretty well over his troubles." She shrugged and wrapped herself tighter in the quilt. "She's sunk so much money in him it's a crime, but he's just a brute and I don't think I can do anything more with him. Of course, if she wants to go on paying me to ride him, O.K., and her other horses are tops, so I haven't any kick, really. You can't have them all perfect."

"What does she bother with him for?" Joanna asked.

"Well, she's cracked, like most horse-show people," Chris said. "They can't resist being spectacular—exhibitionists, or whatever they call it. Got to have something startling, and then more startling, and so on. And I must say this horse is something to see. He's beautiful." Her somewhat bored little voice died away.

Joanna contemplated all this seriously. It seemed to her an arduous yet dramatic way of earning one's living; she did not notice that there was nothing in the least dramatic about the girl on the bed beside her. Chris, for her part, was speculating more directly about Joanna, watching her, appreciating her looks, wondering what she was doing with Phil. Then, because she was not unkind and sensed that Joanna was at loose ends in the strange house, she said to her, suddenly leaving the world of horses for the domestic scene where women cozily collaborate over the comforts of their men, "Is there a fire in the living room? I was too queasy to notice when I came in. If there isn't one, why don't you light it, so it'll be warm when they come in?"

"I'll look," said Joanna. "I didn't notice, either. Can I get you anything?"

"No, I'll be down pretty soon," Chris said. "I've got to start supper."

Joanna went back down the little stairs. There was no fire in the living room, but a broken basket beside the fireplace was half full of logs, and she carefully laid these on the andirons and stuffed in some twigs and old comics and lit them. In a few minutes the tall flames sprang up into the black chimney, shiny with creosote. Joanna sat on the floor and looked around the room. It was the same size as the bedroom above it, but it was comfortable and snug, with plain gray walls and white woodwork. A fat sofa, covered with dirty, flowered linen, stood in front of the fire. There were some big wicker chairs and four little carved Victorian chairs and a round table with big, bowed legs, covered with a red tablecloth. A high, handsome secretary stood against the long wall opposite the fire; its veneer was peeling, and it was filled with tarnished silver cups and ribbon rosettes. A guitar lay on a chair. There were dog hairs on the sofa, and the floor was dirty, and outside the windows there was nothingness. Joanna got up to look at the kitchen fire, put more wood on it, and returned to the living room. Overhead she heard Chris moving around quietly, and she pictured her walking about the barren, dusty bedroom, combing her short black hair, tying her necktie, folding up the quilt, looking in the gloom for a lipstick; and suddenly a dreadful, lonely sadness and longing came over her. The living room was growing dark, too, and she would have lit the big nickel lamp standing on the table but she did not know how to, so she sat there dreaming in the hot, golden firelight. Presently she heard the men's voices outside, and they came into the kitchen and stopped there to talk. Joanna heard the stove lids being rattled. Sandy came to the door and, seeing her, said, "Is Chris all right?"

"Yes, I think so," Joanna said. "She said she was, anyway."

"Guess I'll just see," he said, and went running up the stairs. The spaniel came in from the kitchen to be near the fire. Joanna stroked his back. His wavy coat was damp with fog, and he smelled very strongly of dog; he sat down on the hearth facing the fire, raised his muzzle, and closed his eyes and gave a great sigh of comfort. Then all of a sudden he trotted away and went leaping up the stairs to the bedroom, and Joanna could hear his feet overhead.

Phil came in next, his hair sticking to his forehead. He hung his coat on a chair back and said to Joanna, "How do you like it here?"

"It's wonderful," she said earnestly.

"It seems to me a queer place," he said, lifting the white, fluted china shade off the lamp and striking a match. "Very queer—so far off. We're marooned. I don't feel there's any other place anywhere, do you?"

Joanna shook her head and watched him touch the match to the wick and stoop to settle the chimney on its base. When he put on the shade, the soft yellow light caught becomingly on his red head and his narrow face, with the sharp cheekbones and the small, deep-set blue eyes. Joanna had known him for years, but she realized, looking at him in the yellow light, that she knew almost nothing about him. Before this, he had been Carol's elder brother, but here, in the unfamiliar surroundings, he was somebody real. She looked away from his lighted face, surprised and wondering. He took his pipe out of his coat pocket and came to the sofa and sat down with a sigh of comfort exactly like the dog's, sticking his long, thin, booted feet out to the fire, banishing the dark, making the fog retreat.

Sandy came down the stairs and went toward the kitchen, and

Phil called after him, "Chris O.K.?"

"Yes," Sandy said, going out.

"She's a little crazy," Phil said. "Too much courage and no sense. But she's young. She'll settle down, maybe."

"Are she and Sandy engaged?" Joanna asked.

"Well, no," said Phil. "Sandy's got a wife. She stays in Texas." He paused to light his pipe, and then he said, "That's where he raises his horses, you know; this place is only sort of a salesroom. But he and Chris know each other pretty well."

This seemed obvious to Joanna, who said, "Yes, I know." Phil smoked in silence.

"Doesn't his wife *ever* come here?" Joanna asked after a moment.

"I don't think so," Phil answered.

They could hear Sandy in the kitchen, whistling, and occasionally rattling pans. They heard the pump squeak as he worked the handle, and the water splashed down into the black iron sink. Then he, too, came in to the fire and said to Joanna, smiling down at her, "Are you comfy, and all?"

"Oh *yes*," she said, and flushed with pleasure. "I love your house," she managed to say.

"I'm glad you do. It's kind of a barn of a place, but fine for the little I'm in it." He walked away, pulled the flowered curtains across the windows, and came back to stand before the fire. He looked very solid, small, and cheerful, with his shirtsleeves rolled up, his collar unbuttoned, and his gay, printed tie loosened. He seemed so snug and kind to Joanna, so somehow sympathetic, that she could have leaned forward and hugged him around the knees. But at the idea of doing any such thing she blushed again, and bent to pat the dog.

Sandy took up the guitar and tuned it. He began playing absentmindedly, his stubby fingers straying across the strings as he stared into the fire. Chris came down the stairs. Instead of her long black boots she had on a pair of dilapidated Indian moccasins with a few beads remaining on the toes, and between these and the ends of her breeches' legs were gay blue socks. The breeches were fawn-colored, and she had on a fresh white shirt with the sleeves rolled up. Her curly hair, cropped nearly as short as a boy's, was brushed and shining, and her hard, sallow little face was carefully made up and completely blank. Whether she was happy or disturbed, well or ill, Joanna could see no stranger would be able to tell.

"What about supper?" she asked Sandy.

"Calm yourself," he said. "I'm cook tonight. It's all started." He took her hand to draw her down on the sofa, but she moved away and pulled a cushion off a chair and lay down on the floor, her feet toward the fire and her hands folded, like a child's, on her stomach. Phil had gone into the kitchen, and now he came back carrying a lighted lamp; it dipped wildly in his hand as he set it on the round table beside the other one. The room shone in the low, beneficent light. Sandy, leaning his head against the high, carved back of the sofa, humming and strumming, now sang aloud in a light, sweet voice:

"For I'd rather hear your fiddle
And the tone of one string,
Than watch the waters a–gliding,
Hear the nightingales sing."

The soft strumming went on, and the soft voice, accompanied by Chris's gentle crooning. The fire snapped. Phil handed around some glasses and then went around with a bottle of whiskey he found in the kitchen. He paused at Joanna's glass, smiled at her, and poured her a very small portion.

"If I ever return,
It will be in the spring
To watch the waters a–gliding,
Hear the nightingales sing."

The old air died on a trailing chord.

"That's a lovely song," Joanna said, and then shrank at her sentimentality.

Sandy said, "Yes, it's nice. My mother used to sing it. She knew an awful lot of old songs." He picked out the last bars again on the guitar. Joanna, sitting beside him on the floor, was swept with warmth and comfort.

"My God, the peas!" Sandy said suddenly, in horror, as a loud sound of hissing came from the kitchen. Throwing the guitar down on the sofa, he rushed to rescue the supper.

Joanna and Chris picked their way toward the privy that adjoined the end of the barn nearer the house. They moved in a little circle of light from the kerosene lantern that Chris carried, the batteries of Sandy's big flashlight having turned out to be dead. They were both very full of food, and sleepy, and just a little tipsy. Chris had taken off her socks and moccasins and Joanna her leather sandals, and the soaking grass was cold to their feet, which had so lately been stretched out to the fire. Joanna had never been in a privy in her life, and when Chris opened the door she was astonished at the four neatly covered holes, two large and—on a lower level—two small. Everything was whitewashed; there were pegs to hang things on, and a very strong smell of disinfectant. A few flies woke up and buzzed. Chris set the lantern down on the path and partly closed the door behind them.

There was something cozy about the privy, and they were in no particular hurry to go back to the house. Chris lit a cigarette, and they sat there comfortably in the semidarkness, and Chris talked. She told Joanna about her two years in college, to which she had been made to go by her family. But Chris's love was horses, not gaining an education, and finally she had left and begun to support herself as a professional rider.

"I'd known Sandy ever since I was little," she said. "I used to hang around him when I was a kid, and he let me ride his horses and everything, and when I left college he got me jobs and sort of looked after me."

"He's a darling, isn't he?" Joanna said dreamily, watching the dim slice of light from the open door, and the mist that drifted past it.

"Well, sometimes he is," Chris said. "And sometimes I wish I'd never seen him."

"Oh, *no!*" cried Joanna. "Why?"

"Because he's got so he takes charge too much of the time—you know?" Chris said. "At first I was so crazy about him I didn't care, but now it's gone on so long I'm beginning to see I'm handicapped, in a way. Or that's what I think, anyway. Everybody just assumes I'm his girl. And he's got a wife, you know, and he won't leave her, ever. And then he's not here a lot of the time. But the worst of all is that he's spoiled me; everybody else seems kind of tame and young. So you see it's a mixed pleasure."

Joanna pondered, a little fuzzily. She was not at all sure what it was that Chris was telling her, but she felt she was being talked to as by one worldly soul to another. Now Chris was saying, "He said that would happen, and I didn't care then. He said, 'I'm too *old* for you, Chris, even if I was single, and this way it's hopeless for you.' But I didn't care. I didn't want anybody or anything else and I just plain chased him. And now I don't want anything else, either. So it *is* hopeless. . . . I hope you don't ever love anybody more than he loves you."

"I've never really been in love," Joanna said bravely.

"Well, you will be," Chris said, lighting a second cigarette. The little white interior and their two young, drowsy faces shone for a second in the flash of the match. "First I thought you were coming here because you were Phil's girl, but I soon saw you weren't."

"Oh, *no!*" cried Joanna again. "He's just the brother of a friend of mine, that's all."

"Yes," said Chris. "He always picks racier types than you."

Racy, thought Joanna. I wish *I* was racy, but I'm too scared.

"I've seen some of his girls, and not one of them was as good-looking as you are," Chris went on. "But they were all very dizzy. He has to have that, I guess—he's so sort of restrained himself, with that family and all. I went to a cocktail party at his house once, and it was terrible. Jeepers!" She began to laugh.

Vulgarity is what he likes, then, said Joanna to herself. Perhaps I like it myself, though I don't know that I know what it is. Perhaps my mother would say Chris and Sandy were vulgar, but they don't seem vulgar to me, though I'm glad Mother isn't here to hear their language and some of Sandy's songs.

She gave it up as Chris said, with a yawn, "We'd better go back."

As they went toward the house, it loomed up above them, twice its size, the kitchen windows throwing low beams of light out into the fog. Still there was no wind. In the heavy night air nothing was real, not even Chris and the lantern and the corner of the great wall near the house. Joanna was disembodied, moving through a dream on her bare, numb feet to a house of no substance.

"Let's walk around to the front," she said. "I love the fog."

"O.K.," said Chris, and they went around the corner and stopped by the lilac bushes to listen to the stillness.

But suddenly the dampness reached their bones, and they shivered and screeched and ran back to the back door, with the bobbing lantern smoking and smelling in Chris's hand.

When they came in, Phil looked at them fondly. "Dear little Joanna," he said. "She's all dripping and watery and vaporous, like Undine. What in God's name have you girls been doing?"

"Oh, talking," said Chris.

"Pull up to the fire," Sandy said. "What did you talk about? Us?"

"Yes, dear," said Chris. "We talked about you every single second."

"Joanna's very subdued," remarked Phil. "Did you talk her into a stupor, or what?"

"Joanna doesn't have to talk if she doesn't want to," said Sandy. "I like a quiet woman, myself."

"Do you, now?" said Phil, laughing at Chris, who made a face at him and sat down beside Sandy and gave him a violent hug.

Joanna, blinking, sat on the floor with her wet feet tucked under her, and listened vaguely to the talk that ran to and fro above her. Her head was swimming, and she felt sleepy and wise in the warm lamplight and with the sound of the banter in which she did not have to join unless she wanted to. Suddenly she heard Phil saying, "You know, Joanna, we've got to start along. It seems to me you made a rash promise to your family that you wouldn't be too late getting home, and it's nearly ten now and we've got thirty miles to go." He yawned, stretched, and bent to knock out his pipe on the side of the fireplace.

"I don't want to go," Joanna said.

"Then stay," said Sandy. "There's plenty of room."

But Phil said, getting up, "No, we've got to go. They'd have the police out if we didn't come soon. Joanna's very carefully raised, you know."

"I *love* Joanna," said Chris, hugging Sandy again until he grunted. "I don't care how carefully she was raised, I love her."

"We all love her," Sandy said. "You haven't got a monopoly on her. Come again and stay longer, will you, Joanna? We love you, and you look so nice here in this horrible old house."

They really do like me, Joanna thought, pulling on her sandals. But not as much as I like them. They have a lot of fun all the time, so it doesn't mean as much to them to find somebody they like. But I'll remember this evening as long as I live.

Sadly she went out with them to the station wagon, following the lantern, and climbed in and sat on the clammy leather seat beside Phil. Calling back, and being called to, they drove away, bumping slowly over the little road, and in a second Chris and Sandy and the lantern were gone in the fog.

Joanna let herself in the front door and turned to wave to Phil, who waved back and drove off down the leafy street, misty in the midnight silence. Inland, the fog was not so bad as it had been near the sea, but the trees dripped with the wetness and the sidewalk shone under the street light. She listened to the faraway, sucking sound of Phil's tires die away; then she sighed and closed the door and moved sleepily into the still house, dropping her key into the brass bowl on the hall table. The house was cool, and dark downstairs except for the hall light, and it smelled of the earth in her mother's little conservatory.

Joanna started up the stairs, slowly unfastening the belt of the old trench coat she had borrowed from Phil. The drive back had been a meaningless interval swinging in the night, with nothing to remember but the glow of the headlights so blanketed by the fog that they had had to creep around the curves and down the hills, peering out until their eyes ached. Soon after they had left the farm, they had stopped in a small town while Joanna telephoned her family. Through the open door of the phone booth she had watched Phil sitting on a spindly stool at the little marble counter next to the shelves full of Westerns, drinking a coke. She had a coke herself and she sipped it as the telephone rang far away in her parents' house, while back of the counter a radio played dance music. And twice after that Phil had pulled off the road, once to light his pipe, and once for Joanna to put on his coat. But now, moving up the shallow, carpeted stairs, she was back in the great, cold, dusty house with the sound of Sandy's guitar and the smell of the oil lamps, and the night, the real night, wide and black and empty, only a step away outside.

Upstairs, there was a light in her own room and one in her mother's dressing room. It was a family custom that when she came in late she should put out her mother's light, so now she went into the small, bright room. With her hand on the light chain, she looked around her, at the chintz-covered chaise longue, the chintz-skirted dressing table with family snapshots, both old and recent, arranged under its glass top, the polished furniture, the long mirror, the agreeable clutter of many years of satisfactory married life. On the walls were more family pictures, covering quite a long period of time—enlargements of picnic photographs, of boats, of a few pets. There was Joanna at the age of twelve on a cow pony in Wyoming; her father and uncle in snow goggles and climbing boots on the lower slopes of Mont Blanc, heaven knows how long ago; her sister and brother-in-law looking very young and carefree with their bicycles outside Salisbury Cathedral sometime in the early thirties, judging by her sister's clothes. In all of them the sun shone, and everyone was happy in the world of the pictures, which was as fresh and good and simple as a May morning. She stared at the familiar little scenes on the walls with love—and with a sympathy for them she had never felt before—and then she put out the light and went back along the hall.

In her own room she kicked off her sandals and dropped Phil's coat on a chair. A drawn window shade moved inward and fell back again in the night breeze that rustled the thick, wet trees close outside. Her pajamas lay on the turned-down bed with its tall, fluted posts. Joanna did not stop to brush her teeth or braid her hair; she was in bed in less than two minutes.

In the darkness she heard the wind rising around Sandy's house, breathing over the open hill, whistling softly in the wet, rusted window screens, stirring in the apple trees. She heard the last burning log in the fireplace tumble apart, and a horse kick at his stall out in the barn. If I'd stayed all night, she thought, in the morning when the fog burned off I'd have known how far you could see from the top of the hill.

For in the morning the hot sun would shine from a mild blue sky, the roofs would steam, the horses would gallop and squeal in the pastures between the great walls, and all the nightingales would rise singing out of the short, tough grass.

The Amazing Adventures of Kavalier & Clay, *Michael Chabon's* fifth book, tells the escapades of Jewish trans-Atlantic cousins—Brooklynite Sammy Klayman and Czech refugee Josef Kavalier —who, during the comic book's "golden age" in the 1930s and 1940s, collaborate on boldly plotted and innovatively drawn pulp strips to wage a fantasy war against the satanic Axis Powers. In this selection, the adolescent Josef is spirited from Nazi-occupied Prague under the cover of the Golem. The materialization of an escapist dream of a persecuted people seeking the ultimate weapon and guardian in the midst of a hostile world, the Golem, or homunculus, is a sixteenth-century avatar of Marvel Comics superheroes. According to legend, the hulking creature—three eels high, with the face of a thirty-year-old man, mute, seemingly bereft of reason and impervious to the action of fire, water, or sword—was crafted of riverbank clay by the wonder-working Rabbi Loew of Prague to protect Jews against false accusations of ritual murder.

from *the amazing adventure of kavalier & clay*

MICHAEL CHABON

the pair of young German professors spelunking with their electric torches in the rafters of the Old-New Synagogue, or Altneuschul, had, as it happened, gone away disappointed; for the attic under the stair-stepped gables of the old Gothic synagogue was a cenotaph. Around the turn of the last century, Prague's city fathers had determined to "sanitize" the ancient ghetto. During a moment when the fate of the Altneuschul had appeared uncertain, the members of the secret circle had arranged for their charge to be moved from its ancient berth, under a cairn of decommissioned prayer books in the synagogue's attic, to a room in a nearby apartment block, newly constructed by a member of the circle who, in public life, was a successful speculator in real estate. After this burst of uncommon activity, however, the ghetto-bred inertia and disorganization of the circle reasserted itself. The move, supposed to have been only temporary, somehow was never undone, even after it became clear that the Altneuschul would be spared. A few years later, the old yeshiva in whose library a record of the transfer was stored fell under the wrecking ball, and the log containing the record was lost. As a result, the circle was able to provide Kornblum with only a partial address for the Golem, the actual number of the apartment in which it was concealed having been forgotten or come into dispute. The embarrassing fact was that none of the current members of the circle could remember having laid eyes on the Golem since early 1917.

"Then why move it again?" Josef asked his old teacher, as they stood outside the art nouveau building, long since faded and smudged with thumbprints of soot, to which they had been referred. Josef gave a nervous tug at his false beard, which was making his chin itch. He was also wearing a mustache and a wig, all ginger in color and of good quality, and a pair of heavy round tortoiseshell spectacles. Consulting his image in Kornblum's glass that morning, he had struck himself, in the Harris tweeds purchased for his trip to America, as looking quite convincingly Scottish. It was less clear to him why passing as a Scotsman in the streets of Prague was likely to divert people's attention from his and Kornblum's quest. As with many novices at the art of disguise, he could not have felt more conspicuous if he were naked or wearing a sandwich board printed with his name and intentions.

He looked up and down Nicholasgasse, his heart smacking against his ribs like a bumblebee at a window. In the ten minutes it had taken them to walk here from Kornblum's room, Josef had passed his mother three times, or rather had passed three unknown women whose momentary resemblance to his mother had taken his breath away. He was reminded of the previous summer (following one of the episodes he imagined to have broken his young heart) when, every time he set out for school, for the German Lawn Tennis Club under Charles Bridge, for swimming at the Militär- und Civilschwimmschule, the constant possibility of encountering a certain Fraulein Felix had rendered every street corner and doorway a potential theater of shame and humiliation. Only now *he* was the betrayer of the hopes of another. He had no doubt that his mother, when he passed her, would be able to see right through the false whiskers. "If even *they* can't find it, who could?"

"I am sure they could find it," Kornblum said. He had trimmed his own beard, rinsing out the crackle of coppery red which, Josef had been shocked to discover, he had been using for years. He wore rimless glasses and a wide-brimmed black hat that shadowed his face, and he leaned realistically on a malacca cane. Kornblum had produced the disguises from the depths of his marvelous Chinese trunk, but said that they had come originally from the estate of Harry Houdini, who made frequent, expert use of disguise in his lifelong crusade to gull and expose false mediums. "I suppose the fear is that they will be soon be"—he flourished his handkerchief and then coughed into it—"*obliged* to try."

Kornblum explained to the building superintendent, giving a pair of false names and brandishing credentials and bona fides whose source Josef was never able to determine, that they had been sent by the Jewish Council (a public organization unrelated to, though in some cases co-constituent with, the secret Golem circle) to survey the building, as part of a program to keep track of the movements of Jews into and within Prague. There was, in fact, such a program, undertaken semi-voluntarily and with the earnest dread that characterized all of the Jewish Council's dealings with the Reichsprotektorat. The Jews of Bohemia, Moravia, and the Sudeten were being concentrated in the city, while Prague's own Jews were being forced out of their old homes and into segregated neighborhoods, with two and three families often crowding into a single flat. The resulting turmoil made it difficult for the Jewish Council to supply the protectorate with the accurate information it constantly demanded; hence the need for a census. The superintendent of the building in which the Golem slept, which had been designated by the protectorate for habitation by Jews, found nothing to question in their story or documents, and let them in without hesitation.

Starting at the top and working their way down all five floors to the ground, Josef and Kornblum knocked on every door in the building and flashed their credentials, then carefully took down names and relationships. With so many people packed into each flat, and so many lately thrown out of work, it was the rare door that went unanswered in the middle of the day. In some of the flats, strict concords had been worked out among the disparate occupants, or else there was a happy mesh of temperament that maintained order, civility, and cleanliness. But for the most part, the families seemed not to have moved in together so much as to have collided, with an impact that hurled schoolbooks, magazines, hosiery, pipes, shoes, journals, candlesticks, knickknacks, mufflers, dressmaker's dummies, crockery, and framed photographs in all directions, scattering them across rooms that had the provisional air of an auctioneer's warehouse. In many apartments, there was a wild duplication and reduplication of furnishings: sofas ranked like church pews, enough jumbled dining chairs to stock a large café, a jungle growth of chandeliers dangling from ceilings, groves of torchères, clocks that sat side by side by side on a mantel, disputing the hour. Conflicts, in the nature of border wars, had inevitably broken out. Laundry was hung to demarcate lines of conflict and truce. Dueling wireless sets were tuned to different stations, the volumes turned up in hostile increments. In such circumstances, the scalding of a pan of milk, the frying of a kipper, the neglect of a fouled nappy, could posses incalculable strategic value. There were tales of families reduced to angry silence, communicating by means of hostile notes; three times, Kornblum's simple request for the relationships among occupants resulted in bitter shouting over degrees of cousinage or testamentary disputes that in one case nearly led to a punch being thrown. Circumspect questioning of husbands, wives, great-uncles, and grandmothers brought forth no mention of a mysterious lodger, or of a door that was permanently shut.

When, after four hours of tedious and depressing make-believe, Mr. Krumm and Mr. Rosenblatt, representatives of the Census Committee of the Jewish Council of Prague, had knocked at every flat in the building, there were still three unaccounted for—all, as it turned out, on the fourth floor. But Josef thought he sensed futility—though he doubted his teacher ever would have admitted to it—in the old man's stoop.

"Maybe," Josef began, and then, after a brief struggle, let himself continue the thought, "maybe we ought to give up."

He was exhausted by their charade, and as they came out onto the sidewalk again, crowded with a late-afternoon traffic of schoolchildren, clerks, and tradesmen, housekeepers carrying market bags and wrapped parcels of meat, all of them headed for home, he was aware that his fear of being discovered, unmasked, recognized by his disappointed parents, had been replaced by an acute longing to see them again. At any moment he expected—yearned—to hear his mother calling his name, to feel the moist brush stroke of his father's mustache against his cheek. There was a residuum of summer in the watery blue sky, in the floral smell issuing from the bare throats of passing women. In the last day, posters had gone up advertising a new film starring Emil Jannings, the great German actor and friend of the Reich, for whom Josef felt a guilty admiration. Surely there was time to regroup, consider the situation in the bosom of his family, and prepare a less lunatic strategy. The idea that his previous plan of escape, by the conventional means of passports and visas and bribes, could somehow be revived and put into play started a seductive whispering in his heart.

"You may of course do so," Kornblum said, resting on his cane with a fatigue that seemed less feigned than it had that morning. "I haven't the liberty. Even if I do not send *you*, my prior obligation remains."

"I was just thinking that perhaps I gave up on my other plan too soon."

Kornblum nodded but said nothing, and the silence so counterbalanced the nod as to cancel it out.

"That isn't the choice, is it?" Josef said after a moment. "Between your way and the other way. If I'm really going to go, I have to go your way, don't I? Don't I?"

Kornblum shrugged, but his eyes were not involved in the gesture. They were drawn at the corners, glittering with concern. "In my professional opinion," he said.

Few things in the world carried more weight for Josef than that.

"Then there *is* no choice," he said. "They spent everything they had." He accepted the cigarette the old man offered. "What am I saying—'if I'm going'?" He spat a flake of tobacco at the ground. "I have to go."

"What you have to do, my boy," Kornblum said, "is to try to remember that you are already gone."

They went to the Eldorado Café and sat, nursing butter and egg sandwiches, two glasses of Herbert water, and the better part of a pack of Letkas. Every fifteen minutes, Kornblum consulted his wristwatch, the intervals so regular and precise as to render the gesture superfluous. After two hours they paid their check, made a stop in the men's room to empty their bladders and adjust their getups, then returned to Nicholasgasse 26. Very quickly they accounted for two of the three mystery flats, 40 and 41, discovering that the first, a tiny two-room, belonged to an elderly lady who had been taking a nap the last time the ersatz census takers came to call; and that the second, according to the same old woman, was rented to a family named Zweig or Zwang who had gone to a funeral in Zuerau or Zilina. The woman's alphabetic confusion seemed to be part of a more global uncertainty—she came to the door in her nightgown and one sock, and addressed Kornblum for no obvious reason as Herr Kapitan—encompassing, among many other points of doubt, Apartment 42, the third unaccounted-for flat, about whose occupant or occupants she was unable to provide any information at all. Repeated knocking on the door to 42 over the next hour brought no one. The mystery deepened when they returned to the neighbors in 43, the last of the floor's four flats. Earlier that afternoon, Kornblum and Josef had spoken to the head of this household: two families, the wives and fourteen children of brothers, brought together in four rooms. They were religious Jews. As before, the elder brother came to the door. He was a heavyset man in skullcap and fringes, with a great beard, black and bushy, that looked much more false to Josef than his own. The brother would consent to speak to them only through a four-inch gap, athwart a length of brass chain, as if admitting them might contaminate his home or expose the women and children to untoward influences. But his bulk could not prevent the escape of children's shrieks and laughter, women's voices, the smell of stewing carrots and of onions half-melting in a pan of fat.

"What do you want with that—?" the man said after Kornblum inquired about Apartment 42. He seemed to have second thoughts about the noun he was going to employ, and broke off. "I have nothing to do with that."

"That?" Josef said, unable to contain himself, though Kornblum had enjoined him to play the role of silent partner. "That *what?*"

"I have nothing to say." The man's long face—he was a jewel cutter, with said, exophthalmic blue eyes—seemed to ripple with disgust. "As far as I'm concerned, that apartment is empty. I pay no attention. I couldn't tell you the first thing. If you'll excuse me."

He slammed the door. Josef and Kornblum looked at each other.

"It's forty-two," Josef said as they climbed into the rattling lift.

"We shall find out," Kornblum said. "I wonder."

On their way back to his room, they passed an ash can and into it Kornblum tossed the clipped packet of flimsy on which he and Josef had named and numbered the occupants of the building. Before they had gone a dozen steps, however, Kornblum stopped, turned, and went back. With a practiced gesture, he pushed up his sleeve and reached into the mouth of the rusting drum. His face took on a pinched, stoic blankness as he groped about in the unknown offal that filled the can. After a moment, he brought out the list, now stained with a nasty green blotch. The packet was at least two centimeters thick. With a jerk of his sinewy arms, Kornblum ripped it cleanly in half. He gathered the halves together and tore them into quarters, then tore the gathered quarters into eighths. His mien remained neutral, but with each division and reassembly the wad of paper grew thicker, the force required to tear it correspondingly increased, and Josef sensed a mounting anger in Kornblum as he ripped to smithereens the inventory, by name and age, of every Jew who lived at Nicholasgasse 26. Then, with a gelid showman's smile, he rained the scraps of paper down into the wastebasket, like coins in the famous Shower of Gold illusion.

"Contemptible," he said, but Josef was not sure, then or afterward, whom or what he was talking about—the ruse itself, the occupiers who made it plausible, the Jews who had submitted to it without question, or himself for having perpetrated it.

Well past midnight, after a dinner of hard cheese, tinned smelts, and pimientos, and an evening passed in triangulating the divergent news from the Rundesfunk, Radio Moscow, and the BBC, Kornblum and Josef returned to Nicholasgasse. The extravagant front doors, thick plate glass on an iron frame worked in the form of drooping lilies, were locked, but naturally this presented Kornblum with no difficulty. In just under a minute, they were inside and headed up the stairs to the fourth floor, their rubber-soled shoes silent on the worn carpeting. The sconce lights were on mechanical timers, and had long since turned off for the night. As they proceeded, a unanimous silence seeped from the walls of the stairwell and hallways, as stifling as a smell. Josef felt his way, hesitating, listening for the whisper of his teacher's trousers, but Kornblum moved confidently in darkness. He didn't stop until he reached the door of 42. He struck a light, then gripped the door handle and knelt, using the handle to steady himself. He passed the lighter to Josef. It was hot against the palm. It grew hotter still as Josef kept it burning so that Kornblum could get the string of his pick-wallet untied. When he had unrolled the little wallet, Kornblum looked up at Josef with a question in his eyes, a teacherly amalgam of doubt and encouragement. He tapped the picks with his fingertips. Josef nodded and let the light go out. Kornblum's hand felt for Josef's. Josef took it and helped the old man to his feet with an audible creaking of bones. Then he passed back the lighter and knelt down himself, to see if he still knew how to work over a door.

There was a pair of locks, one mounted on the latch and a second set higher up—a deadbolt. Josef selected a pick tipped with a bent parenthesis and, with a twitch of the torsion wrench, made short work of the lower lock, a cheap three-pin affair. But the dead-

the amazing adventure of kavalier & clay

bolt gave him trouble. He teased and tickled the pins, sought out their resonant frequencies as if the pick were an antenna connected to the trembling inductor of his hand. But there was no signal; his fingers had gone dead. He grew first impatient, then embarrassed, huffing and blowing through his teeth. When he let loose with a hissed *Scheiss*, Kornblum laid a heavy hand on his shoulder, then struck another light. Josef hung his head, slowly stood up, and handed Kornblum the pick. In the instant before the flame of the lighter was again extinguished, he was humbled by the lack of consolation in Kornblum's expression. When he was sealed up in a coffin, in a container car on the platform in Vilna, he was going to have to do a better job.

Seconds after Josef handed over the pick, they were inside Apartment 42. Kornblum closed the door softly behind them and switched on the light. They just had time to remark on the unlikely decision someone had made to decorate the Golem's quarters in a profusion of Louis XV chairs, tiger skins, and ormolu candelabra when a low, curt, irresistible voice said, "Hands up, gents."

The speaker was a woman of about fifty, dressed in a green sateen housecoat and matching green mules. Two younger women stood behind her, wearing hard expressions and ornate kimonos, but the woman in green was the one holding the gun. After a moment, an elderly man emerged from the hallway at the women's back, in stocking feet, his shirttails flapping around him, his broom-straw legs pale and knobby. His seamed, potato-nosed face was strangely familiar to Josef.

"Max," Kornblum said, his face and voice betraying surprise for the first time since Josef had known him. It was then that Josef recognized, in the half-naked old man, the candy-producing magical waiter from his and Thomas's lone night at the Hofzinser Club years before. A lineal descendant, as it later turned out, of the Golem's maker, Rabbi Judah Loew ben Bezalel, and the man who had first brought Kornblum to the attention of the secret circle, old Max Loeb took in the scene before him, narrowing his eyes, trying to place this graybeard in a slouch hat with a commanding stage-trained voice.

"*Kornblum?*" he guessed finally, and his worried expression changed quickly to one of pity and amusement. He shook his head and signaled to the woman in green that she could put down her gun. "I can promise you this, Kornblum, you aren't going to find it here," he said, and then added, with a sour smile, "I've been poking around this apartment for years."

Early the next morning, Josef and Kornblum met in the kitchen of Apartment 42. Here they were served coffee in scalloped Herend cups by Trudi, the youngest of the three prostitutes. She was an ample girl plain and intelligent, studying to be a nurse. After relieving Josef of the burden of his innocence the previous night, in a procedure that required less time than it now took her to brew a pot of coffee, Trudi had pulled on her cherry-pink kimono and gone out to the parlor to study a text on phlebotomy, leaving Josef to the warmth of her goose-down counterpane, the lilac smell of her nape and cheek lingering on the cool pillow, the perfumed darkness of her bedroom, the shame of his contentment.

When Kornblum walked into the kitchen that morning, his eyes and Josef's sought and avoided each other's, and their conversation was monosyllabic; while Trudi was still in the kitchen, they barely drew a breath. It was not that Kornblum regretted having corrupted his young pupil. He had been frequenting prostitutes for decades and held liberal views on the utility and good sense of sexual commerce. Their berths had been more comfortable and far more fragrant then either would have found in Kornblum's cramped room, with its single cot and its clanging pipes. Nevertheless, he was embarrassed, and from the guilty arc of Josef's shoulders and the evasiveness of his gaze, Kornblum inferred that the young man felt the same.

The apartment's kitchen was redolent of good coffee and *eau de lilas*. Wan October sunshine came through the curtain on the window and worked a needlepoint of shadow across the clean pine surface of the table. Trudi was an admirable girl, and the ancient, abused hinges of Kornblum's battered frame seemed to have regained an elastic hum in the embrace of his own partner, Madame Willi—the wielder of the gun.

"Good morning," Kornblum muttered.

Josef blushed deeply. He opened his mouth to speak, but a spasm of coughing seemed to seize him, and his reply was broken and scattered on the air. They had wasted a night on pleasure at a time when so much seemed to depend on haste and self-sacrifice.

Moral discomfort notwithstanding, it was from Trudi that Josef deceived a valuable piece of information.

"She heard some kids talking," he told Kornblum after the girl, leaning down to plant a brief, coffee-scented kiss on Josef's cheek, had padded out of the kitchen and down the hall, to regain her disorderly bed. "There is a window in which no one ever sees a face."

"The *children*," Kornblum said, with a curt shake of his head. "Of course." He looked disgusted with himself for having neglected this obvious source of surprising information. "On what floor is this mysterious window?"

"She didn't know."

"On which side of the building?"

"Again, she didn't know. I thought we could find a child and ask it."

Kornblum gave his head a shake. He took another puff on his Letka, tapped it, turned it over, studied the tiny airplane symbol that was printed on the paper. Abruptly, he stood up and started to go through the kitchen drawers, working his way around the cabinets until he came up with a pair of scissors. He carried the scissors into the gilded parlor, where he began opening and closing cabinets. With gentle, precise movements, he went through the drawers of an ornate sideboard in the dining room. At last, in a table in the front hall, he found a box of notepaper, heavy sheets of rag tinted a soft robin's-egg blue. He returned to the kitchen with paper and scissors and sat down again.

"We tell the people we forgot something," he said, folding a sheet of the stationery in half and cutting it, without hesitation, his hand steady and sure. With a half-dozen strokes, he had snipped the three-pointed outline of a paper boat, the sort that children fold from pieces of newspaper. "We say they have to put one of these in every window. To show they have been counted."

"A boat," Josef said. "A boat?"

"Not a boat," Kornblum said. He put the scissors down, opened the cropped piece of paper at the center pleat, and held up a small blue Star of David.

Josef shivered at the sight of it, chilled by the plausibility of this imaginary directive. "They won't do it," he said, watching as Kornblum pressed the little star against the kitchen windowpane. "They won't comply."

"I would like to hope that you're right, young man," Kornblum said. "But we very much need you to be wrong."

Within two hours, every household in the building had spangled its windows in blue. By means of this base stratagem, the room that contained the Golem of Prague was rediscovered. It was on the top floor of Nicholasgasse 26, at the back; its lone window overlooked in the rear courtyard. A generation of children at play had, like sky-gazing shepherds in ancient fields, perfected a natural history of the windows that looked down like stars upon them; in its perpetual vacancy, this window, like a retrograde planetoid, had attracted attention and fired imaginations. It also turned out to be the only simple means of ingress for the old escape artist and his protégé. There was, or rather there had once been, a doorway, but it had been plastered and papered over, no doubt at the time of the Golem's installment in the room. Since the roof was easily accessible via the main stair, Kornblum felt that it would attract less notice if they lowered themselves, under the cover of darkness, on ropes and came in through the window than if they tried to cut their way in through the door.

Once again they returned to the building after midnight—the third night of Josef's shadow-existence in the city. This time they came dressed in somber suits and derby hats, carrying vaguely medical black bags, all supplied by a member of the secret circle who ran a mortuary. In this funereal garb, Josef lowered himself, hand under leather-gloved hand, down the rope to the ledge of the Golem's window. He dropped much faster than he intended, nearly to the level of the window on the floor below, then managed to arrest his fall with a sudden jerk that seemed to wrench his shoulder from its socket. He looked up and, in the gloom, could just distinguish the outline of Kornblum's head, the expression as unreadable as the fists clutching the other end of the rope. Josef let out a soft sigh between his clenched teeth and pulled himself back up to the Golem's window.

It was latched, but Kornblum had provided him with a length of stout wire. Josef dangled, ankles snaked around the end of the rope, clinging to it with one hand while, with the other, he jabbed the wire up into the gap between the upper, outer sash and the lower, inner one. His cheek scraped against brick, his shoulder burned, but Josef's only thought was a prayer that this time he should not fail. Finally, just as the pain in his shoulder joint was beginning to intrude on the purity of his desperation, Josef succeeded in popping the latch. He fingered the lower sash, eased it up, and swung himself into the room. He stood panting, working his shoulder in circles. A moment later, there was a creaking of rope or old bones, a soft gasp, and then Kornblum's long narrow legs kicked in through the open window. The magician turned on his torch and scanned the room until he found a lightbulb socket, dangling on a looped cord from the ceiling. He bent to reach into his mortician's bag, took out a lightbulb, and handed it to Josef, who went up on tiptoe to screw it in.

The casket in which the Golem of Prague had been laid was the simple pine box prescribed by Jewish law, but wide as a door and long enough to hold two adolescent boys head to toe. It rested across the backs of a pair of stout sawhorses in the center of an empty room. After more than thirty years, the floor of the Golem's room looked new; free of dust, glossy, and smooth. The white paint on the walls was spotless and still carried a sting of fresh emulsion. Hitherto, Josef had been inclined to discount the weirdness in Kornblum's plan of escape, but now, in the presence of this enormous coffin, in this timeless room, he felt an uneasy prickling creep across his neck and shoulders. Kornblum, too, approached the casket with visible diffidence, extending toward its rough pine lid a hand that hesitated a moment before touching. Cautiously he circled the casket, feeling out the nail heads, counting them, inspecting their condition and the condition of the hinges, and of the screws that held the hinges in place.

"All right," he said softly, with a nod, clearly trying to hearten himself as much as Josef. "Let us continue with the remainder of the plan."

The remainder of Kornblum's plan, at whose midpoint they had now arrived, was this:

First, using the ropes, they would convey the casket out of the window, onto the roof, and thence, posing as undertakers, down the stairs and out of the building. At the funeral home, in a room that had been reserved for them, they would prepare the Golem for shipment by rail to Lithuania. They would begin by gaffing the casket, which involved drawing the nails from one side and replacing them with nails that had been trimmed short, leaving a nub just long enough to fix the gaffed side to the rest of the box. That way, when the time came, Josef would be able, without much difficulty, to kick his way out. Applying the sacred principle of misdirection, they would next equip the coffin with an "inspection panel," making a cut across its lid about a third of the way from the end that held the head and equipping this upper third with a latch, so that it could, like the top half of a Dutch door, be opened separately from the lower. This would afford a good view of the dead Golem's face and chest, but not of the portion of the coffin in which Josef would crouch. After that, they would label the casket, following all the complicated regulations and procedures and affixing the elaborate forms necessary for the transshipment of human remains. Forged death certificates and other required papers would have been left for them, properly concealed, in the mortuary's workroom. After the coffin was prepared and documented, they would load it into a hearse and drive it to the train station. While riding in the back of the hearse, Josef was to climb into the coffin alongside the Golem, pulling shut the gaffed panel after him. At the station, Kornblum would check to see that the coffin appeared sealed and would consign it to the care of the porters, who would load it onto the train. When the coffin arrived in Lithuania, Josef, at his earliest opportunity, would kick aside the gaffed panel, roll free, and discover what fate awaited him on the Baltic shore.

Now that they were confronted with the actual materials of the trick however—as was so often the case—Kornblum encountered two problems.

"It's a giant," Kornblum said, with a shake of his head, speaking in a tense whisper. With his miniature crowbar, he had pried loose the nails along one side of the coffin's top and lifted the lid on its creaking, galvanized-tin hinges. He stood peering at the pitiable slab of lifeless and innocent clay. "And it's naked."

"It is very big."

"We'll never get it through the window. And if we do, we'll never get it dressed."

"Why do we have to dress it? It has those cloths, the Jewish scarves," Josef said, pointing to the tallises in which the Golem had been wrapped. They were tattered and stained, and yet gave off no odor of corruption. The only smell Josef could detect arising from the swarthy flesh of the Golem was one too faint to name, acrid and green, that he was only later to identify as the sweet stench, on a summer afternoon in the dog days, of the Moldau. "Aren't Jews supposed to be buried naked?"

"That is precisely the point," Kornblum said. He explained that, according to a recent promulgation, it was illegal to transport even a dead Jew out of the country without direct authority of Reichsprotektor von Neurath. "We must practice the tricks of our trade." He smiled thinly, nodding to the black mortician's bags. "Rouge his cheeks and lips. Fit that dome of his with a convincing wig. Someone will look inside the coffin, and when he does, we want him to see a dead *goyische* giant." He closed his eyes as if envisioning what he wanted the authorities to see, should they order the coffin to be opened. "Preferably in a very nice suit."

"The most beautiful suits I ever saw," said Josef, "belonged to a dead giant."

Kornblum studied him, sensing an implication in the words that he was unable to catch.

"Alois Hora. He was over two meters tall."

"From the Circus Zeletny?" Kornblum said. " 'The Mountain'?"

"He wore suits made in England, on Savile Row. Enormous things."

"Yes, yes, I remember," Kornblum said, nodding. "I used to see him quite often at the Café Continental. Beautiful suits," he agreed.

"I think—" Josef began. He hesitated. He said, "I know where I can find one."

It was not at all uncommon in this era for a doctor who treated glandular cases to maintain a wardrobe of wonders, stocked with underlinens the size of horse blankets, homburgs no bigger than berry bowls, and all manner of varied prodigies of haberdashery and the shoemaker's last. These items, which Josef's father had acquired or been given over the years, were kept in a cabinet in his office at the hospital, with the laudable but self-defeating intention of preventing their becoming objects of morbid curiosity to his children. No visit to their father at his place of work was ever complete without the boys at least making an attempt to persuade Dr. Kavalier to let them see the belt, fat and coiling as an anaconda, of the giant Vaclav Sroubek, or the digitalis-blossom slippers of tiny Miss Petra Frantisek. But after the doctor had been dismissed from his position at the hospital, along with the rest of the Jews on the faculty, the wardrobe of wonders had come home and its contents, in sealed packing boxes, stuffed into a closet in his study. Josef was certain that he would find some of Alois Hora's suits among them.

And so, after living for three days in Prague as a shadow, it was as a shadow that he finally went home. It was well past curfew, and the streets were deserted but for a few long, flag-fendered sedans with impenetrable black windows and, once, a lorry loaded with gray-coated boys carrying guns. Josef went slowly and carefully, inserting himself into doorways, ducking behind a parked car or bench when he heard the clank of gears, or when the fork of passing headlights jabbed at the housefronts, the awnings, the cobbles in the street. In his coat pocket, he carried the picks Kornblum had thought he would need for the job, but when Josef got to the service door of the building off the Graben he found that, as was not uncommonly the case, it had been left propped open with a tin can, probably by some housekeeper taking unauthorized leave, or by a vagabond husband.

Josef met no one in the back hall or on the stairs. There was no baby whimpering for a bottle, no faint air of Weber from a late-night radio, no elderly smoker intent on the nightly business of coughing up his lungs. Although the ceiling lights and wall sconces were lit, the collective slumber of the building seemed even more profound than that of Nicholasgasse 26. Josef found this stillness disturbing. He felt the same prickle on his nape, the creeping of his flesh, that he had felt on entering the Golem's empty room.

As he slunk down the hall, he noticed that someone had discarded a pile of clothes on the carpet outside the door of his family's home. For a preconscious instant, his heart leaped at the thought that, by some dreamlike means, one of the suits he sought had somehow been abandoned there. Then Josef saw that it was not a mere heap of clothing but one actually inhabited by a body—someone drunk, or passed out, or expired in the hallway. A girl, he thought, one of his mother's patients. It was rare, but not unheard of, for an analysand, tossed by tides of transference and desublimation, to seek the safety of Dr. Kavalier's doorstep or, by contrast, inflamed with the special hatred of countertransference, to leave herself there in some desperate condition, as a cruel prank, like a paper sack of dog turds set afire.

But the clothes belonged to Josef himself, and the body inside them was Thomas's. The boy lay on his side, knees drawn to his chest, head pillowed on an arm that reached toward the door, fingers spread with an air of lingering intention, as if he had fallen asleep with a hand on the doorknob, then subsided to the floor. He had on a pair of trousers, charcoal corduroy, shiny at the knee, and a

bulky cable sweater, with a large hole under the arm and a permanent Czechoslovakia-shaped ghost of bicycle grease on the yoke,
which Josef knew his brother liked to put on whenever he was feeling ill or friendless. From the collar of the sweater protruded the
piped lapels of a pajama top. The cuffs of the pajama bottoms poked
out from the legs of the borrowed pants. Thomas's right cheek was
flattened against his outstretched arm, and his breath rattled, regular
and clamorous, through his permanently rheumy nose. Josef smiled
and started to kneel down beside Thomas to wake him, and tease
him, and help him back to bed. Then he remembered that he was
not permitted—could not permit himself—to make his presence
known. He could not ask Thomas to lie to their parents, nor did he
really trust him to do so in any sustained manner. He backed away,
trying to think what could have happened and how best to proceed. How had Thomas gotten himself locked out? Was this who
had left the service door propped open downstairs? What could
have prompted him to risk being out so late when, as everyone
knew, a girl in Vinorhady, not much older than Thomas, had just a
few weeks before sneaked outside to look for her lost dog and been
shot, in a gloomy alley, for violating curfew? There had been official
expressions of regret from von Neurath over the incident, but no
promise that such a thing would not happen again. If Josef could
somehow manage to wake his brother undetected—say by throwing a five-haleru piece at his head from around the corner of the
hallway—would Thomas ring to be let in? Or would he be too
ashamed, and choose to continue to pass the night in the chilly, dark
hall, on the floor? And how would he, Josef, possibly be able to get
to the giant's clothes with his brother lying asleep in the doorway
or else with the whole household awakened and in an uproar over
the boy's waywardness?

These speculations were cut short when Josef stepped on something that crunched, at once soft and rigid, under his heel. His heart
seized, and he looked down, dancing backward in disgust, to see not
a burst mouse but the leather wallet of lock picks that had once
been his reward from Bernard Kornblum. Thomas's eyes fluttered,
and he snuffled, and Josef waited, wincing, to see if his brother
would sink back into sleep. Thomas sat up abruptly. With the back
of his arm he wiped the spittle from his lips, blinked, and gave a
short sigh.

"Oh, dear," he said, looking sleepily unsurprised to find his Brooklyn-bound brother crouched beside him, three days after he was supposed to have departed, in the hallway of their building in the heart of Prague. Thomas opened his mouth to speak again, but Josef covered it with the flat of his hand and pressed a finger to his own lips. He shook his head and pointed at the door.

When Thomas cast his eyes in the direction of the door to their flat, he finally seemed to awaken. His mouth narrowed to a pout, as if he had something sour on his tongue. His thick black eyebrows piled up over his nose. He shook his head and again attempted to say something, and again Josef covered his mouth, less gently this time. Josef picked up his old pick-wallet, which he had not seen in months, perhaps years, and which he had supposed, when he gave the matter any thought at all, to be lost. The lock on the Kavaliers' door was one that, in another era, Josef had successfully picked many times. He got them inside now with little difficulty, and stepped into the front hall, grateful for its familiar smell of pipe smoke and paper-whites, for the distant hum of the electric icebox. Then he stepped into the living room and saw that the sofa and piano had been draped in quilts. The fish tank stood empty of fish and drained of water. The box orange in its putti-crusted terra-cotta pot was gone. Crates stood piled in the center of the room.

"They moved?" he said, in the softest whisper he could manage.

"To Dlouha eleven," Thomas said, in a normal tone. "This morning."

"They moved," Josef said, unable now to raise his voice, though there was no one to hear them, no one to alert or disturb.

"It's a *vile* place. The Katzes are *vile* people."

"The Katzes?" There were cousins of his mother, for whom she had never cared much, who went by this name. "Viktor and Renata?"

Thomas nodded. "And the Mucus Twins." He gave a vast roll of his eyes. "And their *vile* parakeet. They taught it to say 'Up your bum, Thomas.'" He sniffed, snickered when his brother did, and then, with another slow agglomeration of his eyebrows, began to discharge a series of coughing sobs, careful and choked, as if they were painful to let out. Josef took him into his arms, stiffly, and thought suddenly how long it had been since he had heard the sound of Thomas freely crying, a sound that had once been as common in the house as the teakettle whistle or the scratch of their father's match. The weight of Thomas on his knee was unwieldy, his shape awkward and unembraceable; he seemed to have grown from a boy to a youth in just the last three days.

"There's a beastly aunt," Thomas said, "and a moronic brother-in-law due tomorrow from Frydlant. I wanted to come back here. Just for tonight. Only I couldn't work the lock."

"I understand," Josef said, understanding only that, until now, until this moment, his heart had never been broken. "You were born in this flat."

Thomas nodded.

"What a day that was," Josef said, trying to cheer the boy. "I was never so disappointed in my life."

Thomas smiled politely. "Almost the whole building moved," he said, sliding off of Josef's knee. "Only the Kravniks and the Policeks and the Zlatnys are allowed to stay." He wiped at his cheek with a forearm.

"Don't get snot on my sweater," Josef said, knocking his brother's arm to one side.

"You left it."

"I might send for it."

"Why aren't you gone?" Thomas said. "What happened to your ship?"

"There have been difficulties. But I should be on my way tonight. You mustn't tell Mother and Father that you saw me."

"You aren't going to see them?"

The question, the plaintive rasp in Thomas's voice as he asked it, pained Josef. He shook his head. "I just had to dash back here to get something."

"Dash back from where?"

Josef ignored the question. "Is everything still here?"

"Except for some clothes, and some kitchen things. And my tennis racket. And my butterflies. And your wireless." This was a twenty-tube set, built into a kind of heavy valise of oiled pine, that Josef had constructed from parts, amateur radio having succeeded illusion and preceded modern art in the cycle of Josef's passions, as Houdini and then Marconi had given way to Paul Klee and Josef's enrollment at the Academy of Fine Arts. "Mother carried it on her lap in the tram. She said listening to it was like listening to your voice, and she

michael chabon   **51**

would rather have your voice to remember you than your photograph, even."

"And then she said that I never photograph well, anyway."

"Yes, she did, as a matter of fact. The wagon is coming here tomorrow morning for the rest of our things. I'm going to ride with the driver. I'm going to hold the reins. What is it you need? What did you come back for?"

"Wait here," Josef said. He had already revealed too much; Kornblum was going to be very displeased.

He went down the hall to their father's study, checking to make sure that Thomas did not follow, and doing his best to ignore the piled crates, the open doors that ought at this hour to have been long shut, the rolled carpets, the forlorn knocking of his shoe heels along the bare wooden floors. In his father's office, the desk and bookcase had been wrapped in quilted blankets and tied with leather straps, the pictures and curtains taken down. The boxes that contained the uncanny clothing of endocrine freaks had been dragged from the closet and stacked, conveniently, just by the door. Each bore a pasted-on label, carefully printed in his father's strong, regular hand, that gave a precise accounting of the contents of the crate:

DRESSES (5)—MARTINKA
HAT (STRAW)—ROTHMAN
CHRISTENING GOWN—SROUBEK

For some reason, the sight of these labels touched Josef. The writing was as legible as if it had been typeset, each letter shod and gloved with serifs, the parentheses neatly crimped, the wavy hyphens like stylized bolts of lightning. The labels had been lettered lovingly; his father had always expressed that emotion best through troubling with details. In this fatherly taking of pains—in this stubbornness, persistence, orderliness, patience, and calm—Josef had always taken comfort. Here Dr. Kavalier seemed to have composed, on his crates of strange mementos, a series of messages in the very alphabet of imperturbability itself. The labels seemed evidence of all the qualities his father and family were going to require to survive the ordeal to which Josef was abandoning them. With his father in charge, the Kavaliers and the Katzes would doubtless manage to form one of those rare households in which decency and order prevailed. With patience and calm, persistence and stoicism, good hand-writing and careful labeling, they would meet persecution, indignity, and hardship head-on.

But then, staring at the label on one crate, which read

SWORD-CANE—DLUBECK
SHOE TREE—HORA
SUITS (3)—HORA
ASSORTED HANDKERCHIEFS (6)—HORA

Josef felt a bloom of dread in his belly, and all at once he was certain that it was not going to matter one iota how his father and the others behaved. Orderly or chaotic, well inventoried and civil or jumbled and squabbling, the Jews of Prague were dust on the boots of the Germans, to be whisked off with an indiscriminate broom. Stoicism and an eye for detail would avail them nothing. In later years, when he remembered this moment, Josef would be tempted to think that he had suffered a premonition, looking at those mucilage-caked labels, of the horror to come. At the time it was a simpler matter. The hair stood up on the back of his neck with a prickling discharge of ions. His heart pulsed in the hollow of his throat as if someone had pressed there with a thumb. And he felt, for an instant, that he was admiring the penmanship of someone who had died.

"What's that?" Thomas said, when Josef returned to the parlor with one of Hora's extra-large garment bags slung over his shoulder. "What happened? What's wrong?"

"Nothing," said Josef. "Look, Thomas, I have to go. I'm sorry."

"I *know.*" Thomas sounded almost irritated. He sat down cross-legged on the floor. "I'm going to spend the night."

"No, Thomas, I don't think—"

"You don't get to say," Thomas said. "You aren't here anymore, remember?"

The words echoed Kornblum's sound advice, but somehow they chilled Josef. He could not shake the feeling—reportedly common among ghosts—that it was not he but those he haunted whose lives were devoid of matter, sense, future.

"Perhaps you're right," he said after a moment. "You oughtn't to be out in the streets at night, anyway. It's too dangerous."

A hand on each of Thomas's shoulders, Josef steered his brother back to the room they had shared for the last eleven years. With some blankets and a slipless pillow that he found in a trunk, he made up a bed on the floor. Then he dug around in some other crates until he found an old children's alarm clock, a bear's face eared with a pair of brass bells, which he wound and set for five-thirty.

"You have to be back there by six," he said, "or they'll miss you."

Thomas nodded and climbed between the blankets of the makeshift bed. "I wish I could go with you," he said.

"I know," Josef said. He brushed the hair from Thomas's forehead. "So do I. But you'll be joining me soon enough."

"Do you promise?"

"I will make sure of it," Josef said. "I won't rest until I'm meeting your ship in the harbor of New York City."

"On that island they have," Thomas said, his eyelids fluttering. "With the Statue of Liberation."

"I promise," Josef said.

"Swear."

"I swear."

"Swear by the River Styx."

"I swear it," Josef said, "by the River Styx."

Then he leaned down and, to the surprise of both of them, kissed his brother on the lips. It was the first such kiss between them since the younger had been an infant and the elder a doting boy in knee pants.

"Goodbye, Josef," said Thomas.

When Josef returned to Nicholasgasse, he found that Kornblum had, with typical resourcefulness, solved the problem of the Golem's extrication. Into the thin panel of gypsum that had been used to fill the door frame at the time when the Golem was installed, Kornblum, employing some unspeakable implement of the mortuary trade, had cut a rectangle, at floor level, just large enough to accommodate the casket end-on. The obverse of the gypsum panel, out in the hall, was covered in the faded Jugendstil paper, a pattern of tall interlocking poppies, that decorated all the hallways of the building. Kornblum had been careful to cut through this thin outer hide on only three of his rectangle's four sides, leaving at its top a hinge of intact wallpaper. Thus he had formed a serviceable trapdoor.

"What if someone notices?" Josef said after he had finished inspecting Kornblum's work.

This gave rise to another of Kornblum's impromptu and slightly cynical maxims. "People notice only what you tell them to notice," he said. "And then only if you remind them."

They dressed the Golem in the suit that had belonged to the giant Alois Hora. This was hard work, as the Golem was relatively inflexible. It was not as rigid as one might have imagined, given its nature and composition. Its cold clay flesh seemed to give slightly under the pressure of fingertips, and a narrow range of motion, perhaps the faintest memory of play, inhered in the elbow of the right arm, the arm it would have used, as the legend records, to touch the mezuzah on its maker's doorway every evening when it returned from its labors, bringing its Scripture-kissed fingers to its lips. The Golem's knees and ankles, however, were more or less petrified. Furthermore, its hands and feet were poorly proportioned, as is often the case with the work of amateur artists, and much too large for its body. The enormous feet got snagged in the trouser legs, so that getting the pants on was particularly difficult. Finally, Josef had to reach into the coffin and grasp the Golem around the waist, elevating its lower body several inches, before Kornblum could tug the trousers over the feet, up the legs, and around the Golem rather sizable buttocks. They had decided not to bother with underwear, but for the sake of anatomical verisimilitude—in a display of the thoroughness that had characterized his career on the stage—Kornblum tore one of the old tallises in two (kissing it first), gave a series of twists to one of the halves, and tucked the resulting artifact up between the Golem's legs, into the crotch, where there was only a smooth void of clay.

"Maybe it was supposed to be a female," Josef suggested as he watched Kornblum zip the Golem's fly.

"Not even the Maharal could make a woman out of clay," Kornblum said. "For that you need a rib." He stood back, considering the Golem. He gave a tug on one lapel of the jacket and smoothed the billowing pleats of the trousers front. "This is a very nice suit."

It was one of the last Alois Hora had taken delivery of before his death, when his body had been wasted by Marfan's syndrome, and that a perfect fit for the Golem, which was not so large as the Mountain in his prime. Of excellent English worsted, gray and tan, shot with a burgundy thread, it easily could have been subdivided into a suit for Josef and another for Kornblum, with enough left over, as the magician remarked, for a waistcoat apiece. The shirt was of fine white twill, with mother-of-pearl buttons, and the necktie of burgundy silk, with an embossed pattern of cabbage roses, slightly flamboyant, as Hora had like his ties. There were no shoes—Josef had forgotten to search for a pair and in any case none would have been large enough—but if the lower regions of the casket's interior were ever inspected, the trick would fail anyway, shoes or no.

Once it was dressed, its cheeks rouged, its smooth head bewigged, its forehead and eyelids fitted with the tiny eyebrow and eyelash hair pieces employed by gentile morticians in the case of facial burning or certain depilatory diseases, the Golem looked, with its dull grayish complexion the color of boiled mutton, indisputably dead and passably human. There was only the faintest trace of the human handprint on its forehead, from which, centuries before, the name of God had been rubbed away. Now they only had to slide it through the trapdoor and follow it out of the room.

This proved easy enough; as Josef had remarked when he lifted it to get the trousers on, the Golem weighed far less than its bulk and nature would have suggested. To Josef, it felt as if they were struggling, down the hallway, down the stairs, and out the front door of Nicholasgasse 26, with a substantial pine box and a large suit of clothes, and little besides.

"'Mach' bida lo nafsho,'" Kornblum said, quoting Midrash, when Josef remarked on the lightness of their load. "'His soul is a burden unto him.' This is nothing, this." He nodded toward the lid of the coffin. "Just an empty jar. If you were not in there, I would have been obliged to weight it down with sandbags."

The trip out of the building and back to the mortuary in the borrowed Skoda hearse—Kornblum had learned to drive in 1908, he said, taught by Franz Hofzinser's great pupil Hans Kreutzler—came off without incident or an encounter with the authorities. The only person who saw them carrying the coffin out of the building, an insomniac out-of-work engineer named Pilzen, was told that old Mr. Lazarus in 42 had finally died after a long illness. When Mrs. Pilzen came by the flat the next afternoon with a plate of egg cookies in hand, she found a wizened old gentleman and three charming if somewhat improper women in black kimonos, sitting on low stools, with torn ribbons pinned to their clothes and the mirrors covered, a set of conditions that proved bemusing to the clientele of Madame Willi's establishment over the next seven days, some of whom were unnerved and some excited by the blasphemy of making love in a house of the dead.

Seventeen hours after he climbed into the coffin to lie with the empty vessel that once had been animate with the condensed hopes of Jewish Prague, Josef's train approached the town of Oshmyany, on the border between Poland and Lithuania. The two national railway systems employed different gauges of track, and there was to be a sixty-minute delay as passengers and freight were shifted from the gleaming black Soviet-built express of Polish subjugation to the huffing, Czarist-era local of a tenuous Baltic liberty. The big *Josef Stalin*-class locomotive eased all but silently into its berth and uttered a surprisingly sensitive even rueful, sigh. Slowly, for the most part, as if unwilling to draw a tention to themselves by an untoward display of eagerness or nerve the passengers, a good many young men of an age with Josef Kavalier dressed in the belted coats, knickers, and broad hats of Chasidin stepped down onto the platform and moved in an orderly way toward the emigration and customs officers who waited, along with a representative of the local Gestapo bureau, in a room overheated by a roaring pot-bellied stove. The railway porters, a sad crew of spavined of men and weaklings, few of whom looked capable of carrying a hatbox let alone the coffin of a giant, rolled back the doors of the car in which the Golem and its stowaway companion rode, and squinted doubtful at the burden they were now expected to unload and carry twenty-five meters to a waiting Lithuanian boxcar.

Inside the coffin, Josef lay insensible. He had fainted with an excruciating, at times almost pleasurable, slowness over a period of some eight or ten hours, as the rocking of the train, the lack of oxygen, the deficit of sleep and surfeit of nervous upset he had accumulated over the past week, the diminished circulation of his blood, and a strange soporific emanation from the Golem itself that seemed connected to its high-summer, rank-river smell, all conspired to overcome the severe pain in his hips and back, the cramping of his leg and arm muscles, the near-impossibility of urination, the tingling, at times almost jolting numbness of his legs and feet, the growling of his stomach, and the dread, wonder, and uncertainty of the voyage on which he had embarked. When they took the coffin from the train, he did not waken though his dream took on an urgent but inconclusive tinge of peril. He did not come to his senses until a beautiful jet of cold fir-green a singed his nostrils, lighting his slumber with an intensity matched only by the pale shaft of sunlight that penetrated his prison when the "inspection panel" was abruptly thrown open.

Once more it was Kornblum's instruction that saved Josef from losing everything in the first instant. In the first dazzling panic that followed the opening of the panel, when Josef wanted to cry out in pain, rapture, and fear, the word "Oshmyany" seemed to lie cold and rational between his fingers, like a pick that was going, in the end, to free him. Kornblum, whose encyclopedic knowledge of the railroads of this part of Europe was in a few short years to receive a dreadful appendix, had coached him thoroughly, as they worked to gaff the coffin, on the stages and particulars of his journey. He felt the jostle of men's arms, the sway of their hips as they carried the coffin, and this, together with the odor of northern forest and a susurrant snippet of Polish, resolved at the last possible instant into a consciousness of where he was and what must be happening to him. The porters themselves had opened the coffin as they carried it from the Polish train to the Lithuanian. He could hear, and vaguely understand, that they were marveling both at the deadness and giantness of their charge. Then Josef's teeth came together with a sharp porcelain chiming as the coffin was dropped. Josef kept silent and prayed that the impact didn't pop the gaffed nails and send him tumbling out. He hoped that he had been thrown thus into the new boxcar, but feared that it was only impact with the station floor that had filled his mouth with blood from his bitten tongue. The light shrank and winked out, and he exhaled, safe in the airless, eternal dark; then the light blazed again.

"What is this? Who is this?" said a German voice.

"A giant, Herr Lieutenant. A dead giant."

"A dead Lithuanian giant." Josef heard a rattle of paper. The German officer was leafing through the sheaf of forged documents that Kornblum had affixed to the outside of the coffin. "Named Kervelis Hailonidas. Died in Prague the night before last. Ugly bastard."

"Giants are always ugly, Lieutenant," said one of the porters in German. There was general agreement from the other porters, with some supporting cases offered into evidence.

"Great God," said the German officer, "but it's a crime to bury a suit like that in a dirty old hole in the ground. Here, you. Get a crowbar. Open that coffin."

Kornblum had provided Josef with an empty Mosel bottle, into which he was, at rare intervals, to insert the tip of his penis and, sparingly, relieve his bladder. But there was no time to maneuver it into place as the porters began to kick and scrape at the seams of the giant coffin. The inseam of Josef's trousers burned and then went instantly cold.

"There is no crowbar, Herr Lieutenant," one of the porters said. "We will chop it open with an ax."

Josef struggled against a wild panic that scratched like an animal at his rib cage.

"Ah, no," the German officer said with a laugh. "Forget it. I'm tall, all right, but I'm not that tall." After a moment, the darkness of the coffin was restored. "Carry on, men."

There was a pause, and then, with a jerk, Josef and the Golem were lifted again.

"And he's ugly, too," said one of the men, in a voice just audible to Josef, "but he's not *that* ugly."

Some twenty-seven hours later, Josef staggered, dazed, blinking, limping, bent, asphyxiated, and smelling of stale urine, into the sun-tattered grayness of an autumn morning in Lithuania. He watched from behind a soot-blackened pillar of the Vilna station as the two dour-looking confederates of the secret circle claimed the curious, giant coffin from Prague. Then he hobbled around to the house of Kornblum's brother-in-law; on Pylimo Street, where he was received kindly with food, a hot bath, and a narrow cot in the kitchen. It was while staying here, trying to arrange for passage to New York out of Priekule, that he first heard of a Dutch consul in Kovno who was madly issuing visas to Curaçao, in league with a Japanese official who would grant rights of transit via the Empire of Japan to any Jew bound for the Dutch colony. Two days later he was on the Trans-Siberian Express; a week later he reached Vladivostok, and thence sailed for Kobe. From Kobe he shipped to San Francisco, where he wired his aunt in Brooklyn for money for the bus to New York. It was on the steamer carrying him through the Golden Gate that he happened to reach down into the hole in the lining of the right pocket of his overcoat and discover the envelope that his brother had solemnly handed to him almost a month before. It contained a single piece of paper, which Thomas had hastily stuffed into it that morning as they all were leaving the house together for the last time, by way or in lieu of expressing the feelings of love, fear, and hopefulness that his brother's escape inspired. It was the drawing of Harry Houdini, taking a calm cup of tea in the middle of the sky, that Thomas had made in his notebook during his abortive career as a librettist. Josef studied it, feeling as he sailed toward freedom as if he weighed nothing at all, as if every precious burden had been lifted from him.

*If there's anything more gripping than a prison break
story, it's a prison break story that's true. In this case,
the events not only happened, but had as their subject
and chronicler one of the most captivating minds of
the twentieth century. Statesman and man of letters,
Sir Winston Churchill lived life as a constant source of
narrative inspiration. In 1899, the twenty-five-year-old
subaltern took the decisive step—both for his political
and journalistic career—of accepting an invitation to
become the Daily Mail's correspondent in South
Africa, then in the grip of the Boer War. While there,
the intrepid correspondent took part in the major
military actions. He also had the unexpected but
priceless experience of capture and escape, which
instantly won him the reputation of a dashing hero,
a national figure, and even the subject of popular
songs—all of which stood him in good stead when
he stood for Parliament a second time. Wrought with
an impeccable eye for detail and a thoroughly
gentlemanly sense of fair play, Churchill's Boer War
dispatches mark the high point of his journalistic
career.*

from *young winston's wars*

WINSTON S. CHURCHILL

how unhappy is that poor man who loses his liberty! What can the wide world give him in exchange? No degree of material comfort, no consciousness of correct behaviour, can balance the hateful degradation of imprisonment. Before I had been an hour in captivity I resolved to escape. Many plans suggested themselves, were examined and rejected. For a month I thought of nothing else. But the peril and difficulty restrained action. I think that it was the news of the British defeat at Stormberg that clinched the matter. All the news we heard in Pretoria was derived from Boer sources, and was hideously exaggerated and distorted. Every day we read in the *Volksstem*—probably the most amazing tissue of lies ever presented to the public under the name of a newspaper—of Boer victories and of the huge slaughters and shameful flights of the British. However much one might doubt and discount these tales they made a deep impression. A month's feeding on such literary garbage weakens the constitution of the mind. We wretched prisoners lost heart. Perhaps Great Britain would not persevere; perhaps foreign powers would intervene; perhaps there would be another disgraceful, cowardly peace. At the best the war and our confinement would be prolonged for many months. I do not pretend that impatience at being locked up was not the foundation of my determination; but I should never have screwed up my courage to make the attempt without the earnest desire to do something, however small, to help the British cause. Of course, I am a man of peace. I do not fight. But swords are not the only weapons in the world. Something may be done with a pen. So I determined to take all hazards; and, indeed, the affair was one of very great danger and difficulty.

The State Model Schools, the building in which we were confined, is a brick structure standing in the midst of a gravel quadrangle and surrounded on two sides by an iron grille and on two by a
corrugated iron fence about 10 feet high. These boundaries offered
little obstacle to anyone who possessed the activity of youth, but the
fact that they were guarded on the inside by sentries armed with
rifle and revolver fifty yards apart made them a well-nigh insupera-
ble barrier. No walls are so hard to pierce as living walls. I thought
of the penetrating power of gold, and the sentries were sounded.
They were incorruptible. I seek not to deprive them of the credit,
but the truth is that the bribery market in this country has been
spoiled by the millionaires. I could not afford with my slender
resources to insult them heavily enough. So nothing remained but
to break out in spite of them. With another officer who may for the
present—since he is still a prisoner—remain nameless I formed a
scheme. Please to look at the plan.

After anxious reflection and continual watching, it was discovered
that when the sentries near the offices walked about on their beats
they were at certain moments unable to see the top of a few yards of
the wall. The electric lights in the middle of the quadrangle brilliantly lighted the whole place, but cut off the sentries beyond them
from looking at the eastern wall. For behind the lights all seemed by
contrast darkness. The first thing was therefore to pass the two sentries near the offices. It was necessary to hit off the exact moment
when both their backs should be turned together. After the wall was
scaled we should be in the garden of the villa next door. There our
plan came to an end. Everything after this was vague and uncertain.
How to get out of the garden, how to pass unnoticed through the
streets, how to evade the patrols that surrounded the town and, above
all, how to cover the two hundred and eighty miles to the Portuguese frontiers, were questions which would arise at a later stage. All
attempts to communicate with friends outside had failed. We cher-
ished the hope that with chocolate, a little Kaffir knowledge and a
great deal of luck we might march the distance in a fortnight, buying
mealies at the native kraals and lying hidden by day. But it did not
look a very promising prospect.

We determined to try on the night of 11 December, making up
our minds quite suddenly in the morning, for these things are best
done on the spur of the moment. I passed the afternoon in positive

terror. Nothing has ever disturbed me as much as this. There is something appalling in the idea of stealing secretly off in the night like a guilty thief. The fear of detection has a pang of its own. Besides, we knew quite well that on occasion, even on excuse, the sentries—they were armed police—would fire. Fifteen yards is a short range. And beyond the immediate danger lay a prospect of severe hardship and suffering, only faint hopes of success, and the probability at the best of five months in Pretoria Gaol.

The afternoon dragged tediously away. I tried to read Mr. Lecky's *History of England*, but for the first time in my life that wise writer wearied me. I played chess and was hopelessly beaten. At last it grew dark. At seven o'clock the bell for dinner rang and the officers trooped off. Now was the time. But the sentries gave us no chance. They did not walk about. One of them stood exactly opposite the only practicable part of the wall. We waited for two hours, but the attempt was plainly impossible, and so with a most unsatisfactory feeling of relief to bed.

Tuesday, the 12th! Another day of fear, but fear crystallising more and more into desperation. Anything was better than further suspense. Night came again. Again the dinner bell sounded. Choosing my opportunity I strolled across the quadrangle and secreted myself in one of the offices. Through a chink I watched the sentries. For half an hour they remained stolid and obstructive. Then all of a sudden one turned and walked up to his comrade and they began to talk. Their backs were turned. Now or never. I darted out of my hiding-place and ran to the wall, seized the top with my hands and drew myself up. Twice I let myself down again in sickly hesitation, and then with a third resolve scrambled up. The top was flat. Lying on it I had one parting glimpse of the sentries, still talking, still with their backs turned; but, I repeat, fifteen yards away. Then I lowered myself silently down into the adjoining garden and crouched among the shrubs. I was free. The first step had been taken and it was irrevocable.

It now remained to await the arrival of my comrade. The bushes of the garden gave a good deal of cover, and in the moonlight their shadows lay black on the ground. Twenty yards away was the house, and I had not been five minutes in hiding before I perceived that it was full of people; the windows revealed brightly-lighted rooms, and within I could see figures moving about. This was a fresh complication. We had always thought the house unoccupied. Presently—

how long afterwards I do not know, for the ordinary measures of time, hours, minutes and seconds, are quite meaningless on such occasions—a man came out of the door and walked across the garden in my direction. Scarcely ten yards away he stopped and stood still, looking steadily towards me. I cannot describe the surge of panic which nearly overwhelmed me. I must be discovered. I dared not stir an inch. But amid a tumult of emotion, reason, seated firmly on her throne, whispered, "Trust to the dark background." I remained absolutely motionless. For a long time the man and I remained opposite each other, and every instant I expected him to spring forward. A vague idea crossed my mind that I might silence him. "Hush, I am a detective. We expect that an officer will break out here tonight. I am waiting to catch him." Reason—scornful this time—replied: "Surely a Transvaal detective would speak Dutch. Trust to the shadow." So I trusted, and after a spell another man came out of the house, lighted a cigar, and both he and the other walked off together. No sooner had they turned than a cat pursued by a dog rushed into the bushes and collided into me. The startled animal uttered a "miaul" of alarm and darted back again making a horrible rustling. Both men stopped at once. But it was only the cat, and they passed out of the garden gate into the town.

I looked at my watch. An hour had passed since I climbed the wall. Where was my comrade? Suddenly I heard a voice from within the quadrangle say quite loud "All up." I crawled back to the wall. Two officers were walking up and down the other side jabbering Latin words, laughing and talking all manner of nonsense—amid which I caught my name. I risked a cough. One of the officers immediately began to chatter alone. The other said slowly and clearly: "...cannot get out. The sentry suspects. It's all up. Can you get back again?" But now all my fears fell from me at once. To go back was impossible. I could not hope to climb the wall unnoticed. Fate pointed onwards. Besides, I said to myself, "Of course, I shall be recaptured, but I will at least have a run for my money." I said to the officers: "I shall go on alone."

Now, I was in the right mood for these undertakings—that is to say that, thinking failure almost certain, no odds against success affected me. All risks were less than the certainty. A glance at the plan will show that the gate which led into the road was only a few yards from another sentry. I said to myself, *"Toujours l'audace"*: put my hat on my head, strode out into the middle of the garden, walked past the windows of the house without any attempt at concealment, and so went through the gate and turned to the left. I passed the sentry at less than five yards. Most of them knew me by sight. Whether he looked at me or not I do not know, for I never turned my head. But after walking a hundred yards I knew that the second obstacle had been surmounted. I was at large in Pretoria.

I walked on leisurely through the night humming a tune and choosing the middle of the road. The streets were full of burghers, but they paid no attention to me. Gradually I reached the suburbs, and on a little bridge I sat down to reflect and consider. I was in the heart of the enemy's country. I knew no one to whom I could apply for succour. Nearly three hundred miles stretched between me and Delagoa Bay. My escape must be known at dawn. Pursuit would be immediate. Yet all exits were barred. The town was picketed, the country was patrolled, the trains were searched, the line was guarded. I had £75 in my pocket and four slabs of chocolate, but the compass and the map which might have guided me, the opium tablets and meat lozenges which should have sustained me, were in my friend's pockets in the State Model School. Worst of all, I could not speak a word of Dutch or Kaffir, and how was I to get food or direction?

But when hope had departed, fear had gone as well. I formed a plan. I would find the Delagoa Bay railway. Without map or compass I must follow that in spite of the pickets. I looked at the stars. Orion shone brightly. Scarcely a year ago he had guided me when lost in the desert to the bank of the Nile. He had given me water. Now he should lead me to freedom. I could not endure the want of either.

After walking south for half a mile I struck the railroad. Was it the line to Delagoa Bay or the Pietersburg branch? If it were the former it should run east. But as far as I could see this line ran northwards. Still, it might be only winding its way out among the hills. I resolved to follow it. The night was delicious. A cool breeze fanned my face and a wild feeling of exhilaration took hold of me. At any rate I was free, if only for an hour. That was something. The fascination of the adventure grew. Unless the stars in their courses fought for me I could not escape. Where was the need for caution? I marched briskly along the line. Here and there the lights of a picket fire gleamed. Every bridge had its watchers. But I passed them all, making very short detours at the dangerous places, and really taking scarcely any precautions.

As I walked I extended my plan. I could not march three hundred miles to the frontier. I would go by train. I would board a train in motion and hide under the seats, on the roof, on the couplings—anywhere. What train should I take? The first, of course. After walking for two hours I perceived the signal lights of a station. I left the line and, circling round it, hid in the ditch by the track about 200 yards beyond it. I argued that the train would stop at the station and that it would not have got up too much speed by the time it reached me. An hour passed. I began to grow impatient. Suddenly I heard the whistle and the approaching rattle. Then the great yellow headlights of the engine flashed into view. The train waited five minutes at the station and started again with much noise and steaming. I crouched by the track. I rehearsed the act in my mind. I must wait until the engine had passed, otherwise I should be seen. Then I must make a dash for the carriages.

The train started slowly but gathered speed sooner than I had expected. The flaring lights drew swiftly near. The rattle grew into a roar. The dark mass hung for a second above me. The engine driver silhouetted against his furnace glow, the black profile of the engine, the clouds of steam rushed past. Then I hurled myself on the trucks, clutched at something, missed, clutched again, missed again, grasped some sort of handhold, was swung off my feet—my toes bumping on the line, and with a struggle seated myself on the couplings of the fifth truck from the front of the train. It was a goods train, and the trucks were full of sacks, soft sacks covered with coal dust. I crawled on top and burrowed in among them. In five minutes I was completely buried. The sacks were warm and comfortable. Perhaps the engine driver had seen me rush up to the train and would give the alarm at the next station; on the other hand, perhaps not. Where was the train going to? Where would it be unloaded? Would it be searched? Was it on the Delagoa Bay line? What should I do in the morning? Ah, never mind that. Sufficient for the day was the luck thereof. Fresh plans for fresh contingencies. I resolved to sleep, nor can I imagine a more pleasing lullaby than the clatter of the train that carries you at twenty miles an hour away from the enemy's capital.

How long I slept I do not know, but I woke up suddenly with all feelings of exhilaration gone, and only the consciousness of oppressive difficulties heavy on me. I must leave the train before daybreak, so that I could drink at a pool and find some hiding place while it was still dark. Another night I would board another train. I crawled from my cosy hiding place among the sacks and sat again on the couplings. The train was running at a fair speed, but I felt it was time to leave it. I took hold of the iron handle at the back of the truck, pulled strongly with my left hand, and sprang. My feet struck the ground in two gigantic strides, and the next instant I was sprawling in the ditch considerably shaken but unhurt. The train, my faithful ally of the night, hurried on its journey.

It was still dark. I was in the middle of a wide valley, surrounded by low hills and carpeted with high grass drenched in dew. I searched for water in the nearest gully and soon found a clear pool. I was very thirsty, but long after I had quenched my thirst I continued to drink that I might have sufficient for the whole day.

Presently the dawn began to break, and the sky to the east grew yellow and red, slashed across with heavy black clouds. I saw with relief that the railway ran steadily towards the sunrise. I had taken the right line after all.

Having drunk my fill, I set out for the hills, among which I hoped to find some hiding-place, and as it became broad daylight I entered a small group of trees which grew on the side of a deep ravine. Here I resolved to wait till dusk. I had one consolation: no one in the world knew where I was—I did not know myself. It was now four o'clock. Fourteen hours lay between me and the night. My impatience to proceed doubled their length. At first it was terribly cold, but by degrees the sun gained power, and by ten o'clock the heat was oppressive. My sole companion was a gigantic vulture, who manifested an extravagant interest in my condition, and made hideous and ominous gurglings from time to time. From my lofty position I commanded a view of the whole valley. A little tin-roofed town lay three miles to the westward. Scattered farmsteads, each with a clump of trees, relieved the monotony of the undulating ground. At the foot of the hill stood a Kaffir kraal, and the figures of its inhabitants dotted the patches of cultivation or surrounded the droves of goats and cows which fed on the pasture. The railway ran through the middle of the valley, and I could watch the passage of the various trains. I counted four passing each way, and from this I drew the conclusion that the same number would run at night. I marked a steep gradient up which they climbed very slowly, and determined at nightfall to make another attempt to board one of these. During the day I ate one slab of chocolate which, with the heat, produced a violent thirst. The pool was hardly half a mile away, but I dared not leave the shelter of the little wood, for I could see the figures of white men riding or walking occasionally across the valley, and once a Boer came and fired two shots at birds close to my hiding place. But no one discovered me.

The elation and the excitement of the previous night had burnt away, and a chilling reaction followed. I was very hungry, for I had no dinner before starting, and chocolate though it sustains does not satisfy. I had scarcely slept, but yet my heart beat so fiercely and I was so nervous and perplexed about the future that I could not rest. I thought of all the chances that lay against me; I dreaded and detested more than words can express the prospect of being caught and dragged back to Pretoria. I do not mean that I would rather have died than have been retaken, but I have often feared death for much less. I found no comfort in any of the philosophical ideas that some men parade in their hours of ease and strength and safety. They seemed only fair weather friends. I realised with awful force that no exercise of my own feeble wit and strength could save me from my enemies, and that without the assistance of that High Power which interferes more often than we are always prone to admit in the eternal sequence of causes and effects, I could never succeed. I prayed long and earnestly for help and guidance. My prayer, as it seems to me, was swiftly and wonderfully answered. I cannot now relate the strange circumstances which followed, and which changed my nearly hopeless position into one of superior advantage. But after the war is over I shall hope to lengthen this account, and so remarkable will the addition be that I cannot believe the reader will complain.

The long day reached its close at last. The western clouds flushed into fire; the shadows of the hills stretched out across the valley. A ponderous Boer waggon, with its long team, crawled slowly along the track towards the town. The Kaffirs collected their herds and drew around their kraal. The daylight died, and soon it was quite dark. Then, and not till then, I set forth. I hurried to the railway line, pausing on my way to drink at a stream of sweet, cold water. I waited for sometime at the top of the steep gradient in the hope of catching a train. But none came, and I gradually guessed, and I have since found out that I guessed right, that the train I had already travelled in was the only one that ran at night. At last I resolved to walk on and make, at any rate, twenty miles of my journey. I walked for about six hours. How far I travelled I do not know, but I do not expect it was very many miles in the direct line. Every bridge was guarded by armed men; every few miles were gangers' huts; at intervals there were stations with villages clustering round them. All the veldt was bathed in the bright rays of the full moon, and to avoid these dangerous places I had to make wide circuits and often to creep along the ground. Leaving the railroad I fell into bogs and swamps, and brushed through high grass dripping with dew, and so I was drenched to the waist. I had been able to take little exercise during my month's imprisonment, and I was soon tired out with walking, as well as from want of food and sleep. I felt very miserable when I looked around and saw here and there the lights of houses, and thought of the warmth and comfort within them, but knew that they only meant danger to me. After six or seven hours of walking I thought it unwise to go further lest I should exhaust myself, so I lay down in a ditch to sleep. I was nearly at the end of my tether. Nevertheless, by the will of God, I was enabled to sustain myself during the next few days, obtaining food at great risk here and there, resting in concealment by day and walking only at night. On the fifth day I was beyond Middleburg, as far as I could tell, for I dared not inquire nor as yet approach the stations near enough to read the names. In a secure hiding place I waited for a suitable train, knowing that there is a through service between Middleburg and Lourenço Marques.

Meanwhile there had been excitement in the State Model Schools, temporarily converted into a military prison. Early on Wednesday morning—barely twelve hours after I had escaped—my absence was discovered—I think by Doctor Gunning, an amiable Hollander who used often to come and argue with me the rights and wrongs of the war. The alarm was given. Telegrams with my description at great length were despatched along all the railways. A warrant was issued for my immediate arrest. Every train was strictly searched. Everyone was on the watch. The newspapers made so much of the affair that my humble fortunes and my whereabouts were discussed in long columns of print, and even in the crash of the war I became to the Boers a topic all to myself. The rumours in part amused me. It was certain, said the *Standard and Digger's News,* that I had escaped disguised as a woman. The next day I was reported captured at Komati Poort dressed as a Transvaal policeman. There was great delight at this, which was only changed to doubt when other telegrams said that I had been arrested at Bragsbank, at Middleburg and at Bronkerspruit. But the captives proved to be harmless people after all. Finally it was agreed that I had never left Pretoria. I had—it appeared—changed clothes with a waiter, and was now in hiding at the house of some British sympathiser in the capital. On the strength of this all the houses of suspected persons were searched from top to bottom, and these unfortunate people were, I fear, put to a great deal of inconvenience. A special commission was also appointed to investigate "stringently" (a most hateful adjective in such a connection) the causes "which had rendered it possible for the war correspondent of the *Morning Post* to escape."

The *Volksstem* noticed as a significant fact that I had recently become a subscriber to the State Library, and had selected Mill's essay *On Liberty*. It apparently desired to gravely deprecate prisoners having access to such inflammatory literature. The idea will, perhaps, amuse those who have read the work in question.

All these things may provoke a smile of indifference; perhaps even of triumph after the danger is past; but during the days when I was lying up in holes and corners waiting for a good chance to board a train, the causes that had led to them preyed more than I knew on my nerves. To be an outcast, to be hunted, to be under a warrant for arrest, to fear every man, to have imprisonment—not necessarily military confinement either—hanging overhead, to fly the light, to doubt the shadows—all these things ate into my soul and have left an impression that will not perhaps be easily effaced.

On the sixth day the chance I had patiently waited for came. I found a convenient train duly labelled to Lourenço Marques standing in a siding. I withdrew to a suitable spot for boarding it—for I dared not make the attempt in the station—and, filling a bottle with water to drink on the way, I prepared for the last stage of my journey.

The truck in which I ensconced myself was laden with great sacks of some soft merchandise, and I found among them holes and crevices by means of which I managed to work my way into the inmost recess. The hard floor of the truck was littered with gritty coal dust, and made a most uncomfortable bed. The heat was almost stifling. I was resolved, however, that nothing should lure or compel me from my hiding place until I reached Portuguese territory. I expected the journey to take thirty-six hours; it dragged out into two and a half days. I hardly dared sleep for fear of snoring.

I feared lest the trucks should be searched at Komati Poort, and my anxiety as the train approached this neighborhood was very great. To prolong it we were shunted on to a siding for eighteen hours either at Komati Poort or the station beyond it. Once indeed they began to search my truck, but luckily did not search deep enough so that, providentially protected, I reached Delagoa Bay at last, and crawled forth from my place of refuge and of punishment, weary, dirty, hungry but free once more.

Thereafter everything smiled. I found my way to the British Consul, Mr. Ross, who at first mistook me for a fireman off one of the ships in the harbour, but soon welcomed me with enthusiasm. I bought clothes, I washed, I sat down to dinner with a real tablecloth and real glasses; and fortune, determined not to overlook the smallest detail, had arranged that the steamer *Induna* should leave that very night for Durban. It is from the cabin of this little vessel, as she coasts along the sandy shores of Africa, that I write these lines, and the reader who may preserve through this hurried account will perhaps understand why I write them with a feeling of triumph, and better than triumph, a feeling of pure joy.

24 January, 1900

Radical metamorphoses, from one skin color, religion,
or sex, to another, represent the most daring retreats
into another way of life. In Passing, her second novel,
Nella Larsen captures the vicarious fascination with—
and ultimately, rejection of—a childhood friend whose
passage into an "anti-self" signifies something at once
compelling and abhorrent. Drawing deeply on her
own experience as the dark-skinned child of light-
skinned parents, the Harlem Renaissance author
investigates the precarious proposition of escape from
racial stereotyping and class prejudice into the
treacherous terrain of "passing." With an almost
morbid fascination, Irene Redfield studies Clare
Kendry, a bourgeois African-American, who, by dint of
her pale skin and plaint temperament, slips as easily
into the mannerisms of another race as a black hand
into a white glove.

from *passing*

NELLA LARSEN

this is what Irene Redfield remembered.

Chicago. August. A brilliant day, hot, with a brutal staring sun pouring down rays that were like molten rain. A day on which the very outlines of the buildings shuddered as if in protest at the heat. Quivering lines sprang up from baked pavements and wriggled along the shining car tracks. The automobiles parked at the curbs were a dancing blaze, and the glass of the shop windows threw out a blinding radiance. Sharp particles of dust rose from the burning sidewalks, stinging the seared or dripping skins of wilting pedestrians. What small breeze there was seemed like the breath of a flame fanned by slow bellows.

It was on that day of all others that Irene set out to shop for the things which she had promised to take home from Chicago to her two small sons, Brian junior and Theodore. Characteristically, she had put it off until only a few crowded days remained of her long visit. And only this sweltering one was free of engagements till the evening.

Without too much trouble she had got the mechanical airplane for Junior. But the drawing book, for which Ted had so gravely and insistently given her precise directions, had sent her in and out of five shops without success.

It was while she was on her way to a sixth place that right before her smarting eyes a man toppled over and became an inert crumpled heap on the scorching cement. About the lifeless figure a little crowd gathered. Was the man dead or only faint? someone asked her. But Irene didn't know and didn't try to discover. She edged her way out of the increasing crowd, feeling disagreeable damp and sticky and soiled from contact with so many sweating bodies.

For a moment she stood fanning herself and dabbing at her moist face with an inadequate scrap of handkerchief. Suddenly she was aware that the whole street had a wobbly look and realized that she was about to faint. With a quick perception of the need for immediate safety, she lifted a wavering hand in the direction of a cab parked directly in front of her. The perspiring driver jumped out and guided her to his car. He helped, almost lifted her in. She sank down on the hot leather seat.

For a minute her thoughts were nebulous. They cleared.

"I guess," she told her Samaritan, "it's tea I need. On a roof somewhere."

"The Drayton, ma'am?" he suggested. "They do say as how it's always a breeze up there."

"Thank you. I think the Drayton'll do nicely," she told him.

There was that little grating sound of the clutch being slipped in as the man put the car in gear and slid deftly out into the boiling traffic. Reviving under the warm breeze stirred up by the moving cab, Irene made some small attempts to repair the damage that the heat and crowds had done to her appearance.

All too soon the rattling vehicle shot towards the sidewalk and stood still. The driver sprang out and opened the door before the hotel's decorated attendant could reach it. She got out, and thanking him smilingly as well as in a more substantial manner for his kind helpfulness and understanding, went in through the Drayton's wide doors.

Stepping out of the elevator that had brought her to the roof, she was led to a table just in front of a long window whose gently moving curtains suggested a cool breeze. It was, she thought, like being wafted upward on a magic carpet to another world, pleasant, quiet, and strangely remote from the sizzling one that she had left below.

The tea, when it came, was all that she had desired and expected. In fact, so much was it what she had desired and expected that after the first deep cooling drink she was able to forget it, only now and then sipping, a little absently, from the tall green glass, while she surveyed the room about her or looked out over some lower buildings at the bright unstirred blue of the lake reaching away to an undetected horizon.

She had been gazing down for some time at the specks of cars and people creeping about in streets, and thinking how silly they looked, when on taking up her glass she was surprised to find it empty at last. She asked for more tea and, while she waited, began to recall the happenings of the day and to wonder what she was to do about Ted and his book. Why was it that almost invariably he wanted something that was difficult or impossible to get? Like his father. Forever wanting something that he couldn't have.

Presently there were voices, a man's booming one and a woman's slightly husky. A waiter passed her, followed by a sweetly scented woman in a fluttering dress of green chiffon whose mingled pattern of narcissuses, jonquils, and hyacinths was a reminder of pleasantly chill spring days. Behind her there was a man, very red in the face, who was mopping his neck and forehead with a big crumpled handkerchief.

"Oh dear!" Irene groaned, rasped by annoyance, for after a little discussion and commotion they had stopped at the very next table. She had been alone there at the window and it had been so satisfyingly quiet. Now, of course, they would chatter.

But no. Only the woman sat down. The man remained standing, abstractedly pinching the knot of his bright blue tie. Across the small space that separated the two tables his voice carried clearly.

"See you later, then," he declared, looking down at the woman. There was pleasure in his tones and a smile on his face.

His companion's lips parted in some answer, but her words were blurred by the little intervening distance and the medley of noises floating up from the streets below. They didn't reach Irene. But she noted the peculiar caressing smile that accompanied them.

The man said: "Well, I suppose I'd better," and smiled again, and said good-bye, and left.

An attractive-looking woman, was Irene's opinion, with those dark, almost black, eyes and that wide mouth like a scarlet flower against the ivory of her skin. Nice clothes too, just right for the weather, thin and cool without being mussy, as summer things were so apt to be.

A waiter was taking her order. Irene saw her smile up at him as she murmured something—thanks, maybe. It was an odd sort of smile. Irene couldn't quite define it, but she was sure that she would have classed it, coming from another woman, as being just a shade too provocative for a waiter. About this one, however, there was something that made her hesitate to name it that. A certain impression of assurance, perhaps.

The waiter came back with the order. Irene watched her spread out her napkin, saw the silver spoon in the white hand slit the dull gold of the melon. Then, conscious that she had been staring, she looked quickly away.

Her mind returned to her own affairs. She had settled, definitely, the problem of the proper one of two frocks for the bridge party that night, in rooms whose atmosphere would be so thick and hot that every breath would be like breathing soup. The dress decided her thoughts had gone back to the snag of Ted's book, her unseeing eyes far away on the lake, when by some sixth sense she was acutely aware that someone was watching her.

Very slowly she looked around, and into the dark eyes of the woman in the green frock at the next table. But she evidently failed to realize that such intense interest as she was showing might be embarrassing, and continued to stare. Her demeanor was that of one who with utmost singleness of mind and purpose was determined to impress firmly and accurately each detail of Irene's features upon her memory for all time, nor showed the slightest trace of disconcertment at having been detected in her steady scrutiny.

Instead, it was Irene who was put out. Feeling her color heighten under the continued inspection, she slid her eyes down. What, she wondered, could be the reason for such persistent attention? Had she, in her haste in the taxi, put her hat on backwards? Guardedly she felt at it. No. Perhaps there was a streak of powder somewhere on her face. She made a quick pass over it with her handkerchief. Something wrong with her dress? She shot a glance over it. Perfectly all right. *What* was it?

Again she looked up, and for a moment her brown eyes politely returned the stare of the other's black ones, which never for an instant fell or wavered. Irene made a little mental shrug. Oh well, let her look! She tried to treat the woman and her watching with indifference, but she couldn't. All her efforts to ignore her, it, were futile. She stole another glance. Still looking. What strange languorous eyes she had!

And gradually there rose in Irene a small inner disturbance, odious and hatefully familiar. She laughed softly, but her eyes flashed.

Did that woman, could that woman, somehow know that here before her very eyes on the roof of the Drayton sat a Negro?

Absurd! Impossible! White people were so stupid about such

things for all that they usually asserted that they were able to tell; and by the most ridiculous means: fingernails, palms of hands, shapes of ears, teeth, and other equally silly rot. They always took her for an Italian, a Spaniard, a Mexican, or a Gypsy. Never, when she was alone, had they even remotely seemed to suspect that she was a Negro. No, the woman sitting there staring at her couldn't possibly know.

Nevertheless, Irene felt, in turn, anger, scorn, and fear slide over her. It wasn't that she was ashamed of being a Negro, or even of having it declared. It was the idea of being ejected from any place, even in the polite and tactful way in which the Drayton would probably do it, that disturbed her.

But she looked, boldly this time, back into the eyes still frankly intent upon her. They did not seem to her hostile or resentful. Rather, Irene had the feeling that they were ready to smile if she would. Nonsense, of course. The feeling passed, and she turned away with the firm intention of keeping her gaze on the lake, the roofs of the buildings across the way, the sky, anywhere but on that annoying woman. Almost immediately, however, her eyes were back again. In the midst of her fog of uneasiness she had been seized by a desire to outstare the rude observer. Suppose the woman did know or suspect her race. She couldn't prove it.

Suddenly her small fright increased. Her neighbor had risen and was coming towards her. What was going to happen now?

"Pardon me," the woman said pleasantly, "but I think I know you." Her slightly husky voice held a dubious note.

Looking up at her, Irene's suspicions and fears vanished. There was no mistaking the friendliness of that smile or resisting its charm. Instantly she surrendered to it and smiled too, as she said: "I'm afraid you're mistaken."

"Why, of course, I know you!" the other exclaimed. "Don't tell me you're not Irene Westover. Or do they still call you 'Rene?"

In the brief second before her answer, Irene tried vainly to recall where and when this woman could have known her. There, in Chicago. And before her marriage. That much was plain. High school? College? Y.M.C.A. committees? High school, most likely. What white girls had she known well enough to have been familiarly addressed as 'Rene by them? The woman before her didn't fit her memory of any of them. Who was she?

"Yes, I'm Irene Westover. And though nobody calls me 'Rene

any more, it's good to hear the name again. And you—" She hesitated, ashamed that she could not remember, and hoping that the sentence would be finished for her.

"Don't you know me? Not really, 'Rene?"

"I'm sorry, but just at the minute I can't seem to place you."

Irene studied the lovely creature standing beside her for some clue to her identity. Who could she be? Where and when had they met? And through her perplexity there came the thought that the trick which her memory had played her was for some reason more gratifying than disappointing to her old acquaintance, that she didn't mind not being recognized.

And, too, Irene felt that she was just about to remember her. For about the woman was some quality, an intangible something, too vague to define, too remote to seize, but which was, to Irene Redfield, very familiar. And that voice. Surely she'd heard those husky tones somewhere before. Perhaps before time, contact, or something had been at them, making them into a voice remotely suggesting England. Ah! Could it have been in Europe that they had met? 'Rene. No.

"Perhaps," Irene began, "you—"

The woman laughed, a lovely laugh, a small sequence of notes that was like a trill and also like the ringing of a delicate bell fashioned of a precious metal, a tinkling.

Irene drew a quick sharp breath. "Clare!" she exclaimed. "Not really Clare Kendry?"

So great was her astonishment that she had started to rise.

"No, no, don't get up," Clare Kendry commanded, and sat down herself. "You've simply got to stay and talk. We'll have something more. Tea? Fancy meeting you here! It's simply too, too lucky!"

"It's awfully surprising," Irene told her, and, seeing the change in Clare's smile, knew that she had revealed a corner of her own thoughts. But she only said: "I'd never in this world have known you if you hadn't laughed. You are changed, you know. And yet, in a way, you're just the same."

"Perhaps," Clare replied. "Oh, just a second."

She gave her attention to the waiter at her side. "M-mm, let's see. Two teas. And bring some cigarettes. Y-es, they'll be all right. Thanks." Again that odd upward smile. Now Irene was sure that it was too provocative for a waiter.

While Clare had been giving the order, Irene made a rapid mental calculation. It must be, she figured, all of twelve years since she, or anybody that she knew, had laid eyes on Clare Kendry.

After her father's death she'd gone to live with some relatives, aunts or cousins two or three times removed, over on the West Side: relatives that nobody had known the Kendrys possessed until they had turned up at the funeral and taken Clare away with them.

For about a year or more afterward she would appear occasionally among her old friends and acquaintances on the South Side for short little visits that were, they understood, always stolen from the endless domestic tasks in her new home. With each succeeding one she was taller, shabbier, and more belligerently sensitive. And each time the look on her face was more resentful and brooding. "I'm worried about Clare, she seems so unhappy," Irene remembered her mother saying. The visits dwindled, becoming shorter, fewer, and further apart until at last they ceased.

Irene's father, who had been fond of Bob Kendry, made a special trip over to the West Side about two months after the last time Clare had been to see them and returned with the bare information that he had seen the relatives and that Clare had disappeared. What else he had confided to her mother, in the privacy of their own room, Irene didn't know.

But she had had something more than a vague suspicion of its nature. For there had been rumors. Rumors that were, to girls of eighteen and nineteen years, interesting and exciting.

There was the one about Clare Kendry's having been seen at the dinner hour in a fashionable hotel in company with another woman and two men, all of them white. And *dressed*! And there was another which told of her driving in Lincoln Park with a man, unmistakably white, and evidently rich. Packard limousine, chauffeur in livery, and all that. There had been others whose context Irene could no longer recollect, but all pointing in the same glamorous direction.

And she could remember quite vividly how, when they used to repeat and discuss these tantalizing stories about Clare, the girls would always look knowingly at one another and then, with little excited giggles, drag away their eager shining eyes and say with lurking undertones of regret or disbelief some such thing as: "Oh, well, maybe she's got a job or something," or "After all, it mayn't have been Clare," or "You can't believe all you hear."

And always some girl, more matter-of-fact or more frankly malicious than the rest, would declare: "Of course it was Clare! Ruth said it was and so did Frank, and they certainly know her when they see her as well as we do." And someone else would say: "Yes, you can bet it was Clare all right." And then they would all join in asserting that there could be no mistake about its having been Clare, and that such circumstances could mean only one thing. Working indeed! People didn't take their servants to the Shelby for dinner. Certainly not all dressed up like that. There would follow insincere regrets, and somebody would say: "Poor girl, I suppose it's true enough, but what can you expect? Look at her father. And her mother, they say, would have run away if she hadn't died. Besides, Clare always had a—a—having way with her."

Precisely that! The words came to Irene as she sat there on the Drayton roof, facing Clare Kendry. "A having way." Well, Irene acknowledged, judging from her appearance and manner, Clare seemed certainly to have succeeded in having a few of the things that she wanted.

It was, Irene repeated, after the interval of the waiter, a great surprise and a very pleasant one to see Clare again after all those years, twelve at least.

"Why, Clare, you're the last person in the world I'd have expected to run into. I guess that's why I didn't know you."

Clare answered gravely: "Yes. It is twelve years. But I'm not surprised to see you, 'Rene. That is, not so very. In fact, ever since I've been here, I've more or less hoped that I should, or someone. Preferably you, though. Still, I imagine that's because I've thought of you often and often, while you—I'll wager you've never given me a thought."

It was true, of course. After the first speculations and indictments, Clare had gone completely from Irene's thoughts. And from the thoughts of others too—if their conversation was any indication of their thoughts.

Besides, Clare had never been exactly one of the group, just as she'd never been merely the janitor's daughter, but the daughter of Mr. Bob Kendry, who, it was true, was a janitor, but who also, it seemed, had been in college with some of their fathers. Just how or why he happened to be a janitor, and a very inefficient one at that, they none of them quite knew. One of Irene's brothers, who had put the question to their father, had been told: "That's something that doesn't concern you," and given him the advice to be careful not to end in the same manner as "poor Bob."

No, Irene hadn't thought of Clare Kendry. Her own life had been too crowded. So, she supposed, had the lives of other people. She defended her—their—forgetfulness. "You know how it is. Everybody's so busy. People leave, drop out, maybe for a little while there's talk about them, or questions; then, gradually they're forgotten."

"Yes, that's natural," Clare agreed. And what, she inquired, had they said of her for that little while at the beginning before they'd forgotten her altogether?

Irene looked away. She felt the telltale color rising in her cheeks. "You can't," she evaded, "expect me to remember trifles like that over twelve years of marriages, births, deaths, and the war."

There followed that trill of notes that was Clare Kendry's laugh, small and clear and the very essence of mockery.

"Oh, 'Rene!" she cried. "Of course you remember! But I won't make you tell me, because I know just as well as if I'd been there and heard every unkind word. Oh, I know, I know. Frank Danton saw me in the Shelby one night. Don't tell me he didn't broadcast that, and with embroidery. Others may have seen me at other times. I don't know. But once I met Margaret Hammer in Marshall Field's. I'd have spoken, was on the very point of doing it, but she cut me dead. My dear 'Rene, I assure you that, from the way she looked through me, even I was uncertain whether I was actually there in the flesh or not. I remember it clearly, too clearly. It was that very thing which, in a way, finally decided me not to go out and see you one last time before I went away to stay. Somehow, good as all of you, the whole family, had always been to the poor forlorn child that was me, I felt I shouldn't be able to bear that. I mean if any of you, your mother or the boys or—Oh, well, I just felt I'd rather not know it if you did. And so I stayed away. Silly, I suppose. Sometimes I've been sorry I didn't go."

Irene wondered if it was tears that made Clare's eyes so luminous.

"And now, 'Rene, I want to hear all about you and everybody and everything. You're married, I s'pose?"

Irene nodded.

"Yes," Clare said knowingly, "you would be. Tell me about it."

And so for an hour or more they had sat there smoking and drinking tea and filling in the gap of twelve years with talk. That is, Irene did. She told Clare about her marriage and removal to New York, about her husband, and about her two sons, who were having their first experience of being separated from their parents at a summer camp, about her mother's death, about the marriages of her two brothers. She told of the marriages, births, and deaths in other families that Clare had known, opening up, for her, new vistas on the lives of old friends and acquaintances.

Clare drank it all in, these things which for so long she had wanted to know and hadn't been able to learn. She sat motionless, her bright lips slightly parted, her whole face lit by the radiance of her happy eyes. Now and then she put a question, but for the most part she was silent.

Somewhere outside, a clock struck. Brought back to the present, Irene looked down at her watch and exclaimed: "Oh, I must go, Clare!"

A moment passed during which she was the prey of uneasiness. It had suddenly occurred to her that she hadn't asked Clare anything about her own life and that she had a very definite unwillingness to do so. And she was quite well aware of the reason for that reluctance. But, she asked herself, wouldn't it, all things considered, be the kindest thing not to ask? If things with Clare were as she—as they all—had suspected, wouldn't it be more tactful to seem to forget to inquire how she had spent those twelve years?

If? It was that "if" which bothered her. It might be, it might just be, in spite of all gossip and even appearances to the contrary, that there was nothing, had been nothing, that couldn't be simply and innocently explained. Appearances, she knew now, had a way sometimes of not fitting facts, and if Clare hadn't—Well, if they had all been wrong, then certainly she ought to express some interest in what had happened to her. It would seem queer and rude if she didn't. But how was she to know? There was, she at last decided, no way; so she merely said again, "I must go, Clare."

"Please, not so soon, 'Rene," Clare begged, not moving.

Irene thought: "She's really almost too good-looking. It's hardly any wonder that she—"

"And now, 'Rene dear, that I've found you, I mean to see lots and lots of you. We're here for a month at least. Jack, that's my husband, is here on business. Poor dear! In this heat. Isn't it beastly? Come to dinner with us tonight, won't you?" And she gave Irene a curious little sidelong glance and a sly, ironical smile peeped out on her full red lips, as if she had been in the secret of the other's thoughts and was mocking her.

Irene was conscious of a sharp intake of breath, but whether it was relief or chagrin that she felt, she herself could not have told. She said hastily: "I'm afraid I can't, Clare. I'm filled up. Dinner and bridge. I'm so sorry."

"Come tomorrow instead, to tea," Clare insisted. "Then you'll see Margery—she's just ten—and Jack too, maybe, if he hasn't got an appointment or something."

From Irene came an uneasy little laugh. She had an engagement for tomorrow also and she was afraid that Clare would not believe it. Suddenly, now, that possibility disturbed her. Therefore it was with a half-vexed feeling at the sense of undeserved guilt that had come upon her that she explained that it wouldn't be possible because she wouldn't be free for tea, or for luncheon or dinner either. "And the next day's Friday when I'll be going away for the weekend, Idlewild, you know. It's quite the thing now." And then she had an inspiration.

"Clare!" she exclaimed. "Why don't you come up with me? Our place is probably full up—Jim's wife has a way of collecting mobs of the most impossible people—but we can always manage to find room for one more. And you'll see absolutely everybody."

In the very moment of giving the invitation she regretted it. What a foolish, what an idiotic impulse to have given way to! She groaned inwardly as she thought of the endless explanations in which it would involve her, of the curiosity, and the talk, and the lifted eyebrows. It wasn't, she assured herself, that she was a snob, that she cared greatly for the petty restrictions and distinctions with which what called itself Negro society chose to hedge itself about; but that she had a natural and deeply rooted aversion to the kind of front-page notoriety that Clare Kendry's presence in Idlewild, as her guest, would expose her to. And here she was, perversely and against all reason, inviting her.

But Clare shook her head. "Really, I'd love to, 'Rene," she said, a little mournfully. "There's nothing I'd like better. But I couldn't. I mustn't, you see. It wouldn't do at all. I'm sure you understand. I'm simply crazy to go, but I can't." The dark eyes glistened and there was a suspicion of a quaver in the husky voice. "And believe me, 'Rene, I do thank you for asking me. Don't think I've entirely forgotten just what it would mean for you if I went. That is, if you still care about such things."

All indication of tears had gone from her eyes and voice, and Irene Redfield, searching her face, had an offended feeling that behind what was now only an ivory mask lurked a scornful amusement. She looked away, at the wall far beyond Clare. Well, she deserved it, for, as she acknowledged to herself, she *was* relieved. And for the very reason at which Clare had hinted. The fact that Clare had guessed her perturbation did not, however, in any degree lessen that relief. She was annoyed at having been detected in what might seem to be an insincerity; but that was all.

The waiter came with Clare's change. Irene reminded herself that she ought immediately to go. But she didn't move.

The truth was, she was curious. There were things that she wanted to ask Clare Kendry. She wished to find out about this hazardous business of "passing," this breaking away from all that was familiar and friendly to take one's chance in another environment, not entirely strange, perhaps, but certainly not entirely friendly. What, for example, one did about background, how one accounted for oneself. And how one felt when one came into contact with other Negroes. But she couldn't. She was unable to think of a single question that in its context or its phrasing was not too frankly curious, if not actually impertinent.

As if aware of her desire and her hesitation, Clare remarked thoughtfully: "You know, 'Rene, I've often wondered why more colored girls, girls like you and Margaret Hammer and Esther Dawson and—oh, lots of others—never "passed" over. It's such a frightfully easy thing to do. If one's the type, all that's needed is a little nerve."

"What about background? Family, I mean. Surely you can't just drop down on people from nowhere and expect them to receive you with open arms, can you?"

"Almost," Clare asserted. "You'd be surprised, 'Rene, how much easier that is with white people than with us. Maybe because there are so many more of them, or maybe because they are secure and so don't have to bother. I've never quite decided."

nella larsen   **85**

Irene was inclined to be incredulous. "You mean that you didn't have to explain where you came from? It seems impossible."

Clare cast a glance of repressed amusement across the table at her. "As a matter of fact, I didn't. Though I suppose under any other circumstances I might have had to provide some plausible tale to account for myself. I've a good imagination, so I'm sure I could have done it quite creditably, and credibly. But it wasn't necessary. There were my aunts, you see, respectable and authentic enough for anything or anybody."

"I see. They were 'passing' too."

"No. They weren't. They were white."

"Oh!" And in the next instant it came back to Irene that she had heard this mentioned before; by her father or, more likely, her mother. They were Bob Kendry's aunts. He had been a son of their brother's, on the left hand. A wild oat.

"They were nice old ladies," Clare explained, "very religious and as poor as church mice. That adored brother of theirs, my grandfather, got through every penny they had after he'd finished his own little bit."

Clare paused in her narrative to light another cigarette. Her smile, her expression, Irene noticed, was faintly resentful.

"Being good Christians," she continued, "when Dad came to his tipsy end, they did their duty and gave me a home of sorts. I was, it was true, expected to earn my keep by doing all the housework and most of the washing. But do you realize, 'Rene, that if it hadn't been for them I shouldn't have had a home in the world?"

Irene's nod and little murmur were comprehensive, understanding.

Clare made a small mischievous grimace and proceeded. "Besides, to their notion, hard labor was good for me. I had Negro blood and they belonged to the generation that had written and read long articles headed: 'Will the Blacks Work?' Too, they weren't quite sure that the good God hadn't intended the sons and daughters of Ham to sweat because he had poked fun at old man Noah once when he had taken a drop too much. I remember the aunts telling me that that old drunkard had cursed Ham and his sons for all time."

Irene laughed. But Clare remained quite serious.

"It was more than a joke, I assure you, 'Rene. It was a hard life for a girl of sixteen. Still, I had a roof over my head, and food, and clothes—such as they were. And there were the Scriptures, and talks on morals and thrift and industry and the loving-kindness of the good Lord."

"Have you ever stopped to think, Clare," Irene demanded, "how much unhappiness and downright cruelty are laid to the loving-kindness of the Lord? And always by His most ardent followers, it seems."

"Have I?" Clare exclaimed. "It, they, made me what I am today. For, of course, I was determined to get away, to be a person and not a charity or a problem, or even a daughter of the indiscreet Ham. Then, too, I wanted things. I knew I wasn't bad-looking and that I could 'pass.' You can't know, 'Rene, how, when I used to go over to the South Side, I used almost to hate all of you. You had all the things I wanted and never had had. It made me all the more determined to get them, and others. Do you, can you understand what I felt?"

She looked up with a pointed and appealing effect, and, evidently finding the sympathetic expression on Irene's face sufficient answer, went on. "The aunts were queer. For all their Bibles and praying and ranting about honesty, they didn't want anyone to know that their darling brother had seduced—ruined, they called it—a Negro girl. They could excuse the ruin, but they couldn't forgive the tar brush. They forbade me to mention Negroes to the neighbors, or even to mention the South Side. You may be sure that I didn't. I'll bet they were good and sorry afterwards."

She laughed and the ringing bells in her laugh had a hard metallic sound.

"When the chance to get away came, that omission was of great value to me. When Jack, a schoolboy acquaintance of some people in the neighborhood, turned up from South America with untold gold, there was no one to tell him that I was colored, and many to tell him about the severity and the religiousness of Aunt Grace and Aunt Edna. You can guess the rest. After he came, I stopped slipping off to the South Side and slipped off to meet him instead. I couldn't manage both. In the end I had no great difficulty in convincing him that it was useless to talk marriage to the aunts. So on the day that I was eighteen we went off and were married. So that's that. Nothing could have been easier."

"Yes, I do see that for you it was easy enough. By the way! I wonder why they didn't tell Father that you were married? He went over to find out about you when you stopped coming over to see us. I'm sure they didn't tell him. Not that you were married."

Clare Kendry's eyes were bright with tears that didn't fall. "Oh, how lovely! To have cared enough about me to do that. The dear sweet man! Well, they couldn't tell him because they didn't know it. I took care of that, for I couldn't be sure that those consciences of theirs wouldn't begin to work on them afterward and make them let the cat out of the bag. The old things probably thought I was living in sin, wherever I was. And it would be about what they expected."

An amused smile lit the lovely face for the smallest fraction of a second. After a little silence she said soberly: "But I'm sorry if they told your father so. That was something I hadn't counted on."

"I'm not sure that they did," Irene told her. "He didn't say so, anyway."

"He wouldn't, 'Rene dear. Not your father."

"Thanks. I'm sure he wouldn't."

"But you've never answered my question. Tell me, honestly, haven't you ever thought of 'passing'?"

Irene answered promptly: "No. Why should I?" And so disdainful was her voice and manner that Clare's face flushed and her eyes glinted. Irene hastened to add: "You see, Clare, I've everything I want. Except, perhaps, a little more money."

At that Clare laughed, her spark of anger vanished as quickly as it had appeared. "Of course," she declared, "that's what everybody wants, just a little more money, even the people who have it. And I must say I don't blame them. Money's awfully nice to have. In fact, all things considered, I think, 'Rene, that it's even worth the price."

Irene could only shrug her shoulders. Her reason partly agreed, her instinct wholly rebelled. And she could not say why. And though conscious that if she didn't hurry away, she was going to be late to dinner, she still lingered. It was as if the woman sitting on the other side of the table, a girl she had known, who had done this rather dangerous and, to Irene Redfield, abhorrent thing successfully and had announced herself well satisfied, had for her a fascination, strange and compelling.

Clare Kendry was still leaning back in the tall chair, her sloping shoulders against the carved top. She sat with an air of indifferent assurance, as if arranged for, desired. About her clung that dim suggestion of polite insolence with which a few women are born and which some acquire with the coming of riches or importance.

Clare, it gave Irene a little prick of satisfaction to recall, hadn't got that by passing herself off as white. She herself had always had it.

Just as she'd always had that pale gold hair, which, unsheared still, was drawn loosely back from a broad brow, partly hidden by the small close hat. Her lips, painted a brilliant geranium red, were sweet and sensitive and a little obstinate. A tempting mouth. The face across the forehead and cheeks was a trifle too wide, but the ivory skin had a peculiar soft luster. And the eyes were magnificent! Dark, sometimes absolutely black, always luminous, and set in long, black lashes. Arresting eyes, slow and mesmeric, and with, for all their warmth, something withdrawn and secret about them.

Ah! Surely! They were Negro eyes! Mysterious and concealing. And set in that ivory face under that bright hair, there was about them something exotic.

Yes, Clare Kendry's loveliness was absolute, beyond challenge, thanks to those eyes which her grandmother and later her mother and father had given her.

Into those eyes there came a smile and over Irene the sense of being petted and caressed. She smiled back.

"Maybe," Clare suggested, "you can come Monday, if you're back. Or, if you're not, then Tuesday."

With a small regretful sigh, Irene informed Clare that she was afraid she wouldn't be back by Monday and that she was sure she had dozens of things for Tuesday, and that she was leaving Wednesday. It might be, however, that she could get out of something Tuesday.

"Oh, do try. Do put somebody else off. The others can see you any time, while I—why, I may never see you again! Think of that, 'Rene! You'll have to come. You'll simply have to! I'll never forgive you if you don't."

At that moment it seemed a dreadful thing to think of never seeing Clare Kendry again. Standing there under the appeal, the caress, of her eyes, Irene had the desire, the hope, that this parting wouldn't be the last.

"I'll try, Clare," she promised gently. "I'll call you—or will you call me?"

"I think, perhaps, I'd better call you. Your father's in the book, I know, and the address is the same. Sixty-four eighteen. Some memory, what? Now remember, I'm going to expect you. You've got to be able to come."

Again that peculiar mellowing smile.

"I'll do my best, Clare."

Irene gathered up her gloves and bag. They stood up. She put out her hand. Clare took and held it.

"It has been nice seeing you again, Clare. How pleased and glad Father'll be to hear about you!"

"Until Tuesday, then," Clare Kendry replied. "I'll spend every minute of the time from now on looking forward to seeing you again. Good-bye, 'Rene dear. My love to your father, and this kiss for him."

The sun had gone from overhead, but the streets were still like fiery furnaces. The languid breeze was still hot. And the scurrying people looked even more wilted than before Irene had fled from their contact.

Crossing the avenue in the heat, far from the coolness of the Drayton's roof, away from the seduction of Clare Kendry's smile, she was aware of a sense of irritation with herself because she had been pleased and a little flattered at the other's obvious gladness at their meeting.

With her perspiring progress homeward this irritation grew, and she began to wonder just what had possessed her to make her promise to find time, in the crowded days that remained of her visit, to spend another afternoon with a woman whose life had so definitely and deliberately diverged from hers; and whom, as had been pointed out, she might never see again.

Why in the world had she made such a promise?

As she went up the steps to her father's house, thinking with what interest and amazement he would listen to her story of the afternoon's encounter, it came to her that Clare had omitted to mention her marriage name. She had referred to her husband as Jack. That was all. Had that, Irene asked herself, been intentional?

Clare had only to pick up the telephone to communicate with her, or to drop her a card, or to jump into a taxi. But she couldn't reach Clare in any way. Nor could anyone else to whom she might speak of their meeting.

"As if I should!"

Her key turned in the lock. She went in. Her father, it seemed, hadn't come in yet.

Irene decided that she wouldn't, after all, say anything to him about Clare Kendry. She had, she told herself, no inclination to speak of a person who held so low an opinion of her loyalty, or her discretion. And certainly she had no desire or intention of making the slightest effort about Tuesday. Nor any other day for that matter.

She was through with Clare Kendry.

To stake everything on a chance for a better life one must be either an idiot or insane. Terminal despair can turn the biggest rationalist or the most cringing coward into either. And, given a desperate enough set of circumstances, both will opt for the madness of escape. By comparison with their ordeals, the flights into holidays, affairs, work, narcotics, or religion, which also go under the name of "escape," are just self-indulgent exercises in evasive maneuvering. No time in memory has been cursed with more or grimmer displacements of suffering humanity than the twentieth century, when every border in existence has been defiled by the blood and tears of people fleeing persecution, poverty, starvation, and humiliation. Reporter Michael Finkel takes us into the hearts and minds and fear-ridden bodies of refugees from Haiti who embark on a journey that will take them either to the mythical promised land of America, or to a dreadful, slow and painful death on the high seas.

desperate passage

MICHAEL FINKEL

down in the hold, beneath the deck boards, where we were denied most of the sun's light but none of its fire, it sometimes seemed as if there were nothing but eyes. The boat was twenty-three feet long, powered solely by two small sails. There were forty-one people below and five above. All but myself and a photographer were Haitian citizens fleeing their country, hoping to start a new life in the United States. The hold was lined with scrap wood and framed with hand-hewn joists, as in an old mine tunnel, and when I looked into the darkness it was impossible to tell where one person ended and another began. We were compressed together, limbs entangled, heads upon laps, a mass so dense there was scarcely room for motion. Conversation had all but ceased. If not for the shifting and blinking of eyes there'd be little sign that anyone was alive.

Twenty hours before, the faces of the people around me seemed bright with the prospect of reaching a new country. Now, as the arduousness of the crossing became clear, their stares conveyed the flat helplessness of fear. David, whose journey I had followed from his hometown of Port-au-Prince, buried his head in his hands. He hadn't moved for hours. "I'm thinking of someplace else," is all he would reveal. Stephen, who had helped round up the passengers, looked anxiously out the hold's square opening four feet over our heads, where he could see a corner of the sail and a strip of cloudless sky. "I can't swim," he admitted softly. Kenton, a thirteen-year-old boy, sat in a puddle of vomit and trembled as though crying, only there were no tears. I was concerned about the severity of Kenton's dehydration and could not shake the thought that he wasn't going to make it. "Some people get to America, and some people die," David had said. "Me, I'll take either one. I'm just not taking Haiti anymore."

It had been six weeks since David had made that pronouncement. This was in mid-March of 2000, in Port-au-Prince, soon after Haiti's national elections had been postponed for the fifth time and the country was entering its second year without a parliament or regional officials. David sold mahogany carvings on a street corner not far from the United States embassy. He spoke beautiful English, spiced with pitch-perfect sarcasm. His name wasn't really David, he said, but it's what people called him. He offered no surname. He said he'd once lived in America but had been deported. He informed me, matter-of-factly, that he was selling souvenirs in order to raise funds to pay a boat owner to take him back.

David was not alone in his desire to leave Haiti. In the previous six months, Haitians had been fleeing their country in numbers unseen since 1994, when a military coup tried to oust Jean-Bertrand Aristide, who was president at the time. Haiti's poverty level, always alarming, in recent years has escalated to even higher levels. Today, nearly 80 percent of Haitians live in abject conditions. Fewer than one in fifty has a steady wage-earning job; per capita income hovers around $250, less than one-tenth the Latin American average. Haitians once believed that Aristide might change things, but he was no longer in power, and the endless delays in elections, the recent spate of political killings, and the general sense of spiraling violence and corruption has led to a palpable feeling of despair. In February, the U.S. State Department released the results of a survey conducted in nine Haitian cities. Based on the study, two-thirds of Haitians— approximately 4,690,000 people—"would leave Haiti if given the means and opportunity." If they were going to leave, though, most would have to do so illegally; each year, the United States issues about ten thousand immigration visas to Haitian citizens, satisfying about one-fifth of 1 percent of the estimated demand.

To illegally enter America, Haitians typically embark on a two-step journey, taking a boat first to the Bahamas and then later to Florida. In the first five months of 2000, the United States and Bahamian Coast Guards picked up more than a thousand Haitians, most on marginally seaworthy vessels. This was twice the number caught in all of 1999. Late April was an especially busy time. On

April 22, the U.S. Coast Guard rescued 200 Haitians after their boat ran aground near Harbor Island, in the Bahamas. Three days later, 123 Haitian migrants were plucked from a sinking ship off the coast of Great Inagua Island. Three days after that, 278 Haitians were spotted by Bahamian authorities on a beach on Flamingo Cay, stranded after their boat had drifted for nearly a week. By the time rescuers arrived, 14 people had died from dehydration; as many as 18 others had perished during the journey. These were merely the larger incidents. Most boats leaving Haiti carry fewer than 50 passengers.

Such stories did not deter David. He said he was committed to making the trip, no matter the risks. His frankness was unusual. Around foreigners, most Haitians are reserved and secretive. David was boastful and loud. It's been said that Creole, the lingua franca of Haiti, is 10 percent grammar and 90 percent attitude, and David exercised this ratio to utmost effectiveness. It also helped that he was big, well over six feet and bricked with muscle. His head was shaved bald; a sliver of mustache shaded his upper lip. He was twenty-five years old. He used his size and his personality as a form of self-defense: the slums of Port-au-Prince are as dangerous as any in the world, and David, who had once been homeless for more than a year, had acquired the sort of street credentials that lent his words more weight than those of a policeman or soldier. He now lived in a broken-down neighborhood called Project Droullard, where he shared a one-room hovel with thirteen others—the one mattress was suspended on cinder blocks so that people could sleep not only on but also beneath it. David was a natural leader, fluent in English, French, and Creole. His walk was the chest-forward type of a boxer entering the ring. Despite his apparent candor, it was difficult to know what was really on his mind. Even his smile was ambiguous—the broader he grinned, the less happy he appeared.

The high season for illegal immigration is April through September. The seas this time of year tend to be calm, except for the occasional hurricane. Last May I mentioned to David that I, along with a photographer named Chris Anderson, wanted to document a voyage from Haiti to America. I told David that if he was ready to make the trip, I'd pay him $30 a day to aid as guide and translator. He was skeptical at first, suspicious that we were working undercover for the CIA to apprehend smugglers. But after repeated assurances, and after showing him the supplies we'd brought for the voyage—self-inflating life vests (including one for David), vinyl rain jackets, waterproof flashlights, Power Bars, and a first-aid kit—his wariness diminished. I offered him an advance payment of one day's salary.

"Okay," he said. "It's a deal." He promised he'd be ready to leave early the next morning.

David was at our hotel at 5:30 A.M., wearing blue jeans, sandals, and a T-shirt and carrying a black plastic bag. Inside the bag was a second T-shirt, a pair of socks, a tin bowl, a metal spoon, and a Bible. In his pocket was a small bundle of money. This was all he took with him. Later, he bought a toothbrush.

David opened his Bible and read Psalm 23 aloud: *Yea, though I walk through the valley of the shadow of death.* Then we walked to the bus station, sidestepping the stray dogs and open sewers. We boarded an old school bus, thirty-six seats, seventy-two passengers, and headed north, along the coast, to Île de la Tortue—Turtle Island—one of the three major boatbuilding centers in Haiti. David knew the island well. A year earlier, he'd spent a month there trying to gain a berth on a boat. Like many Haitians who can't afford such a trip, he volunteered to work. Seven days a week, he hiked deep into the island's interior, where a few swatches of forest still remained, and hacked down pine trees with a machete, hauling them back to be cut and hammered into a ship. For his efforts, David was served one meal a day, a bowlful of rice and beans. After thirty days of labor there was still no sign he'd be allowed onto a boat, so he returned to his mahogany stand in Port-au-Prince.

The bus rattled over the washboard roads and the sun bore down hard, even at 7:00 in the morning, and the men in the sugarcane fields were shirtless and glistening. A roadside billboard, faded and peeling, advertised Carnival Cruise Lines. LES BELLES CROISIÈRES, read the slogan—the Beautiful Cruises. At noon, we transferred to the bed of a pickup truck, the passing land gradually surrendering fertility until everything was brown. Five hours later the road ended at the rough-edged shipping town of Port-de-Paix, where we boarded a dilapidated ferry and set off on the hourlong crossing to Île Tortue, a fin-shaped wisp of land twenty miles long and four miles wide. Here, said David, is where he'd begin his trip to America.

There are at least seven villages on Île Tortue—its population is about 30,000—but no roads, no telephones, no running water, no electricity, and no police. Transportation is strictly by foot, via a web of thin trails lined with cactus bushes. David walked the trails, up and down the steep seafront bluffs, until he stopped at La Vallée, a collection of huts scattered randomly along the shore. On the beach I counted seventeen boats under construction. They looked like the skeletons of beached whales. Most were less than thirty feet long, but two were of the same cargo-ship girth as the boat that had tried a rare Haiti-to-Florida nonstop last January but was intercepted by the Coast Guard off Key Biscayne. Three hundred ninety-five Haitians, fourteen Dominicans, and two Chinese passengers were shoehorned aboard, all of whom were returned to Haiti. According to survivors' reports, ten people had suffocated during the crossing, the bodies tossed overboard.

The boats at La Vallée were being assembled entirely with scrap wood and rusty nails; the only tools I saw were hammers and machetes. David said a boat left Île Tortue about once every two or three days during the high season. He thought the same was true at the other two boatbuilding spots—Cap-Haïtien, in the north, and Gonaïves, in the west. This worked out to about a boat a day, forty or more Haitians leaving every twenty-four hours.

The first step in getting onto a boat at Île Tortue, David said, is to gain the endorsement of one of the local officials, who are often referred to as elders. Such approval, he explained, is required whether you are a foreigner or not—and foreigners occasionally come to Haiti to arrange their passage to America. A meeting with the elder in La Vallée was scheduled. David bought a bottle of five-star rum as an offering, and we walked to his home.

The meeting was tense. David, Chris, and I crouched on miniature wooden stools on the porch of the elder's house, waiting for him to arrive. About a dozen other people were present, all men. They looked us over sharply and did not speak or smile. When the official appeared, he introduced himself as Mr. Evon. He did not seem especially old for an elder, though perhaps I shouldn't have been surprised; the average life expectancy for men in Haiti is less than fifty years. When Haitian men discuss serious matters, they tend to sit very close and frequently touch each other's arms. David placed both his hands upon Mr. Evon and attested, in Creole, to the availability of funds for the trip and to our honesty.

"What are your plans?" asked Mr. Evon.

"To go to America," David said. "To start my life."

"And if God does not wish it?"

"Then I will go to the bottom of the sea."

That evening, several of the men who had been present during our interview with Mr. Evon came to visit, one at a time. They were performing what David called a *vit ron*—a quick roundup, trying to gather potential passengers for the boat they were each affiliated with. David chose an amiable man named Stephen Bellot, who claimed to be filling a ship that was likely to leave in a matter of days. Stephen was also a member of one of the more prominent families on Île Tortue. He was twenty-eight years old, lanky and loose-limbed, with rheumy eyes and a wiggly way of walking that made me think, at times, that he'd make an excellent template for a cartoon character. In many ways, he seemed David's opposite. Where David practically perspired bravado, Stephen was tentative and polite. His words were often lost in the wind, and he had a nervous habit of rubbing his thumbs across his forefingers, as if they were little violins. He had been raised on Île Tortue and, though he'd moved to Port-au-Prince to study English, he seemed to lack David's city savvy. In Port-au-Prince, Stephen had worked for several years as a high school teacher—chemistry and English were his specialties. He was paid $35 a month. He'd returned to Île Tortue six months before in order to catch a boat to America. The prospect of leaving, he admitted, both inspired and intimidated him. "I've never been anywhere," he told me. "Not even across the border to the Dominican Republic." He said he'd set up a meeting with a boat owner the next day.

The boat owner lived on the mainland, in Port-de-Paix. Stephen's mother and brother and grandmother and several of his cousins lived in a small house nearby, and Stephen took us there while he went off to find the captain. An open sewer ran on either side of the two-room cinder-block home; insects formed a thrumming cloud about everyone's head. There was a TV but no electricity. The lines had been down for some time, and nobody knew when they'd be repaired. Sleep was accomplished in shifts—at all times, it seemed, four or five people were in the home's one bed. The sole decoration was a poster advertising Miami Beach. We waited there for eleven hours. The grandmother, bone thin, sat against a wall and did not move. Another woman scrubbed clothing with a washboard and stone. "Everyone in Haiti has been to prison," David once said, "because Haiti is a prison."

The captain arrived at sunset. His name was Gilbert Marko; he was thirty-one years old. He was wearing the nicest clothing I'd seen in Haiti—genuine Wrangler blue jeans, a gingham button-down shirt, and shiny wingtips. He had opaque eyes and an uncommonly round head, and tiny, high-set ears. There was an air about him of scarcely suppressed intensity, like a person who has recently eaten a jalapeño pepper. The meeting went well. David explained that his decision to leave had not been a hasty one—he mentioned his previous trip to Île Tortue and his time in America. Stephen said we all understood the risks. Both David and Stephen declared their support for us. This seemed good enough for Gilbert. He said he'd been to the Bahamas many times. He had seven children by five women and was gradually trying to get everyone to America. He spoke excellent English, jingly with Bahamian rhythms.

His boat, he said, was new—this would only be its second crossing. There would be plenty of water and food, he insisted, and no more than twenty-five passengers. He was taking family members and wanted a safe, hassle-free trip. His boat was heading to Nassau, the Bahamian capital. The crossing could take four days if the wind was good, and as many as eight days if it was not. We'd have no engine.

Most people who make it to America, Gilbert explained, do so only after working in the Bahamas for several months, usually picking crops or cleaning hotel rooms. According to Gilbert, the final segment of the trip, typically a ninety-minute shot by powerboat from the Bimini Islands, Bahamas, to Broward Beach, Florida, costs about $3,000 a person. Often, he said, an American boat owner pilots this leg—ten people in his craft, a nice profit for a half-day's work.

Eventually, talk came around to money for Gilbert's segment of the trip. Nothing in Haiti has a set price, and the fee for a crossing is especially variable, often depending on the quality of the boat. Virtually every Haitian is handing over his life savings. The price most frequently quoted for an illegal trip to the Bahamas was 10,000 gourdes—about $530. Fees ten times as high had also been mentioned. Rumor on Île Tortue was that the two Chinese passengers on the Key Biscayne boat had paid $20,000 apiece. Gilbert said that a significant percentage of his income goes directly to the local elders, who in turn make sure that no other Haitian authorities become overly concerned with the business on Île Tortue.

After several hours of negotiations, Gilbert agreed to transport Chris and me for $1,200 each, and David and Stephen, who were each given credit for rounding us up, for $300 each.

Gilbert had named his boat *Believe in God*. It was anchored (next to the *Thank You Jesus*) off the shore of La Vallée, where it had been built. If you were to ask a second-grader to draw a boat, the result would probably look a lot like the *Believe in God*. It was painted a sort of brackish white, with red and black detailing. The mast was a thin pine, no doubt dragged out of the hills of Île Tortue. There was no safety gear, no maps, no life rafts, no tool kit, and no nautical instruments of any type save for an ancient compass. The deck boards were misaligned. With the exception of the hold, there was no shelter from the elements. Not a single thought had been given to comfort. It had taken three weeks to build, said Gilbert, and had cost $4,000. It was his first boat.

Gilbert explained that he needed to return to Port-de-Paix to purchase supplies, but that it'd be best if we remained on the boat. The rest of his passengers, he said, were waiting in safe houses. "We'll be set to go in three or four hours," he said as he and his crew boarded a return ferry.

Time in Haiti is an extraordinary flexible concept, so when eight hours passed and there was no sign of our crew, we were not concerned. Night came, and still no word. Soon, twenty-four hours had passed since Gilbert's departure. Then thirty. David became convinced that we had been set up. We'd handed over all our money and everyone had disappeared. Boat-smuggling cons were nothing new. The most common one, David said, involved sailing around Haiti and the Dominican Republic two or three times and then dropping everyone off on a deserted Haitian island and telling them they're in the Bahamas. A more insidious scam, he mentioned, involved taking passengers a mile out to sea and then tossing them overboard. It happens, he insisted. But this, said David, was a new one. He was furious, but for a funny reason. "They stole all that money," he said, "and I'm not even getting any."

David was wrong. After dark, Gilbert and his crew docked a ferry alongside the *Believe in God*. They had picked up about thirty other

Haitians—mostly young, mostly male—from the safe houses, and the passengers huddled together as if in a herd, each clutching a small bag of personal belongings. Their faces registered a mix of worry and confusion and excitement—the mind-jumble of a life-altering moment. Things had been terribly delayed, Gilbert said, though he offered no further details. I saw our supplies for the trip: a hundred-pound bag of flour, two fifty-five-gallon water drums, four bunches of plantains, a sack of charcoal, and a rooster in a card-board box. This did not seem nearly enough for what could be a weeklong trip, but at least it was something. I'd been told that many boats leave without any food at all.

The passengers transferred from the ferry to the *Believe in God*, and Gilbert sent everyone but his crew down to the hold. We pushed against one another, trying to establish small plots of territo-ry. David's size in such a situation was suddenly a disadvantage—he had difficulty contorting himself to fit the parameters of the hold and had to squat with his knees tucked up against his chest, a little-boy position. For the first time since I'd met him he appeared weak, and more than a bit tense. Throughout our long wait, David had been a study in nonchalance. "I'm not nervous; I'm not excited; I'm just ready to leave," he'd said the previous day. Perhaps now, as the gravity of the situation dawned on him, he realized what he was about to undergo.

"Wasn't it like this last time you crossed?" I asked. David flashed me an unfamiliar look and touched my arm and said, "I need to tell you something," and finally, in the strange confessional that is the hold of a boat, he told me a little of his past. The first time he'd gone to America, he said, he'd flown on an airplane. He was nine years old. His mother had been granted an immigration visa, and she took David and his two brothers and a sister to Naples, Florida. Soon after, his mother died of AIDS. He had never known his father. He fell into bad company, and at age seventeen spent nine months in jail for stealing a car. At nineteen, he served a year and five days in jail for selling marijuana and then was deported. That was seven years ago. In Naples, he said, his friends had called him Six-Four, a moniker bestowed because of his penchant for stealing 1964 Chevy Impalas. He admitted to me that if he returned to Naples, where his sister lived, he was concerned he'd have to become Six-Four again in order to afford to live there. In America, he mentioned, there is shame in poverty—a shame you don't feel in Haiti. "People are always looking at the poor Haitians who just stepped off their banana boat," he said. This was something, he suggested, that Stephen might find a painful lesson.

The view from the hold, through the scuttle, was like watching a play from the orchestra pit. Gilbert handed each crew member an envelope stuffed with money, as if at a wedding. Nobody was satisfied, of course, and an argument ensued that lasted into the dawn. Down in the hold, where everyone was crushed together, frustration mounted. Occasionally curses were yelled up. When it was clear there was no more money to distribute, the crew demanded spots on the boat for family members. Gilbert acquiesced, and the crew left the ship to inform their relatives. Soon there were thirty-five people on board, then forty. Hours passed. There was no room in the hold to do anything but sit, and so that is what we did. People calmed down. Waiting consumes a significant portion of life in Haiti, and this was merely another delay. The sun rode its arc; heat escaping through the scuttle blurred the sky. A container of water was passed about, but only a few mouthfuls were available for each person. Forty-two people were aboard. Then forty-six. It was difficult to breathe, as though the air had turned to gauze. David and Stephen could not have been pressed closer to each other if they'd been wrestling. There had been murders on these journeys, and suicides and suffocations. Now I could see why. "We came to this country on slave boats," David said, "and we're going to leave on slave boats."

There was a sudden pounding of feet on the deck and a man— an old man, with veiny legs and missing teeth—dropped headfirst into the hold. Gilbert jumped after him, seized the old man by his hair, and flung him out. I heard the hollow sounds of blows being landed, and then a splash, and the attempted stowaway was gone.

Everything was quiet for a moment, a settling, and then there was again commotion on deck, but it was choreographed commotion, and the sails were raised, a mainsail and a bed-sheet-sized jib, two wedges of white against the cobalt sky. We'd already been in the hold ten hours, but still the boat did not leave. There was a clipped squawk from above, and the rooster was slaughtered. Then Gilbert came down to our quarters—he'd tied a fuchsia bandanna about his head—and crawled to the very front, where there was a tiny door with a padlock. He stuck his head inside the cubby and hung a few flags, sprayed perfumed water, and chanted. "Voodoo prayers," said David. When he emerged he crawled through the hold and methodically sprinkled the top of everyone's head with the perfume. Then he climbed onto the deck and barked a command, and the *Believe in God* set sail.

The poorest country and the richest country in the Western Hemisphere are separated by six hundred miles of open ocean. It's a treacherous expanse of water. The positioning of the Caribbean Islands relative to the Gulf Stream creates what is known as a Venturi effect—a funneling action that can result in a rapid buildup of wind and waves. Meteorologists often call the region "hurricane alley." For a boat without nautical charts, the area is a minefield of shallows and sandbars and reefs. It is not uncommon for inexperienced sailors to become sucked into the Gulf Stream and fail to reach their destination. "If you miss South Florida," said Commander Christopher Carter of the Coast Guard, who has sixteen years' experience patrolling the Caribbean, "your next stop is North Carolina. Then Nova Scotia. We've never found any migrants alive in Nova Scotia, but we've had ships wash ashore there."

Initially, the waves out past the tip of Île Tortue were modest, four or five feet at most, the whitecaps no more than a froth of curlicues. Still, the sensation in the hold was of tumbling unsteadiness. The hold was below the waterline, and the sloshing of the surf was both amplified and distorted—the sounds of digestion, it occurred to me, and I thought more than once of Jonah, trapped in the belly of a whale. When the boat was sideswiped by an especially aggressive wave, the stress against the hull invariably produced a noise like someone stepping on a plastic cup. Water came in through the cracks. Every time this happened, David and Stephen glanced at each other and arched their eyebrows, as if to ask, Is this the one that's going to put us under? When building a boat, David had said, it was common to steal nails from other ships, hammer them straight and reuse them. I wondered how many nails had been pulled from our boat. As the waves broke upon us, the hull boards bellied and bowed, straining against the pressure. There was a pump aboard, a primitive one, consisting of a rubber-wrapped broom handle and a plastic pipe that ran down to the bottom of the hold. Someone on deck continuously had to work the broom handle up and down, and still we were sitting in water. The energy of the ocean against the precariousness of our boat seemed a cruel mismatch.

Nearly everyone in the hold kept their bags with them at all times; clearly, a few of the possessions were meant to foster good luck. One man repeatedly furled and unfurled a little blue flag upon which was drawn a *vévé*—a symbolic design intended to invoke a voodoo spirit. Stephen fingered a necklace, carved from a bit of coconut, that a relative had brought him from the Bahamas. Another man read from a scrap of a paperback book, Chapters 29 through 33 of a work called *Garden of Lies*. David often held his Bible to his chest. I had my own charm. It was a device called an Emergency Position-Indicating Radio Beacon, or EPIRB. When triggered, an EPIRB transmits a distress signal to the Coast Guard via satellite, indicating its exact position in the water. I was assured by the company that manufactured the beacon that if I activated it anywhere in the Caribbean, help would be no more than six hours away. The EPIRB was a foot tall, vaguely cylindrical, and neon yellow. I kept it stashed in my backpack, which I clasped always in my lap. Nobody except Chris, the photographer, knew it was there.

The heat in the hold seemed to transcend temperature. It had become an object, a weight—something solid and heavy, settling upon us like a dentist's X-ray vest. There was no way to shove it aside. Air did not circulate, wind was shut out. Thirst was a constant dilemma. At times, the desire to drink crowded out all other notions. Even as Gilbert was sending around a water container, my first thought was when we'd have another. We had 110 gallons of water on board, and forty-six people. In desert conditions, it's recommended that a person drink about one gallon per day. It was as hot as any desert down there. Hotter. That meant we had a two-day supply. But we were merely sitting, so perhaps half a gallon would be enough. That's four days. The trip, though, could take eight days. If it did we'd be in serious trouble.

Finding a comfortable position in the hold was hopeless. The hull was V-shaped, and large waves sent everyone sliding into the center, tossing us about like laundry. I exchanged hellos with the people around me—Wesley and Tijuan and Wedell and Andien— but there seemed nothing further to say. Every hour, an electronic watch chirped from somewhere in the dark. From here and there came the murmurs of sleep. The occasional, taut conversations between Stephen and David consisted primarily of reveries about reaching America. David said that he wanted to work in the fields, picking tomatoes or watermelon. His dream was to marry an American woman. Stephen's fantasy was to own a pickup truck, a red one.

The rules of the boat had been established by Gilbert. Eight people were allowed on deck at once; the rest had to remain in the hold. Six spots were reserved by Gilbert and the crew. The other two were filled on a rotating basis—a pair from the deck switched with a pair from the hold every twenty minutes or so. This meant each person would be allowed out about once every six hours. A crowded deck, Gilbert explained, would interfere with the crew and rouse the suspicions of passing boats. More important, people were needed in the hold to provide ballast—too much weight up top and the boat would tip.

Of the forty-six people on the boat, five were women. They were crammed together into the nether reaches of the hold, visible only as silhouettes. The farther back one crawled into the hold, the hotter it got. Where the women were it must have been crippling. Occasionally they braided one another's hair, but they appeared never to speak. They were the last to be offered time on deck, and their shifts seemed significantly shorter than those of the men.

The oldest person on the boat was a forty-year-old passenger named Desimeme; the youngest was thirteen-year-old Kenton. The average age was about twenty-five. Unlike the migrants of the early nineties, who tended more heavily to be families and rural peasants, most Haitian escapees are now young, urban males. The reason for this shift is probably an economic one. In recent years, according to people on Île Tortue, the price for a crossing has become vastly inflated, and women and farmers are two of Haiti's lowest-paid groups.

Two hours after leaving, the seasickness began. There was a commotion in the rear of the hold, and people started shouting, and a yellow bucket—at one time it was a margarine container—was tossed below. It was passed back. The man who was sick filled it up, and the bucket was sent forward, handed up, dumped overboard and passed back down. A dozen pairs of hands reached for it. The yellow bucket went back and forth. It also served as our bathroom, an unavoidable humiliation we each had to endure. Not everyone could wait for the bucket to arrive, and in transferring the container in pitching seas it was sometimes upended. The contents mingled with the water that sloshed ankle-deep about the bottom of the hold. The stench was overpowering.

One of the sickest people on board was Kenton, the thirteen-year-old boy. He lay jackknifed next to me in the hold, clutching his stomach, too ill to grab for the bucket. I slipped him a seasickness pill, but he was unable to keep it down. Kenton was a cousin of one of the crew members. He had been one of the last people to board the boat. In the scramble to fill the final spots, there was no room for both him and his parents, so he was sent on alone. His parents, I'd overheard, had promised that they'd be on the very next boat, and when Kenton boarded he was bubbly and smiling, as if this were going to be a grand adventure. Now he was obviously petrified, but also infused with an especially salient dose of Haitian mettle—as he grew weaker he kept about him an iron face. Never once did he cry out. He had clearly selected a favorite shirt for the voyage: a New York Knicks basketball jersey.

This did not seem like the appropriate time to eat, but dinner was ready. The boat's stove, on deck, was an old automobile tire rim filled with charcoal. There was also a large aluminum pot and a ladle. The meal consisted of dumplings and broth—actually, boiled flour balls and hot water. Most people had brought a bowl and spoon with them, and the servings were passed about in the same manner as the bucket. When the dumplings were finished, Hanson, one of the crew members, came down into the hold. He was grasping a plastic bag that was one of his personal possessions. Inside the bag was an Île Tortue specialty—ground peanuts and sugar. He produced a spoon from his pocket, dipped it into the bag, and fed a spoonful to the man nearest him, carefully cupping his chin as if administering medicine. Then he wormed his way through the hold, inserting a heaping spoon into everyone's mouth. His generosity was appreciated, but the meal did little to help settle people's stomachs. The yellow bucket was again in great demand.

Hours trickled by. There was nothing to do, no form of diversion. The boat swayed, the sun shone, the heat intensified. People were sick; people were quiet. Eyes gradually dimmed. Everyone seemed to have withdrawn into themselves, as in the first stages of shock. Heads bobbed and hung, fists clenched and opened. Thirst was like a tight collar about our throats. It was the noiselessness of the suffering that made it truly frightening—the silent panic of deep fear.

Shortly before sunset, when we'd been at sea nearly twelve hours, I was allowed to take my second stint on deck. By now there was nothing around us but water. The western sky was going red and our shadows were at full stretch. The sail snapped and strained against its rigging; the waves, at last, sounded like waves. Gilbert was standing at the prow, gazing at the horizon, a hand cupped above his eyes, and as I watched him a look of concern came across his face. He snapped around, distressed, and shouted one word: "Hamilton!" Everyone on deck froze. He shouted it again. Then he pointed to where he'd been staring, and there, in the distance, was a ship of military styling, marring the smooth seam between sea and sky. Immediately, I was herded back into the hold.

A Hamilton, Stephen whispered, is Haitian slang for a Coast Guard ship—it's also, not coincidentally, the name of an actual ship. The news flashed through the hold, and in reflexive response everyone crushed deeper into the rear, away from the opening, as though this would help avoid detection. Gilbert paced the deck, manic. He sent two of the crew members down with us, and then he, too, descended. He burrowed toward his cubby, shoving people aside, unlocked the door, and wedged himself in. And then he began to chant, in a steady tone both dirgelike and defiant. The song paid homage to Agwe, the voodoo spirit of the sea, and when Gilbert emerged, still chanting, several people in the hold took up the tune, and then he climbed up and the crew began chanting, too. It was an ethereal tune, sung wholly without joy, a signal of desperate unity that seemed to imply we'd sooner drift to Nova Scotia than abandon our mission. Some of these people, it seemed, really were willing to sacrifice their lives to try and get to America. Our captain was one of them.

Over the singing came another sound, an odd buzz. Then there were unfamiliar voices—non-Haitian voices, speaking French. In the hold, people snapped out of their stupor. Stephen grabbed his necklace. David chewed on the meat of his hand. I stood up and peeked out. The buzz was coming from a motorized raft that had pulled beside us. Six people were aboard, wearing orange life vests imprinted with the words U.S. COAST GUARD. Gilbert was sitting atop one of our water drums, arms folded, flashing our interlopers a withering look. Words were shouted back and forth—questions from the Coast Guard, blunt rejoinders from Gilbert.

"Where are you headed?"

"Miami."

"Do you have docking papers?"

"No."

"What are you transporting?"

"Rice."

"Can we have permission to board?"

"No."

There was nothing further. In the hold everyone was motionless. People tried not to breathe. Some had their palms pushed together in prayer. One man pressed his fingertips to his forehead. Soon I heard the buzz again, this time receding, and the Coast Guard was gone. Gilbert crouched beside the scuttle and spoke. This had happened on his last crossing, he said. The Coast Guard just comes and sniffs around. They were looking for drugs, but now they've gone. Then he mentioned one additional item. As a precaution, he said, nobody would be allowed onto the deck, indefinitely.

The reaction to this news was subtle but profound. There was a general exhalation, as if we'd each been kicked in the stomach, and then a brief burst of conversation—more talking than at any time since we'd set sail. The thought of those precious minutes on deck had been the chief incentive for enduring the long hours below. With Gilbert's announcement, something inside of me—some scaffolding of fortitude—broke. We'd been at sea maybe fourteen hours; we had a hundred to go, minimum. Ideas swirled about my head, expanding and consuming like wildfire. I thought of drowning, I thought of starving, I thought of withering from thirst.

Then, as if he'd read my mind, David took my right hand and held it. He held it a long time, and I felt calmer. He looked at my eyes; I looked at his. This much was clear: David wasn't willing to heed his own words. He wasn't prepared to die. He was terrified, too. This wasn't something we discussed until much later, though he eventually admitted it.

When David let go of my hand, the swirling thoughts returned. I wrestled with the idea of triggering the EPIRB. People were weak—I was weak—and it occurred to me that I had the means to save lives. But though pressing the button might lead to our rescue, it would certainly dash everyone's dreams. There was also the concern that I'd be caught setting it off, the repercussions of which I did not want to ponder. I made a decision.

"Chris," I said. I was whispering.

"Yes."

"I'm going to use the thing."

"Don't."

"Don't?"

"No, don't. Wait."

"How long?"

"Just wait."

"I don't think I can."

"Just wait a little."

"Okay. I'll wait a little."

I waited a little, a minute at a time. Four more hours passed. Then, abruptly, the buzz returned. Two buzzes. This time there was no conversation, only the clatter of Coast Guard boots landing on our deck. At first, it seemed as though there might be violence. The mood in the hold was one of reckless, nothing-to-lose defiance. I could see it in the set of people's jaws, and in the vigor that suddenly leaped back into their eyes. This was our boat; strangers were not invited—they were to be pummeled and tossed overboard, like the old man who had tried to stow away. Then lights were shined into the hold, strong ones. We were blinded. There was no place for us to move. The idea of revolt died as quickly as it had ignited. Eighteen hours after we'd set sail, the trip was over.

Six at a time, we were loaded into rubber boats and transported to the Coast Guard cutter *Forward*, a ship 270 feet long and nine stories high. It was 4:00 in the morning. Nobody struggled, no weapons were drawn. We were frisked and placed in quarantine on the flight deck, in a helicopter hangar. Three Haitians were so weak from dehydration that they needed assistance walking. The Coast Guard officers were surprised to see journalists on board, but we were processed with the Haitians. We were each supplied with a blanket, a pair of flip-flops, and a toothbrush. We were given as much water as we could drink. We were examined by a doctor. The *Forward*'s crew members wore two layers of latex gloves whenever they were around us.

The *Forward's* commanding officer, a nineteen-year Coast Guard veteran named Dan MacLeod, came onto the flight deck. He pulled me aside. The Coast Guard, he said, had not lost sight of our boat since we'd first been spotted. He'd spent the previous four hours contacting Haitian authorities, working to secure an S.N.O.—a Statement of No Objection—that would permit the Coast Guard to stop a Haitian boat in international waters. When David and Stephen learned of this, they were furious. There is the feeling among many Haitians of abandonment by the United States—or worse, of manipulation. American troops helped restore Aristide to power, then they vanished. Now, because there is democracy in Haiti, the United States has a simple excuse for rejecting Haitian citizenship claims: Haitians are economic, not political migrants. For those Haitians who do enter America illegally—the United States Border Patrol estimates that between 6,000 and 12,000 do so each year—it is far better to try to seep into the fabric of the Haitian-American community than to apply for asylum. In 1999, 92 percent of Haitian asylum claims were rejected.

As soon as the Haitian government granted permission, the Coast Guard had boarded our boat. Though illegal migrants were suspected to be on board—two large water barrels seemed a bit much for just a crew—the official reason the boat had been intercepted, Officer MacLeod told me, was because we were heading straight for a reef. "You were off course from Haiti about two degrees," he said. "That's not bad for seat-of-the-pants sailing, but you were heading directly for the Great Inagua reef. You hadn't altered your course in three hours, and it was dark out. When we boarded your vessel you were 2,200 yards from the reef. You'd have hit it in less than forty minutes."

Our boat running against a reef could have been lethal. The hull, probably, would have split. The current over the reef, Officer MacLeod informed me, is unswimmably strong. The reef is as sharp as a cheese grater. The EPIRB would not have helped.

Even if we'd managed to avoid the reef—if, by some good fortune, we'd changed course at the last minute—we were still in danger. Officer MacLeod asked me if I'd felt the boat become steadier as the night progressed. I said I had. "That's the first sure sign you're sinking," he said. There was more. "You were in three-to-four-foot seas. At six-foot seas, you'd have been in a serious situation, and six-foot seas are not uncommon here. Six-foot seas would've taken that boat down." When I mentioned that we'd expected the trip to take four or five days, Officer MacLeod laughed. "They were selling you a story," he said. In the eighteen hours since leaving Haiti, we had covered thirty miles. We'd had excellent conditions. The distance from Haiti to Nassau was 450 miles. Even with miraculous wind, it could have taken us ten days. The doctor on board said we'd most likely have been dealing with fatalities within forty-eight hours.

The next day, it turned out, was almost windless. It was hotter than ever. And the seas were choppy—seven feet at times, one officer reported. Another high-ranking officer added one more bit of information: a Coast Guard ship hadn't been in these waters at any time in the past two weeks. The *Forward* happened to be heading in for refueling when we were spotted.

Our trip, it appeared, had all the makings of a suicide mission. If there had been no EPIRB and no Coast Guard, it's very likely that the *Believe in God* would have vanished without a trace. And our craft, said Officer MacLeod, was one of the sturdier sailboats he has seen—probably in the top 20 percent. Most boats that make it, he mentioned, have a small motor. I wondered how many Haitians have perished attempting such a crossing. "That's got to be a very scary statistic," said Ron Labrec, a Coast Guard public affairs officer, though he wouldn't hazard a guess. He said it's impossible to accurately determine how many migrants are leaving Haiti and what percentage of them make it to shore.

But given the extraordinary number of people fleeing on marginal sailboats, it seems very likely that there are several hundred unrecorded deaths each year. Illegal migration has been going on for decades. It is not difficult to imagine that there are thousands of Haitian bodies on the bottom of the Caribbean.

We spent two days on the *Forward*, circling slowly in the sea, while it was determined where we would be dropped off. On May 16, everyone was deposited on Great Inagua Island and turned over to Bahamian authorities. Chris and I were released and the Haitians were placed in a detention center. The next day they were flown to Nassau and held in another detention center, where they were interviewed by representatives of the United Nations High Commission for Refugees. None were found to qualify for refugee status.

As for the *Believe in God*, the boat came to a swift end. The night we were captured, we stood along the rail of the flight deck as the

Forward's spotlight was trained on our boat. It looked tiny in the ink-dark sea. The sail was still up, though the boat was listing heavily. Officer MacLeod had just started telling me about its unseaworthiness. "Watch," he said. With nobody pumping water from it, the hold had been filling up fast. As I looked, the mast leaned farther and farther down, as if bowing to the sea, until it touched the water. Then the boat slowly began to sink.

After two weeks in the Nassau detention center, all forty-four Haitians were flown to Port-au-Prince. They received no punishment from Haitian authorities. The next morning, Gilbert returned to Île Tortue, already formulating plans for purchasing a second boat and trying to cross once more. Stephen also went home to Île Tortue, but was undecided as to whether he'd try the journey again. David went back to Port-au-Prince, back to his small mahogany stand, back to his crumbling shack, where his personal space consisted of a single nail from which he hung the same black plastic bag he'd had on the boat. He said he felt lucky to be alive. He said he would not try again by boat, not ever. Instead, he explained, he was planning on sneaking overland into the Dominican Republic. There were plenty of tourists there and he'd be able to sell more mahogany. He told me he was already studying a new language, learning from a Spanish translation of *The Cat in the Hat* that he'd found in the street.

The idea of running off to a deserted island strikes
such a deep chord in us that just thinking of one is
enough to send a soothing current of alpha waves
coursing through our tension-ridden limbs. The cliché
version, as featured on countless calendars, coffee-
table books, and postcards, invariably depicts a black
silhouette of palm trees jutting from a platter of land
adrift on a Technicolor ground of sea and sky. But
what if, D. H. Lawrence asks here, all those longed-for
qualifies of the island getaway—inaccessability,
immunity from intrusion, control over one's own
inviolable domain—bring us all the more inexorably
face-to-face with something absolutely inescapable?
What if that expanse of sea and space that insulates
against the cares and unpleasantness
of life ends up threatening to suffocate us?

the man who loved islands

D. H. LAWRENCE

1

there was a man who loved islands. He was born on one, but it didn't suit him, as there were too many other people on it, besides himself. He wanted an island all of his own: not necessarily to be alone on it, but to make it a world of his own.

An island, if it is big enough, is no better than a continent. It has to be really quite small, before it *feels* like an island; and this story will show how tiny it has to be, before you can presume to fill it with your own personality.

Now circumstances so worked out that this lover of islands, by the time he was thirty-five, actually acquired an island of his own. He didn't own it as freehold property, but he had a ninety-nine years' lease of it, which, as far as a man and an island are concerned, is as good as everlasting. Since, if you are like Abraham, and want your offspring to be numberless as the sands of the sea-shore, you don't choose an island to start breeding on. Too soon there would be over-population, overcrowding, and slum conditions. Which is a horrid thought, for one who loves an island for its insulation. No, an island is a nest which holds one egg, and one only. This egg is the islander himself.

The island acquired by our potential islander was not in the remote oceans. It was quite near at home, no palm trees nor boom of surf on the reef, nor any of that kind of thing; but a good solid dwelling-house, rather gloomy, above the landing-place, and beyond, a small farmhouse with sheds, and a few outlying fields. Down on the little landing-bay were three cottages in a row, like coastguards' cottages, all neat and whitewashed.

What could be more cosy and home-like? It was four miles if you walked all round your island, through the gorse and the black-thorn bushes, above the steep rocks of the sea and down in the little glades where the primroses grew. If you walked straight over the two humps of hills, the length of it, through the rocky fields where the cows lay chewing, and through the rather sparse oats, on into the gorse again, and so to the low cliffs' edge, it took you only twenty minutes. And when you came to the edge, you could see another, bigger island lying beyond. But the sea was between you and it. And as you returned over the turf where the short, downland cowslips nodded, you saw to the east still another island, a tiny one this time, like the calf of the cow. This tiny island also belonged to the islander.

Thus it seems that even islands like to keep each other company.

Our islander loved his island very much. In early spring, the little ways and glades were a snow of blackthorn, a vivid white among the Celtic stillness of close green and grey rock, blackbirds calling out in the whiteness their first long, triumphant calls. After the blackthorn and the nestling primroses came the blue apparition of hyacinths, like elfin lakes and slipping sheets of blue, among the bushes and under the glade of trees. And many birds with nests you could peep into, on the island all your own. Wonderful what a great world it was!

Followed summer, and the cowslips gone, the wild roses faintly fragrant through the haze. There was a field of hay, the foxgloves stood looking down. In a little cove, the sun was on the pale granite where you bathed, and the shadow was in the rocks. Before the mist came stealing, you went home through the ripening oats, the glare of the sea fading from the high air as the fog-horn started to moo on the other island. And then the sea-fog went, it was autumn, the oat-sheaves lying prone, the great moon, another island, rose golden out of the sea, and rising higher, the world of the sea was white.

So autumn ended with rain, and winter came, dark skies and dampness and rain, but rarely frost. The island, your island, cowered dark, holding away from you. You could feel, down in the wet, sombre hollows, the resentful spirit coiled upon itself, like a wet dog coiled in gloom, or a snake that is neither asleep nor awake. Then in the night, when the wind left off blowing in great gusts and volleys, as at sea, you felt that your island was a universe, infinite and old as the darkness; not an island at all, but an infinite dark world where all the souls from all the other bygone nights lived on, and the infinite distance was near.

Strangely, from your little island in space, you were gone forth into the dark, great realms of time, where all the souls that never die veer and swoop on their vast, strange errands. The little earthly island has dwindled, like a jumping-off place, into nothingness, for you have jumped off, you know not how, into the dark wide mystery of time, where the past is vastly alive, and the future is not separated off.

This is the danger of becoming an islander. When, in the city, you wear your white spats and dodge the traffic with the fear of death down your spine, then you are quite safe from the terrors of infinite time. The moment is your little islet in time, it is the spatial universe that careers round you.

But once isolate yourself on a little island in the sea of space, and the moment begins to heave and expand in great circles, the solid earth is gone, and your slippery, naked dark soul finds herself out in the timeless world, where the chariots of the so-called dead dash down the old streets of centuries, and souls crowd on the footways that we, in the moment, call bygone years. The souls of all the dead are alive again, and pulsating actively around you. You are out in the other infinity.

Something of this happened to our islander. Mysterious "feelings" came upon him that he wasn't used to; strange awareness of old, far-gone men, and other influences; men of Gaul, with big moustaches, who had been on his island, and had vanished from the face of it, but not out of the air of night. They were there still, hurtling their big, violent, unseen bodies through the night. And there were priests, with golden knives and mistletoe; then other priests with a crucifix; then pirates with murder on the sea.

Our islander was uneasy. He didn't believe, in the day-time, in any of this nonsense. But at night it just was so. He had reduced himself to a single point in space, and, a point being that which has neither length nor breadth, he had to step off it into somewhere else. Just as you must step into the sea, if the waters wash your foothold away, so he had, at night, to step off into the other worlds of undying time.

He was uncannily aware, as he lay in the dark, that the blackthorn grove that seemed a bit uncanny even in the realm of space and day, at night was crying with old men of an invisible race, around the altar stone. What was a ruin under the hornbeam trees by day, was a moaning of blood-stained priests with crucifixes, on the ineffable night. What was a cave and a hidden beach between coarse rocks, became in the invisible dark the purple-lipped imprecation of pirates.

To escape any more of this sort of awareness, our islander daily concentrated upon his material island. Why should it not be the Happy Isle at last? Why not the last small isle of the Hesperides, the perfect place, all filled with his own gracious, blossom-like spirit? A minute world of pure perfection, made by man himself.

He began, as we begin all our attempts to regain Paradise, by spending money. The old, semi-feudal dwelling-house he restored, let in more light, put clear lovely carpets on the floor, clear, flower-petal curtains at the sullen windows, and wines in the cellars of rock. He brought over a buxom housekeeper from the world, and a soft-spoken, much-experienced butler. These two were to be islanders.

In the farmhouse he put a bailiff, with two farm-hands. There were Jersey cows, tinkling a slow bell, among the gorse. There was a call to meals at midday, and the peaceful smoking of chimneys at evening, when rest descended.

A jaunty sailing-boat with a motor accessory rode in the shelter in the bay, just below the row of three white cottages. There was also a little yawl, and two row-boats drawn up on the sand. A fishing-net was drying on its supports, a boatload of new white planks stood criss-cross, a woman was going to the well with a bucket.

In the end cottage lived the skipper of the yacht, and his wife and son. He was a man from the other, large island, at home on this sea. Every fine day he went out fishing, with his son, every fair day there was fresh fish in the island.

In the middle cottage lived an old man and wife, a very faithful couple. The old man was a carpenter, and man of many jobs. He was always working, always the sound of his plane or his saw; lost in his work, he was another kind of islander.

In the third cottage was a mason, a widower with a son and two daughters. With the help of his boy, this man dug ditches and built fences, raised buttresses and erected a new outbuilding, and hewed stone from the little quarry. One daughter worked at the big house.

It was a quiet, busy little world. When the islander brought you over as his guest, you met first the dark-bearded, thin, smiling skipper, Arnold, then his boy Charles. At the house, the smooth-lipped butler who had lived all over the world valeted you, and created that curious creamy-smooth, disarming sense of luxury around you which only a perfect and rather untrustworthy servant can create. He disarmed you and had you at his mercy. The buxom housekeeper smiled and treated you with the subtly respectful familiarity that is only dealt out to the true gentry. And the rosy maid threw a glance at you, as if you were very wonderful, coming from the great outer world. Then you met the smiling but watchful bailiff, who came from Cornwall, and the shy farm-hand from Berkshire, with his clean wife and two little children: then the rather sulky farmhand from Suffolk. The mason, a Kent man, would talk to you by the yard if you let him. Only the old carpenter was gruff and elsewhere absorbed.

Well then, it was a little world to itself, and everybody feeling very safe, and being very nice to you, as if you were really something special. But it was the islander's world, not yours. He was the Master. The special smile, the special attention was to the Master. They all knew how well off they were. So the islander was no longer Mr. So-and-so. To everyone on the island, even to you yourself, he was "the Master".

Well, it was ideal. The Master was no tyrant. Ah, no! He was a delicate, sensitive, handsome Master, who wanted everything perfect and everybody happy. Himself, of course, to be the fount of this happiness and perfection.

But in his way, he was a poet. He treated his guests royally, his servants liberally. Yet he was shrewd, and very wise. He never came the boss over his people. Yet he kept his eye on everything, like a shrewd, blue-eyed young Hermes. And it was amazing what a lot of knowledge he had at hand. Amazing what he knew about Jersey cows, and cheese-making, ditching and fencing, flowers and gardening, ships and the sailing of ships. He was a fount of knowledge about everything, and this knowledge he imparted to his people in an odd, half-ironical, half-portentous fashion, as if he really belonged to the quaint, half-real world of the gods.

They listened to him with their hats in their hands. He loved white clothes; or creamy white; and cloaks, and broad hats. So, in fine weather, the bailiff would see the elegant tall figure in creamy-white serge coming like some bird over the fallow, to look at the weeding of the turnips. Then there would be a doffing of hats, and a few minutes of whimsical, shrewd, wise talk, to which the bailiff answered admiringly, and the farm-hands listened in silent wonder, leaning on their hoes. The bailiff was almost tender, to the Master.

Or, on a windy morning, he would stand with his cloak blowing in the sticky sea-wind, on the edge of the ditch that was being dug to drain a little swamp, talking in the teeth of the wind to the man below, who looked up at him with steady and inscrutable eyes.

Or at evening in the rain he would be seen hurrying across the yard, the broad hat turned against the rain. And the farm-wife would hurriedly exclaim: "The Master! Get up, John, and clear him a place on the sofa." And then the door opened, and it was a cry of: "Why, of all things, if it isn't the Master! Why, have ye turned out then, of a night like this, to come across to the like of we?" And the bailiff took his cloak, and the farm-wife his hat, the two farm-hands drew their chairs to the back, he sat on the sofa and took a child up near him. He was wonderful with children, talked to them simply wonderful, made you think of Our Saviour Himself, said the woman.

He was always greeted with smiles, and the same peculiar deference, as if he were a higher, but also frailer being. They handled him almost tenderly, and almost with adulation. But when he left, or when they spoke of him, they had often a subtle, mocking smile on their faces. There was no need to be afraid of "the Master." Just let him have his own way. Only the old carpenter was sometimes sincerely rude to him; so he didn't care for the old man.

It is doubtful whether any of them really liked him, man to man, or even woman to man. But then it is doubtful if he really liked any of them, as man to man, or man to woman. He wanted them to be happy, and the little world to be perfect. But anyone who wants the world to be perfect must be careful not to have real likes or dislikes. A general goodwill is all you can afford.

The sad fact is, alas, that general goodwill is always felt as something of an insult, by the mere object of it; and so it breeds a quite special brand of malice, Surely general good-will is a form of egoism, that it should have such a result!

Our islander, however, had his own resources. He spent long hours in his library, for he was compiling a book of references to all the flowers mentioned in the Greek and Latin authors. He was not a great classical scholar; the usual public-school equipment. But there are such excellent translations nowadays. And it was so lovely, tracing flower after flower as it blossomed in the ancient world.

So the first year on the island passed by. A great deal had been done. Now the bills flooded in, and the Master, conscientious in all things, began to study them. The study left him pale and breathless. He was not a rich man. He knew he had been making a hole in his capital to get the island into running order. When he came to look, however, there was hardly anything left but hole. Thousands and thousands of pounds had the island swallowed into nothingness.

But surely the bulk of the spending was over! Surely the island would now begin to be self-supporting, even if it made no profit! Surely he was safe. He paid a good many of the bills, and took a little heart. But he had had a shock, and the next year, the coming year, there must be economy, frugality. He told his people so in simple and touching language. And they said: "Why, surely! Surely!"

So, while the wind blew and the rain lashed outside, he would sit in his library with the bailiff over a pipe and pot of beer, discussing farm projects. He lifted his narrow, handsome face, and his blue eyes became dreamy. "*What* a wind!" It blew like cannon-shots. He thought of his island, lashed with foam, and inaccessible, and he exulted....No, he must not lose it. He turned back to the farm projects with the zest of genius, and his hands flicked white emphasis, while the bailiff intoned: "Yes, sir! Yes, sir! You're right, Master!"

But the man was hardly listening. He was looking at the Master's blue lawn shirt and curious pink tie with the fiery red stone, at the enamel sleeve-links, and at the ring with the peculiar scarab. The brown searching eyes of the man of the soil glanced repeatedly over the fine, immaculate figure of the Master, with a sort of slow, calculating wonder. But if he happened to catch the Master's bright, exalted glance, his own eye lit up with a careful cordiality and deference, as he bowed his head slightly.

Thus between them they decided what crops should be sown, what fertilizers should be used in different places, which breed of pigs should be imported, and which line of turkeys. That is to say, the bailiff, by continually cautiously agreeing with the Master, kept out of it, and let the young man have his own way.

The Master knew what he was talking about. He was brilliant at grasping the gist of a book, and knowing how to apply his knowledge. On the whole, his ideas were sound. The bailiff even knew it. But in the man of the soil there was no answering enthusiasm. The brown eyes smiled their cordial deference, but the thin lips never changed. The Master pursed his own flexible mouth in a boyish versatility, as he cleverly sketched in his ideas to the other man, and the bailiff made eyes of admiration, but in his heart he was not attending, he was only watching the Master as he would have watched a queer, caged animal, quite without sympathy, not implicated.

So, it was settled, and the Master rang for Elvery, the butler, to bring a sandwich. He, the Master, was pleased. The butler saw it, and came back with anchovy and ham sandwiches, and a newly opened bottle of vermouth. There was always a newly opened bottle of something.

It was the same with the mason. The Master and he discussed the drainage of a bit of land, and more pipes were ordered, more special bricks, more this, more that.

Fine weather came at last; there was a little lull in the hard work on the island. The Master went for a short cruise in his yacht. It was not really a yacht, just a little bit of a thing. They sailed along the coast of the mainland, and put in at the ports. At every port some friend turned up, the butler made elegant little meals in the cabin. Then the Master was invited to villas and hotels, his people disembarked him as if he were a prince.

And oh, how expensive it turned out! He had to telegraph to the bank for money. And he went home again to economise.

The marsh-marigolds were blazing in the little swamp where the ditches were being dug for drainage. He almost regretted, now, the work in hand. The yellow beauties would not blaze again.

Harvest came, and a bumper crop. There must be a harvest-home supper. The long barn was now completely restored and added to. The carpenter had made long tables. Lanterns hung from the beams of the high-pitched roof. All the people of the island were assembled. The bailiff presided. It was a gay scene.

Towards the end of the supper the Master, in a velvet jacket, appeared with his guests. Then the bailiff rose and proposed "The Master! Long life and health to the Master!" All the people drank the health with great enthusiasm and cheering. The Master replied with a little speech: They were on an island in a little world of their own. It depended on them all to make this world a world of true happiness and content. Each must do his part. He hoped he himself did what he could, for his heart was in his island, and with the people of his island.

The butler responded: As long as the island had such a Master, it could not help but be a little heaven for all the people on it. This was seconded with virile warmth by the bailiff and the mason, the skipper was beside himself. Then there was dancing, the old carpenter was fiddler.

But under all this, things were not well. The very next morning came the farm-boy to say that a cow had fallen over the cliff. The Master went to look. He peered over the not very high declivity, and saw her lying dead on a green ledge under a bit of late-flowering broom. A beautiful, expensive creature, already looking swollen. But what a fool, to fall so unnecessarily!

It was a question of getting several men to haul her up the bank, and then of skinning and burying her. No one would eat the meat. How repulsive it all was!

This was symbolic of the island. As sure as the spirits rose in the human breast, with a movement of joy, an invisible hand struck malevolently out of the silence. There must not be any joy, nor even any quiet peace. A man broke a leg, another was crippled with rheumatic fever. The pigs had some strange disease. A storm drove the yacht on a rock. The mason hated the butler, and refused to let his daughter serve at the house.

Out of the very air came a stony, heavy malevolence. The island itself seemed malicious. It would go on being hurtful and evil for weeks at a time. Then suddenly again one morning it would be fair, lovely as a morning in Paradise, everything beautiful and flowing. And everybody would begin to feel a great relief, and a hope for happiness.

Then as soon as the Master was opened out in spirit like an open flower, some ugly blow would fall. Somebody would send him an anonymous note, accusing some other person on the island. Somebody else would come hinting things against one of his servants.

"Some folks think they've got an easy job out here, with all the pickings they make!" the mason's daughter screamed at the suave butler, in the Master's hearing. He pretended not to hear.

"My man says this island is surely one of the lean kine of Egypt, it would swallow a sight of money, and you'd never get anything back out of it," confided the farm-hand's wife to one of the Master's visitors.

The people were not contented. They were not islanders. "We feel we're not doing right by the children," said those who had children. "We feel we're not doing right by ourselves," said those who had no children. And the various families fairly came to hate one another.

Yet the island was so lovely. When there was a scent of honeysuckle and the moon brightly flickering down on the sea, then even the grumblers felt a strange nostalgia for it. It set you yearning, with a wild yearning; perhaps for the past, to be far back in the mysterious past of the island, when the blood had a different throb. Strange floods of passion came over you, strange violent lusts and imaginations of cruelty. The blood and the passion and the lust which the island had known. Uncanny dreams, half-dreams, half-evocated yearnings.

The Master himself began to be a little afraid of his island. He felt here strange, violent feelings he had never felt before, and lustful desires that he had been quite free from. He knew quite well now that his people didn't love him at all. He knew that their spirits were secretly against him, malicious, jeering, envious, and lurking to down him. He became just as wary and secretive with regard to them.

But it was too much. At the end of the second year, several departures took place. The housekeeper went. The Master always blamed self-important women most. The mason said he wasn't going to be monkeyed about any more, so he took his departure, with his family. The rheumatic farm-hand left.

And then the year's bills came in, the Master made up his accounts. In spite of good crops, the assets were ridiculous, against the spending. The island had again lost, not hundreds but thousands of pounds. It was incredible. But you simply couldn't believe it! Where had it all gone?

The Master spent gloomy nights and days going through accounts in the library. He was thorough. It became evident, now the housekeeper had gone, that she had swindled him. Probably everybody was swindling him. But he hated to think it, so he put the thought away.

He emerged, however, pale and hollow-eyed from his balancing of unbalanceable accounts, looking as if something had kicked him in the stomach. It was pitiable. But the money had gone, and there was an end of it. Another great hole in his capital. How could people be so heartless?

It couldn't go on, that was evident. He would soon be bankrupt. He had to give regretful notice to his butler. He was afraid to find out how much his butler had swindled him. Because the man was such a wonderful butler, after all. And the farm bailiff had to go. The Master had no regrets in that quarter. The losses on the farm had almost embittered him.

The third year was spent in rigid cutting down of expenses. The island was still mysterious and fascinating. But it was also treacherous and cruel, secretly, fathomlessly malevolent. In spite of all its fair show of white blossom and bluebells, and the lovely dignity of foxgloves bending their rose-red bells, it was your implacable enemy.

With reduced staff, reduced wages, reduced splendour, the third year went by. But it was fighting against hope. The farm still lost a good deal. And once more there was a hole in that remnant of capital. Another hole in that which was already a mere remnant round the old holes. The island was mysterious in this also: it seemed to pick the very money out of your pocket, as if it were an octopus with invisible arms stealing from you in every direction.

Yet the Master still loved it. But with a touch of rancour now.

He spent, however, the second half of the fourth year intensely working on the mainland, to be rid of it. And it was amazing how difficult he found it, to dispose of an island. He had thought that everybody was pining for such an island as his; but not at all. Nobody would pay any price for it. And he wanted now to get rid of it, as a man who wants a divorce at any cost.

It was not till the middle of the fifth year that he transferred it, at a considerable loss to himself, to an hotel company who were willing to speculate in it. They were to turn it into a handy honeymoon-and-golf island.

There, take that, island which didn't know when it was well off. Now be a honeymoon-and-golf island!

2

The Second Island

The islander had to move. But he was not going to the mainland. Oh, no! He moved to the smaller island, which still belonged to him. And he took with him the faithful old carpenter and wife, the couple he never really cared for; also a widow and daughter, who had kept house for him the last year; also an orphan lad, to help the old man.

The small island was very small; but being a hump of rock in the sea, it was bigger than it looked. There was a little track among the rocks and bushes, winding and scrambling up and down around the islet, so that it took you twenty minutes to do the circuit. It was more than you would have expected.

Still, it was an island. The islander moved himself, with all his books, into the commonplace six-roomed house up to which you had to scramble from the rocky landing-place. There were also two joined-together cottages. The old carpenter lived in one, with his wife and the lad, the widow and daughter lived in the other.

At last all was in order. The Master's books filled two rooms. It was already autumn, Orion lifting out of the sea. And in the dark nights, the Master could see the lights on his late island, where the hotel company were entertaining guests who would advertise the new resort for honeymoon-golfers.

On his lump of rock, however, the Master was still master. He explored the crannies, the odd hand-breadths of grassy level, the steep little cliffs where the last harebells hung and the seeds of summer were brown above the sea, lonely and untouched. He peered down the old well. He examined the stone pen where the pig had been kept. Himself, he had a goat.

Yes, it was an island. Always, always underneath among the rocks the Celtic sea sucked and washed and smote its feathery greyness. How many different noises of the sea! Deep explosions, rumblings, strange long sighs and whistling noises; then voices, real voices of people clamouring as if they were in a market, under the waters: and again, the far-off ringing of a bell, surely an actual bell! Then a tremendous trilling noise, very long and alarming, and an undertone of hoarse gasping.

On this island there were no human ghosts, no ghosts of any ancient race. The sea, and the spume and the weather, had washed them all out, washed them out so there was only the sound of the sea itself, its own ghost, myriad-voiced, communing and plotting and shouting all winter long. And only the smell of the sea, with a few bristly bushes of gorse and coarse tufts of heather, among the grey, pellucid rocks, in the grey, more-pellucid air. The coldness, the greyness, even the soft, creeping fog of the sea, and the islet of rock humped up in it all, like the last point in space.

Green star Sirius stood over the sea's rim. The island was a shadow. Out at sea a ship showed small lights. Below, in the rocky cove, the row-boat and the motor-boat were safe. A light shone in the carpenter's kitchen. That was all.

Save, of course, that the lamp was lit in the house, where the widow was preparing supper, her daughter helping. The islander went in to his meal. Here he was no longer the Master, he was an islander again and he had peace. The old carpenter, the widow and daughter were all faithfulness itself. The old man worked while ever there was light to see, because he had a passion for work. The widow and her quiet, rather delicate daughter of thirty-three worked for the Master, because they loved looking after him, and they were infinitely grateful for the haven he provided them. But they didn't call him "the Master." They gave him his name: "Mr. Cathcart, sir!" softly and reverently. And he spoke back to them also softly, gently, like people far from the world, afraid to make a noise.

The island was no longer a "world." It was a sort of refuge. The islander no longer struggled for anything. He had no need. It was as if he and his few dependents were a small flock of sea-birds alighted on this rock, as they travelled through space, and keeping together without a word. The silent mystery of travelling birds.

He spent most of his day in his study. His book was coming along. The widow's daughter could type out his manuscript for him, she was not uneducated. It was the one strange sound on the island, the typewriter. But soon even its spattering fitted in with the sea's noises, and the wind's.

The months went by. The islander worked away in his study, the people of the island went quietly about their concerns. The goat had a little black kid with yellow eyes. There were mackerel in the sea. The old man went fishing in the row-boat with the lad, when the weather was calm enough; they went off in the motor-boat to the biggest island for the post. And they brought supplies, never a penny wasted. And the days went by, and the nights, without desire, without ennui.

The strange stillness from all desire was a kind of wonder to the islander. He didn't want anything. His soul at last was still in him, his spirit was like a dim-lit cave under water, where strange sea-foliage expands upon the watery atmosphere, and scarcely sways, and a mute fish shadowily slips in and slips away again. All still and soft and uncrying, yet alive as rooted seaweed is alive.

The islander said to himself: "Is this happiness?" He said to himself: "I am turned into a dream. I feel nothing, or I don't know what I feel. Yet it seems to me I am happy."

Only he had to have something upon which his mental activity could work. So he spent long, silent hours in his study, working not very fast, nor very importantly, letting the writing spin softly from him as if it were drowsy gossamer. He no longer fretted whether it were good or not, what he produced. He slowly, softly spun it like gossamer, and if it were to melt away as gossamer in autumn melts, he would not mind. It was only the soft evanescence of gossamy things which now seemed to him permanent. The very mist of eternity was in them. Whereas stone buildings, cathedrals for example, seemed to him to howl with temporary resistance, knowing they must fall at last; the tension of their long endurance seemed to howl forth from them all the time.

Sometimes he went to the mainland and to the city. Then he went elegantly, dressed in the latest style, to his club. He sat in a stall at the theatre, he shopped in Bond Street. He discussed terms for publishing his book. But over his face was that gossamy look of having dropped out of the race of progress, which made the vulgar city people feel they had won it over him, and made him glad to go back to his island.

He didn't mind if he never published his book. The years were blending into a soft mist, from which nothing obtruded. Spring came. There was never a primrose on his island, but he found a winter-aconite. There were two little sprayed bushes of blackthorn, and some wind-flowers. He began to make a list of the flowers of his islet, and that was absorbing. He noted a wild currant bush and watched for the elder flowers on a stunted little tree, then for the first yellow rags of the broom, and wild roses. Bladder campion, orchids stitchwort, celandine, he was prouder of them than if they had been people on his island. When he came across the golden saxifrage, so inconspicuous in a damp corner, he crouched over it in a trance, he knew not for how long, looking at it. Yet it was nothing to look at. As the widow's daughter found, when he showed it her.

He had said to her in real triumph:

"I found the golden saxifrage this morning."

d. h. lawrence   **129**

The name sounded splendid. She looked at him with fascinated brown eyes, in which was a hollow ache that frightened him a little.

"Did you, sir? Is is a nice flower?"

He pursed his lips and tilted his brows.

"Well—not showy exactly. I'll show it you if you like."

"I should like to see it."

She was so quiet, so wistful. But he sensed in her a persistency which made him uneasy. She said she was so happy: really happy. She followed him quietly, like a shadow, on the rocky track where there was never room for two people to walk side by side. He went first, and could feel her there, immediately behind him, following so submissively, gloating on him from behind.

It was a kind of pity for her which made him become her lover: though he never realised the extent of the power she had gained over him, and how *she* willed it. But the moment he had fallen, a jangling feeling came upon him, that it was all wrong. He felt a nervous dislike of her. He had not wanted it. And it seemed to him, as far as her physical self went, she had not wanted it either. It was just her will. He went away, and climbed at the risk of his neck down to a ledge near the sea. There he sat for hours, gazing all jangled at the sea, and saying miserably to himself: "We didn't want it. We didn't really want it."

It was the automatism of sex that had caught him again. Not that he hated sex. He deemed it, as the Chinese do, one of the great life-mysteries. But it had become mechanical, automatic, and he wanted to escape that. Automatic sex shattered him, and filled him with a sort of death. He thought he had come through, to a new stillness of desirelessness. Perhaps beyond that there was a new fresh delicacy of desire, an unentered frail communion of two people meeting on untrodden ground.

Be that as it might, this was not it. This was nothing new or fresh. It was automatic, and driven from the will. Even she, in her true self, hadn't wanted it. It was automatic in her.

When he came home, very late, and saw her face white with fear and apprehension of his feeling against her, he pitied her, and spoke to her delicately, reassuringly. But he kept himself remote from her.

She gave no sign. She served him with the same silence, the same hidden hunger to serve him, to be near where he was. He felt her love following him with strange, awful persistency. She claimed nothing. Yet now, when he met her bright, brown, curiously vacant eyes, he saw in them the mute question. The question came direct at him, with a force and a power of will he never realised.

So he succumbed, and asked her again.

"Not," she said, "if it will make you hate me."

"Why should it?" he replied, nettled. "Of course not."

"You know I would do anything on earth for you."

It was only afterwards, in his exasperation, he remembered what she said, and was more exasperated. Why should she pretend to do this for *him*? Why not herself? But in his exasperation, he drove himself deeper in. In order to achieve some sort of satisfaction, which he never did achieve, he abandoned himself to her. Everybody on the island knew. But he did not care.

Then even what desire he had left him, and he felt only shattered. He felt that only with her will had she wanted him. Now he was shattered and full of self-contempt. His island was smirched and spoiled. He had lost his place in the rare, desireless levels of Time to which he had at last arrived, and he had fallen right back. If only it had been true, delicate desire between them, and a delicate meeting on the third rare place where a man might meet a woman, when they were both true to the frail, sensitive, crocus-flame of desire in them. But it had been no such thing: automatic, an act of will, not of true desire, it left him feeling humiliated.

He went away from the islet, in spite of her mute reproach. And he wandered about the continent, vainly seeking a place where he could stay. He was out of key; he did not fit in the world any more.

There came a letter from Flora—her name was Flora—to say she was afraid she was going to have a child. He sat down as if he were shot, and he remained sitting. But he replied to her: "Why be afraid? If it is so, it is so, and we should rather be pleased than afraid."

At this very moment, it happened there was an auction of islands. He got the maps, and studied them. And at the auction he bought, for very little money, another island. It was just a few acres of rock away in the north, on the outer fringe of the isles. It was low, it rose low out of the great ocean. There was not a building, not even a tree on it. Only northern sea-turf, a pool of rain-water, a bit of sedge, rock, and sea-birds. Nothing else. Under the weeping wet western sky.

He made a trip to visit his new possession. For several days, owing to the seas, he could not approach it. Then, in a light sea-mist, he landed, and saw it hazy, low, stretching apparently a long way. But it was illusion. He walked over the wet, springy turf, and dark-grey sheep tossed away from him, spectral, bleating hoarsely. And he came to the dark pool, with the sedge. Then on in the dampness, to the grey sea sucking angrily among the rocks.

This was indeed an island.

So he went home to Flora. She looked at him with guilty fear, but also with a triumphant brightness in her uncanny eyes. And again he was gentle, he reassured her, even he wanted her again, with that curious desire that was almost like toothache. So he took her to the mainland, and they were married, since she was going to have his child.

They returned to the island. She still brought in his meals, her own along with them. She sat and ate with him. He would have it so. The widowed mother preferred to stay in the kitchen. And Flora slept in the guest-room of his house, mistress of his house.

His desire, whatever it was, died in him with nauseous finality. The child would still be months coming. His island was hateful to him, vulgar, a suburb. He himself had lost all his finer distinction. The weeks passed in a sort of prison, in humiliation. Yet he stuck it out, till the child was born. But he was meditating escape. Flora did not even know.

A nurse appeared, and ate at table with them. The doctor came sometimes, and, if the sea were rough, he too had to stay. He was cheery over his whisky.

They might have been a young couple in Golders Green.

The daughter was born at last. The father looked at the baby, and felt depressed, almost more than he could bear. The millstone was tied round his neck. But he tried not to show what he felt. And Flora did not know. She still smiled with a kind of half-witted triumph in her joy, as she got well again. Then she began again to look at him with those aching, suggestive, somehow impudent eyes. She adored him so.

This he could not stand. He told her that he had to go away for a time. She wept, but she thought she had got him. He told her he had settled the best part of his property on her, and wrote down for her what income it would produce. She hardly listened, only looked at him with those heavy, adoring, impudent eyes. He gave her a cheque-book, with the amount of her credit duly entered. This did arouse her interest. And he told her, if she got tired of the island, she could choose her home wherever she wished.

She followed him with those aching, persistent brown eyes, when he left, and he never even saw her weep.

He went straight north, to prepare his third island.

3

The Third Island

The third island was soon made habitable. With cement and the big pebbles from the shingle beach, two men built him a hut, and roofed it with corrugated iron. A boat brought over a bed and table, and three chairs, with a good cupboard, and a few books. He laid in a supply of coal and paraffin and food—he wanted so little.

The house stood near the flat shingle bay where he landed, and where he pulled up his light boat. On a sunny day in August the men sailed away and left him. The sea was still and pale blue. On the horizon he saw the small mail-steamer slowly passing northwards, as if she were walking. She served the outer isles twice a week. He could row out to her if need be, in calm weather, and he could signal her from a flagstaff behind his cottage.

Half a dozen sheep still remained on the island, as company; and he had a cat to rub against his legs. While the sweet, sunny days of the northern autumn lasted, he would walk among the rocks, and over the springy turf of his small domain, always coming to the ceaseless, restless sea. He looked at every leaf, that might be different from another, and he watched the endless expansion and contraction of the water-tossed seaweed. He had never a tree, not even a bit of heather to guard. Only the turf, and tiny turf-plants, and the sedge by the pool, the seaweed in the ocean. He was glad. He didn't want trees or bushes. They stood up like people, too assertive. His bare, low-pitched island in the pale blue sea was all he wanted.

He no longer worked at his book. The interest had gone. He liked to sit on the low elevation of his island, and see the sea; nothing but the pale, quiet sea. And to feel his mind turn soft and hazy, like the hazy ocean. Sometimes, like a mirage, he would see the shadow of land rise hovering to northwards. It was a big island beyond. But quite without substance.

He was soon almost startled when he perceived the steamer on the near horizon, and his heart contracted with fear, lest it were going to pause and molest him. Anxiously he watched it go, and not till it was out of sight did he feel truly relieved, himself again. The tension of waiting for human approach was cruel. He did not want to be approached. He did not want to hear voices. He was shocked by the sound of his own voice, if he inadvertently spoke to his cat. He rebuked himself for having broken the great silence. And he was irritated when his cat would look up at him and mew faintly, plaintively. He frowned at her. And she knew. She was becoming wild, lurking in the rocks, perhaps fishing.

But what he disliked most was when one of the lumps of sheep opened its mouth and baa-ed its hoarse, raucous baa. He watched it, and it looked to him hideous and gross. He came to dislike the sheep very much.

He wanted only to hear the whispering sound of the sea, and the sharp cries of the gulls, cries that came out of another world to him. And best of all, the great silence.

He decided to get rid of the sheep when the boat came. They were accustomed to him now, and stood and stared at him with yellow or colourless eyes, in an insolence that was almost cold ridicule. There was a suggestion of cold indecency about them. He disliked them very much. And when they jumped with staccato jumps off the rocks, and their hoofs made the dry, sharp hit, and the fleece flopped on their square backs, he found them repulsive, degrading.

The fine weather passed, and it rained all day. He lay a great deal on his bed, listening to the water trickling from his roof into the zinc water-butt, looking through the open door at the rain, the dark rocks, the hidden sea. Many gulls were on the island now: many seabirds of all sorts. It was another world of life. Many of the birds he had never seen before. His old impulse came over him, to send for a book, to know their names. In a flicker of the old passion, to know the name of everything he saw, he even decided to row out to the steamer. The names of these birds! He must know their names, otherwise he had not got them, they were not quite alive to him.

But the desire left him, and he merely watched the birds as they wheeled or walked around him, watched them vaguely, without discrimination. All interest had left him. Only there was one gull, a big, handsome fellow, who would walk back and forth, back and forth in front of the open door of the cabin, as if he had some mission there. He was big, and pearl-grey, and his roundnesses were as smooth and lovely as a pearl. Only the folded wings had shut black pinions, and on the closed black feathers were three very distinct white dots, making a pattern. The islander wondered very much, why this bit of trimming on the bird out of the far, cold seas. And as the gull walked back and forth, back and forth in front of the cabin, strutting on pale-dusky gold feet, holding up his pale yellow beak, that was curved at the tip, with curious alien importance, the man wondered over him. He was portentous, he had a meaning.

Then the bird came no more. The island, which had been full of sea-birds, the flash of wings, the sound and cut of wings and sharp eerie cries in the air, began to be deserted again. No longer they sat like living eggs on the rocks and turf, moving their heads, but scarcely rising into flight round his feet. No longer they ran across the turf among the sheep, and lifted themselves upon low wings. The host had gone. But some remained, always.

The days shortened, and the world grew eerie. One day the boat came: as if suddenly, swooping down. The islander found it a violation. It was torture to talk to those two men, in their homely clumsy clothes. The air of familiarity around them was very repugnant to him. Himself, he was neatly dressed, his cabin was neat and tidy. He resented any intrusion, the clumsy homeliness, the heavy-footedness of the two fishermen was really repulsive to him.

The letters they had brought he left lying unopened in a little box. In one of them was his money. But he could not bear to open even that one. Any kind of contact was repulsive to him. Even to read his name on an envelope. He hid the letters away.

And the hustle and horror of getting the sheep caught and tied and put in the ship made him loathe with profound repulsion the whole of the animal creation. What repulsive god invented animals and evil-smelling men? To his nostrils, the fishermen and the sheep alike smelled foul; an uncleanness on the fresh earth.

He was still nerve-racked and tortured when the ship at last lifted sail and was drawing away, over the still sea. And sometimes, days after, he would start with repulsion, thinking he heard the munching of sheep.

The dark days of winter drew on. Sometimes there was no real day at all. He felt ill, as if he were dissolving, as if dissolution had already set in inside him. Everything was twilight, outside, and in his mind and soul. Once, when he went to the door, he saw black heads of men swimming in his bay. For some moments he swooned unconscious. It was the shock, the horror of unexpected human approach. The horror in the twilight! And not till the shock had undermined him and left him disembodied, did he realise that the black heads were the heads of seals swimming in. A sick relief came over him. But he was barely conscious, after the shock. Later on, he sat and wept with gratitude, because they were not men. But he never realised that he wept. He was too dim. Like some strange, ethereal animal, he no longer realised what he was doing.

Only he still derived his single satisfaction from being alone, absolutely alone, with the space soaking into him. The grey sea alone, and the footing of his sea-washed island. No other contact. Nothing human to bring its horror into contact with him. Only space, damp, twilit, sea-washed space! This was the bread of his soul.

For this reason, he was most glad when there was a storm, or when the sea was high. Then nothing could get at him. Nothing could come through to him from the outer world. True, the terrific violence of the wind made him suffer badly. At the same time, it swept the world utterly out of existence for him. He always liked the sea to be heavily rolling and tearing. Then no boat could get at him. It was like eternal ramparts round his island.

He kept no track of time, and no longer thought of opening a book. The print, the printed letters, so like the depravity of speech, looked obscene. He tore the brass label from his paraffin stove. He obliterated any bit of lettering in his cabin.

His cat had disappeared. He was rather glad. He shivered at her thin, obtrusive call. She had lived in the coal-shed. And each morning he had put her a dish of porridge, the same as he ate. He washed her saucer with repulsion. He did not like her writhing about. But he fed her scrupulously. Then one day she did not come for her porridge; she always mewed for it. She did not come again.

He prowled about his island in the rain, in a big oilskin coat, not knowing what he was looking at, nor what he went out to see. Time had ceased to pass. He stood for long spaces, gazing from a white, sharp face, with those keen, far-off blue eyes of his, gazing fiercely and almost cruelly at the dark sea under the dark sky. And if he saw the labouring sail of a fishing-boat away on the cold waters, a strange malevolent anger passed over his features.

Sometimes he was ill. He knew he was ill, because he staggered as he walked, and easily fell down. Then he paused to think what it was. And he went to his stores and took out dried milk and malt, and ate that. Then he forgot again. He ceased to register his own feelings.

The days were beginning to lengthen. All winter the weather had been comparatively mild, but with much rain, much rain. He had forgotten the sun. Suddenly, however, the air was very cold, and he began to shiver. A fear came over him. The sky was level and grey, and never a star appeared at night. It was very cold. More birds began to arrive. The island was freezing. With trembling hands he made a fire in his grate. The cold frightened him.

And now it continued, day after day, a dull, deathly cold. Occasional crumblings of snow were in the air. The days were greyly longer, but no change in the cold. Frozen grey daylight. The birds passed away, flying away. Some he saw lying frozen. It was as if all life were drawing away, contracting away from the north, contracting southwards. "Soon," he said to himself, "it will all be gone, and in all these regions nothing will be alive." He felt a cruel satisfaction in the thought.

Then one night there seemed to be a relief; he slept better, did not tremble half-awake, and writhe so much, half-conscious. He had become so used to the quaking and writhing of his body, he hardly noticed it. But when for once it slept deep, he noticed that.

He woke in the morning to a curious whiteness. His window was muffled. It had snowed. He got up and opened his door, and shuddered. Ugh! How cold! All white, with a dark leaden sea, and black rocks curiously speckled with white. The foam was no longer pure. It seemed dirty. And the sea ate at the whiteness of the corpse-like land. Crumbles of snow were silting down the dead air.

On the ground the snow was a foot deep, white and smooth and soft, windless. He took a shovel to clear round his house and shed. The pallor of morning darkened. There was a strange rumbling of far-off thunder in the frozen air, and through the newly-falling snow, a dim flash of lightning. Snow now fell steadily down in the motionless obscurity.

He went out for a few minutes. But it was difficult. He stumbled and fell in the snow, which burned his face. Weak, faint, he toiled home. And when he recovered, took the trouble to make hot milk.

It snowed all the time. In the afternoon again there was a muffled rumbling of thunder, and flashes of lightning blinking reddish through the falling snow. Uneasy, he went to bed and lay staring fixedly at nothingness.

Morning seemed never to come. An eternity long he lay and waited for one alleviating pallor on the night. And at last it seemed the air was paler. His house was a cell faintly illuminated with white light. He realised the snow was walled outside his window. He got up, in the dead cold. When he opened his door, the motionless snow stopped him in a wall as high as his breast. Looking over the top of it, he felt the dead wind slowly driving, saw the snow-powder lift and travel like a funeral train. The blackish sea churned and champed, seeming to bite at the snow, impotent. The sky was grey, but luminous.

He began to work in a frenzy, to get at his boat. If he was to be shut in, it must be by his own choice, not by the mechanical power of the elements. He must get to the sea. He must be able to get at his boat.

But he was weak, and at times the snow overcame him. It fell on him, and he lay buried and lifeless. Yet every time he struggled alive before it was too late, and fell upon the snow with the energy of fever. Exhausted, he would not give in. He crept indoors and made coffee and bacon. Long since he had cooked so much. Then he went at the snow once more. He must conquer the snow, this new, white brute force which had accumulated against him.

He worked in the awful, dead wind, pushing the snow aside, pressing it with his shovel. It was cold, freezing hard in the wind, even when the sun came out for a while, and showed him his white, lifeless surroundings, the black sea rolling sullen, flecked with dull spume, away to the horizons. Yet the sun had power on his face. It was March.

He reached the boat. He pushed the snow away, then sat down under the lee of the boat, looking at the sea, which swirled nearly to his feet, in the high tide. Curiously natural the pebbles looked, in a world gone all uncanny. The sun shone no more. Snow was falling in hard crumbs, that vanished as if by a miracle as they touched the hard blackness of the sea. Hoarse waves rang in the shingle, rushing up at the snow. The wet rocks were brutally black. And all the time the myriad swooping crumbs of snow, demonish, touched the dark sea and disappeared.

During the night there was a great storm. It seemed to him he could hear the vast mass of snow striking all the world with a ceaseless thud; and over it all, the wind roared in strange hollow volleys, in between which came a jump of blindfold lightning, then the low roll of thunder heavier than the wind. When at last the dawn faintly discoloured the dark, the storm had more or less subsided, but a steady wind drove on. The snow was up to the top of his door.

Sullenly, he worked to dig himself out. And he managed through sheer persistency to get out. He was in the tail of a great drift, many feet high. When he got through, the frozen snow was not more than two feet deep. But his island was gone. Its shape was all changed, great heaping white hills rose where no hills had been, inaccessible, and they fumed like volcanoes, but with snow powder. He was sickened and overcome.

His boat was in another, smaller drift. But he had not the strength to clear it. He looked at it helplessly. The shovel slipped from his hands, and he sank in the snow, to forget. In the snow itself, the sea resounded.

Something brought him to. He crept to his house. He was almost without feeling. Yet he managed to warm himself, just that part of him which leaned in snow-sleep over the coal fire. Then again he made hot milk. After which, carefully, he built up the fire.

The wind dropped. Was it night again? In the silence, it seemed he could hear the panther-like dropping of infinite snow. Thunder rumbled nearer, crackled quick after the bleared reddened lightning. He lay in bed in a kind of stupor. The elements! The elements! His mind repeated the word dumbly. You can't win against the elements.

How long it went on, he never knew. Once, like a wraith, he got out and climbed to the top of a white hill on his unrecognisable island. The sun was hot. "It is summer," he said to himself, "and the time of leaves." He looked stupidly over the whiteness of his foreign island, over the waste of the lifeless sea. He pretended to imagine he saw the wink of a sail. Because he knew too well there would never again be a sail on that stark sea.

As he looked, the sky mysteriously darkened and chilled. From far off came the mutter of the unsatisfied thunder, and he knew it was the signal of the snow rolling over the sea. He turned, and felt its breath on him.

In 1937, forty-one-year-old academic, poet and
mother of two Eugenia Semyonovna Ginzburg was
arrested on the charge of "participation in a Trotskyist
terrorist group." She was sentenced to statutory ten
years' hard labor in the "gold-and-death" camps of
Kolyma in the far north of Siberia. Journey into the
Whirlwind, the first of a two-volume memoir,
chronicles the culture of institutionalized betrayal that
was the Stalinist terror, when, as Sir Isaiah Berlin
recalled, "Nobody knew who was friend and who was
foe," and one person out of every twenty households
could expect to be arrested, and, eventually,
"disappeared" in the sprawling network of penal
colonies. Among the burgeoning testimony of terror—
books such as Alexander Solzhenitsyn's The Gulag
Archipelago, Roy Medvedev's Let History Judge,
Nadezhda Mandelstam's Hope Against Hope, or
Robert Conquest's The Great Terror—Eugenia
Ginzburg's Journey into the Whirlwind is a work of
exquisite literature. Animated by a driving curiosity
and amazement at the obscene horrors spawned by
Stalin's gigantomanic cult of personality, Ginzburg
here offers a testimonial to the discovery that the only
escape from the paralyzing, all-pervading fear that
cripples the body, drains the spirit, and warps the soul,
lies through art.

from *journey into the whirlwind*

EUGENIA SEMYONOVNA GINZBURG

in one of Knut Hamsun's novels there is a character called
Captain Glan with a dog answering to the name of Aesop. Although
the whole spirit of our prison life was permeated by "Aesopian language," Julia, clearly overestimating our warders' education, was
frightened of using this expression aloud. Thus it was that we came
to use the term "Glan's dog" for the methods of allegory, fable, and
double-talk in which we became adept for the purpose of convers-
ing on forbidden topics and, especially, corresponding with the
outside world. This meant with my mother, since Julia had no close
relatives and was therefore debarred from writing.

The writing of my fortnightly letters was a momentous event for
which we prepared long beforehand, weighing every word.

It was a difficult task to write something that would be fully
intelligible to my mother without attracting the vigilance of the
prison censor, who would return without compunction any letter
in which he detected the slightest ambiguity. This happened, for
instance, when I asked my mother, in all sincerity, to make sure that
Vasya was vaccinated. Any reference to illness was suspected of containing a hidden meaning.

We wrote with regulation pencils made of Bakelite with lead
refills that needed no sharpening: we were not allowed any sharp
objects such as penknives. The letters were put in envelopes in the
censor's office.

In order to give Mother as much news as possible and to find out
about my husband and children and all our friends and relatives, I
used a device we had invented of writing in the third person. This
involved long preparation, including the choice of a code name for

myself. We eventually decided that I should be called "Eva" which sounded a little like "Genia"; and in due course I wrote a letter containing the cryptic sentence:

"Don't worry so much about the children, especially little Eva. After all, she's not alone, and I'm sure her aunt looks after her quite well."

My mother caught on at once and replied that indeed she hoped that Eva would be all right, but didn't I think her aunt was a bit strait-laced? Would she allow the child to get about and see her friends? This was in order to find out whether I was in solitary confinement.... From this point on, our system worked beautifully. By writing about ourselves as though we were children we got all kinds of strictly forbidden information past the censor without arousing his suspicions. Thus, when Mother wrote, "Paul hasn't taken his exams yet," I understood that my husband had not yet been tried and sentenced. The fact that my sister's husband, Shura Korolyov, had been disgraced and arrested was conveyed as follows. First my mother wrote: "Shura has a new job, he's working in a garage." Since he had been a history professor, this could only mean that he had been expelled from the Party. In her next letter she wrote, "Shura's staying with little Paul now," which could only mean one thing.

We corresponded in this way for two years. From Mother's full accounts of my children's doings I concluded that they were all right, and this gave me strength to endure everything. Long afterward, at Kolyma, I learned that at the time when Mother had written, "We had a New Year's party for Vasya," he had in fact been in a home for prisoners' children, where he was registered under the wrong surname. For months the family despaired of finding him, until my husband's brother succeeded, in 1938, in tracing him at Kostroma. It was a mercy that I knew none of this at Yaroslavl.

We also used "Aesopian language" in our notes and conversations. We were allowed to buy two notebooks a month from the prison store and to write in them anything we liked. But since they had to be handed to the censor as soon as they were full, we could not use them, for example, to write verses in as we should have wished.

Our prison experience illustrated the fact that any husband being in the position of Robinson Crusoe will, as it were, retrace the development of the species, passing through the various stages of technical progress. We made a needle out of fishbone, and thread out of our own hair. We invented a system of shorthand for writing verses

(I have completely forgotten it now) and brought to exquisite perfection the technique of wall tapping, which in the awful stillness of this place was far more dangerous than in the cellars at Kazan.

When I had written my verses I used to learn them by heart, then rub them out with bread crumbs and substitute algebra sums or conjugations of French verbs. But the main object of our subterfuges was, of course, to overcome the strict isolation from the world and from one another which was one of the prison's basic laws.

From the authorities' point of view, the ideal was that each of us should feel as though she were the only inmate of the prison. Since they had had to put two of us in one cell, I was at least assured of the existence of Julia Karepova. But who were our neighbors? By listening intently to the vague sounds that came through the walls on either side of us, we decided that they were both "solitaries," without an extra bunk in their cells. No doubt the more important prisoners were kept as long as possible without company.... Our neighbor to the right paced incessantly up and down, the creaking of her heavy prison boots being audible even through the three-foot wall. When we asked her name and how long she was in for, she countered by asking which party we belonged to. When we replied that we were Communists, she retorted, "No member of that Party is a friend of mine," and banged the wall with her fist, after which she ignored us for fully two years. She was evidently a Menshevik or a Social Revolutionary of the same stamp as Mukhina at Kazan.

With our neighbor to the left, on the other hand, we were able to strike up regular communication. Almost every day we exchanged "telegrams" composed in such a style that the authorities would not have understood them even if they had intercepted them. Her name was Olga Orlovskaya; she was a journalist from Kuibyshev and the ex-wife of a certain Lenzner, who had played an important role in the Trotskyist opposition. Although she was a keen Party member and had been divorced from Lenzner for many years, she was arrested for association with him. She had now been several months in a solitary cell and was delighted to be in contact with us. We "spoke" to each other during mealtimes, when the silence was broken by the clatter of ladles and tin bowls. Our chief topics of discussion were furnished by the local newspaper, the *Northern Worker*, to which we were allowed to subscribe out of the fifty rubles which our families had sent us.

What a newspaper it was! If any reader were to pick it up today, he would think he had gone mad. The process of rooting out "enemies of the people" had become quite stereotyped. For instance, one would read an article about the slackness of a district committee secretary who had stated that there were no culprits left to arrest in his district. The writer expressed indignation at such softness toward "hostile elements" and cast doubt on the secretary's own loyalty. Several times a month, full-page spreads would be devoted to the trials of local leaders. The drab columns bristled with bold-type references to the "supreme penalty" and to "sentences carried out," interspersed with fulsome praise of "true sons of the people" and "simple Soviet folk."

The elections to the Supreme Soviet were about to be held, the first under the new constitution. The candidate for Yaroslavl was Zimin, the first secretary of the regional committee, whose predecessor in that office had just been arrested. Every issue of the newspaper contained photographs of Zimin in various poses and eulogistic accounts of his services. A few months after the elections, Zimin was arrested together with the entire bureau of the regional committee, and the *Northern Worker* devoted pages to denouncing "the arch-spy Zimin, who wormed his way into the higher command of the Party."

We got the impression that whole layers of society were being eliminated even before Kaganovish used this very term in noting with satisfaction that the government had "liquidated several layers" in its campaign to stamp out the after-effects of sabotage.

Olga and I discussed all these matters through the wall in "Aesopian language." Her replies testified to her keen intelligence and journalist's flair for summing things up in a vivid phrase. We communicated in this way for two years. But only in 1939, on the way to Kolyma, did I discover that in spite of everything she worshiped Stalin. In her solitary cell at Yaroslavl she had written a poem to him which began:

Stalin, my golden sun,
If death should be my fate,
I will die, a petal on the road
Of our great country.

This was not really out of the ordinary, for I met many people in the camp who managed to combine a shrewd sense of what was going on in the country at large with a religious cult of Stalin.

Julia, who had a taste for detective stories, got so carried away by her "Aesopian" techniques that even I could not always understand her intricate allusions. She became even more careful after Olga warned us that she had been deprived of books as a punishment for certain underlinings which she had not in fact made. From then on we scrutinized all our books with the utmost care before returning them.

Julia's language became still more "Aesopian" after she got it into her head that a microphone might be concealed in a niche in the wall above her bed. I tried vainly to convince her that this would hardly be necessary from our jailors' point of view, since we had already been investigated, tried, and sentenced as enemies of the people, and they could not expect to get any further evidence out of us. Julia continued to be terrified of "Nicky" (her name for the niche), and invented such grotesque ways of preserving the secrecy of our conversations that I sometimes burst out laughing, hiding my head under the straw pillow so as not to attract attention.

But in spite of all our efforts and precautions, the heavy hand of the prison authorities fell on us at last. The punishments which they dispensed, like our sentences themselves, were not proportionate to any misdeeds of ours but were meted out according to a plan, a prearranged formula. And in this plan a key date was the first of December—the third anniversary of Kirov's murder.

•

The underground punishment cell

As usual, misfortune struck when we were least expecting it: indeed, we were feeling particularly cheerful that day.

In the morning they had brought us food from the prison store: a pound of sugar, a quarter of a pound of meat, and some cucumbers that had found their way there. These were yellow, wizened, and frightfully bitter. Julia, with her background of old-fashioned housekeeping, was carried away by an ingenious plan for pickling them.

"It's perfectly sensible! We can ask the day and the night warder, and the one tomorrow morning, for a pinch of salt each. For the next three days we won't take any hot water, or if we do, we'll pour it into the slop pail. Then we can salt them in the hot-water jug, and in three days' time they'll be delicious."

"Honestly, Julia, I ought to write a poem in your honor."

"Yes, I think you might. You write about everything under the sun except your faithful cellmate."

So I tried my hand at classical elegiacs:

Not in iambics I sing thee, nor yet with the frivolous
    trochee;
No, elegiacs of old fitly echo thy praise.
E'en though Vesuvius again should erupt and astonish
    nations,
Thou on its summit shouldst yet pickle and salt with a will.

Just then, as we were bubbling with suppressed laughter, the key turned in the door. My heart jumped into my throat: any visit at an unscheduled time could only mean trouble. It was the block warder, ordering me to go with him. There had been a few such occasions since our arrival, when we were taken to be fingerprinted or to the dentist. But for the dentist one had to apply beforehand, so what could this be?

As I walked down the stairs I could hear Julia coughing to express alarm and sympathy. We passed the first floor and still went down and down. Clearly this was more than a mere formality. The continuing descent was ominous. How many underground floors could there be?

Finally we came to a halt in a sort of narrow dungeon, where I saw the stout, stocky figure of the senior warder we called the "Nabob." He had a dark, swarthy face with startlingly pale eyes, and spoke with a strong Ukrainian accent. Having checked who I was, he pulled out a register and announced that the governor had given orders for me to be confined in an underground punishment cell for five days "for continuing counter-revolutionary activity in prison by writing her name on the washroom wall."

The charge was a manifest lie: I had not written my name, and should have been very foolish to do so. We knew perfectly well that each time we left the washroom the warder who mounted guard outside looked in to make sure we had not planted a bomb there. His other duty was to hand each of us a single square of newspaper, which responsible task he performed with a suitably solemn and impassive air.

All this flashed through my head, and I tried to point out to the Nabob that no one but an idiot would try to write on the wall in these circumstances. He paid no attention, but ordered me to confirm by signing the book that I had been informed of the governor's instructions.

"Certainly not! I won't sign any such lying nonsense. Anyway, what's all this about counter-revolutionary activity?" As I quoted these words from the charge, I suddenly realized their point. I saw in my mind's eye the passage in Major Weinstock's twenty-two commandments which said that prisoners who continued counter-revolutionary activity were liable to a new trial. If I had acknowledged the order, it would look as though I were confirming its truth, and I should be giving them an excuse to re-try me and probably, this time, condemn me to death.

"I won't sign it. It's a trick!"

"All right, don't, it'll be the worse for you. Come on now, get undressed."

"What!"

"Undress, I said. You have to wear special clothes in the punishment cell. Come on, look sharp!"

He urged me forward into a sort of triangular stone space. There was no lamp or window, and the only light came from the open door. There was a damp and chilly draft: clearly the place was not heated. A narrow plank bed was fixed a few inches above the floor, and on it were the rags I was supposed to change into: the greasy remnant of a soldier's overcoat, and enormous bast sandals.

"I won't!"

"Oh, yes, you will, or we'll put you into a worse place," said the Nabob in sudden rage, and before I knew what was happening he started to undress me by force. I felt his paws on my breast. I heard myself scream wildly, and broke loose from him. This time it was more than I could stand. I shouted and struggled even more desperately than I had in the Black Maria after my trial. Then I had hit my head against the wall, seeking to harm no one except myself; but this time I was so beside myself that I tried to fight the Nabob, who could have felled me with one blow of his fist. I scratched and bit and kicked him in the stomach, uttering frightful words:

"You fascist scum—just you wait, you'll be punished one day!"

Suddenly I felt a sharp pain, so excruciating that I almost lost consciousness. The Nabob had twisted my arms back and bound my hands together with a towel. Through my daze I saw a wardress rush over to help him. She undressed me down to my prison shirt, even taking out my hairpins. Then everything became a blur, and I sank into a black abyss where everything seemed on fire.

When I came to myself I was freezing with cold. The toes of my left foot were so numb that I could not feel them. I had in fact got second-degree frostbite, and to this day my foot swells and aches every winter.

My whole body throbbed with pain. I lay on my back on the low plank bed, almost naked, with my shirt and the grubby coat over me. But my hands were unbound—the wardress must have had the decency to do that before she threw me in here.

I looked into the darkness but could see absolutely nothing, not a glimmer of any kind. Then I heard the tramp of military boots approaching. The little window in the door was unlocked, and a blessed stream of light flowed in. At least I could see, I was not blind! Now that I knew this I should be less afraid of staring into the dark.

"Water," said my guard, offering me a dirty, rusted mug. The water was coated with a film of grease. I swallowed two mouthfuls and used the rest to wash with, wiping my face and hands meticulously and drying them with the top of my shirt. Now I was once more a human being and not a grimy, hunted animal.

"Here's some bread."

"I won't eat it."

"Why?"

"It's too filthy to eat here."

"I'll tell the supervisor."

He went away, but did not shut the window quite so tightly as before, so that a gleam of electric light was visible around the edge. I fixed my eyes on it and felt immensely relieved.

What I must do was to keep count of the days and nights so that they did not all merge into one. They had just offered me bread: this would be the first day, and so I made a rent in the hem of my shirt. When there were five of them I would be let out.

How palatial our cell would seem! I wondered if they had treated Julia like this too. She had trouble with her lungs as it was....

It was impossible to sleep because of the cold and the rats. They scuttled past my face and I clouted them with the huge sandals. What was I to do? Of course—there was always poetry!

I recited Pushkin, Blok, Nekrasov, and Tyutchev. Then I composed a poem of my own—actually without a pencil! It was called "The Punishment Cell."

> This is no fantasy of a mad producer
> Or something dreamed by Edgar Allan Poe.
> As it dies away, I really hear
> The tread of my jailors' boots.
>
> In their drunken jackals' zeal
> How vicious they are, and vile . . .
> In my cold stone cell
> Darkness descends on me.
>
> Can a soul in hell be more lost?
> I must drink my cup to the dregs,
> But at least I am not alone
> In my calvary.
>
> A flagstone is my only cushion,
> But Pushkin, sitting in one corner,
> Sings me a song
> About Gurzuf at night.
>
> And, unseen by any guard,
> Another priceless friend
> Comes into my cell—
> His name is Alexander Blok.

Poetry, at least, they could not take away from me! They had taken my dress, my shoes and stockings, and my comb, they had left me half naked and freezing, but this it was not in their power to take away, it was and remained mine. And I should survive even this dungeon.

•

Comunista Italiana

There were now four tears in the hem of my shirt: four times I had been offered bread, and four times refused it. I was beginning to get the hang of my new cell: I could recognize the Nabob's steps and his hoarse whisper, and the sounds when the guard was changed. I was able to deduce that the cellar contained no less than five "black holes" similar to mine.

In the same way, I at once recognized the loping, camel-like gait of the prison governor. When my door opened, I turned toward the wall so as not to look at his sneering face. He waited to see whether I would give any sign of life, and I waited for him to shout "Stand up!" But he addressed me with Olympian calm:

"Are you aware that hunger strikes are forbidden here?"

I said nothing. Even in my own cell I had refused to talk to this brute—and I certainly wasn't going to do so here!

"I repeat: do you know that in this prison, hunger-striking is regarded as a continuation of counter-revolutionary activity?"

I bit my lips hard and remained silent.

"You refused to acknowledge the detention order or to accept food. That is sufficient ground for me to make a report on your behavior to the judicial authorities. Do you realize this?"

He could go to the devil or shoot me on the spot, I was not going to utter a word. What had I to lose? Wouldn't I be better off in the grave than here?

He paused for another few moments, then turned on his heel (I remembered from his monthly visits how shiny his boots were) and disappeared. The door closed again, but suddenly the little window opened and I saw Yaroslavsky's friendly face with its rosy cheeks and sharp pig's bristles. He whispered rapidly:

"You'd better take the bread or they'll do you in, they really will...." Then, though he had been about to say something more, he slammed the window to again. Someone was coming along the corridor.

I heard the sound of several feet, muffled cries, and a shuffling noise as though a body were being pulled along the stone floor. Then there was a shrill cry of despair; it continued for a long while on the same note, and stopped abruptly.

It was clear that someone was being dragged into a punishment cell and was offering resistance.... The cry rang out again and stopped suddenly, as though the victim had been gagged.

I prayed, as Pushkin once did, "Please God, may I not go mad! Rather grant me prison, poverty, or death." The first sign of approaching madness must surely be the urge to scream like that on a single continuous note. I must conquer it and preserve the balance of my mind by giving it something to do. So I began again to recite verses to myself. I composed more of my own and said them over and over so as not to forget them, and above all not to hear that awful cry.

But it continued—a penetrating, scarcely human cry which seemed to come from the victim's very entrails, to be viscous and tangible as it reverberated in the narrow space. Compared with it, the cries of a woman in labor were sweet music. They, after all, express hope as well as anguish, but here there was only a vast despair.

I felt such terror as I had not experienced since the beginning of my wanderings through this inferno. I felt that at any moment I should start screaming like my unknown neighbor, and from that it could only be a step to madness.

Suddenly the monotonous howl began to be punctuated by shouted words, though I could not make them out. I got up and, dragging my enormous sandals, crept to the door and put my ear close to it. I must find out what the wretched woman was saying.

"What's the matter? Fallen down or something?" came Yaroslavsky's voice from the corridor. He again half opened the window of my cell, and as the light gleamed I could hear words pronounced fairly clearly in a foreign language. Could it be Carola? No, it did not sound like German.

Yaroslavsky looked upset. It was indeed a beastly job for this peasant youth with his fresh face and porcine bristles. I am sure that if he had not been afraid of the accursed Nabob he would have helped both me and this woman who was screaming. At present the Nabob was evidently not there, for instead of slamming the window Yaroslavsky held it open and whispered:

"You'll be back in your cell tomorrow. Only one more night to go. What about a bit of bread, eh?"

I wanted to thank him for these words and above all for his kind expression, but I was afraid of scaring him by too much familiarity. So I only whispered: "What's the matter with her? It's terrible to hear."

He shrugged and said: "They haven't got the guts, these foreigners, they just can't take it. She's only just come in, and yet she makes all that fuss. The Russians are different, they don't kick up a row. Look at you for instance, you've got five days and you're not crying...."

At that moment I heard clearly, in the midst of the wailing, the words *"Comunista Italiana, Comunista Italiana!"* So that was it! No doubt she had fled from Mussolini just as Klara, my cellmate at Butyrki, had fled from Hitler.

Yaroslavsky hastily shut the window and coughed severely. It must be the Nabob—but no, there was more than one person. I heard the Italian's door opened, and a kind of slithering sound which I could not identify. Why did it remind me of flower beds? Good God, it was a hose! So Vevers had not been joking when he had said to me: "We'll hose you down with freezing water and then shove you in a punishment cell."

The wails became shorter as the victim gasped for breath. Soon it was a tiny shrill sound, like a gnat's. The hose played again; then I heard blows being struck, and the iron door was slammed to. Dead silence.

According to my reckoning, we were now on the eve of December the fifth—Constitution Day.... I do not remember how I spent the rest of that night. But I can still hear the exact sound of the Italian woman's thin piping voice as I write now, a quarter of a century later....

Yaroslavsky had gone off duty. The door was flung open. Before I could see who it was, I realized with brutal clarity what I myself looked like, crouching on that filthy, frozen, stone floor, disheveled and covered by a dirty smock, with enormous sandals on my blue, frostbitten feet. A hunted animal—who could wish to live after such an experience?

Apparently one could. The person in the doorway was the wardress called Dumpling. Her cheeks and chin were dimpled, her hair fell in cheerful ringlets onto her prison uniform, she smelled overpoweringly of scented soap and strong eau de Cologne. She said something in a kindly voice. At first I could only take in the sound of her speech—could there really be such a thing as a kind, pleasant, friendly human voice? Gradually I understood what she was saying.

"You're going back to your cell now. It's nearly supper-time. Tomorrow you can have a wash in the shower room."

"Supper? I thought it was morning."

She helped me to take off the smock and put on the gray-blue prison uniform again. How nice and comfortable it seemed! At once I felt warmer, and for the first time in five days I stopped shivering. I tried to put on my stockings but somehow could not—they seemed terribly long, and I could not remember how to pull them on. She helped me again and said: "Come along." We came to a space off which three or four cell doors opened. Outside each one was a pair of down-at-heel shoes—evidently there were not enough regulation boots to go around. But what was this? A pair of exquisite high-heeled shoes, size three at the outside—evidently the Italian woman's; and I thought of that slight, graceful figure, and the hose torture....

Soon I was being taken up the stairs which I used to go up every day after my walk. Suddenly I stopped in agonizing uncertainty: was it to the right or to the left? I began to be frightened. I must be losing my reason after all. I had followed this route every single day for three and a half months. Why had I suddenly forgotten it?

"To the right," Dumpling whispered. I tried to turn, but now I lost all sense of direction and slowly collapsed on the stairs. Evidently I was not made of iron after all.

As I sank into unconsciousness, the last sound that rang in my head was that piercing shriek and the words *"Comunista Italiana! Comunista Italiana!"*

•

"Next year in Jerusalem"

Everything on earth comes to an end, and so did the accursed year 1937. As December wore to a close we were both suffering in health as a result of our experience in the punishment cells: I had frostbitten feet and Julia's lungs had got much worse.

The newspapers were full of reports of the first elections held under the new constitution and the new electoral law.

Day and night we were tormented by the thought: Does our disappearance from life mean nothing to anyone? I imagined my ex-university colleagues voting. Did none of them remember me? And what about the people I had worked with on the newspaper? But no doubt the turnover there had been a hundred per cent.

Even now—we asked ourselves—after all that has happened to us, would we vote for any other than the Soviet system, which seemed as much a part of us as our hearts and as natural to us as breathing? Everything I had in the world—the thousands of books I had read, memories of my youth, and the very endurance which was now keeping me from going under—all this had been given me by the Soviet system, and the revolution which had transformed my world while I was still a child. How exciting life had been and how gloriously everything had begun! What in God's name had happened to us all?

"Julia! Wake up! Listen, don't you think 'he' must have gone mad? They say that megalomania and persecution mania go together.... Suppose, like Boris Godunov, he really does 'dream of slaughtered infants all night long'?"

Julia mumbled something unintelligible. Why had I wakened her up just to say that, especially when she had not got over her spell in the punishment cell?

Illness, however, did not prevent Julia from preparing to see the New Year in. Each day she set aside one of the two lumps of sugar we were given, and for more than a week she had been jealously saving half an ounce of butter out of the seven ounces (for three months) which we had bought from the prison store.

"We must do the thing properly. You know, there's a saying that the way you see it in makes the whole year good or bad for you. And you must write some special New Year verses."

"I wouldn't be in too much of a hurry to rejoice if I were you. For all we know, they'll be celebrating the New Year in an even bigger way than the first of December—the anniversary of Kirov's murder. I shouldn't be surprised if they've invented a special kind of punishment cell for the occasion!"

All the same, as the New Year drew closer we both looked forward to it with impatience. We felt, superstitiously, that the fresh air of 1938 might blow away the nightmares of 1937.

As was always the case before dates of any significance, the prison regime increased in severity. More and more often we heard the click of the peephole, the malevolent hiss "Stop talking." The library for some reason was not functioning, and we knew almost by heart the books we had had for the past month. One of them was the volume of poems by Nekrasov, which Julia could not bring herself to part with.... I reflected once again on the power which literature exerts on us in that state of spiritual composure which prison life induces, and which makes us strive, devoutly and humbly, to drink in an author's words to the full. I have never loved human beings so devotedly as in those months and years when, cast away in the inhuman land and imprisoned behind stone walls, I absorbed every line of print as though it were a message radioed from Earth, my distant mother and homeland, where I had lived with my human brothers and sisters, and where they lived still.

Even Nekrasov's most hackneyed lines were now as moving as a letter, charged with emotion, from a distant friend. I used to read to Julia "Knight for an Hour" and "The Russian Women." Strange to say, the passages which struck one most forcibly were those which one had previously hardly noticed. For example, "Sleep is for others, not for me"—the poet's exclamation on a moonlit, frosty night when he "longed to sob upon a distant grave." I had learned these lines at school and they had merged with dozens of other lines describing landscapes and the feelings they aroused, without making any deep impression on me; but now...! Outside our cell window was that very same frosty night, and however cold it might be we never closed the chink through which a trickle of fresh air came in to us, and with it our beggar's dole from the table of life. It also brought with it Nekrasov's tingling frosty night, and I felt as if no one before us could have fully appreciated the words: "Sleep is for others, not for me."

Apart from Nekrasov, one of the books on our little table hinged to the wall was a volume of poems by Selvin-sky. In it we happened to read some lines about the destiny of the Jewish people, their stubbornness and vitality, and the ancient greeting: "Next year in Jerusalem!" I took this as the theme of the New Year verses Julia had asked me for:

And again, like gray-haired Jews,
We shall cry out eagerly
With voices cracked and weak:
Next year in Jerusalem!

Clinking our prison mugs
We shall drain them dry—
There is no sweeter wine
Than the wine of hope!

Comrade, be of good cheer,
Our prison food is not manna from heaven
But, like the gray-haired Jews,
We believe in the Promised Land.

We may be poor and persecuted,
But on New Year's Eve
We'll cry:
Next year in Jerusalem.

So at last New Year's Eve arrived—our first in prison. If we had
known then that no less than seventeen of them lay before us—if,
on a television screen in our cell, we had beheld even one of the
scenes we were to endure in the next seventeen years—I doubt if
we should have greeted this one with such fortitude. Luckily, the
future was closed to us, and hope lulled us with its childish babble.
In defiance of logic and common sense, we were confident that
before the year was out we should be "in Jerusalem."

Lying on our prison beds, we did our best to gauge the passage of
time. It was not easy—not for nothing had Vera Figner entitled her
memoirs of solitary confinement "When the Clock Stopped." But
during the fateful minutes when that extraordinary year was vanishing
into the abyss of time, giving place to a new one which would, we
believed, be its righteous judge, we were able to count the steps of
time by many intangible signs: the beating of our hearts, the warder's
expression as he looked through the peephole. Prompted by some
sixth sense, we simultaneously stretched out our hands from under the
gray, prickly blankets and clinked together our tin mugs, which we
had previously filled with sugar and water. Luckily, the warders did not
notice our illegal gesture, and we were able to drink the toast in peace,
eating our bread with its thin spread of butter—a truly Lucullan feast!

I read my poem triumphantly to Julia, and we fell asleep dreaming sweetly of the months to come. Next year in Jerusalem!

The oppression of guerilla combat in the vermin-laced
jungles of Vietnam screams for release: psychological,
in the form of locoweed-induced alternate realities
and delusional projections and mind-travel into
photographs from sweethearts at home; and physical
escape, negotiated through tolerable self-mutilation,
and followed by evacuation to freedom, through
cloud- and napalm-laced skies, and destruction. The
penultimate destination—before home or death—
leads to military hospitals, far from the torments of
the front where cute little geishas tended to wounds
that made escape possible. Tim O'Brien's 1987 story
offers an unsentimental, startlingly compelling
inventory of the totems and relics of coherence that
soldiers carry into the field of battle as gateways to
alternate realities.

the things they carried

TIM O'BRIEN

first lieutenant Jimmy Cross carried letters from a girl named Martha, a junior at Mount Sebastian College in New Jersey. They were not love letters, but Lieutenant Cross was hoping, so he kept them folded in plastic at the bottom of his rucksack. In the late afternoon, after a day's march, he would dig his foxhole, wash his hands under a canteen, unwrap the letters, hold them with the tips of his fingers, and spend the last hour of light pretending. He would imagine romantic camping trips into the White Mountains in New Hampshire. He would sometimes taste the envelope flaps, knowing her tongue had been there. More than anything, he wanted Martha to love him as he loved her, but the letters were mostly chatty, elusive on the matter of love. She was a virgin, he was almost sure. She was an English major at Mount Sebastian, and she wrote beautifully about her professors and roommates and midterm exams, about her respect for Chaucer and her great affection for Virginia Woolf. She often quoted lines of poetry; she never mentioned the war, except to say, Jimmy, take care of yourself. The letters weighed ten ounces. They were signed "Love, Martha," but Lieutenant Cross understood that "Love" was only a way of signing and did not mean what he sometimes pretended it meant. At dusk, he would carefully return the letters to his rucksack. Slowly, a bit distracted, he would get up and move among his men, checking the perimeter, then at full dark he would return to his hole and watch the night and wonder if Martha was a virgin.

The things they carried were largely determined by necessity. Among the necessities or near necessities were P-38 can openers, pocket knives, heat tabs, wrist watches, dog tags, mosquito repellent, chewing gum, candy, cigarettes, salt tablets, packets of Kool-Aid, lighters, matches, sewing kits, Military Payment Certificates, C rations, and two or three canteens of water. Together, these items weighed between fifteen and twenty pounds, depending upon a man's habits or rate of metabolism. Henry Dobbins, who was a big man, carried extra rations; he was especially fond of canned peaches in heavy syrup over pound cake. Dave Jensen, who practiced field hygiene, carried a toothbrush, dental floss, and several hotel-size bars of soap he'd stolen on R&R in Sydney, Australia. Ted Lavender, who was scared, carried tranquilizers until he was shot in the head outside the village of Than Khe in mid-April. By necessity, and because it was SOP, they all carried steel helmets that weighed five pounds including the liner and camouflage cover. They carried the standard fatigue jackets and trousers. Very few carried underwear. On their feet they carried jungle boots—2.1 pounds—and Dave Jensen carried three pairs of socks and a can of Dr. Scholl's foot powder as a precaution against trench foot. Until he was shot, Ted Lavender carried six or seven ounces of premium dope, which for him was a necessity. Mitchell Sanders, the RTO, carried condoms. Norman Bowker carried a diary. Rat Kiley carried comic books. Kiowa, a devout Baptist, carried an illustrated New Testament that had been presented to him by his father, who taught Sunday school in Oklahoma City, Oklahoma. As a hedge against bad times, however, Kiowa also carried his grandmother's distrust of the white man, his grandfather's old hunting hatchet. Necessity dictated. Because the land was mined and booby-trapped, it was SOP for each man to carry a steel-centered, nylon-covered flak jacket, which weighed 6.7 pounds, but which on hot days seemed much heavier. Because you could die so quickly, each man carried at least one large compress bandage, usually in the helmet band for easy access. Because the nights were cold, and because the monsoons were wet, each carried a green plastic poncho that could be used as a raincoat or ground sheet or makeshift tent. With its quilted liner, the poncho weighed almost two pounds, but it was worth every ounce. In April, for instance, when Ted Lavender was shot, they used his poncho to wrap him up, then to carry him across the paddy, then to lift him into the chopper that took him away.

They were called legs or grunts.

To carry something was to "hump" it, as when Lieutenant Jimmy

Cross humped his love for Martha up the hills and through the swamps. In its intransitive form, "to hump" meant "to walk," or "to march," but it implied burdens far beyond the intransitive.

Almost everyone humped photographs. In his wallet, Lieutenant Cross carried two photographs of Martha. The first was a Kodachrome snapshot signed "Love," though he knew better. She stood against a brick wall. Her eyes were gray and neutral, her lips slightly open as she stared straight-on at the camera. At night, sometimes, Lieutenant Cross wondered who had taken the picture, because he knew she had boyfriends, because he loved her so much, and because he could see the shadow of the picture taker spreading out against the brick wall. The second photograph had been clipped from the 1968 Mount Sebastian yearbook. It was an action shot—women's volleyball—and Martha was bent horizontal to the floor, reaching, the palms of her hands in sharp focus, the tongue taut, the expression frank and competitive. There was no visible sweat. She wore white gym shorts. Her legs, he thought, were almost certainly the legs of a virgin, dry and without hair, the left knee cocked and carrying her entire weight, which was just over one hundred pounds. Lieutenant Cross remembered touching that left knee. A dark theater, he remembered, and the movie was *Bonnie and Clyde*, and Martha wore a tweed skirt, and during the final scene, when he touched her knee, she turned and looked at him in a sad, sober way that made him pull his hand back, but he would always remember the feel of the tweed skirt and the knee beneath it and the sound of the gunfire that killed Bonnie and Clyde, how embarrassing it was, how slow and oppressive. He remembered kissing her good night at the dorm door. Right then, he thought, he should've done something brave. He should've carried her up the stairs to her room and tied her to the bed and touched that left knee all night long. He should've risked it. Whenever he looked at the photographs, he thought of new things he should've done.

What they carried was partly a function of rank, partly of field specialty.

As a first lieutenant and platoon leader, Jimmy Cross carried a compass, maps, code books, binoculars, and a .45-caliber pistol that weighed 2.9 pounds fully loaded. He carried a strobe light and the responsibility for the lives of his men.

As an RTO, Mitchell Sanders carried the PRC-25 radio, a killer, twenty-six pounds with its battery.

As a medic, Rat Kiley carried a canvas satchel filled with morphine and plasma and malaria tablets and surgical tape and comic books and all the things a medic must carry, including M&M for especially bad wounds, for a total weight of nearly twenty pounds.

As a big man, therefore a machine gunner, Henry Dobbins carried the M-60, which weighed twenty-three pounds unloaded, but which was almost always loaded. In addition, Dobbins carried between ten and fifteen pounds of ammunition draped in belts across his chest and shoulders.

As PFCs or Spec 4s, most of them were common grunts and carried the standard M-16 gas-operated assault rifle. The weapon weighed 7.5 pounds unloaded, 8.2 pounds with its full twenty-round magazine. Depending on numerous factors, such as topography and psychology, the riflemen carried anywhere from twelve to twenty magazines, usually in cloth bandoliers, adding on another 8.4 pounds at minimum, fourteen pounds at maximum. When it was available, they also carried M-16 maintenance gear—rods and steel brushes and swabs and tubes of LSA oil—all of which weighed about a pound. Among the grunts, some carried the M-79 grenade launcher, 5.9 pounds unloaded, a reasonably light weapon except for the ammunition, which was heavy. A single round weighed ten ounces. Their typical load was twenty-five rounds. But Ted Lavender, who was scared, carried thirty-four rounds when he was shot and killed outside Than Khe, and he went down under an exceptional burden, more than twenty pounds of ammunition, plus the flak jacket and helmet and rations and water and toilet paper and tranquilizers and all the rest, plus the unweighed fear. He was dead weight. There was no twitching or flopping. Kiowa, who saw it happen, said it was like watching a rock fall, or a big sandbag or something—just boom, then down—not like the movies where the dead guy rolls around and does fancy spins and goes ass over teakettle—not like that, Kiowa said, the poor bastard just flat-fuck fell. Boom. Down. Nothing else. It was a bright morning in mid-April. Lieutenant Cross felt the pain. He blamed himself. They stripped off Lavender's canteens and ammo, all the heavy things, and Rat Kiley said the obvious, the guy's dead, and Mitchell Sanders used his radio to report one U.S. KIA and to request a chopper. Then they wrapped Lavender in his poncho. They carried him out to a dry paddy, established security, and sat smoking the dead man's dope until the chopper came. Lieutenant Cross kept to himself. He pictured Martha's smooth young face, thinking he loved her more than anything, more than his men, and now Ted Lavender was dead because he loved her so much and could not stop thinking about her. When the dust-off arrived, they carried Lavender aboard. Afterward they burned Than Khe. They marched until dusk, then dug their holes, and that night Kiowa kept explaining how you had to be there, how fast it was, how the poor guy just dropped like so much concrete. Boom-down, he said. Like cement.

In addition to the three standard weapons—the M-60, M-16, and M-79—they carried whatever presented itself, or whatever seemed appropriate as a means of killing or staying alive. They carried catch-as-catch-can. At various times, in various situations, they carried M-14s and CAR-15s and Swedish Ks and grease guns and captured AK-47s and Chi-Coms and RPGs and Simonov carbines and black-market Uzis and .38-caliber Smith & Wesson handguns and 66 mm LAWs and shotguns and silencers and blackjacks and bayonets and C-4 plastic explosives. Lee Strunk carried a slingshot; a weapon of last resort, he called it. Mitchell Sanders carried brass knuckles. Kiowa carried his grandfather's feathered hatchet. Every third or fourth man carried a Claymore anti-personnel mine—3.5 pounds with its firing device. They all carried fragmentation grenades—fourteen ounces each. They all carried at least one M-18 colored smoke grenade—twenty-four ounces. Some carried CS or tear-gas grenades. Some carried white-phosphorus grenades. They carried all they could bear, and then some, including a silent awe for the terrible power of the things they carried.

In the first week of April, before Lavender died, Lieutenant Jimmy Cross received a good-luck charm from Martha. It was a simple pebble, an ounce at most. Smooth to the touch, it was a milky-white color with flecks of orange and violet, oval-shaped, like a miniature egg. In the accompanying letter, Martha wrote that she had found the pebble on the Jersey shoreline, precisely where the land touched water at high tide, where things came together but also separated. It was this separate-but-together quality, she wrote, that had inspired her to pick up the pebble and to carry it in her breast pocket for several days, where it seemed weightless, and then to send it through the mail, by air, as a token of her truest feelings for him. Lieutenant Cross found this romantic. But he wondered what her truest feelings were, exactly, and what she meant by separate-but-together. He wondered how the tides and waves had come into play on that afternoon along the Jersey shoreline when Martha saw the pebble and bent down to rescue it from geology. He imagined bare feet. Martha was a poet, with the poet's sensibilities, and her feet would be brown and bare, the toenails unpainted, the eyes chilly and somber like the ocean in March, and though it was painful, he wondered who had been with her that afternoon. He imagined a pair of shadows moving along the strip of sand where things came together but also separated. It was phantom jealousy, he knew, but he couldn't help himself. He loved her so much. On the march, through the hot days of early April, he carried the pebble in his mouth, turning it with his tongue, tasting sea salts and moisture. His mind wandered. He had difficulty keeping his attention on the war. On occasion he would yell at his men to spread out the column, to keep their eyes open, but then he would slip away into daydreams, just pretending, walking barefoot along the Jersey shore, with Martha, carrying nothing. He would feel himself rising. Sun and waves and gentle winds, all love and lightness.

What they carried varied by mission.

When a mission took them to the mountains, they carried mosquito netting, machetes, canvas tarps, and extra bug juice.

If a mission seemed especially hazardous, or if it involved a place they knew to be bad, they carried everything they could. In certain heavily mined AOs, where the land was dense with Toe Poppers and Bouncing Betties, they took turns humping a twenty-eight-pound mine detector. With its headphones and big sensing plate, the equipment was a stress on the lower back and shoulders, awkward to handle, often useless because of the shrapnel in the earth, but they carried it anyway, partly for safety, partly for the illusion of safety.

On ambush, or other night missions, they carried peculiar little odds and ends. Kiowa always took along his New Testament and a pair of moccasins for silence. Dave Jensen carried night-sight vitamins high in carotin. Lee Strunk carried his slingshot; ammo, he claimed, would never be a problem. Rat Kiley carried brandy and

M&M's. Until he was shot, Ted Lavender carried the starlight scope, which weighed 6.3 pounds with its aluminum carrying case. Henry Dobbins carried his girlfriend's pantyhose wrapped around his neck as a comforter. They all carried ghosts. When dark came, they would move out single file across the meadows and paddies to their ambush coordinates, where they would quietly set up the Claymores and lie down and spend the night waiting.

Other missions were more complicated and required special equipment. In mid-April, it was their mission to search out and destroy the elaborate tunnel complexes in the Than Khe area south of Chu Lai. To blow the tunnels, they carried one-pound blocks of pentrite high explosives, four blocks to a man, sixty-eight pounds in all. They carried wiring, detonators, and battery-powdered clackers. Dave Jensen carried earplugs. Most often, before blowing the tunnels, they were ordered by higher command to search them, which was considered bad news, but by and large they just shrugged and carried out orders. Because he was a big man, Henry Dobbins was excused from tunnel duty. The others would draw numbers. Before Lavender died there were seventeen men in the platoon, and whoever drew the number seventeen would strip off his gear and crawl in head first with a flashlight and Lieutenant Cross's .45-caliber pistol. The rest of them would fan out as security. They would sit down or kneel, not facing the hole, listening to the ground beneath them, imagining cobwebs and ghosts, whatever was down there—the tunnel walls squeezing in—how the flashlight seemed impossibly heavy in the hand and how it was tunnel vision in the very strictest sense, compression in all ways, even time, and how you had to wiggle in— ass and elbows—a swallowed-up feeling—and how you found yourself worrying about odd things—will your flashlight go dead? Do rats carry rabies? If you screamed, how far would the sound carry? Would your buddies hear it? Would they have the courage to drag you out? In some respects, though not many, the waiting was worse than the tunnel itself. Imagination was a killer.

On April 16, when Lee Strunk drew the number seventeen, he laughed and muttered something and went down quickly. The morning was hot and very still. Not good, Kiowa said. He looked at the tunnel opening, then out across a dry paddy toward the village of Than Khe. Nothing moved. No clouds or birds or people. As they waited, the men smoked and drank Kool-Aid, not talking much, feeling sympathy for Lee Strunk but also feeling the luck of the draw. You win some, you lose some, said Mitchell Sanders, and sometimes you settle for a rain check. It was a tired line and no one laughed.

Henry Dobbins ate a tropical chocolate bar. Ted Lavender popped a tranquilizer and went off to pee.

After five minutes, Lieutenant Jimmy Cross moved to the tunnel, leaned down, and examined the darkness. Trouble, he thought—a cave-in maybe. And then suddenly, without willing it, he was thinking about Martha. The stresses and fractures, the quick collapse, the two of them buried alive under all that weight. Dense, crushing love. Kneeling, watching the hole, he tried to concentrate on Lee Strunk and the war, all the dangers, but his love was too much for him, he felt paralyzed, he wanted to sleep inside her lungs and breathe her blood and be smothered. He wanted her to be a virgin and not a virgin, all at once. He wanted to know her. Intimate secrets—why poetry? Why so sad? Why that grayness in her eyes? Why so alone? Not lonely, just alone—riding her bike across campus or sitting off by herself in the cafeteria. Ever dancing, she danced alone—and it was the aloneness that filled him with love. He remembered telling her that one evening. How she nodded and looked away. And how, later, when he kissed her, she received the kiss without returning it, her eyes wide open, not afraid, not a virgin's eyes, just flat and uninvolved.

Lieutenant Cross gazed at the tunnel. But he was not there. He was buried with Martha under the white sand at the Jersey shore. They were pressed together, and the pebble in his mouth was her tongue. He was smiling. Vaguely, he was aware of how quiet the day was, the sullen paddies, yet he could not bring himself to worry about matters of security. He was beyond that. He was just a kid at war, in love. He was twenty-two years old. He couldn't help it.

A few moments later Lee Strunk crawled out of the tunnel. He came up grinning, filthy but alive. Lieutenant Cross nodded and closed his eyes while the others clapped Strunk on the back and made jokes about rising from the dead.

Worms, Rat Kiley said. Right out of the grave. Fuckin' zombie.

The men laughed. They all felt great relief.

Spook City, said Mitchell Sanders.

Lee Strunk made a funny ghost sound, a kind of moaning, yet very happy, and right then, when Strunk made that high happy moaning sound, when he went *Ahhooooo*, right then Ted Lavender was shot in the head on his way back from peeing. He lay with his mouth open. The teeth were broken. There was a swollen black bruise under his left eye. The cheekbone was gone. Oh shit, Rat Kiley said, the guy's dead. The guy's dead, he kept saying, which seemed profound—the guy's dead. I mean really.

The things they carried were determined to some extent by superstition. Lieutenant Cross carried his good-luck pebble. Dave Jensen carried a rabbit's foot. Norman Bowker, otherwise a very gentle person, carried a thumb that had been presented to him as a gift by Mitchell Sanders. The thumb was dark brown, rubbery to the touch, and weighed four ounces at most. It had been cut from a VC corpse, a boy of fifteen or sixteen. They'd found him at the bottom of an irrigation ditch, badly burned, flies in his mouth and eyes. The boy wore black shorts and sandals. At the time of his death he had been carrying a pouch of rice, a rifle, and three magazines of ammunition.

You want my opinion, Mitchell Sanders said, there's a definite moral here.

He put his hand on the dead boy's wrist. He was quiet for a time, as if counting a pulse, then he patted the stomach, almost affectionately, and used Kiowa's hunting hatchet to remove the thumb.

Henry Dobbins asked what the moral was.

Moral?

You know. *Moral.*

Sanders wrapped the thumb in toilet paper and handed it across to Norman Bowker. There was no blood. Smiling, he kicked the boy's head, watched the flies scatter, and said, It's like with that old TV show—Paladin. Have gun, will travel.

Henry Dobbins thought about it.

Yeah, well, he finally said. I don't see no moral.

There it *is*, man.

Fuck off.

They carried USO stationery and pencils and pens. They carried Sterno, safety pins, trip flares, signal flares, spools of wire, razor blades, chewing tobacco, liberated joss sticks and statuettes of the smiling Buddha, candles, grease pencils, *The Stars and Stripes*, fingernail clippers, Psy Ops leaflets, bush hats, bolos, and much more.

Twice a week, when the resupply choppers came in, they carried hot chow in green Mermite cans and large canvas bags filled with iced beer and soda pop. They carried plastic water containers, each with a two-gallon capacity. Mitchell Sanders carried a set of starched tiger fatigues for special occasions. Henry Dobbins carried Black Flag insecticide. Dave Jensen carried empty sandbags that could be filled at night for added protection. Lee Strunk carried tanning lotion. Some things they carried in common. Taking turns, they carried the big PRC-77 scrambler radio, which weighed thirty pounds with its battery. They shared the weight of memory. They took up what others could no longer bear. Often, they carried each other, the wounded or weak. They carried infections. They carried chess sets, basketballs, Vietnamese-English dictionaries, insignia of rank, Bronze Stars and Purple Hearts, plastic cards imprinted with the Code of Conduct. They carried diseases, among them malaria and dysentery. They carried lice and ringworm and leeches and paddy algae and various rots and molds. They carried the land itself— Vietnam, the place, the soil—a powdery orange-red dust that covered their boots and fatigues and faces. They carried the sky. The whole atmosphere, they carried it, the humidity, the monsoons, the stink of fungus and decay, all of it, they carried gravity. They moved like mules. By daylight they took sniper fire, at night they were mortared, but it was not battle, it was just the endless march, village to village, without purpose, nothing won or lost. They marched for the sake of the march. They plodded along slowly, dumbly, leaning forward against the heat, unthinking, all blood and bone, simple grunts, soldiering with their legs, toiling up the hills and down into the paddies and across the rivers and up again and down, just humping, one step and then the next and then another, but no volition, no will, because it was automatic, it was anatomy, and the war was entirely a matter of posture and carriage, the hump was everything, a kind of inertia, and kind of emptiness, a dullness of desire and intellect and conscience and hope and human sensibility. Their principles were in their feet. Their calculations were biological. They had no sense of strategy or mission. They searched the villages without knowing what to look for, not caring, kicking over jars of rice, frisking children and old men, blowing tunnels, sometimes setting fires and sometimes not, then forming up and moving on to the next village, then other villages, where it would always be the same.

They carried their own lives. The pressures were enormous. In the heat of early afternoon, they would remove their helmets and flak jackets, walking bare, which was dangerous but which helped ease the strain. They would often discard things along the route of march. Purely for comfort, they would throw away rations, blow their Claymores and grenades, no matter, because by nightfall the resupply choppers would arrive with more of the same, then a day or two later still more, fresh watermelons and crates of ammunition and sunglasses and woolen sweaters—the resources were stunning—sparklers for the Fourth of July, colored eggs for Easter. It was the great American war chest—the fruits of science, the smokestacks, the canneries, the arsenals at Hartford, the Minnesota forests, the machine shops, the vast fields of corn and wheat—they carried like freight trains; they carried it on their backs and shoulders—and for all the ambiguities of Vietnam, all the mysteries and unknowns, there was at least the single abiding certainty that they would never be at a loss for things to carry.

After the chopper took Lavender away, Lieutenant Jimmy Cross led his men into the village of Than Khe. They burned everything. They shot chickens and dogs, they trashed the village well, they called in artillery and watched the wreckage, then they marched for several hours through the hot afternoon, and then at dusk, while Kiowa explained how Lavender died, Lieutenant Cross found himself trembling.

He tried not to cry. With his entrenching tool, which weighed five pounds, he began digging a hole in the earth.

He felt shame. He hated himself. He had loved Martha more than his men, and as a consequence Lavender was now dead, and this was something he would have to carry like a stone in his stomach for the rest of the war.

All he could do was dig. He used his entrenching tool like an ax, slashing, feeling both love and hate, and then later, when it was full dark, he sat at the bottom of his foxhole and wept. It went on for a long while. In part, he was grieving for Ted Lavender, but mostly it was for Martha, and for himself, because she belonged to another world, which was not quite real, and because she was a junior at Mount Sebastian College in New Jersey, a poet and a virgin and uninvolved, and because he realized she did not love him and never would.

Like cement, Kiowa whispered in the dark. I swear to God—boom-down. Not a word.

I've heard this, said Norman Bowker.

A pisser, you know? Still zipping himself up. Zapped while zipping.

All right, fine. That's enough.

Yeah, but you had to see it, the guy just—

I *heard*, man. Cement. So why not shut the fuck *up*?

Kiowa shook his head sadly and glanced over at the hole where Lieutenant Jimmy Cross sat watching the night. The air was thick and wet. A warm, dense fog had settled over the paddies and there was the stillness that precedes rain.

After a time Kiowa sighed.

One thing for sure, he said. The Lieutenant's in some deep hurt. I mean that crying jag—the way he was carrying on—it wasn't fake or anything, it was real heavy-duty hurt. The man cares.

Sure, Norman Bowker said.

Say what you want, the man does care.

We all got problems.

Not Lavender.

No, I guess not. Bowker said. Do me a favor, though.

Shut up?

That's a smart Indian. Shut up.

Shrugging, Kiowa pulled off his boots. He wanted to say more, just to lighten up his sleep, but instead he opened his New Testament and arranged it beneath his head as a pillow. The fog made things seem hollow and unattached. He tried not to think about Ted Lavender, but then he was thinking how fast it was, no drama, down and dead, and how it was hard to feel anything except surprise. It seemed un-Christian. He wished he could find some great sadness, or even anger; but the emotion wasn't there and he couldn't make it happen. Mostly he felt pleased to be alive. He liked the smell of the New Testament under his cheek, the leather and ink and paper and glue, whatever the chemicals were. He liked hearing the sounds of night. Even his fatigue, it felt fine, the stiff muscles and the prickly awareness of his own body, a floating feeling. He enjoyed not being dead. Lying there, Kiowa admired Lieutenant Jimmy Cross's capacity for grief. He wanted to share the man's pain, he wanted to care as Jimmy Cross cared. And yet when he closed his eyes, all he could think was Boom-down, and all he could feel was the pleasure of having his boots off and the fog curling in around him and the damp soil and the Bible smells and the plush comfort of night.

After a moment Norman Bowker sat up in the dark.

What the hell, he said. You want to talk, *talk*. Tell it to me.

Forget it.

No, man, go on. One thing I hate, it's a silent Indian.

For the most part they carried themselves with poise, a kind of dignity. Now and then, however, there were times of panic, when they squealed or wanted to squeal but couldn't, when they twitched and made moaning sounds and covered their heads and said Dear Jesus and flopped around on the earth and fired their weapons blindly and cringed and sobbed and begged for the noise to stop and went wild and made stupid promises to themselves and to God and to their mothers and fathers, hoping not to die. In different ways, it happened to all of them. Afterward, when the firing ended, they would blink and peek up. They would touch their bodies, feeling shame, then quickly hiding it. They would force themselves to stand. As if in slow motion, frame by frame, the world would take on the old logic—absolute silence, then the wind, then sunlight, then voices. It was the burden of being alive. Awkwardly, the men would reassemble themselves, first in private, then in groups, becoming soldiers again. They would repair the leaks in their eyes. They would check for casualties, call in dust-offs, light cigarettes, try to smile, clear their throats and spit and begin cleaning their weapons. After a time someone would shake his head and say, No lie, I almost shit my pants, and someone else would laugh, which meant it was bad, yes, but the guy had obviously not shit his pants, it wasn't that bad, and in any case nobody would ever do such a thing and then go ahead and talk about it. They would squint into the dense, oppressive sunlight. For a few moments, perhaps, they would fall silent, lighting a joint and tracking its passage from man to man, inhaling, holding in the humiliation. Scary stuff, one of them might say. But then someone else would grin or flick his eyebrows and say, Roger-dodger, almost cut me a new asshole, *almost*.

There were numerous such poses. Some carried themselves with a sort of wistful resignation, others with pride or stiff soldierly discipline or good humor or macho zeal. They were afraid of dying but they were even more afraid to show it.

They found jokes to tell.

They used a hard vocabulary to contain the terrible softness. *Greased*, they'd say. *Offed, lit up, zapped while zipping.* It wasn't cruelty, just stage presence. They were actors and the war came at them in 3-D. When someone died, it wasn't quite dying, because in a curious way it seemed scripted, and because they had their lines mostly memorized, irony mixed with tragedy, and because they called it by other names, as if to encyst and destroy the reality of death itself. They kicked corpses. They cut off thumbs. They talked grunt lingo. They told stories about Ted Lavender's supply of tranquilizers, how the poor guy didn't feel a thing, how incredibly tranquil he was.

There's a moral here, said Mitchell Sanders.

They were waiting for Lavender's chopper, smoking the dead man's dope.

The moral's pretty obvious, Sanders said, and winked. Stay away from drugs. No joke, they'll ruin your day every time.

Cute, said Henry Dobbins.

Mind-blower, get it? Talk about wiggy—nothing left, just blood and brains.

They made themselves laugh.

There it is, they'd say, over and over, as if the repetition itself were an act of poise, a balance between crazy and almost crazy, knowing without going. There it is, which meant be cool, let it ride, because oh yeah, man, you can't change what can't be changed, there it is, there it absolutely and positively and fucking well *is*.

They were tough.

They carried all the emotional baggage of men who might die. Grief, terror, love, longing—these were intangibles, but the intangibles had their own mass and specific gravity, they had tangible weight. They carried shameful memories. They carried the common secret of cowardice barely restrained, the instinct to run or freeze or hide, and in many respects this was the heaviest burden of all, for it could never be put down, it required perfect balance and perfect posture. They carried their reputations. They carried the soldier's greatest fear, which was the fear of blushing. Men killed, and died, because they were embarrassed not to. It was what had brought them to the war in the first place, nothing positive, no dreams of glory or honor, just to avoid the blush of dishonor. They died so as not to die of embarrassment. They crawled into tunnels and walked point and advanced under fire. Each morning, despite the unknowns, they made their legs move. They endured. They kept humping. They did not submit to the obvious alternative, which was simply to close the eyes and fall. So easy, really. Go limp and tumble to the ground and let the muscles unwind and not speak and not budge until your buddies picked you up and lifted you into the chopper that would roar and dip its nose and carry you off to the world. A mere matter of falling, yet no one ever fell. It was not courage, exactly; the object was not valor. Rather, they were too frightened to be cowards.

By and large they carried these things inside, maintaining the masks of composure. They sneered at sick call. They spoke bitterly about guys who had found release by shooting off their own toes or fingers. Pussies, they'd say. Candyasses. It was fierce, mocking talk, with only a trace of envy or awe, but even so, the image played itself out behind their eyes.

They imagined the muzzle against flesh. They imagined the quick, sweet pain, then the evacuation to Japan, then a hospital with warm beds and cute geisha nurses.

They dreamed of freedom birds.

At night, on guard, staring into the dark, they were carried away by jumbo jets. They felt the rush of takeoff. *Gone!* they yelled. And then velocity, wings and engines, a smiling stewardess—but it was more than a plane, it was a real bird, a big sleek silver bird with feathers and talons and high screeching. They were flying. The weights fell off, there was nothing to bear. They laughed and held on tight, feeling the cold slap of wind and altitude, soaring, thinking *It's over, I'm gone!*—they were naked, they were light and free—it was all lightness, bright and fast and buoyant, light as light, a helium buzz in the brain, a giddy bubbling in the lungs as they were taken up over the clouds and the war, beyond duty, beyond gravity and mortification and global entanglements—*Sin loi!* they yelled, *I'm sorry, motherfuckers, but I'm out of it, I'm goofed, I'm on a space cruise, I'm gone!*—and it was a restful, disencumbered sensation, just riding the light waves, sailing that big silver freedom bird over the mountains and oceans, over America, over the farms and great sleeping cities and cemeteries and highways and the golden arches of McDonald's. It was flight, a kind of fleeing, a kind of falling, falling higher and higher, spinning off the edge of the earth and beyond the sun and through the vast, silent vacuum where there were no burdens and where everything weighed exactly nothing. *Gone!* they screamed, *I'm sorry but I'm gone!* And so at night, not quite dreaming, they gave themselves over to lightness, they were carried, they were purely borne.

On the morning after Ted Lavender died, First Lieutenant Jimmy Cross crouched at the bottom of his foxhole and burned Martha's letters. Then he burned the two photographs. There was a steady rain falling, which made it difficult, but he used heat tabs and Sterno to build a small fire, screening it with his body, holding the photographs over the tight blue flame with the tips of his fingers.

He realized it was only a gesture. Stupid, he thought. Sentimental, too, but mostly just stupid.

Lavender was dead. You couldn't burn the blame.

Besides, the letters were in his head. And even now, without photographs, Lieutenant Cross could see Martha playing volleyball in her white gym shorts and yellow T-shirt. He could see her moving in the rain.

When the fire died out, Lieutenant Cross pulled his poncho over his shoulders and ate breakfast from a can.

There was no great mystery, he decided.

In those burned letters Martha had never mentioned the war, except to say, Jimmy, take care of yourself. She wasn't involved. She signed the letters "Love," but it wasn't love, and all the fine lines and technicalities did not matter.

The morning came up wet and blurry. Everything seemed part of everything else, the fog and Martha and the deepening rain.

It was a war, after all.

Half smiling, Lieutenant Jimmy Cross took out his maps. He shook his head hard, as if to clear it, then bent forward and began planning the day's march. In ten minutes, or maybe twenty, he would rouse the men and they would pack up and head west, where the maps showed the country to be green and inviting. They would do what they had always done. The rain might add some weight, but otherwise it would be one more day layered upon all the other days.

He was realistic about it. There was that new hardness in his stomach.

No more fantasies, he told himself.

Henceforth, when he thought about Martha, it would be only to think that she belonged elsewhere. He would shut down the daydreams. This was not Mount Sebastian, it was another world, where there were no pretty poems or midterm exams, a place where men died because of carelessness and gross stupidity. Kiowa was right. Boom-down, and you were dead, never partly dead.

Briefly, in the rain, Lieutenant Cross saw Martha's gray eyes gazing back at him.

He understood.

It was very sad, he thought. The things men carried inside. The things men did or felt they had to do.

He almost nodded at her, but didn't.

Instead he went back to his maps. He was now determined to perform his duties firmly and without negligence. It wouldn't help Lavender, he knew that, but from this point on he would comport himself as a soldier. He would dispose of his good-luck pebble. Swallow it, maybe, or use Lee Strunk's slingshot, or just drop it along the trail. On the march he would impose strict field discipline. He would be careful to send out flank security, to prevent straggling or bunching up, to keep his troops moving at the proper pace and at the proper interval. He would insist on clean weapons. He would confiscate the remainder of Lavender's dope. Later in the day, perhaps, he would call the men together and speak to them plainly. He would accept the blame for what had happened to Ted Lavender. He would be a man about it. He would look them in the eyes, keeping his chin level, and he would issue the new SOPs in a calm, impersonal tone of voice, an officer's voice, leaving no room for argument or discussion. Commencing immediately, he'd tell them, they would no longer abandon equipment along the route of march. They would police up their acts. They would get their shit together, and keep it together, and maintain it neatly and in good working order.

He would not tolerate laxity. He would show strength, distancing himself.

Among the men there would be grumbling, of course, and maybe worse, because their days would seem longer and their loads heavier, but Lieutenant Cross reminded himself that his obligation was not to be loved but to lead. He would dispense with love; it was not now a factor. And if anyone quarreled or complained, he would simply tighten his lips and arrange his shoulders in the correct command posture. He might give a curt little nod. Or he might not. He might just shrug and say Carry on, then they would saddle up and form into a column and move out toward the villages of Than Khe.

At the flash of a skirt, Mickey the barber launches
erotic escape fantasies that unravel even as they scale
the heights of passion. Packaged in the defective,
over-ripe body of a reluctant momma's boy, the
author of these scripts sets about turning fancy into
fact, looking for a love visionary enough to melt the
excesses and plug the shortfalls of all-too-solid-flesh.
Filled with vaguely mythical overtones, Saunders' story
is just too hilarious and rich—in the sense of being
packed with satisfying insights and delicious verbal
virtuosity—for right-brain analysis.

the barber's unhappiness

GEORGE SAUNDERS

mornings the barber left his stylists inside and sat out front of his shop, drinking coffee and ogling every woman in sight. He ogled old women and pregnant women and women whose photographs were passing on the sides of buses and, this morning, a woman with close-cropped black hair and tear-stained cheeks, who wouldn't be half bad if she'd just make an effort, clean up her face a little and invest in some decent clothes, some white tights and a short skirt maybe, knee boots and a cowboy hat and a cigarillo, say, and he pictured her kneeling on a crude Mexican sofa in a little mud hut, daring him to take her, and soon they'd screwed their way into some sort of bean field while gaucho guys played soft guitars, although actually he'd better put the gaucho guys behind some trees or a rock wall so they wouldn't get all hot and bothered from watching the screwing and swoop down and stab him and have their way with Miss Hacienda as he bled to death, and, come to think of it, forget the gauchos altogether, he'd just put some soft guitars on the stereo in the hut and leave the door open, although actually what was a stereo doing in a Mexican hut? Were there outlets? Plus how could he meet her? He could compliment her hair, then ask her out for coffee. He could say that, as a hair-care professional, he knew a little about hair, and boy did she ever have great hair, and by the way did she like coffee? Except they always said no. Lately no no no was all he got. Plus he had zero access to a bean field or mud hut. They could do it in his yard, but it wouldn't be the same, because Jeepers had basically made of it a museum of poop, plus Ma would call 911 at the first hint of a sexy moan.

Miss Hacienda passed through a gap in a hedge and disappeared into the Episcopal church.

Why was she going into church on a weekday? Maybe she had a problem. Maybe she was knocked up. Maybe if he followed her into the church and told her he knew a little about problems, having been born with no toes, she'd have coffee with him. He was tired of going home to just Ma. Lately she'd been falling asleep with her head on his shoulder while they watched TV. Sometimes he worried that somebody would look in the window and wonder why he'd married such an old lady. Plus sometimes he worried that Ma would wake up and catch him watching the black girl in the silver bikini riding her horse through that tidal pool in slow motion on 1-900-DREMGAL. He wondered how Miss Hacienda would look in a silver bikini in slow motion. Although if she was knocked up she shouldn't be riding a horse. She should be sitting down, taking it easy. Somebody should be bringing her a cup of tea. She should move in with him and Ma. He wouldn't rub it in that she was knocked up. He'd be loving about it. He'd be a good friend to her and wouldn't even try to screw her, and pretty soon she'd start wondering why not and start really wanting him. He'd be her labor coach and cheerfully change diapers in the wee hours and finally when she'd lost all the pregnancy weight she'd come to his bed and screw his brains out in gratitude, after which he'd have a meditative smoke by the window and decide to marry her. He nearly got tears in his eyes thinking of how she'd get tears in her eyes as he went down on one knee to pop the question, a nice touch the dolt who'd knocked her up wouldn't have thought of in a million years, the nimrod, and that S.O.B. could drive by as often as he wanted, deeply regretting his foolishness as the baby frolicked in the yard, it was too late, they were a family, and nothing would ever break them up.

But he'd have to remember to stick a towel under the door while meditatively smoking or Ma would have a cow, because after he smoked she always claimed everything smelled like smoke, and made him wash every piece of clothing in the house. And they'd better screw quietly if they weren't married, because Ma was old-fashioned. It was sort of a pain living with Ma. But Miss Hacienda had better be prepared to tolerate Ma, who was actually pretty good company when she stayed on her meds, and so what if she was nearly eighty and went around the house flossing in her bra? It was her damn house. He'd better never hear Miss Hacienda say a word against Ma, who'd paid his way through barber college, like for example asking why Ma had thick sprays of gray hair growing out of her ears, because that would kill Ma, who was always reminding the gas man she'd been a dish in high school. How would Miss Hacienda like it if after a lifetime of hard work she got wrinkled and forgetful and some knocked-up slut dressed like a Mexican cowgirl moved in and started complaining about her ear hair? Who did Miss Hacienda think she was, the Queen of Sheba? She could go into labor in the damn Episcopal church for all he cared, he'd keep wanking it in the pantry on the little milking stool for the rest of his life before he'd let Ma be hurt, and that was final.

As Miss Hacienda came out of the church she saw a thick-waisted, beak-nosed, middle-aged man rise angrily from a wooden bench and stomp into Mickey's Hairport, slamming the door behind him.

Next morning Ma wanted an omelette. When he said he was running late, she said never mind in a tone that made it clear she was going to accidentally on purpose burn herself again while ostensibly making her own omelette. So he made the omelette. When he asked was it good, she said it was fine, which meant it was bad and he had to make pancakes. So he made pancakes. Then he kissed her cheek and flew out the door, very, very late for Remedial Driving School.

Remedial Driving School was being held in what had been a trendy office park in the Carter years and was now a flat white overgrown stucco bunker with tinted windows and a towable signboard that said "Driving School." Inside was a conference table that smelled like a conference table sitting in direct sunlight with some spilled burned coffee on it.

"Latecomers will be beaten," said the Driving School instructor.

"Sorry," said the barber.

"Joking!" said the instructor, thrusting a wad of handouts at the barber, who was trying to get his clip-ons off. "What I was just saying was that, our aim is, we're going to be looking at some things or aspects, in terms of driving? Meaning safety, meaning, is speeding something we do in a vacuum, or could it involve a pedestrian or fatality or a family out for a fun drive, and then here you come, speeding, with the safety or destiny of that family not held firmly in your mind, and what happens next? Who knows?"

"A crash?" said someone.

"An accident?" said someone else.

"I didn't hit nobody," said a girl in a T-shirt that said 'Buggin.'
"Cop just stopped me."

"But I'm talking the possibility aspect?" the instructor said kindly.

"Oh," said the Buggin' girl, who now seemed chastened and convinced.

Outside the tinted window were a little forest and a stream and an insurance agency and a FedEx drop-off tilted by some pipeline digging. There were six students. One was the barber. One was a country boy with a briefcase, who took laborious notes and kept asking questions with a furrowed brow, as if, having been caught speeding, he was now considering a career in law enforcement. Did radar work via sonar beams? How snotty did someone have to get before you could stun them with your stun gun? Next to the country boy was the Buggin' girl. Next to the Buggin' girl was a very, very happy crew-cut older man in a cowboy shirt and bolo tie who laughed at everything and seemed to consider it a great privilege to be here at the driving school on this particular day with this particular bunch of excellent people, and who by the end of the session had proposed holding a monthly barbecue at his place so they wouldn't lose touch. Across the table from the Happy Man was a white-haired woman who kept making sly references to films and books the barber had never heard of and rolling her eyes at things the instructor said, while writing "Help Me!" and "Beam Me Up!" on her notepad and shoving it across the table for the Happy Man to read, which seemed to make the Happy Man uncomfortable.

Next to the white-haired woman was a pretty girl. A very pretty girl. Wow. One of the prettiest girls the barber had ever seen. Boy was she pretty. Her hair was crimped and waist-length and her eyes were doelike and Egyptian and about her there was a sincerity and intelligence that made it hard for him to look away. She certainly looked out of place here at the conference table, with one hand before her in a strip of sunlight which shone on a very pretty turquoise ring that seemed to confirm her as someone exotic and darkish and schooled in things Eastern, someone you could easily imagine making love to on a barge on the Nile, say, surrounded by thousands of candles that smelled weird, or come to think of it maybe she was American Indian, and he saw her standing at the door of a tepee wearing that same sincere and intelligent expression as he came home from the hunt with a long string of dead rabbits, having been accepted into the tribe at her request after killing a cute rabbit publicly to prove he was a man of the woods, or actually they had let him skip the rabbit part because he had spoken to them so frankly about the white man's deviousness and given them secret information about an important fort after first making them promise not to kill any women or children. He pictured one of the braves saying to her, as she rubbed two corncobs together in the dying sunlight near a spectacular mesa, that she was lucky to have the barber, and silently she smiled, rubbing the corncobs together perhaps a little faster, remembering the barber naked in their tepee, although on closer inspection it appeared she was actually probably Italian.

The girl looked up and caught him staring at her. He dropped his eyes and began leafing through his course materials.

The instructor asked did anyone know how many Gs a person pulled when he or she went through a windshield at eighty miles per after hitting a cow.

No one knew.

The instructor said quite a few.

The Happy Man said he'd had a feeling it was quite a few, which was why, wasn't it, that people died?

"So what's my point?" the instructor said, pointing with his pointer to an overhead of a cartoon man driving a little car toward a tombstone while talking gaily on a car phone. "Say we're feeling good, very good, or bad, which is the opposite, say we've just had a death or a promotion or the birth of a child or a fight with our wife or spouse. Because what we then maybe forget is that two tons of car is what you are inside of, driving, and I hope not speeding, although for the sake of this pretend example I'm afraid we have to assume yes, you are, which is how this next bad graphic occurs."

Now on the overhead the cartoon man's body parts were scattered and his car phone was flying up to Heaven on little angel wings. The barber looked at the pretty girl again. She smiled at him. His heart began to race. This never happened. They never smiled back. Well, she was young. Maybe she didn't know better than to smile back at an older guy she didn't want. Or maybe she wanted him. Maybe she'd had it with young horny guys just out for quick rolls in the hay, and wanted someone old enough to really appreciate her, who didn't come too quickly and owned his own business and knew how to pick up after himself. He hoped she was a strict religious virgin who'd never had a roll in the hay. Not that he hoped she was frigid. He hoped she was the kind of strict religious virgin who, once married, would let it all hang out, and when not letting it all hang out would move with quiet dignity in conservative clothes so that no one would suspect how completely and totally she could let it all hang out when she chose to, and that she came from a poor family and could therefore really appreciate the hard work that went into running a small business, and maybe even had some accounting experience and could help with the books. Although truthfully, even if she'd had hundreds of rolls in the hay and couldn't add a stinking row of figures, he didn't care, she was so pretty, they'd work it out, assuming of course she'd have him, and with a sinking heart he thought of his missing toes. He remembered that day at the lake with Mary Ellen Kovski, when it had been over a hundred degrees and he'd sat on a beach chair fully dressed, claiming to be chilly. A crowd of Mary Ellen's friends had gathered to help her undress him and throw him in, and in desperation he'd whispered to her about his toes, and she'd gone white and called off her friends and two months later married Phil Anpesto, that idiotic bean-pole. Oh, he was tired of hiding his toes. Maybe this girl had a wisdom beyond her years. Maybe her father had a deformity, a glass eye or a facial scar, maybe through long years of loving this kindly but deformed man she had come to almost need the man she loved to be somewhat deformed. Not that he liked the idea of her trotting after a bunch of deformed guys, and also not that he considered himself deformed, exactly, although, admittedly, ten barely discernible bright-pink nubs were no picnic. He pictured her lying nude in front of a fireplace, so comfortable with his feet that she'd given each nub a pet name, and sometimes during lovemaking she got a little carried away and tried to lick his nubs, although certainly he didn't expect that, and in fact found it sort of disgusting, and for a split second he thought somewhat less of her, then pictured himself gently pulling her up, away from his feet, and the slightly shamed look on her face made him forgive her completely for the disgusting thing she'd been about to do out of her deep deep love for him.

The instructor held up a small bloodied baby doll, which he then tossed across the room into a trunk.

"Blammo," he said. "Let's let that trunk represent a tomb, and it's your fault, from speeding. How then do you feel?"

"Bad," said the Buggin' girl.

The pretty girl passed the barber the Attendance Log, which had to be signed to obtain Course Credit and Associated Conviction Waivers/Point Reductions.

They looked frankly at each other for what felt like a very long time.

"Hokay!" the instructor said brightly. "I suppose I don't have to grind you into absolute putty, so now it's a break, so you don't view me as some sort of Marquis de Sade requiring you to watch gross visuals and graphics until your mind rots out."

The barber took a deep breath. He would speak to her. Maybe buy her a soda. The girl stood up. The barber got a shock. Her face was the same lovely exotic intelligent slim Cleopatran face, but her body seemed scaled to a head twice the size of the one she had. She was a big girl. Her arms were round and thick. Her mannerisms were a big girl's mannerisms. She hunched her shoulders and tugged at her smock. He felt a little miffed at her for having misled him and a little miffed at himself for having ogled such a fatty. Well, not a fatty, exactly, her body was O.K., it seemed solid enough, it was just too big for her head. If you could somehow reduce the body to put it in scale with the head, or enlarge the head and shrink down the entire package, then you'd have a body that would do justice to that beautiful, beautiful face that he, even now, tidying up his handouts, was regretting having lost.

"Hi," she said.

"Hello," he said, and went outside and sat in his car, and when she came out with two Cokes he pretended to be cleaning his ashtray until she went away.

A month or so later the barber sat stiffly at a wedding reception at the edge of a kind of mock Japanese tearoom at the Hilton while some goof-ball inside a full-body PuppetPlayers groom costume, complete with top hat and tails and a huge yellow felt head and three-fingered yellow felt hands, was making vulgar thrusting motions with his hips in the barber's direction, as if to say: Do you like to do this? Have you done this? Can you show me how to do this, because soon I'm going to have to do this with that PuppetPlayers bride over there!

Everyone was laughing and giving the barber inexplicable

thumbs-ups as the PuppetPlayers groom then dragged the PuppetPlayers bride across the dance floor and introduced her to the barber, and she appeared to be very taken with him, and sat on his lap and forced his head into her yellow felt cleavage, which was stained with wine and had a big cigarette burn at the neckline. Then the PuppetPlayers newlyweds sprinted across the room and bowed low before the real newlyweds, Arnie and Evelyn, who were sitting sullenly on the bandstand, apparently in the middle of a snit.

"Mickey!" Uncle Edgar shouted to the barber. "Mickey, you should've boffed that puppet broad! So what if she's a puppet! You're no prize! You're going to be choosy? Think of it! Think of it! Arnie's half your age!"

"Edgar, for Christ's sake, you're embarrassing him!" shouted Aunt Jean. "It's like you're saying he's old! Like he's an old maid, only he's a guy! See what I mean? You think that's nice?"

"I am!" shouted Uncle Edgar. "I am saying that! He's a damned old lady! I don't mean no offense! I'm just saying, Get out and live! I love him! That's why I'm saying! The sun's setting! Pork some young babe, and if you like it, if you like the way she porks, what the hell, put down roots! What do you care? Love you can learn! But you gotta start somewhere! I mean, my God, even these little so-and-sos here are trying to get some of it!"

And Uncle Edgar threw a dinner roll at a group of four adolescent boys whom the barber vaguely remembered having once pulled around the block in a little red wagon. The boys gave Uncle Edgar the finger and said that not only were they trying to get some of it, they were actually getting some of it, and not always from the same chick, and sometimes more than once a day, and sometimes right after football practice, and quite possibly in the near future from a very hot shop teacher they had reason to believe would probably give it to all of them at once if only they approached it the right way.

"Holy Cow!" shouted Uncle Edgar. "Let me go to that school!"

"Edgar, you pig, be logical!" shouted Aunt Jean. "Just because Mickey's not married don't mean he ain't getting any! He could be getting some from a lady friend, or several lady friends, lady friends his own age, who already know the score, whose kids are full grown! You don't know what goes on in his bed at night!" Now the PuppetPlayers groom was trying to remove the real bride's garter, and some little suited boys were walking a ledge along a goldfish stream that separated the Wedding Area from Okinawa Memories, where several clearly non-Japanese women in kimonos were hustling drinks. The little suited boys began prying up the screen that kept the goldfish from going over a tiny waterfall, to see if they would die in a shallow pond near the Vending Area.

"For example, those kids torturing those fish," shouted Uncle Edgar. "You know who those kids are? Them are Brendan's kids. You know who Brendan is? He's Dick's kid. You remember Dick? Your second cousin the same age as you, man! Remember I took you guys to the ballgame and he threw up in my Rambler? So them kids are Dick's grandkids, and here Dick's the same age as you, which means you're old enough to be a grandpa, Grandpa, but you ain't even a pa yet, which I don't know how you feel about it but I think is sort of sad or weird!"

"You do, but maybe he don't!" shouted Aunt Jean. "Why do you think everything you think is everything everybody else thinks? Plus Dick's no saint and neither are those kids! Dick was a teen dad and Brendan was a teen dad and probably those kids on the ledge are going to be teen dads as soon as they finish killing those poor fish!"

"Agreed!" shouted Uncle Edgar. "Hey, I got no abiding love for Dick! You want to have a fight with me at a wedding over my feelings for Dick, whose throwing up in my Rambler was just the start of the crap he's pulled on me? All's I'm saying is, there's no danger of Mickey here being a teen dad, and he better think about what I'm saying and get on the stick before his shooter ain't a viable shooter no more!"

"I'm sure you start talking about the poor guy's shooter at a wedding!" shouted Aunt Jean. "You're drunk!"

"Who ain't?" shouted Uncle Edgar, and the table exploded in laughter and one of the adolescents fell mock-drunk off his chair and when this got a laugh all the other adolescents fell mock-drunk off their chairs.

The barber excused himself and walked quickly out of the Wedding Area past three stunning girls in low-cut white gowns, who stood in what would have been shade from the fake overhanging Japanese cherry trees had the trees been outside and had it been daytime.

In the bathroom the Oriental theme receded and all was shiny chrome. The barber peed, mentally defending himself against Uncle

Edgar. First off, he'd had plenty of women. Five. Five wasn't bad. Five was more than most guys, and for sure it was more than Uncle Edgar, who'd married Jean right out of high school and had a lower lip like a fish. Who would Uncle Edgar have had him marry? Sara DelBianco, with her little red face? Ellen Wiest, that tall drink of water? Ann DeMann, who was sway-backed and had claimed he was a bad screw? Why in the world was he, a successful small businessman, expected to take advice from someone who'd spent the best years of his life transferring partial flanges from one conveyor belt to another while spraying them with a protective solvent mist?

The barber wet his comb the way he'd been wetting his comb since high school and prepared to slick back his hair. A big vital man with a sweaty face came in and whacked the barber on the back as if they were old pals. In the mirror was a skeletal mask that the barber knew was his face but couldn't quite believe was his face, because in the past his face could always be counted on to amount to more than the sum of its parts when he smiled winningly, but now when he smiled winningly he looked like a corpse trying to appear cheerful in a wind tunnel. His eyes bulged, his lips were thin, his forehead wrinkles were deep as stick lines in mud. It had to be the lighting. He was ugly. He was old. How had this happened? Who would want him now?

"You look like hell," thundered the big man from a stall, and the barber fled the mirror without slicking back his hair.

As he rushed past the stunning girls, a boy in a fraternity sweatshirt came over. Seeing the barber, he made a comic geriatric coughing noise in his throat, and one of the girls giggled and adjusted her shoulder strap as if to keep the barber from seeing down her dress.

A few weeks before the wedding, the barber had received in the mail a greeting card showing a cowboy roping a steer. The barber's name was scrawled across the steer's torso and "Me (Mr. Jenks)" across the cowboy.

"Here's hoping you will remember me from our driving school," said a note inside, "and attend a small barbecue at my home. My hope being to renew those acquaintances we started back then, which I found enjoyable and which since the loss of my wife I've had far too few of. Please come and bring nothing. As you can see from the cover, I am roping you in, not to brand you but only to show you my hospitality, I hope. Your friend, Larry Jenks."

Who was Jenks? Was Jenks the Happy Man? The barber threw the card in the bathroom trash, imagining the Driving School kooks seated glumly on folding chairs in a trailer house. For a week or so the card sat there, cowboy side up, vaguely reproaching him. Then he took out the trash.

A few days after the wedding, he received a second card from Jenks, with a black flower on the front.

"A good time was had by all," it said. "Sorry you were unable to attend. Even the younger folks, I think, enjoyed. Many folks took home quite a few sodas, because, as I am alone now, I never could have drank that many sodas in my life. This note, on a sadder note, and that is why the black flower, is to inform you that Eldora Ronsen is moving to Seattle. You may remember her as the older woman to your immediate right. She is high up in her company and just got higher, which is good for her but bad for us, as she is such a super-gal. Please join us Tuesday next, Corrigan's Pub, for farewell drinks, map enclosed, your friend, Larry Jenks."

Tuesday next was tomorrow.

"Well, you can't go," Ma said. "The girls are coming over."

The girls were the Rosary and Altar Society. When they came over he had to wait on them hand and foot while they talked about which priest they would marry if only the priests weren't priests. When one lifted her blouse to show her recent scar, he had to say it was the worst scar ever. When one asked if her eye looked rheumy, he had to get very close to her rheumy eye and say it looked non-rheumy to him.

"Well, I think I might want to go," he said.

"I just said you can't," she said. "The girls are coming."

She was trying to guilt him. Once she'd faked a seizure when he tried to go to Detroit for a hair show.

"Ma," he said. "I'm going."

"Mr. Big Shot," she said. "Bullying an old lady."

"I'm not bullying you," he said. "And you're not old."

"Oh, I'm young, I'm a tiny baby," she said, tapping her dentures.

That night he dreamed of the pretty but heavy girl. In his dream she was all slimmed down. Her body looked like the body of Daisy Mae in the "Li'l Abner" cartoon. She came into the shop in cut-off jeans, chewing a blade of grass, and said she found his accomplishments amazing, especially considering the hardships he'd had to overcome, like his dad dying young and his mother being so nervous, and then she took the blade of grass out of her mouth and put it on the magazine table and stretched out across the Waiting Area couch while he undressed, and seeing his unit she said it was the biggest unit she'd ever seen, and arched her back in a sexy way, and then she called him over and gave him a deep warm kiss on the mouth that was so much like the kiss he'd been waiting for all his life that it abruptly woke him.

Sitting up in bed, he missed her. He missed how much she loved and understood him. She knew everything about him and yet still liked him. His gut sort of ached with wanting.

In his boyhood mirror he caught sight of himself and flexed his chest the way he used to flex his chest in the weight-lifting days, and looked so much like a little old man trying to take a dump in his bed that he hopped up and stood panting on the round green rug.

Ma was blundering around in the hallway. Because of the dream, he had a partial bone. To hide his partial bone, he kept his groin behind the door as he thrust his head into the hall.

"I was walking in my sleep," Ma said. "I'm so worried I was walking in my sleep."

"What are you worried about?" he said.

"I'm worried about when the girls come," she said.

"Well, don't worry," he said. "It'll be fine."

"Thanks a million," she said, going back into her room. "Very reassuring."

Well, it would be fine. If they ran out of coffee, one of the old ladies could make coffee, if they ran out of snacks they could go a little hungry, if something really disastrous happened they could call him at Corrigan's, he'd leave Ma the number.

Because he was going.

In the morning he called Jenks and accepted the invitation, while Ma winced and clutched her stomach and pulled over a heavy wooden chair and collapsed into it.

Corrigan's was meant to feel like a pub at the edge of a Scottish golf course, there was a roaring fire, and many ancient-looking golf clubs hanging above tremendous tables of a hard plastic material meant to appear gnarled and scarred, and kilted waitresses with names like

Heather and Zoe were sloshing chicken wings and fried cheese and lobster chunks into metal vats near an aerial photo of the Old Course at St. Andrews, Scotland.

The barber was early. He felt it was polite to be early, except when he was late, at which time he felt being early was anal. Where the heck was everybody? They weren't very polite. He looked down at his special shoes. They were blocky and black and had big removable metal stays in the sides and squeaked when he walked.

"Sorry we're late!" Mr. Jenks shouted, and the Driving School group settled in around the long gnarled table.

The pretty but heavy girl hung her purse across the back of her chair. Her hair looked like her hair in the dream and her eyes looked like her eyes in the dream, and as for her body he couldn't tell, she was wearing a muumuu. But certainly facially she was pretty. Facially she was very possibly the prettiest girl here. Was she? If aliens came down and forced each man to pick one woman to reproduce with in a chain-link enclosure while they took notes, would he choose her, based solely on face? Here was a woman with a good rear but a doglike face, and there was a woman with a nice perm but a blop at the end of her nose, and there was the Buggin' girl, who looked like a chicken, and the white-haired woman, whose face was all wrinkled, and here was the pretty but heavy girl. Was she the prettiest? Facially? He thought she very possibly was.

He regarded her fondly from across the table, waiting for her to catch him regarding her fondly, so he could quickly avert his eyes, so she'd know he was still possibly interested, and then she dropped her menu and bent to retrieve it and the barber had a chance to look briefly down her dress.

Well, she definitely had something going on in the chest category. So facially she was the prettiest in the room, plus she had decent boobs. Attractive breasts. The thing was, would she want him? He was old. Oldish. When he stood up too fast, his knee joints popped. Lately his gums had started to bleed. Plus he had no toes. Although why sell himself short? Who was perfect? He wasn't perfect and she wasn't perfect but they obviously had some sort of special chemistry, based on what had happened at the Driving School, and, anyway, what the heck, he wasn't proposing, he was just considering possibly trying to get to know her somewhat better.

In this way, he decided to ask the pretty but heavy girl out.

How to do it, that was the thing. How to ask her. He could get her alone and say her hair looked super. While saying it looked super, he could run a curl through his fingers in a professional way, as if looking for split ends. He could say he'd love a chance to cut such excellent hair, then slip her a card for One Free Cut and Coffee. That had worked with Sylvia Reynolds, a bank teller with crow's-feet and a weird laugh who turned out to be an excellent kisser. When she'd come in for her Free Cut and Coffee, he'd claimed they were out of coffee and taken her to Bean Men Roasters. A few dates later they'd got carried away, because of her excellent kissing, and done more than he ever would've imagined doing with someone with crow's-feet and a weird laugh and strangely wide hips, and when he'd got home that night and had a good hard look inside the locket she'd given him after they'd done it, he'd instantly felt bad, because wow could you ever see the crow's-feet in that picture. As he looked at Sylvia standing in that bright sun-lit meadow in the picture, her head thrown back, joyfully laughing, her crow's-feet so very pronounced, an image had sprung into his mind of her coming wide-hipped toward him while holding a baby, and suddenly he'd been deeply disappointed in himself for doing it with someone so unusual-looking, and to insure that he didn't make matters worse by inadvertently doing it with her a second time he'd sort of never called her again, and had even switched banks.

He glanced at the pretty but heavy girl and found her making her way toward the ladies'.

Now was as good a time as any.

He waited a few minutes, then excused himself and stood outside the ladies', reading ads posted on a corkboard, until the pretty but heavy girl came out.

He cleared his throat and asked was she having fun?

She said yes.

Then he said wow did her hair look great. And in terms of great hair, he knew what he was talking about, he was a professional. Where did she have it cut? He ran one of her curls through his fingers, as if looking for split ends, and said he'd love the chance to work with such dynamite hair, and took from his shirt pocket the card for One Free Cut and Coffee.

"Maybe you could stop by sometime," he said.

"That's nice of you," she said, and blushed.

So she was a shy girl. Sort of cutely nerdy. Not exactly confident. That was too bad. He liked confidence. He found it sexy. On the other hand, who could blame her, he could sometimes be very intimidating. Also her lack of confidence indicated he could perhaps afford to be a little bit bold.

"Like, say, tomorrow?" he said. "Like, say, tomorrow at noon?"

"Ha," she said. "You move quick."

"Not too quick, I hope," he said.

"No," she said. "Not too quick."

So he had her. By saying he wasn't moving too quick, wasn't she implicitly implying that he was moving at exactly the right speed? All he had to do now was close the deal.

"I'll be honest," he said. "I've been thinking about you since Driving School."

"You have?" she said.

"I have," he said.

"So you're saying tomorrow?" she said, blushing again.

"If that's O.K. for you," he said.

"It's O.K. for me," she said.

Then she started uncertainly back to the table, and the barber raced into the men's. Yes! Yes yes yes. It was a date. He had her. He couldn't believe it. He'd really played that smart. What had he been worried about? He was cute, women had always considered him cute, never mind the thin hair and minor gut, there was just something about him women liked.

Wow she was pretty, he had done very very well for himself.

Back at the table, Mr. Jenks was taking Polaroids. He announced his intention of taking six shots of the Driving School group, one for each member to keep, and the barber stood behind the pretty but heavy girl, with his hands on her shoulders, and she reached up and gave his wrist a little squeeze.

At home old-lady cars were in the driveway, and old-lady coats were piled on the couch, and the house smelled like old lady, and the members of the Rosary and Altar Society were gathered around the dining-room table looking frail. The barber could never keep them straight. There was a crone in a lime pants suit, and another crone in a pink pants suit, and two crones in blue pants suits. As he came in they began asking Ma why was he out so late, why hadn't he been here to help, wasn't he normally a fairly good son? And Ma said yes, he was normally a fairly good son, except he hadn't given her any grandkids yet and often wasted water by bathing twice a day.

"My son had that problem," said one of the blue crones. "His wife once pulled me aside."

"Has his wife ever pulled you aside?" the pink crone said to Ma.

"He's not married," said Ma.

"Maybe the not married is related to the bathing too often," said the lime crone.

"Maybe he holds himself aloof from others," said the blue crone. "My son held himself aloof from others."

"My daughter holds herself aloof from others," said the pink crone.

"Does she bathe too often?" said Ma.

"She doesn't bathe too often," said the pink crone. "She just thinks she's smarter than everyone."

"Do you think you're smarter than everyone?" asked the lime crone severely, and thank God at that moment Ma reached up and pulled him down by the shirt and roughly kissed his cheek.

"Have a good time?" she said, and the group photo fell out of his pocket and into the dip.

"Very nice," he said.

"Who are these people?" Ma said, wiping a bit of dip off the photo with her finger. "Are these the people you went to meet? Who is this you're embracing? This big one."

"I'm not embracing her, Ma," he said. "I'm just standing behind her. She's a friend."

"She's big," Ma said. "You smell like beer."

"Actually I don't consider her big," said the barber, in a tone of disinterested interest.

"Whatever you say," said the lime crone.

"He's been drinking," said Ma.

Oh he didn't care what they thought, he was happy. He jokingly snatched the photo away and dashed up to his room, taking two stairs at a time.

Gabby Gabby Gabby, her name was Gabby, short for Gabrielle.

Tomorrow they had a date for lunch. Breakfast, rather. They'd moved it up to breakfast. While they'd been kissing against her car, she'd said she wasn't sure she could wait until lunch to see him again. He felt the same way. Even breakfast seemed a long time to wait. He wished she was sitting next to him on the bed right now, holding his hand, listening to the sounds of the crones cackling as they left. In his mind, he stroked her hair and said he was glad he'd finally found her, and she said she was glad to have been found, she'd never dreamed that someone so distinguished, with such a broad chest and wide shoulders, could love a girl like her. Was she happy? he tenderly asked. Oh, she was so happy, she said, so happy to be sitting next to this accomplished, distinguished man in this amazing house, which in his mind was not the current house, a pea-green ranch with a tilted cracked sidewalk, but a mansion, on a lake, with a smaller house nearby for Ma, down a very very long wooded path, and he'd paid cash for the mansion with money he'd made from his international chain of barbershops, each of which was an exact copy of his current barbershop, and when he and Gabby visited his London, England, shop, leaving Ma behind in the little house, his English barbers would always burst into applause and say, "Jolly good, jolly good," as the happy couple walked in the door.

"I'm leaving you the dishes, Romeo," Ma shouted from the bottom of the stairs.

Early next morning, he sat in the bath, getting ready for his date. Here was his floating weenie, like some kind of sea creature. He danced his nubs nervously against the tiles, like Fred Astaire dancing on a wall, and swirled the washrag through the water, holding it by one corner, so that it, too, was like a sea creature, a blue ray, a blue monogrammed ray that now crossed the land that was his belly and attacked the sea creature that was his weenie, and remembering what Uncle Edgar had said at the wedding about his shooter not being viable, he gave his shooter a good, hard, reassuring shake, as if congratulating it for being so very viable. It was a great shooter, perfectly fine, in spite of what Ann DeMann had once said about him being a bad screw, it had got hard quick last night and stayed hard throughout the kissing, and wow he wished Uncle Edgar could have seen that big boner.

Oh, he felt good, in spite of a slight hangover he was very happy.

Flipping his unit carelessly from side to side with thumb and forefinger, he looked at the group photo, which he'd placed near the sink. God, she was pretty. He was so lucky. He had a date with a pretty young girl. Ma was nuts, Gabby wasn't big, no bigger than any other girl. Not much bigger, anyway. How wide were her shoulders compared to, say, the shoulders of the Buggin' girl? Well, he wasn't going to dignify that with a response. She was perfect just the way she was. He leaned out of the tub to look closer at the photo. Well, Gabby's shoulders were maybe a little wider than the Buggin' girl's shoulders. Definitely wider. Were they wider than the shoulders of the white-haired woman? Actually, in the photo they were even wider than the shoulders of the country boy.

Oh, he didn't care, he just really liked her. He liked her laugh and the way she had of raising one eyebrow when skeptical, he liked the way that, when he moved his hand to her boob as they leaned against her car, she let out a happy little sigh. He liked how, after a few minutes of kissing her while feeling her boobs, which were super, very firm, when he dropped his hand down between her legs she said she thought that was probably enough for one night, which was good, it showed good morals, it showed she knew when to call it quits.

Ma was in her room, banging things around.

Because for a while there last night he'd been worried. Worried she wasn't going to stop him. Which would have been disappointing. Because she barely knew him. He could've been anybody. For a few minutes there against the car, he'd wondered if she wasn't a little on the easy side. He wondered this now. Did he want to wonder this now? Wasn't that sort of doubting her? No, no, it was fine, there was no sin in looking at things honestly. So was she? Too easy? Why had she so quickly agreed to go out with him? Why so willing to give it away so easily to some old guy she barely knew? Some old balding guy she barely knew? Well, he thought he might know why. Possibly it was due to her size. Possibly the guys her own age had passed her by, due to the big bod, and, nearing thirty, she'd heard her biologic clock ticking and decided it was time to lower her standards, which, possibly, was where he came in. Possibly, seeing him at the Driving School, she'd thought, since all old guys like young girls, big bods notwithstanding, this old pear-shaped balding guy can ergo be had no problem.

Was that it? Was that how it was?

"Some girl just called," Ma said, leaning heavily against the bathroom door. "Some girl, Gabby or Tabby or something? Said you had a date. Wanted you to know she's running late. Is that the same girl?

The same fat girl you were embracing?"

Sitting in the tub, he noticed that his penis was gripped nervously in his fist, and let it go, and it fell to one side, as if it had just passed out.

"Do the girl a favor, Mickey," Ma said. "Call it off. She's too big for you. You'll never stick with her. You never stick with anyone. You couldn't even stick with Ellen Wiest, for crying out loud, who was so wonderful, you honestly think you're going to stick with this Tabby or Zippy or whatever?"

Of course Ma had to bring up Ellen Wiest. Ma had loved Ellen, who had a regal face and great manners and was always kissing up to Ma by saying what a great mother Ma was. He remembered the time he and Ellen had hiked up to Butternut Falls and stood getting wet in the mist, holding hands, smiling sweetly at each other, which had really been fun, and she'd said she thought she loved him, which was nice, except wow she was tall. You could hold hands with her for only so long before your back started to hurt. Plus they'd had that fight on the way down. Well, there were a lot of things about Ellen that Ma wasn't aware of, such as her nasty temper, and he remembered Ellen storming ahead of him on the trail, glaring back now and then, just because he'd made a funny remark about her blocking out the sun, and hadn't he also said something about her being able to eat leaves from the tallest of the trees they were passing under? Well, that had been funny, it had all been in fun, why did she have to get so mad about it? Where was Ellen now? Hadn't she married Ed Trott? Well, Trott could have her. Trott was probably suffering the consequences of being married to Miss Thin Skin even now, and he remembered having recently seen Ed and Ellen at the ValueWay, Ellen pregnant and looking so odd, with her big belly pressing against the cart as she craned that giraffelike neck down to nuzzle Ed, who had a big stupid happy grin on his face like he was the luckiest guy in the world.

The barber stood up angrily from the tub. Here in the mirror were his age-spotted deltoids and his age-spotted roundish pecs and his strange pale love handles.

Ma resettled against the door with a big whump.

"So what's the conclusion, lover boy?" she said. "Are you cancelling? Are you calling up and cancelling?"

"No, I'm not," he said.

"Well, poor her," Ma said.

South Street was an old wagon road.

Cars took the bend too fast. Often he scowled at the speeding cars on his way to work, imagining the drivers laughing to themselves about the way he walked. Because on days when his special shoes hurt he sort of minced. They hurt today. He shouldn't have worn the thin gray socks. He was mincing a bit but trying not to, because what if Gabby drove up South on her way to meet him at the shop and saw him mincing?

He turned up Lincoln Avenue and passed the Liquor Mart, and La Belle Époque, the antique store with the joyful dog inside, and as always the joyful dog sprang over the white settee and threw itself against the glass, and then there was Gabby, down the block, peering into his locked shop, and he corrected his mincing and began walking normally, though it killed.

Did she like the shop? He took big bold steps with his head thrown back so he'd look happy. Happy and strong, with all his toes. With all his toes, in the prime of his life. Did she notice how neat the shop was? How professional? Or did she notice that four of the chairs were of one type and the fifth was totally different? Did it seem to her that the shop was geared to old blue-hairs, which was something he'd once heard a young woman say as he took out the trash?

How did she look? Did she look good?

It was still too far to tell.

Now she saw him. Her face brightened, she waved like a little girl. Oh, she was pretty. It was as if he'd known her forever. She looked so hopeful. But, oops. Oh my God, she was big. She'd dressed all wrong, tight jeans and a tight shirt. As if testing him. Jesus, this was the biggest he'd ever seen her look. What was she doing, testing him, trying to look her worst? Here was an alley, should he swerve into the alley and call her later? Or not. Not call her later? Forget the whole thing? Pretend last night had never happened? Although now she'd seen him. And he didn't want to forget the whole thing. Last night for the first time in a long time he'd felt like someone other than a guy who wanks it on the milking stool in his mother's pantry. Last night he'd bought a pitcher for the Driving School group and Jenks had called him a sport. Last night she'd said he was a sexy kisser.

Thinking about forgetting last night gave him a pit in his stomach. Forgetting last night was not an option. What were the options?

Well, she could trim down. That was an option. Maybe all she needed was someone to tell her the simple truth, someone to sit her down and say, Look, you have an incredibly beautiful intelligent face, but from the neck down, sweetie, wow, we've got some serious work to do. And after their rank talk she'd send him flowers with a card that said, Thanks for your honesty, let's get this thing done. And every night as she stood at the mirror in her panties and bra he'd point out places that needed improvement, and the next day she'd energetically address those areas in the gym, and soon the head-bod discrepancy would be eliminated, and he imagined her in a fancy dress at a little table on a veranda, a veranda by the sea, thanking him for the honeymoon trip, she came from a poor family and had never even been on a vacation, much less a six-week tour of Europe, and then she'd say, Honey, why not put down that boring report on how much your international chain of barbershops earned us this month and join me in the bedroom so I can show you how grateful I am, and in the bedroom she'd start stripping, and was good at it, not that she'd ever done it before, no, she hadn't, she was just naturally good at it, and when she was done there she was, with her perfect face and the Daisy Mae body, smiling at him with unconditional love.

It wouldn't be easy. It would take hard work. He knew a little about hard work, having made a barbershop out of a former pet store. Tearing out a counter, he'd found a dead mouse. From a sump pump he'd pulled three hardened snakes. But he'd never quit. Because he was a worker. He wasn't afraid of hard work. Was she a worker? He didn't know. He'd have to find out.

They'd find out together.

She stood beside his wooden bench, under his shop awning, and the shadow of her wild mane fell at his feet.

What a wild ride this had been, how much he had learned about himself already!

"Here I am," she said, with a shy, pretty smile.

"I'm so glad you are," he said, and bent to unlock the door of the shop.

*Few childhood pleasures are as keen as waking up in
the morning to fever (not too high) and being told to
stay home from school. Propped up on pillows, sheets
tucked tightly, you listen to the muffled sounds of the
world going about its business. In the stillness and
inaction, you become aware of yourself in an
unfamiliar way: the hands seem narrower; the legs
longer; the swishing in your ears louder. You feel a
rush of freedom, won without any effort on your part.
You've been let loose on an endless, sweet, delicious
day of delirious daydreams packed with fantastic plot
lines in which you play the starring role. John Updike
explores what happens when a nasty fracture snaps a
successful, happily married lawyer out of the "auto-
pilot" of his life. This is the story about the ability to
escape, without a scratch, reproach, or scornful
rebuke, the customary emotional entanglements that
make sexual affairs treacherous. The protagonist finds
he has purchased a round-trip, all expenses paid
ticket into a never-never-land of paramourous lust,
from which he can disengage with none of the usual
consequences. It's a story about having your cake
and eating it too.*

baby's first step

JOHN UPDIKE

glenn morrissey had been an utterly faithful husband until, at the age of thirty-six, he broke his leg playing touch football on the Mall in Washington, D.C., where he lived, as a lawyer employed by the Bureau of Weights and Measures. A heavy young black man had been standing on the sidelines, watching the scrimmage of lawyers and lobbyists and bureaucrats who each fall Sunday assembled down near the Hirshhorn for their afternoon tussle, and since he seemed to be alone, and the sides were uneven, he was invited to play. Assigned to cover Glenn on an out-and-in button-hook pass pattern, he slipped on the soft earth in changing direction and fell against Glenn's braced leg as the ball spiralled toward them. Glenn heard the bone pop—a muscle-muffled *snap*. But the young black picked himself up and scrambled back to the defensive huddle without even an apology, and it took a while for the other players to believe that Glenn, still lying there astonished, was truly injured and could no longer play. He hopped off the field and induced a close friend, Bud Jorgenson, a red-bearded specialist in ethnic art for the Smithsonian Institution, to help him hop the two blocks down 7th Street to his parked car. Glenn drove it back one-footed to his home in Adams-Morgan, a neo-colonial of powdery brick with a sideways view of Rock Creek Park. His wife, Stacey, was out back, giving the roses their fall pruning; she laughed when she saw him hopping toward her and heard his aggrieved voice cry out, "Look what those bad boys did to me!" It was only an hour later, after a trip to Sibley Memorial Hospital and a reading of his X-rays, that she took his injury seriously. His right tibia had been fractured vertically, splitting off the exterior tuberosity, with a messy involvement of the interosseous cartilage that would necessitate an operation, a week in the hospital, and three months in a cast.

Still, Glenn didn't consciously hold Stacey's underreaction against her—she was right; he was a boyish hypochondriac who had cried wolf too often—or the fact that that very night, with him settled and doped in his hospital bed, she went alone to a cocktail party at the Romanian Embassy, where the hors d'oeuvres were famously lavish. He no more had it in him to blame his wife for anything than he would blame himself; he knew her from the inside out—every motive, every reaction—just as he knew himself. In fact, he found her *more* predictable than he did his own self, which still had some depths and twists that took him unawares. You land, it seemed to him, on the shore of your own being in total innocence, like an explorer who was looking for something else, and it takes decades to penetrate inland and map the mountain passes and trace the rivers to their sources. Even then, there are large blanks, where monsters roam.

Being hospitalized, for the first time in his life—measuring out in pills his capacity for pain, sleeping on his back, submitting his most intimate functions to the care and scrutiny of nurses, learning shamelessness and becoming intensely, solicitously conscious of his own body, as well as doing all the forced entertaining, of doctors and visitors, that a hospital patient must do—opened up a new side of his being, a new stretch of potential. He took it all pretty well, was his verdict on himself. He was less of a sissy than he had thought. And then he endured being on crutches, having to carry his papers and possessions in a canvas tote bag while keeping his grip on the sponge-wrapped rungs of the crutches as he levered himself up and down stairs. He compressed, as it were, his physical activity, at home and the office, into a restricted yet still-effective mold—a smaller, more considered version of his previous life, which had been lived without proper appreciation of the miraculous powers of his body.

The late-winter day came when his orthopedist removed the last of a series of gray, itchy, odorous, scribbled-upon casts and pronounced him whole again. Glenn could hardly believe, even though he had taken a few experimental steps in the doctor's office, that he was free to walk on no more support than his own fallible bones. He felt, without the crutches, dizzyingly tall, and oddly vaporous below the waist. He was floating, he was gliding, and when he stepped into the waiting room he thought the other patients were looking up at him as if at a man on stilts. "Baby's first step," he joked, to a woman whose stare seemed especially nonplussed. But her expression remained stupid, and he realized that she didn't see anything extraordinary about him—just a man walking on his own two legs, as most men do.

That night, he and Stacey had a dinner party to attend, at the home of one of the bureau's chief calibrators; as Glenn stepped into the house he seemed still to be miraculously gliding, like Fred Astaire across a polished ballroom floor. He kissed his hostess with particular warmth; he was back among the living, the ambulatory. The party seemed to be his coming-out party, and he the belle of the evening, to whom everything, as to Shakespeare's Miranda, was new. The unknown woman in finespun metallic red sitting next to him at the dinner table was, he realized, alive just as he was; her thorax held the same complex of arteries and veins pounding with blood, clean and unclean, bluish and bright.

"Do I know you?" he asked her, sliding into his chair.

"We met in the living room." Her smile was dazzling, in a lipstick that also seemed metallic. "I'm the wife of your host's brother. My husband and I live in the Midwest."

"The Midwest's a big place."

Vast areas seemed to lie all about him, waiting to be explored. This woman contained patches of ambivalence and vacancy, he realized. We all hold uncertainties yearning to be clarified. There is more play in the human situation than he in his old innocence had dreamed.

"The Minneapolis–St. Paul area," she said.

"Twin Cities," he said, pleased with himself. "I love the way people from there pronounce it—so quickly, all those syllables. How do you stand the winters?"

"We go underground. We have skyways. Our feet never touch the snow."

There was a sparkle, a shimmer, to the skin of her face, its microscopic epidermal grain, as well as to her red dress and her lipstick. Even the transparent fuzz on her upper lip sparkled as it lifted in the tension of a smile. He felt her rising to the challenge his inner space presented to her; she somehow sensed, Glenn was convinced, his

recent initiation, via suffering, into a freemasonry of human exploration and exchange. Their conversation, as the courses came and
went by candlelight and the wine glasses were rhythmically refilled,
became so heated that they had to keep reminding themselves to
turn to the dinner partner on their other side, for courtesy's sake.
Her knee momentarily rested against his healed knee without
apparent awareness; to emphasize a point she smartly tapped the
back of his hand. How delightful she was, how wonderfully quick
to perceive and respond, to parry and thrust! As they sat side by side
at the dining table, Glenn kept picturing their two chests full of
pumping blood, two barrels brimming with mystery.

"Are you in Washington for long?"

"The National Gallery and all those others—I could be happy
here forever! But I must fly back tomorrow, on United at eleven-
forty. My husband is going on to New York on business first thing
in the morning. Our twelve-year-old daughter takes riding lessons
and is doing dressage in a show and would never forgive me if I
weren't there. She'd be in psychoanalysis forever. You know how it
is—one of those moments that won't come again."

"I know," he said, not sure, in his rapture with her, that he did.

The next day, on the excuse of some research at the Library of
Congress, he took a taxi to National Airport to see his dinner-mate
off. Dressed in a trim travelling suit, carrying a small navy-blue
overnight bag whose many-compartmented capacity was left limp
by her gossamer party clothes, she did not seem surprised to see
him. In the human clutter of the obsolescing old airport, with its
spaces and shops like those of a railroad terminal, and its traffic of
robed and sandalled visitors from all points of the globe, they walked
back and forth, Glenn still marvelling at the ease with which his
healed leg carried him. With every step, he seemed to be floating.
The caged volume of her chest hung beside his; they had their arms
about each other's waists like teenagers lounging back from the
beach. As they walked, he carried her bag, which seemed weightless,
and she talked about her children's activities—the girl's equestrian
lessons, and the two boys' hockey practices, which took place at
ungodly hours at a distant rink. "The sacrifices one makes! But you
must, because some day they will be gone." The message was clear:
she was committed, her life was a thousand miles away. The lapel of
her travelling suit held a small brooch of cloisonné enamel, like a

badge of membership in a society whose insignia he could not quite make out. The club of secret dissatisfaction.

He thought of kissing her, but here, in this international clutter, this traffic, it would have been awkward; it was enough to have her head beside his shoulder, so close he could smell on her the morning dew of her face lotion. She was nervous about missing the plane, and he should be back in his office. At the first boarding call, they reported to her gate; he passed her feather-light suitcase into her hand; they hugged, pressing their chests together; he bent his face to her shoulder and kissed the padded cloth. "Will you forget me?" she asked hurriedly in his ear, in a voice gone husky.

"Why would I do that?"

"You'll have all those others."

"What others?" he asked.

"You'll see." Adroitly she backed off and melted into the boarding line; Glenn missed some of the expressive nuances of her darting, apologetic farewell gestures, for his eyes, amazingly, had mustered tears. More gratifying still, in the few seconds of their embrace he had felt behind his fly the furtive pang of an erection commencing, the tingling throb of the areolar spaces embarking upon engorgement. He was alive, he was full of passion—a barrel waiting to be tapped.

They never met again; she had been a false dawn. Perhaps every major campaign in life needs a false start, a dry run, a resetting of the compass. Riding lessons in Minneapolis were a mere obstructive detail; the possibilities had been established. In the carnival of Washington, with its constant demonstrations, its litter of yesterday's placards, its picketing maniacs and widespread dangerous neighborhoods, there is room for romance and anarchic adventure. All those women, the wives underemployed and the employed women usually single, and all those demure side streets, frothy with flowering azalea and cherry, and the constant parties, and the seething of political gossip, of discontent, of official turnover and hoped-for advancement. War is a well-known aphrodisiac, and Washington is always at war. As the men rise and fall on the ladders of power, women are stimulated to take chances. The touch of Southern indolence in the air helps. Los Angeles and New York, by comparison, are too much in love with work—sex, like lunch, is tightly harnessed to business.

Stacey's best friend was a similarly lean, attractive, exercise-and cause-conscious mother of two, named Andrea Jorgenson. Bud was her husband; he travelled to third-world countries for the Smithsonian, bringing back sculptures made mostly, it seemed, of hair and straw. Andrea had appeared to Glenn rather opaque and standardized hitherto; now, as he turned upon her the powerful beam of his new knowledge—we are all full of warm darkness, unformed and inquisitive—her bones began to glow. It was a simple series of knight's moves, on the skewed chessboard of L'Enfant's city plan, to give her his ear at a party or two (his head bowed like that of a doctor listening to her heartbeat with a stethoscope), and then to indicate with a minute pressure of his hand during a fund-raising ball that a certain unspoken path was open, and then to suggest that, now that her children were both in boarding school and she was working toward a Ph.D. at Georgetown University, she write a paper, with his help, on the failure of metrication in the United States. From there it was just a few pushed pawns to lunches *à deux* downtown, and finally to his afternoon infiltration of her home and occupation of her bed. Bud was off in Mali and Chad, dodging civil wars.

Glenn had been in the Jorgensons' house in Woodley Park many times, as a married guest of the couple, but had never seen it in the quiet of the day, as a possessor of sorts. These chairs and tables, curtains and rugs had all been selected and tended by a sensibility akin to Stacey's yet distinctly other. The bathroom had little beribboned jars of potpourri set about, and pink toilet paper with a quilted texture, and a padded seat to match, and a long-handled brush and a loofah on the sill where the bathtub met the tiles, so he felt invited to picture Andrea scrubbing and buffing herself to a sub-epithelial rosiness, within a sloshing pond of suds. The tub and sink were of some black substance like polished slate or lava, and large mirrors here and there made the sight of one's naked body unavoidable. Andrea was a closet sybarite, just as Stacey was a closet ascetic, though, seeing the two women side by side at a lunch table, one would think them identical.

Andrea fancied not the prim pastel bed linen Stacey preferred but splashy hot-colored floral patterns. She provided, once, in his honor, purple satin sheets, which were disconcertingly slippery; the pillows squirted out from under their bodies like greased pigs. On the walls, even in the bedroom, hairy, hollow-eyed masks stared down, and on bookshelves and table tops carved fertility symbols thrust buttocks in one direction and breasts in the other. The violence of the African artifacts made Glenn slightly uncomfortable. Andrea's absent husband seemed to be present in them, staring through the eye-holes of grimacing masks.

Strange to say, part of the pleasure of Andrea's house was leaving it behind. Glenn would slip out the back door, stride quickly, purposefully along the side of the house like a meter reader up from the basement, and, with relaxing breath, walk the slant sidewalk to his car, parked for discretion's sake in the next block of hushed Washington homes—their gables politely looking the other way, their neo-classic porchlets void of daytime visitors, their walls of powdery or painted brick and plantings both lush and trimmed all conspiring with him to keep his secret, as he, a white man in a business suit, exercised his American right to walk wherever he wished.

One day after three months of such visits, he must have, in his post-coital relaxation, confided something admiring about the décor, because Andrea said, with a jarring vehemence, "God, if Bud brings back one more Ashanti fertility doll or Bambara antelope headdress, I think I'll scream. I honestly think I might leave him if he gets any more African."

Glenn was jarred because he wanted to think that Andrea's marriage, like his own, was basically happy. "Really?"

"Really. What I'm *really* scared he's going to bring back from these trips is AIDS. The whole continent is lousy with it. I'm terrified of sleeping with him."

"But—do you think he...?"

He didn't finish; she snorted at his delicacy. "People do," she said, her angry gesture taking in their naked bodies, on the wrinkled sheet, with its dangerous-looking pattern of red roses and green thorns. "It's human nature, darling."

"You know, that didn't come home to me until I broke my leg last year." He went on, as if selling her husband back to her, "Bud was so nice that day; he was the only one who cared. Not even Stacey cared." The accident had happened in the fall; this was May, on the verge of uncomfortable summer heat; soon, people would be leaving the District for the mountains, for the shore. "Where would you go if you left him?"

The question was idle, but her answer was not. Andrea propped herself up on an elbow to give it. Though they had closed the Venetian blinds, the bedroom was still bright, the sharp spring sunlight clamoring at the windows like a noisy pack of children. Her face—her fine, lean, well-cared-for face, whereon sun and chronic social animation had engraved tiny wrinkles, at the corners of her eyes and mouth—confronted him with that female openness and depth of interrogation which remind men of the dark, of the ocean, of the night sky, of everything swallowing and terminating. But her manner of speaking was girlish, embarrassed, offhand. "With you somewhere?" She primly wrapped the top of the sheet around her breasts and settled her mussed fair head back on the pillow to hear his answer.

Again, there was a muffled *snap*. He had entered more new territory, barren stretches of disappointment and recrimination, under skies gray with tears. He tried to picture it—her in a house of his, them in a house of theirs—and couldn't. What he liked possessing was a woman's accoutrements—her clothes, her blue overnight bag, her distant daughter's riding lessons, her husband's appointment calendar, her exotic black-tubbed bathroom, her entire *nest*. What he wanted was for women to stay put, planted in American plenty, while he ambulated from one to another carrying no more baggage than the suit on his back and the car keys in his pocket. In the years to come, long after Andrea had sunk back angrily into her nest of roses and hairy masks, Glenn experienced a light-headed bliss whenever his feet glided across an illicit threshold, on what felt like stilts.

Everything about this impeccably crafted story vibrates
with the tension of contrary impulses, of antagonistic
realities. Set at the juncture of two centuries and two
civilizations, "The Son" skims along the unruffled
surface of seemingly impeccable conjugality. In the
arid, relentless heat of North Africa, strange states of
consciousness, and even stranger magical spells,
disable willpower so that transgressive desires can
send out roots deep into the soul to bear, by and by,
a poisoned fruit. With characteristically consummate
tact, Ivan Bunin explores the enigmatic, subtle feints
of a respectable married woman poised, with
a lingering backward glance, to escape the
incarceration of matrimonial bliss.

the son

IVAN BUNIN

mme. marot had been born and had grown up in Lausanne, in a strict, honest, and industrious family. She did not marry early, but when she did, hers was a love match. In the March of 1876, among the passengers of the old French steamer *Auvergne*, sailing from Marseilles to Italy, was a newly married couple. The days were calm, cool; the sea, all silvery mirrors, lost itself in the misty spring distances; the newly-married couple scarcely ever left the deck. And all admired them, all beheld their happiness with amiable smiles: he showed his happiness in an alert, keen glance, in the necessity for motion, in an animated amiability to all those around him; she by that joyous interest, with which she assimilated every trifle....This newly married pair was the Marots.

He was some ten years her senior; he was short in height, swarthy of face, with curly hair; his hand was thin, and his voice sonorous. But in her one sensed an admixture of some blood other than that of the Latins. She seemed just the least trifle too tall, although her waist was splendid; though her hair was dark, her eyes were a grayish blue. They travelled through Naples, Palermo and Tunis to the Algerian town of Constantine, where Monsieur Marot had obtained a rather prominent appointment. And life in Constantine those fourteen years which had passed since that happy spring, had given them everything with which people are usually content: a competence, domestic harmony, healthy and handsome children.

During these fourteen years the Marots had changed very much in appearance: his face had become as black as an Arab's, he had grown gray and dried up from work, from travelling, from tobacco, and from the sun,—many took him for a native of Algeria; nor would any one have recognized her as the woman who had been a passenger upon the steamer *Auvergne:* then, even in the shoes she put outside the door at night, there had been the enchantment of youth; now she too had glints of silver in her hair, her skin had grown finer and more aureate, her hands had become thinner, and in her care of them, in the dressing of her hair, in her linen, in her apparel, she already betrayed a certain superfluous nicety. Their relations had changed as well, of course, although none would have said that it was for the worse. And each one led an individual existence: his time was taken up with work,—he still remained as passionate, and, at the same time, as sober a man as he had been before; she had to take care of him, of the children—two very pretty girls, of whom the elder was by now almost a young lady,—and everybody unanimously declared that there was not in all Constantine a better housekeeper, a better mother, or a more charming person to chat with in a drawing room, than Mme. Marot.

Their house stood on a quiet and clean street. From the second story, out of the front rooms, always in semidarkness on account of the closed Venetian blinds, could be seen Constantine, famed all over the world for its picturesqueness: this ancient Arabian stronghold, which had become a French city, lies upon sloping crags. The windows of the living rooms, shady and cool, looked out upon the garden,—there, in a perpetual blaze and glare, dozed age-old eucalypti, sycamores, palms, behind their enclosures of high walls. The master of the house frequently absented himself on matters connected with his work. As for the mistress, she led that confined existence to which, in the colonies, the wives of all Europeans are condemned. On Sundays she invariably attended church. On week days she rarely went out and restricted herself to a small, choice circle. She read, busied herself with embroidery, chatted with the children or took part in their lessons; sometimes, putting the dark-eyed Marie, her younger daughter, on her knees, and playing on the pianoforte with one hand, she would sing old-fashioned French songs, to make the long African day seem shorter, while the hot wind entered in a flood from the garden through the wide-open windows.... Constantine, under the pitiless blaze of the sun and with all its shutters closed, seemed at these hours a dead city: only the roller-birds called out behind the walls of the gardens, and plaintively, with the nostalgia of colonial lands, sounded the trumpets of the buglers on the knolls beyond the city, where at times the cannons made the earth shake with a dull rumble, and one saw the white helmets of the soldiers twinkling.

The days in Constantine passed monotonously, but no one ever remarked that Mme. Marot was oppressed by this. In her character, exquisite and chaste, never appeared any heightened sensitiveness, nor any surplus nervousness. Her health could not be called robust, but it never caused any alarm to Monsieur Marot. Only one incident had struck him: once, in Tunis, and Arab magician had put her so rapidly into a profound sleep, that she had great difficulty in coming back to herself. But this had been still at the time of their journey from France; since that time she had not experienced any such sharp declines of will power, any such unwholesome susceptibility. And Monsieur Marot was happy, tranquil, and convinced that her soul was undisturbed and like an open book to him. And so it really was, even during the last—the fourteenth—year of his domestic life....But now there appeared in Constantine a certain Emile du Buys.

Emile du Buys, son of Mme. Bonnet, an old and close friend of the Marots, was only nineteen years of age. Mme. Bonnet, the widow of an engineer, had also a daughter, Eliza, besides Emile, who was born of the first marriage. He had grown up in Paris and was already reading law; but, above all, he was taken up with the composition of verses which were comprehensible to him alone, and had attached himself to a non-existent school of poetry, "The Seekers." In the May of 1889 Eliza was preparing for the altar, but took sick and died a few days after. Emile, who had never up to now been in Constantine, had come for the funeral. It is easy to understand how touched Mme. Marot was by this death,—this death of a girl who was already trying on the bridal veil; everyone also knows how under such circumstances intimacy is established even between people who have scarce come to know one another. In addition, Emile was in reality only a boy to Mme. Marot. Shortly after the funeral, Mme. Bonnet went to France, to her relatives. Emile remained in Constantine, at the suburban county house of his late stepfather,—at the Villa Hassim, as it was called in the town,—and began to visit the Marots almost daily. No matter what sort of a chap he may have been, or whatever he may have pretended to be, he was, never the less, very young, very sensitive, and had need of people with whom he might seek shelter for a time. "And isn't it strange," said some, "Mme. Marot has become unrecognizable! How animated she has become; how she has improved in looks!"

However, these allusions were unfounded. At first all it amounted to was that her existence became a trifle gayer, and that her girls became more playful and coquettish, for Emile, every minute forgetting his grief and that virus with which, as he thought, the *fin de siècle* had envenomed him, fussed for hours at a time with them, altogether as their equal. Of course he was, after all, a man, a Parisian, and not altogether of an ordinary nature; he had participated in that life which Parisian writers lead, so inaccessible to common mortals; frequently, with a certain somnambulistic expressiveness, he would read strange but sonorous verses; and, perhaps, it was precisely thanks to him that the step of Mme. Marot became lighter and quicker, her house apparel just the least trifle smarter, and the nuances of her voice kindlier and more mocking; there may have been, after all, a drop of purely feminine joy in her soul over the fact that here was a man whom it was possible to lord it over somewhat, with whom it was possible to speak with a half jesting sententiousness, with that freedom which was so naturally permitted by the difference in their years. And also over the fact that here was one who was so devoted to her entire household,—where, however, the first person for him (this, of course was revealed very quickly) was still none other than she. But then, how commonplace all this is! Yet for the most part he was merely pitiful to her.

He, who sincerely deemed himself a poet born, wanted to resemble a poet in appearance as well; he wore his hair long, and tossed back; he dressed with an artistic sobriety; he had fine brown hair, which went well with his pale face, just as his black clothes did; but this pallor was too anæmic, with a yellow tinge; his eyes glittered constantly, but, because of his enervated face, they seemed feverish; and his chest was so thin and flat, his legs were so thin, his hands so bony, that one became somewhat ill at ease when he would grow immoderately lively and would run through the street or garden, bending somewhat forward, as though he were sliding, in order to hide his defect,—he had one leg shorter than the other. In society he was disagreeable, supercilious; he tried to be enigmatic, negligent; or, at times, exquisitely impertinent, audacious, at others disdainfully absent-minded and independent in all things; but only too frequently he did not sustain his rôles to the end,—he would forget his part and begin speaking with a certain naïve candour and impulsiveness. And, of course, he could not manage to hide his feelings for long, to dissemble as an unbeliever in love and happiness on this earth: the entire house soon knew of his being in love. He had already begun to bore the master of the house with his visits; he began to bring, every day, bouquets of the rarest flowers from his villa, to sit at the Marots' from morn till night, to recite verses more and more incomprehensible,—the children heard him, more than once, abjuring some one to die with him; while at nights he took to disappearing in the native quarters, in those dives where the Arabs, wrapped up in their dirty white *bournouses*, avidly watch stomach dances and drink the most pungent of liquors....To put it briefly, not even a month and a half had gone before his inamoration had passed into God only knows what.

His nerves ceased entirely to serve him. Once he sat through almost an entire day in silence; then got up, took his hat, and went out,—and half an hour later was brought in from the street in a dreadful condition: he was writhing in hysterics; he was sobbing so vehemently that he frightened both the children and the domestics. But Mme. Marot, it seemed, did not attach any special significance even to this transport. She herself was restoring him back to consciousness, herself hastily untying his cravat and persuading him to be a man, and she only smiled when he, without any restraint whatsoever before her husband, caught at her hands, covering them with kisses and vowing his disinterested devotion. Still, it was necessary to put an end to all this. And so when Emile, whom the children had soon missed, again made his appearance several days after the fit, already calmed, even though he resembled a man who had gone through a severe illness, Mme. Marot gently told him all that is usually said in such cases.

"My friend, you are really like a son to me," she had said to him, uttering for the first time this word, "son," and really feeling almost a maternal tenderness toward him. "Do not, then, put me in a ridiculous and painful position."

"But I swear to you that you are mistaken!" he exclaimed, with earnest vehemence. "I am only devoted to you; I only want to see you, and no more!"

And he suddenly fell down on his knees,—they were in the garden on a calm, sultry, dusky evening,—impulsively seized her by her hips, on the verge of fainting from passion....And gazing upon his hair, upon his white, slender neck, she, with anguish and rapture, reflected:

"Ah,—yes, yes, I could have had a son almost the same as he!"

Still, from that time until his very departure for France, he committed no more insane actions. Essentially this was bad; it may have signified that his passion had become deeper. But outwardly everything had changed for the better,—only one other time he could not restrain himself. After dinner one Sunday, in the presence of several strangers, he said to her, without at all reflecting that this might attract attention:

"I most earnestly entreat you to grant me one minute...."

She got up and went with him into the empty, half-dark parlour. He walked up to the window, through which the evening light penetrated from outside in narrow longitudinal streaks, and, looking her straight in the face, said:

"To-day is the anniversary of my father's death. I love you!"

She turned to go away. Frightened, he hastened to add as she was going away:

"Forgive me,—this is the first time and the last!"

And truly, she heard no new admissions from him. "I was enchanted by her confusion," he wrote in his diary that evening, in his choice and grandiloquent style; "I vowed to violate her peace no more: for am I not beatified even as it is?" He continued going into the town,—he only slept at the Villa Hassim; and his behaviour varied, but he always observed a greater or lesser degree of seemliness. At times he was, as formerly, inappropriately playful, naïve, romping with the children in the garden; most frequently of all, however, he sat near her and "drank in her presence," read newspapers and novels to her, and "was happy because she listened to him." "The children did not interfere with us," he wrote of these days, "their voices, laughter, bustle, their very beings, seemed to serve as the finest of conductors for our emotions; thanks to them these emotions were still more enchanting; we held the commonest of every day conversations, but something else could be heard in them,—our happiness; yes,—yes; she, too was happy, I affirm this. She liked to hear me declaim; of evenings, from the balcony, we contemplated Constantine lying at our feet in the blue radiance of the moon...."

Finally, in August, Mme. Marot insisted upon his going away, return-ing to his studies,—and won; and *en route* he entered in his diary: "I am going away! Going away, empoisoned by the bitter delight of parting! She has bestowed upon me, in parting, a bit of velvet rib-bon that she had worn about her neck as a girl. When the last minute came, she gave me her blessing, and I saw a humid sparkle in her eyes when she said: 'Farewell, dear son of mine!...'"

Whether he was right in his conjecture that Mme. Marot also was happy in August, is not known. But that his departure proved painful to her is beyond a doubt. This word "son," which had stirred her even previously, now took on such a sound for her that she could not hear it in peace. Even formerly, upon meeting friends on her way to church, who would jestingly say to her: "What should you pray about, Mme. Marot; you are without sin and happy as it is!" she had, more than once, replied with a sad smile: "I complain to God because he has deprived me of a son..." Now the thought of a son, of that happiness which he would have ceaselessly given her by his mere existence in this world, never left her. And once, shortly after the departure of Emile, she had said to her husband:

"Now I have comprehended everything! I now know surely, that every mother ought to have a son; that every woman who has no son, if she will but ponder upon herself, will check up her entire life, will see that she is unhappy. You are a man, you cannot feel this, but it is so....Oh, how tenderly and passionately one can love a son!"

She was very kind to her husband that fall. Occasionally, when she would be left alone with him, she would shyly say to him:

"Hector, listen....I am ashamed now to ask you about it,—but still....Do you ever recall the March of 'seventy-six?...Ah, if only you and I had a son!"

"All this confused me very much," Monsieur Marot would say subsequently,—"it confused me all the more because she began to grow very thin. She was growing weaker, was becoming more and more silent and gentle in manner. She went less and less often to her friends,—she avoided going to the city unless it were unavoid-able....I do not doubt that some dreadful and incomprehensible ail-ment was taking possession of her soul and body!" While the *bonne* added that, whenever Mme. Marot went out of the house that fall, she always put on a thick white veil,—something she had never done before; that, returning home, she would immediately raise her veil in front of a mirror and would intently scrutinize her tired face. It is superfluous to explain that which went on in her soul at this time. But did she want to see Emile, did he write to her, and did she reply to him? He presented two dispatches at court, purporting to be addressed to him, in answer to his letters. One was dated the tenth of November: "You are driving me mad. Calm yourself. Let me have immediate news of yourself." The other, the twenty-third of December: "No, no, do not come, I implore you. Think of me, love me, as a mother." But the certainty of these dispatches having been sent by her could not be proven, of course. One thing only is certain,—that from September until January Mme. Marot led a distressed, troubled, painful existence.

The late autumn of that year in Constantine was cold and rainy. Then, as is always the case in Algeria, a ravishing spring came on. And an animation,—that beatific, exquisite headiness which is experienced at the time of the blossoming of spring by people who have already left their youth behind them,—again began to return to Mme. Marot. She again began to go out; rode out a great deal with her children, went with them to the garden of the deserted Villa Hassim; she contemplated an excursion to Algiers,—to show her children Blidah, near which, in the mountains, there is a wooded ravine, a spot beloved of monkeys....And so things went right up to the seventeenth of January in the year of 1890. On the seventeenth of January, she awoke from some unusually joyous and tender emotion, which, so it had seemed to her, had stirred her all night long. In the large room where she slept alone during the absence of her husband, who had gone away for a long time on matters connected with his post, it was almost dark because of the Venetian blinds and the window curtains. Still, by that blueish pallor which penetrated from behind them, one could gather that it was still early. And, in confirmation, the little clock on the night-table pointed to six. With an enjoyable sense of the morning freshness entering from the garden, she rolled up in a light blanket and turned to the wall.... "Why do I feel so fine?" she thought, dozing off. And, like dim, beautiful visions, pictures of Italy, of Sicily, began to appear before her, pictures of that distant spring when she was sailing in a cabin whose windows looked out on deck, upon the chill silvery shimmer of the sea; a cabin with portieres of red silk, shrivelled and faded by time, and with a high threshold glittering with brass that had been worn down by many years of cleaning....Then she saw the limitless bays of the sea; lagoons; lowlands; a great Arabian town, all white, with flat roofs, and with undulating mistily blue knolls and foot-hills beyond it. This was Tunis, in which she had been but once, on that very same spring when she had been in Naples, and in Palermo....But here a wave of cold seemed to go through her,—and, with a shiver, she opened her eyes. It was already going on nine o'clock; one could hear the voices of the children, the voice of their *bonne*. She arose, threw on a *peignoir*, and, stepping out on the balcony, descended into the garden and sat down on a rocker, standing in the sand near a round table underneath a mimosa in blossom, spreading its golden canopy over-head, its fragrance heavy in the sun. The maid brought her coffee. She again began to think of Tunis, and recalled that strange experience she had gone through, that sweet fear and that beatific abnega-tion of her will which was like that of pre-mortal moments,—an experience she had undergone in that pale blue city in the warm, rosy dusk, half-reclining in a rocker on the roof of a house, vaguely seeing the dark face of the Arab hypnotist and magician who was squatting on his heels before her, lulling her to sleep with his barely audible, monotonous sing-song, and the slow movements of his thin hands. And suddenly, even as she was thinking thus and mechanically gazing with eyes wide-open upon a bright silvery spark with which a teaspoon in a glass of water was aflame, she suddenly lost con-science. And when she came to with a start, Emile was standing over her. All that took place subsequent to this unexpected meeting is known from the words of Emile himself,—from his story, from his answers to interrogations. "Yes, I dropped into Constantine as though from heaven!" he had said. "I had come because I had comprehend-ed that the powers of heaven itself could not stop me. On the morn-ing of the seventeenth of January, straight from the station, without any word of warning, I appeared at the house of Monsieur Marot and ran into the garden. I was dumbfounded by that which met my eyes; but I had scarce made a step when she came to. She, it seemed, was also amazed, both by the unexpectedness of my appearance, and that which she had just been through; but she did not even emit an exclamation. Having looked at me, like a person just awakened from a deep sleep, she got up from her seat, putting her hair in order.

" 'That's the very presentiment I had,' she said, somehow without any expression. 'You did not obey me!'

"And with an accustomed gesture, having buttoned the *peignoir* at her breast, she took my head in both her hands and kissed me twice on the forehead.

"I lost my head from rapture and passion, but she gently put me aside and said:

"'Let us go; I am not dressed,—I shall return at once, go to the children....'

"'But, for God's sake, what was the matter with you?' I asked, ascending after her to the balcony.

"'Oh, a mere nothing—a slight trance. I had gazed too long at a glittering tea-spoon,' she was answering, getting control of herself, and beginning to speak with more animation. 'But what have you done, what have you done!'

"I did not find the children anywhere; the house was empty and quiet; I sat down in the parlour. Suddenly I heard her begin singing in a distant room in a strong, sonorous voice, but I did not then comprehend all the horror of that sound, because I was all atremble with a nervous ague. I had not slept all night; I had counted the minutes as the train had sped me toward Constantine; I jumped into the first *fiacre* I had met upon running out of the depot; I did not expect to reach the height of the city....I knew, I, too, had a premonition, that my arrival would be fatal for us; but still I could not expect that which I had seen in the garden, this mystical meeting, and such a sharp change in her attitude toward me! After ten minutes, she came out with her hair dressed, in a light-gray dress of an iris tint.

"Ah,' said she, as I was kissing her hand, 'but I had forgotten that to-day is Sunday, and that the children are in church; but then, I have over-slept....The children will go to the pine grove after church,—were you ever there?'

"And, without waiting for my answer, she rang, ordered some coffee to be served to me, and, sitting down, began to look at me intently, and, without listening, began to question me as to how I had lived, what I had been doing. She started to speak about herself, of the fact that after two or three months, which had been very bad for her, during which she had aged dreadfully,—these words were uttered with sort of incomprehensible smile,—she was feeling well, as young as never before....I replied, I listened, but did not understand a great deal; both of us said anything but that which we wanted to say; my hands grew chill from the nearness of that other fearful, inevitable hour. I do not deny that I was struck as if by lightning when she had said 'I have aged....' I suddenly saw that she was right: in the thinness of her hands, and of the faded, even though really rejuvenated face, in the slenderness of certain outlines of the body, I caught certain signs of that which compels our hearts to contract so painfully, and even somehow awkwardly,—yet all the more passionately,—at the sight of an aging woman. 'Ah, yes, how rapidly and sharply she had changed!' I reflected. But she was beautiful, never the less. I was growing intoxicated as I gazed upon her. I had grown accustomed to dreaming of her without end; I had not forgotten that moment, when on the evening of the eleventh of July, I had first embraced her knees. Her hands, too, were slightly trembling, when she was putting her *coiffure* in order, smiling, and gazing at me; and suddenly—you will understand all the catastrophic force of this moment!—suddenly, this smile was distorted, somehow; and, with difficulty, but firmly, she uttered:

"'Still, you ought to go home, to rest up from the journey; your appearance is dreadful; you have such suffering, fearful eyes and such burning lips, that I no longer have the strength to see them....Do you wish me to?—I shall go there in your company....'

"And, without letting me answer, she got up and went away to get her hat and cloak....

"We arrived quickly at the Villa Hassim. I lingered near the entrance, in order to pluck some flowers. She did not wait for me, opening the door herself. I had no servants; there was only the caretaker,—he did not see us. When I stepped into the ante-room, hot and half dark because of the closed Venetian blinds, and offered her the flowers, she kissed them, then embracing me with one hand, she kissed me. From emotion her lips were hot, but her voice was clear.

"But listen...how shall we...have you anything with you?' she asked.

"I did not at first understand her,—so had this first kiss, this first familiar 'you' overwhelmed me,—and I mumbled:

"'What do you want to say?'

"She took a step back.

"'What!' she said in astonishment, almost sternly. 'Can you possibly have thought that I...that we can live after this? Have you anything with you that we may die?'

"I recovered my wits and hastened to show her a revolver loaded with five bullets, with which I never parted.

"She rapidly went on, from room to room. The semi-darkness was everywhere. Hearing only the rustle of her silken skirts, I followed after her, with that confusion of all the senses with which a naked man goes on a sultry day into the sea. Finally we arrived at the end of our journey; she threw off her cloak and began to untie the ribbons of her hat. Her hands were still trembling, and once more I remarked through the dusk something pitiful and tired in her face....

"But she died without wavering. During the last moments she became transformed. Kissing me, and leaning back in order to see my face, she told me, in a whisper, a few more words so tender and touching that I have not the strength to repeat them.

"I wanted to go to pluck some more flowers, in order to strew our funeral couch with them. She did not let me, she was hurried, she was saying: 'No, no, it is not necessary...there are plenty of flowers...here are your flowers'—and she kept on repeating:

"'And so, I charge you, by all that you hold sacred, that you kill me!'

"'Yes, and then myself,' said I, not for a second doubting my resolution.

"'Oh, I believe you, I believe you!' she answered, by now as if in a trace....

"A minute before her death she said, very quietly, but simply: 'My God, this is a deed without a name!'

"And again:

"'Where are the flowers you gave me? Kiss me—for the last time.'

"She herself put the muzzle of the revolver up to her temple. I wanted to shoot, but she stopped me:

"'No, that isn't right,—let me show you the right way. Here, so, my child....And *afterward* make the sign of the cross over me, and lay the flowers upon my breast....'

"When I fired, she moved her lips slightly. I fired once more....

"She lay there, calm; in her extinguished gaze there was some bitter beatitude. Her hair was spread out; a tortoise shell comb was thrown upon the floor. Swaying, I got up, to put an end to myself. But, despite the Venetian blinds, it was light in the room; and in this light, and amid this quiet which had suddenly arisen all about me, I distinctly saw her face, already grown pallid....And here a sudden madness possessed me,—I dashed to the window, throwing apart, flinging open the shutters, and began to shout, and to shoot into the air....The rest you know...."

In the spring, five years ago, travelling over Algeria, the writer of these lines visited Constantine. He often recalls now those evenings, rainy and chill, but spring evenings never the less, which he passed by the fireplace in the reading room of a certain old and homelike French hotel. Upon the heavy, elaborate étagères there lay tattered illustrated journals—in them one could find some faded portraits of Mme. Marot, at different ages,—among them, one taken in Lausanne, when she was a girl....Her story is told here again, through a strong desire of telling it in my own way.

On the stairs, pilloried in the bannisters of his own
house, a spectator to his own life and to an
outrageous series of family scandals in the making,
the protagonist of "Jamaica" is going nowhere. As the
members of his hyper-dysfunctional family plot their
getaways from the mighty fortress of normalcy he has
erected, the pater familias mutters, "Hoc feci"—"This
have I wrought." Schickler's hilarious parable on the
pitfalls of domesticity pushes every escape button in
our psyche. After all, there comes a point in the life of
every middle-class American when the good 'n' plenty
that comes with affluence is just so much stuff—a
trap for the soul, an encumbrance for the mind, a
deep freeze for the heart—that threatens to turn the
family into an airless canyon of lovelessness and
boredom. But—and here's the radiant twist—the ties
that bind are also a connection. Blessed are the stuck,
for they will glimpse the sweetness of sticking it out.

jamaica

DAVID SCHICKLER

my name is Everett Dose, and once a month my wife, Jillian, hosts a meeting of the Gorgon Book Club in our living room. The Gorgons are six women. Two, Luce Winningham and Gwen Kirkle, are divorcées. One, Dorry Smith, is a semi-professional archer. My wife, Jillian, is the fourth Gorgon, and the fifth is our daughter, Theresa, who lives with her boyfriend and has a severely pierced face. I have mentioned to Jillian several times that the mythological Gorgons were only three in number and petrifyingly ugly, and that the book club is therefore misnamed, especially considering Luce Winningham's fetching Peter Pan haircut and her perky disdain for brassieres. When I offer such commentary, Jillian reminds me that N.F.L. football is a brutal mystery to her and tells me to take out the garbage.

I'm forty-four now, and I've built a decent life for Jillian and myself and our two children. (My son, Thomas, is twelve, blind, and polite.) For eighteen years, I've edited news for a local television network, WAOK, here in Chicago. If the mayor complains about graft, the White Sox, and Internet porn, I trim which footage gets aired (the porn). If a guy on a ledge blathers his unhinged woes, I consider his case, and do or do not grant him a continuance. I mix in occasional shots of newborn pandas or of glasnost, but I'm usually editing plight. Last week, on Route 94, a Skokie man in a Datsun hit a twelve-point buck, cutting its legs clean off. The poor chump (the man, I mean) ended up at the morgue with antlers up his nose, and I had to air still shots of a deer torso shoved through a windshield.

Still, grim as my calling can be, I make enough money to shield my family from most of the traumas I dice and chop at AOK. Our house has an antique staircase, and Jillian knits pleasant, pastel-colored sweaters for Thomas and our dachshund, T.J. Yes, disorder can creep in: we have mice in our basement and walls. In response, however, my son and I are training T.J. to hunt the little vermin. It's a difficult process involving an alarm whistle and the Pavlovian encouragement of dog biscuits, but some night soon my dachshund will race to Jillian's feet and drop from his jaws a mouse with a snapped neck, and my mastery of this household will be publicly confirmed.

As for the Gorgons, it surprises me not at all that they hold their powwows in my living room, because it's a damn fine living room. Currently, it's decorated for Christmas. There's a brick hearth with frosted holly on the mantel, and a ten-foot-high tree that I felled myself. Every year, little blind Thomas trims the tree with no help from anyone: I watch and weep with joy at the life, the home I've created. So what if Jillian banishes me to my upstairs den on Gorgon nights? I'm more comfortable there anyway, especially because of the sixth and final Gorgon, Abigail Van Roost.

Abigail, Jillian, and I attended the same high school in Cicero. Abby and Jillian were friends, and in junior year Abby and I, as track-and-field teammates, fell in love. Abby was a hurdler, I was a pole-vaulter, and each day after practice we walked down to the Nathan Gandy Apothecary, where I bought Heath bars for Abby and fucked her behind the Dumpster. Those were high old times, but they ended tragically our senior year. Abby's father, Jared, managed a down-in-the-mouth chicken-packing warehouse, and on snowy winter afternoons Abby often set up her hurdles in the warehouse and practiced her sprints there. One day, in mid-workout, Abby skidded out and somehow got herself run over by a forklift. Her legs were crushed completely and her face got, well, mangled, and she's been in a wheelchair ever since. Jared Van Roost closed his already faltering business, I (out of cowardice) split with Abby and took up with Jillian, and now most Chicagoans are patrons of Cheeper Chicken, a Toronto-based poultry outfit that has made disturbingly strong inroads into the American heartland. Anyway, the silver lining (which it's sometimes my job to find) is that Abby married Dr. Bob Beach, a wealthy dermatologist, and now when Dr. Bob drops Abby by for Gorgon nights both her skin and her demeanor positively glow. She apparently bears no ill will toward me or Jillian, but I still find myself ashamed whenever I see her. My boy Thomas, on the other hand, is Abby's bosom buddy. He loves to sit cross-legged beside Abby's wheelchair, and the Gorgons always choose books that are available in Braille or on audiotape so that my little man can keep up.

It's eight o'clock right now, and I'm sitting in my den, where I've just finished reading "Meet Your Maker," the best-selling potboiler that the Gorgons will discuss at eight-thirty. "Meet Your Maker" is the latest novel by the Chicago native Joseph Hederal recounting the adventures of Detective Wesley Truth, a broad-shouldered Buddhist gumshoe who meditates his way around the Windy City, solving homicides and bedding housewives. When I tell Jillian that it makes no sense for a Buddhist to carry nunchakus, Jillian tells me that Wesley Truth is a dark, complex man and that Eastern religions are full of surprises.

I step out of my den and descend a third of the way downstairs. I sit on the stairs and gaze down through the banisters. Jillian's in the kitchen, breaking out almond cookies and brandy and icing her famous Chocolate Chaos cake. She has already set around the coffee table the giant throw pillows on which the Gorgons will recline. In his basket near the roaring hearth, T.J. the dachshund stretches and yawns. Beneath the glittering tree, among wrapped Christmas gifts, sits Thomas, facing the door, waiting for Abby. I try to ignore the fact that T.J. and Thomas are wearing matching sweaters that feature hyper-enthused elves somersaulting down ice hills. I lean my forehead against two bannisters, wishing to join the warm cheer on the other side of the bars. Staring at all the bounty below, I recall a Latin phrase from my old school days.

"*Hoc feci*," I say softly.

I press my forehead harder against the bannisters, like a child at a windowpane. I made this, I made all that I'm seeing. Light spangles off the tree ornaments. T.J. sighs. Proud tears brim in my eyes.

"*Hoc feci.*" I strain forward even more, whispering my incantation, my credo. Then, quite suddenly, my head pops between the bannisters. "Ouch!"

Thomas cocks his head in several directions. Many blind folk have uncanny senses of smell and hearing, and can determine your position from the slightest movement. Thomas isn't one of those folk.

"Dad?" he says.

"I'm on the stairs, buddy." I pull my head back, but it stays budged. "I'm stuck."

Jillian enters the living room, sets the brandy bottle on the coffee table, and sees me. "Everett," she says, "go away."

"I can't, Jills. I'm stuck. Look." I slide my head down, aligning it with the skinniest parts of the bannisters, and tug myself backward. The bannisters, which are made of the finest Indonesian teak, thump against my skull. They do not release me. "This is the darnedest thing," I say.

Jillian puts her hands on her hips. "Stop playing, Everett. Go upstairs at once."

"I'm not playing. Watch." I wiggle my head. I shuck and jive it back and forth, but no dice. I start laughing.

"You're not amusing me," says my wife.

I roll my wrists over the handrail, and make a long face, like a man in the stocks.

"What's wrong with Dad?" Thomas says.

Jillian stares up at me. "Everett, you know you're not welcome at book club. If you stop clowning and go upstairs this minute, I'll give you a Popsicle later. All right?"

A Popsicle is Jillian's code word for a blow job. It is a rare offer, and an even rarer event.

"Jillian, I'm not kidding. I'm stuck. I got my head in here, and I can't get it out. It's like a Christmas miracle or something."

"I want a Popsicle," Thomas says.

Jillian marches up the stairs. T.J. follows her.

"What you're claiming is against the laws of physics, Everett." Jillian grabs my shoulders and starts yanking me backward, clumping my head against the bannisters. My mouse-alarm whistle, which I wear inside my shirt on a necklace, digs at my clavicle.

"Not really." I cough. "It's like when you push a cork into a wine bottle by mistake, and you can't extract it. Also, what you're doing really hurts."

T.J., who likes to lick my face, starts whining because he can't get at me. Instead, he nibbles my ankle.

"I'm all right, boy," I say. And I am. For some reason, I feel great. It's my staircase, after all.

Jillian keeps tugging. It's not that my wife hates me, by the way. Just last Friday night, I bowled a two-forty-three at Sycamore Lanes, and Jillian congratulated me twice the next day, without any prompting.

"This is one for the books," I say.

"Come on, you," Jillian mutters at my skull. She folds my ears closed, making my head an aerodynamic bullet.

I hear a distant pinging. "Is that the doorbell?"

Jillian lets go of my ears. "Thomas," she grunts, "get the door."

Thomas does, and in walks his sister, Theresa, who is nineteen and sleeping with a thirty-five-year-old truck driver named Huey.

"Hi, sweetheart." I wave to Theresa.

Theresa kisses Thomas on the head. She scowls up at me. "Go away, Everett," she says.

"I believe my name is Dad."

Jillian has fetched some Vaseline and is anointing my entire head. I try to be civil with Theresa.

"How's Huey?" I say. It pains me to ask this, because every time I think of Theresa and her scruffy, lecherous man friend I picture my daughter in a four-way with Huey and two other truckers named Dewey and Louie. It is an unhealthy image.

"How'd you get like that?" demands Theresa.

My wife grabs me by the waist of my pants and hauls hard, placing unwelcome pressure on my testicles.

"Jillian, enough," I say, losing patience.

With a snort, my wife stops. I don't blame her for not wanting me at Gorgon Club. When she joins me for nights out with the guys, calamity strikes. One time two years ago, Jillian accompanied me and my buddies to Sycamore Lanes and proceeded to bowl an eleven. I'm talking eleven points total, for ten frames, with smirking, beer-filled men as witnesses. Nine one-pin frames followed by a final, mighty two-pin frame. That's marriage.

Luce Winningham and the ever platinum-blond Gwen Kirkle walk through the door, which Thomas has left open.

"Health and happiness to all!" announces Gwen, who runs a vitamin shop and supports animal rights. I immediately detect Luce Winningham's perfume.

Jillian leans close to my ear. "You better behave," she whispers.

"Oh. Hi, Everett." Gwen is looking up at me, frowning. She's angry that I televised photos of a legless, windshield-encrusted deer.

Jillian sweeps downstairs, hugs her divorced pals. "Welcome,

Gorgons."

"I smell Luce Winningham," Thomas says.

"Good call, son," I say, though we all smell her.

Luce and Gwen stare up at me. Gwen's low neckline is a holiday treat. Despite her pro-kasha diet and my taste for raw-sirloin sandwiches, I've thought often over the years that Gwen and I were on the verge of a torrid affair. Finally, at a cocktail party this past August, Gwen pulled me into a coatroom. I braced myself, expecting Gwen to kiss me and ruin my marriage, but she ended up asking if I realized that garlic and cholesterol are natural enemies.

"What're you doing, Everett?" Luce says.

"You have goop on your head," Gwen says.

I shrug and smile. Swabbed in Vaseline, I feel like a newborn baby.

"I'm caught," I tell the women. I say it loud and I say it proud.

Half an hour later, all the Gorgons have arrived and I'm still stuck. As the women munch almond cookies, they discuss "Meet Your Maker," in which Wesley Truth saves a young, slinky Ugandan woman during a stickup at Lieberman's Deli. The stickup (which is really part of a sinister international conspiracy) becomes a shootout, which claims the life of Mr. Lieberman's beloved canary, Midge. Wesley Truth conks his head on the meat slicer and later comes to in the warehouse loft of the sloe-eyed Ugandan woman, Spella, who's just out of the shower. Wesley remembers nothing except that he's a Buddhist and Spella's a fox. As Spella towels off, she confesses that a Ugandan bounty hunter, Mr. Dropsy, wants her unborn baby for fiendish purposes. Wesley realizes that he must empty himself of selfish desires and kick ass on Spella's behalf.

"Give me a break." I swivel my neck, which is getting stiff. "Real men don't chase Ugandan tail. Real men have wives."

"Please be quiet, Everett," begs Jillian.

"Real men have wives, huh?" Luce glares at me. "Does that mean real women have husbands?" Luce is touchy because her ex-mate, Norbert Wilco, left her last year for a girl in clown college. Luce is thirty-nine and desperate to have babies and now her former husband is screwing someone whose nose will honk when squeezed.

"Let's toast the holidays," says Abby, the matriarchal, peacemaking Gorgon, albeit the thief of my virginity. She sits in her wheelchair, close to the tree, tousling my blind son's hair. Abby's chair appears to be a new, all-chrome gizmo, perhaps an early Christmas gift from plucky Bob Beach, M.D.

"What I'd like to know," I say, "is who names a canary Midge?"

Jillian sighs and rubs her temples.

Abby, undeterred, raises her brandy glass. "To togetherness."

The Gorgons clink glasses. School's out till after New Year, so Luce, a kindergarten teacher, is refilling her glass regularly, and Theresa is on her third amaretto. Dorry Smith sits cross-legged on her throw pillow, abstaining from alcohol and wearing a green tunic. Slung across Dorry's back is a bow and a quiver of arrows. Dorry's husband, an English clothing-store owner named Ben, died ten years ago, and in her grief Dorry became a consummate Anglophile. This began with a taste for tea and tennis, and evolved into a fascination with Robin Hood. The crazy wench now walks the streets of Chicago year-round wearing her weapons in memoriam.

"Everett may have a point," Dorry says. "The canary pushed the envelope. Authors too often introduce a pet to garner unearned sympathy."

T.J. is nosing at my ass, as if I were his fellow-mutt.

Gwen glares at Dorry. "The canary's death was gratuitous, that's all."

The Gorgons are silent. They know never to question Gwen's defense of an animal. Gwen's second husband, Frederick, did not know this, and when he spayed Gwen's cat, Soybean, without her permission Gwen kicked Frederick viciously in the balls and served him papers.

"Let's change tacks and consider Spella," Abby suggests. She wheels herself forward between Dorry and Gwen, and pats each of them affectionately on the wrist. Her chrome hot rod flashes in the hearth light, like the ride of some god, some arbiter.

I clear my throat. "Hey there, Abby. Cool wheels."

Abby ignores me, her eyes on the Gorgons. "Is Spella weak in her reliance on Wesley?"

"A chariot of fire," I say. "Ha."

"Spella is pregnant yet horny," Theresa says. "I respect that."

Luce frowns. Theresa rubs her belly, as if to tell us something.

I decide to get literary. "Wesley Truth's amnesia was absurd. Absurd and hackneyed." I speak loudly, for the women are far from me. "It's not easy for a man to forget who he is."

Jillian sighs. We don't have blistering fights, she and I, but a few months ago she said to me, please, let's try sleeping in separate beds. I said to her, please, let's don't.

Thomas asks what "hackneyed" means.

I say, "It means tired out, son. Tired out from overuse."

Dorry thrusts her chin my way. "You know, I can chop him out of there, Jillian." Dorry adjusts the folds of her tunic to reveal a utility belt. Lo and behold, she's packing a small axe, as well as a sheathed dagger and a cell phone.

"No, leave him be," my wife says. "We'll pretend he's not there."

Abby claps her hands. "I know. Let's all be quiet for two minutes, and everyone think of one word, one totally perfect word, to describe how Wesley Truth made you feel when you read this novel."

The room falls silent. The scents of pine and Luce Winningham are in the air. I've been hunkered in a squat all this time, but now, to stretch my back, I lie on my stomach along one step of the stairs and coax my arms through the bannisters. I prop my head on my hands like a boy before a campfire, and look down on the women. T.J., in his elfin sweater, flops one step below me.

As the women think, I watch Abby as she gazes at the hearth fire. Her jawbones jut at severe, post-accident angles, but she looks perfectly content. If I were editing her profile for AOK, for, say, an inspirational piece about cripples, I would crop the picture so as to feature from above her fine poise in the wheelchair, the arch of her back, the firelight in her hair. In fact, back in my polevaulting days, I sought this view of Abby every afternoon as I speared myself fifteen feet into the sky, and Abby stood beside the cushioned pit below, watching me. I would freeze for a snapshot second, at the top of my arc, and gaze down at my girl, her hair a bell on her shoulders, her eyes a clear path to mine. Thinking of those days, and looking at the Gorgons now, I am reminded suddenly of a sunny afternoon on my honeymoon, in Jamaica, when Jillian and I went snorkeling. We investigated a shipwreck. The ship was small, and only about twenty feet underwater, and it had been sunk on purpose by the resort owners so that it could be discovered again and again by people like us. Anyway, at one point Jillian was by the ship and I was up on the surface, getting air. I aimed my mask down to check on my bride, and, as I did, Jillian, three fathoms deep, looked up at me, and just then some sort of translucent, yellow, gelatinous ocean creature swam in between us. This leviathan or what have you glided quickly by, but while it was there I saw straight through its diaphanous body, and beheld a shimmering, glinty version of my wife. She was still Jillian, in a black one-piece, with full breasts and crooked teeth and all the other joys I'd married, but around the edges she had waving squiggles and snakes of golden light shooting out from her hair. This vision soon vanished, but, while it was real, I was overwhelmed, and immobile, and unable to breathe.

"Lonely," Gwen said. "Wesley made me feel lonely. He had three separate lovers this time around."

"He's cruising for an S.T.D.," I snort. "The next book will be 'Cure Your Crabs.'"

My wife points at me. "Ignore that man."

"Adventurous," Luce Winningham says. According to Jillian, Luce used to skinny-dip with Norbert Wilco, the Lothario of clowns.

"Well armed," Dorry says.

"Fat," Jillian sighs. "Spella was, what, a size two?"

"Jealous," Abby says. "I was jealous of Wesley's amnesia. He seemed to have a new lease on life. I mean, he slept with Spella and killed anyone who tried to harm her, and he did it all without feeling guilt or remorse." Abby leans forward. Her left cheekbone, the one that got most squashed by the forklift, contains a hollow that the light from my Christmas-tree bulbs cannot fill. "Imagine living like that," Abby says. "Imagine the possibilities."

Theresa lifts her studded brows. "Sexy."

"I'd be scared stiff," Jillian says. She looks at me almost accusingly as she says this, but she tucks her hair behind her ears, a gesture she knows I like. She made that same move on our first date. We were in the balcony of a movie house, and I was halfway into the yawn-stretch-the-arms-grab-the-girl ploy when Jillian's hand shot up to protect her hair and maybe her heart. I knew then that I would never have Jillian, body and soul, unless I married her. That hair tuck: I couldn't resist it.

"Scared stiff?" says Abby. "Why? You could be anybody you wanted."

"Unless you were blind," Thomas observes.

Another silence. The Gorgons shift about on their cushions. At work, it's my job to splice out moments—unsure pauses—like the one I'm witnessing. I pet T.J. behind the ears, and stare at each Gorgon, trying to read her thoughts. I imagine that Luce is dreaming of a Barnum & Baileyless world, Abby is mourning her legs, and Jillian is sitting on the steps of some church, some building I wish I believed in.

"I'm just glad to see Wesley eating better," Gwen says cheerfully. "Remember two books ago, in 'Pick Your Poison,' he was obsessed with prime rib."

The other women glare at Gwen. She's somehow killed a moment, a contemplative vibe.

"Hey, ladies," I call out. "Everett here, checking in."

Thomas grins. "Hey, Dad."

"Howdy, buddy."

Theresa cuts her eyes at me. "Enough fucking interruptions, Everett."

"Theresa," Jillian says, "don't say 'fuck' to your father."

Theresa folds her arms on her chest. My wife's guests don't move. The firewood spits in an unjolly way.

"Time for Chaos," Jillian says, as brightly as she can. She heads for the kitchen.

I should explain about Theresa. She's a decent person—she works at a home, helping old people die well—but she hates Christmas, and she hates me at Christmastime. It's my fault. Thirteen years ago, when Theresa was six and Jillian was pregnant with Thomas, we found out that Thomas would be born blind. The doctor showed Jillian and me a sonogram, showed us the lumps where Thomas's eyes should have been growing, and it killed me. I wanted to explain it to Theresa, to teach her before Thomas's birth that ours is a broken world, to brace her for forklift accidents and divorces and blindness and all the other awful news I stare at daily. So I wrote Theresa a story called "Tink on the Blink" and read it to her on Christmas Eve. "Tink on the Blink" was a story in which Tinkerbell is having fun in Never Never Land with the Lost Boys when suddenly she develops pancreatic cancer. She ends up in the hospital on life support. The Lost Boys gather round loyally and hold Tink's little hand and clap and sing about how fervently they believe in fairies, but despite the warm love of friends Tinkerbell flatlines, her wings fall off, and she dies. In retrospect, this story may have been a mite harsh for a six-year-old. Theresa freaked out and had nightmares, and we took her to a child psychologist and Jillian would barely speak to me for a month, until Thomas was born and he built some peace between us.

"This cake is divine," gushes Luce.

Dorry licks her fork. "Yes, divine."

Jillian brings me some Chaos. She hands it to me carefully, so as not to wake T.J., who's dozing at my side. I hold my fork in one trapped hand and my plate in the other.

"Thank you," I tell Jillian.

While the Gorgons ingest chocolate, the talk returns (I'm gratified to say) to my question of whether Wesley Truth is a real man.

"Hell yes, he's a real man," Luce says.

"He's both spiritual and primordial," Gwen says.

"He's a fighter," Dorry says.

"But he never breaks so much as a bone," Abby says.

Theresa nudges Luce. "He's got pecs like my Huey."

"Fictional pecs," I say. "Wesley Truth has fictional pecs, and fictional sex. He never faces unmitigated sadness. He never gets abandoned, or...or crushed or intimidated or embarrassed or anything. He's *not* a real man. He's bullshit."

"You know what I think, Everett?" Jillian says. "I think if you were a real man you would've debannistered yourself by now. You would've engineered some escape."

I wish I could wink at my son. I wish that just once a week I could lower one eyelid at the only other man in the house, and have that lowered eyelid mean "Uh-oh, Mom's mad."

"Maybe I'm happy like this, Jillian," I joke, patting the bannisters that hold me. "Maybe, even better than Wesley Truth, I can accept whatever bleak fix life puts me in."

"Actually," Luce says, munching a cookie, "that's a really nice staircase."

"It's Indonesian teak," I say.

"Everett." My Gorgon wife's voice is shaking. "Nothing about you is better than Wesley Truth." Something I never would have expected—a tear—drips onto Jillian's check. If I could get to Jillian, I'd wipe that tear clear, splice it out. But I'm stuck.

"Hey, Jills. I was just talking. Jills?"

Jillian stares at the fire. Glaring at me, Luce throws an arm around

Jillian's shoulder and gives my wife a squeeze. I feel something then that Wesley Truth doesn't feel: I feel remorse.

"I'm sorry, Jills," I say.

"I would never want amnesia," Theresa decides. "I've had such great times with Huey, I want to remember them all."

"There's a mouse," Gwen Kirkle says, casually. She points to the floor under the tree, and, sure enough, there's a mouse killing time among the gifts. Luce Winningham screams.

Jillian leaps to her feet. "Everett, goddammit, you said you'd caught them all."

I spring into action. Given my circumstances, I do this by yanking out my necklace and blowing the whistle. Beside me, T.J. jumps up. So does Thomas. Luce screams again, doubly confused.

Jillian stares at my whistle. "What the Christ is that?"

I ignore my wife, and point out the intruder below. T.J. follows my finger, howls in recognition, races downstairs.

"Wait," pleads Gwen, the canary-lover.

"Kill it," Luce squeals.

"Easy, Gorgons," Jillian says.

Abby grips her wheelchair, ready to roll. The mouse scurries behind the couch, but I'm out to prove myself.

"Get him, T.J.," I yell. "To the woodbox, Thomas."

My son zips to the hearth and plunks himself inside the woodbox, cutting off what I've long suspected is the mice's access from the basement to our living room. Gwen Kirkle is on her feet now, a righteous panic in her eyes. She stands between T.J. and the couch, but the dachshund, still howling, slips between her legs.

"Everett, what's T.J. doing?" Jillian says.

T.J. disappears behind the couch.

"Let the mouse coexist!" Gwen sobs.

"Good dog," I call. T.J. may wear silly, emasculating sweaters, but in his blood run the hunting instincts of the dachshunds of old, the great Prussian rabbit hunters.

"Go, T.J.," Thomas says.

I'm up in a crouch now, grasping the bannisters, my eyes peeled. My shoulders ache, but I sneer at the pain. Theresa is standing on the hearth, watching the couch, and I don't mind seeing dread in my daughter's eyes. She has always feared rodents, and I wonder if Huey the trucker, or Dr. Bob Beach, or Joseph Hederal himself could respond to this crisis as quickly as we Dose men have.

"There it goes," shrieks Luce.

The mouse charges toward the woodbox, with T.J. on its tail, and Gwen right behind the dachshund.

"He's rolling to you, Thomas."

"Ten-four, Dad."

"Watch out for Gwen Kirkle." I don't want my son kicked in the stones.

"Roger, Dad."

There's a whistling sound. With a life-ending thunk, the mouse is pinned to the wall by an arrow. All eyes fall on Dorry, who stands like a crusader beneath the Yule tree, her bow drawn, the string still humming. Her face is grim and bold.

Thomas still has his body tensed, his hands close to the floor. "Did something go down?" he says.

Luce Winningham exhales. "Whoa. Nice shot, Dorry."

T.J. pads over to the piniomed mouse, sniffs it, looks up at me sadly. I glare at Dorry.

"Damn." Theresa giggles. "Not a creature is stirring, I guess."

"What went down?" Thomas asks.

Gwen Kirkle sniffles. "Dorothy Smith killed one of God's little lambs, Thomas. That's what went down."

Abby uncaps the armrest of her wheelchair. From a snazzy little storage tube, she pulls out several Kleenex and hands them to Gwen.

Dorry fetches her arrow and cleans it. "Mice are standard house-hold pests, Gwen. Their feces are a health hazard."

As Dorry wraps the mouse in a cocktail napkin, I protest her use of lethal force. "T.J. was handling the situation, Dorry. It was his kill."

Dorry takes the mouse out to our garage trash receptacle.

Gwen wipes her nose. "Is that true about the feces?"

When the archer returns, Theresa says, "Dorry Smith, our hero."

I feel my face go crimson.

At ten-thirty, Thomas yawns. Jillian allowed him three sips of brandy tonight.

"I'm hackneyed," Thomas says.

"We all are," Dorry says.

T.J. is curled in his basket. The time for book talk—for all talk—

has passed. Luce Winningham stares at the fire embers, thinking, maybe, of Norbert Wilco, the man with whom she will not be opening Christmas gifts. Or perhaps she is thinking of her car, which is parked in our driveway and which will bear her away tonight. It's a Corsica, with a broken heater. I tried to fix the heater last week, and failed.

Gwen nudges Theresa. "Will Huey be home on Christmas?"

My daughter shakes her head. Her ears, which were naked in her childhood, are riddled with black adornments like buckshot.

"He'll be on a West Coast run," Theresa says. "Hauling kelp."

The Gorgons say nothing, as if kelp were a subject they had long ago exhausted. Bits of chocolate cake lie on the plates. The women slump in their places, sated and moody. I think about Nirvana, which, according to Buddha, is when nothing happens and you don't care about anything. Dorry says she has to go.

Luce gets to her feet. "We all do."

Thomas pads up the stairs, gives me a kiss, trundles to his bedroom. The women stand. Before they don their coats, they engage in yet another ritual of which I'll never be a part: the Gorgon goodbye hug. It appears to be a simple ceremony of each woman embracing every other, but I suspect that each Gorgon hug contains a mingling of female powers, possibly a trading of spiritual recipes.

"Goodbye, Gwen." I wave a hand between the bannisters. "Goodbye, Luce. Goodbye, Dorry."

None of them bid me adieu, although Dorry, who could have put me under her axe blade tonight, gives a slight bow. Then they're gone, and just my wife and daughter remain. Jillian holds up Theresa's coat so Theresa can wriggle her arms down the sleeves.

"Bye, Theresa," I say. "I love you."

My daughter cinches her scarf around her neck. She doesn't look up. "As long as you have nothing good to say about Huey, Everett, I have nothing good to say to you."

She clomps out the door, and Jillian shuts it.

"Well." I'm still caught, by the way. I'm looming over the room like a hunchback.

Jillian doesn't speak. She moves about the living room, collecting used glasses and plates on a tray. There's no music coming from our stereo. There hasn't been all night.

"Jills?" I feel suddenly panicked, sinful. "I'm sorry about the mouse, Jills. And, hey, the Chaos was delicious."

I get no reply. Jillian picks crumbs off the coffee table. Normally, at this time of night, I'm downstairs in front of the television, looking forward to sports highlights, and Jillian is in our bed with Joseph Hederal. It's Christmastime, though, and, as I said, it is sometimes my job to find the silver lining. So I risk it.

"Jillian," I say, "remember when we snorkeled around that shipwreck?"

Jillian freezes. We've never discussed that day. My wife turns slowly. In the light from the tree, she holds my gaze. I don't expect her to cry, and she doesn't.

I draw a breath. "Remember that things? That...amazing thing that came between us?"

I hold the bars and watch my woman. I need her to remember this. T.J. shifts in his basket. It tweaks the cramp in my neck for me to smile at my wife, but I do it. She smiles back, almost shyly, for just a moment. Then she fades into the kitchen with the tray.

"All right, Everett," I whisper to myself. "All right."

My dachshund yawns. A crystal ornament falls from the tree and shatters, reminding me that I'm not Wesley Truth. I might not get that Popsicle, either, but I will get unstuck, I'm sure, soon enough, and get back to editing news, capably, and crooning Sinatra in the shower, badly. What I mean is, I hope to gain Heaven someday, but for now I'm here in Chicago, and I'm warm and I'm married and I'm home.

In an age of numerical tourism, packaged vacations, and formula getaways, where does one turn for that customized, getting-away-from-it-all experience that, ever since Byron's Childe Harold's voyage of self-discovery, is the only respectable way to recharge one's batteries? Grover Amen's nameless New Yorker suffers an identity crisis that only a mega-dose of authenticity can cure. Like most of us, he has only two weeks to do it: on a budget, in an exotic, but not too remote, not too hostile, outpost of mind-blowing hedonism. And, like most of us, he tries to make it happen by the book, in this case, Bradley Smith's fortuitously titled Escape to the West Indies.

escape

GROVER AMEN

many americans suffer these days from the identity problem—from not knowing who or what they are—and I used to have nothing but contempt for such people, until last summer, when I, too, succumbed. I suspect that this was caused by my staying up night after night, drinking beer and watching old television movies in a Second Avenue bar, but, at any rate, I came to feel that my identity was in jeopardy and that the feverish unreality of life in New York was chiefly to blame. With great reluctance—for I usually rebelled against holidays and refused to go anywhere—I decided to devote one summer vacation to a sober and merciless rediscovery of my true self. I could see that, to attain objection, I would have to get as far away from New York—and, in fact, from everything American as possible. But where could I go, I only had two weeks and hardly any money, which eliminated most of the world, and I had just about decided to scrap the project before it began when I happened to find, in a Times Square bookshop, a travel guide entitled *Escape to the West Indies,* by Bradley Smith. "The fabled islands of the Caribbean," the dust jacket said, "provide lush tropical beauty, mountains and valleys to explore, exotic plants and birds to admire...and complete escape from the humdrum, the usual, and the familiar." I bought the book. It was a revelation. I had never thought of going to the West Indies in the summer, merely because I do not like heat. But I gathered from "Escape to the West Indies" that temperatures down there, even during August, were not much higher than in New York. Furthermore, the Leeward and Windward Islands of the Caribbean became almost devoid of tourists during the summer, and were a perfect sanctuary for serious travellers wishing to relax, meditate, and take spiritual inventory. It was just the place for me.

I resolved to go the first week of August, taking precautions to avoid any stopovers at such tourist traps as Bermuda, Jamaica, St. Thomas, and Barbados, and following an itinerary which, by way of a relatively offbeat air route through Antigua, Martinique, and St. Lucia, would take me eventually to Pigeon Island, an isolated beachcomber's paradise accessible only by rowboat. I was all set to go only the barest necessities omitted the electric shaver able transformer for different current and foreign plugs for different types of sockets recommended by *Escape to the West Indies*. I got some bad news. Because of a clerical error made by the airline, my flight chart had to be slightly altered and I would have to stop overnight at Bermuda—the very kind of tourist trap I had most hoped to avoid.

Arriving there about noon, I decided to rent a small motor bicycle and investigate as much of the place as possible. Riding along the south shore, I even had an illusory sense of exhilaration and freedom, and I would stop every so often to study an inviting cove or have a swim in the clear, seductive water. But I was not taken in. The entire setup was shamelessly commercial and confirmed my worst suspicions. There was only one consolation. I felt that the stopoff at Bermuda probably served as a good transition between New York and the real West Indies. I'd been warned that too sudden a change from the nervous life of the city to the serene tempo of Caribbean days could bring on a state of mild psychological shock known as "tropical trauma," in which the sun's intensity could cause the euphoric beauty of the physical environment to seem unreal.

I was therefore relieved to find, on landing at Antigua the next morning, that the sun was not too intense. I did have trouble with a cabdriver, who, on learning that I was American, wanted to take me to some new hotel, a place with a reputation for a steel band, calypso music, and girls. I explained to him that that was not what I had in mind at all, that I had come down simply for solitude, meditation, and spiritual inventory. He then informed me that the hotel where I had a reservation was strictly for squares and that I sounded more like a Canadian than an American.

My reception at the hotel was detached and businesslike. I told the proprietress that though I was an American on vacation, the most modest room in the place would suit my needs. She acquainted me, with the house rules. Breakfast was served from seven-thirty to nine-thirty, lunch from twelve to one-thirty, and dinner, at which a jacket and tie were required, from six to eight. Afternoon tea was extra, the bar closed at eleven, and the water closet was down the hall to the right.

After inspecting my room, which was clean and modest, I headed for the bar. I had feared that even on this remote island some back-slapping party might turn up. But the bar was deserted. It consisted of a sort of shelf in front of which were two prim wooden chairs. I sat down on one of these and punched a bell marked "Service." Promptly, the proprietress appeared, unlocked a padlocked door over the shelf, and prepared me a mint swizzle. She told me that if I wanted another I could fix it myself, and explained that the bar, during the summer slack, operated on the honor.

A few swizzles later, I felt a first inkling of serenity, and the mood deepened after. I moved to the dining room, where in the tropical breezes and flickering candlelight, I savored a delectable flying-fish stew, the house specialty. The proprietress now assumed the role of waitress, but most of the time she remained aloof, and I had the entire dining room—a lofty, windy place full of stuffed game fish, potted palms, Victorian chandeliers, and baroque murals—all to myself. My sense of liberation and reunion with reality was augmented by a small bird of exotic plumage that flew in through the window, and, lighting on my table, pecked at the food on my plate. By the time dessert came, the bird and I had established mutual trust and affection. After supper, it flew away and I returned to the bar, where, at eleven sharp, the proprietress reappeared, announced the last call with a rap on a school bell, and padlocked the supplies.

Next morning, after a generous breakfast of porridge and fried flying fish, I wasted no time in initiating my project. I wanted to meditate, and soon I discovered a perfectly secluded spot. Shielded from the white sky, the shore, and the hotel grounds proper by thick clusters of poinsettia, immortelle, and other tropical foliage, it provided a perfect sanctuary. Many memorable hours I spent in that one spot, reviewing with rustic objectivity the meaning of my life. The mornings were usually invigoratingly damp; a dense mist with a slight trace of salt from the Caribbean discernible in its touch would cover me like a smoke screen. But I came to enjoy the afternoons most, when, a bottle of rum cradled in my arms, I would watch the mist rise slightly, and twigs, tropical clumps of verdure and moss, and exotic insects gradually become visible. Sometimes, my bottle empty at my side, I would sink into a delicious reverie or slumber, from which I would be awakened toward twilight by the gentle sound, and even gentler touch, of dripping from the trees. Only one thing was wrong. I knew that I had to get on the Pigeon Island, and that stopping too long anywhere else was a shirking of responsibility. Regretfully, I left Antigua after five days.

At Martinique, I was grateful to find that the skies were clear, almost blue, despite my spiritual exhilaration in my forays into the foliage had brought on a troublesome sinus condition, which I hoped a little sun might improve. My only fear was of the language barrier, for although ten years of studying French back in school had made me fluent reader of Proust, I still had trouble saying anything in the language. But I was spared humiliation by an extraordinary stroke of good luck. On the ferry that took me from Fort-de-France to L'Anse Mitan Inn, where I was to stay, were several other passengers, including a young Swiss fellow named Michel, who worked in New York and was on a mission much the same as mine. He spoke German, French, and English impeccably. As I was exercising my French on the ferry driver, Michel stepped in to help. "I understand how difficult it is for Americans in a foreign country," he said. "They get isolated by the language barrier." And he promised that when we got to L'Anse Mitan he would keep an eye on me.

Since it was essential for the success of my project to retain a feeling of privacy, I was apprehensive, for I sensed a friendship budding. But my fears were soon allayed. As Michel and I dined together that evening on the patio of L'Anse Mitan, I found that we shared identical views on travelling. He was particularly incensed, as was I, with the typical "American tourist," and said that his brief stay on the island of St. Thomas, which I had avoided for that very reason, had been all but ruined by a pharmaceutical salesman whom he had encountered. "A know-it-all fellow, who thought I couldn't get along on my own because I was Swiss," said Michel. "I could not get rid of him. He had a wretched little Thunderbird, and would drive around in it from hotel to hotel buying everybody drinks, playing the big shot, and trying to pick up American girls. Just one or two Americans like that can ruin a whole island." Michel added that he had escaped the pharmaceutical salesman's clutches by renting a Ford, with which he had made a thorough exploration of the real St. Thomas, "Fantastic!" he said. "Once you get away from the cocktail parties and the hotels, the island's virgin wilderness—nothing American about it. Why, you might almost be in Hawaii."

French food, though, I found strange, for our dinner consisted solely of bread, goat cheese, and bananas, but Michel explained that this was because the French, unlike Americans, eat their main meal in the middle of the day. As supper progressed, I found that Michel was a perceptive observer of many other aspects of the international scene. Under the influence of Martinique wine, my tongue, too, was loosened, and we had quite a bout of it, handying witticisms back and forth. When it came to America, I was content to let Michel hold forth, for, being a foreigner, he had the advantage of critical objectivity. This was a point that Michel himself stressed over the crackers and goat cheese. "Americans, and especially American intellectuals," he explained, "are too subjective to have the slightest conception of what art is. They are afraid of life, and in art they find a subjective refuge for their warped, minor emotions. The poetry of today is, in fact, the poetry of minor emotions, psychiatric confession, and ratiocination. You Americans are all victims of the cult of self-expression. Art should not be an expression of personality but a transcendence of personality—almost, indeed, an escape, from personality." He looked up and added, by way of elaboration, "But, of course, only those who have a personality know what it is to wish to escape it."

I remarked that the poet T. S. Eliot had somewhere made a comparable observation.

"Mr. Eliot will live, if he lives at all," said Michel, "in his role as critic. Unfortunately, his own poetry is a complete contradiction of his criticism."

When the subject of contemporary authors had been provocatively covered, we settled down to a practical discussion of plans for the next day. At first, I was opposed to any major geographical exploration; feeling it might interfere with my mission. But I soon persuaded myself that, after my extended meditations on Antigua, it would do no harm to spend one day in an informal outing. It might even contribute to a certain psychological balance.

I retired to my room early, but awoke a few hours later after a weird nightmare. I felt peculiar and dry, and, on rising to get a drink of mineral water from in his flask (the tap water was contaminated), almost collapsed from dizziness. Coming down with some strange tropical disease was the one thing I dreaded and had taken every precaution to avoid. I had packed a thermometer, and, on taking my temperature, found that it was almost a hundred and one degrees. I decided to wake Michel up and ask his advice. (The owners of the inn had seemed rather hostile when I arrived.) I knocked gingerly on Michel's door; and, getting no response, entered the room and tugged at his mosquito netting. I tugged too hard, for just as Michel sat bolt upright the netting collapsed on him. He uttered an oath in German, and while I helped to extricate him from the netting I explained my predicament. "Sorry to wake you," I said. "But I don't want to ruin my whole vacation by getting sick, and I thought maybe I should wake up the owners and get them to call a doctor."

He shook his head, saying that this would constitute a ridiculous imposition, and then subjected me to exhaustive questioning about my recent activities. In; the course of the interrogation, I mentioned that I had had a booster typhoid shot before leaving Antigua.

"Aha! I might have guessed it," he said. "This always happen to Americans. You aren't supposed to have anything alcoholic to drink for forty-eight hours after a typhoid shot. It often brings on a brief but intense case of typhoid fever. All travellers except Americans know about this, which is why doctor giving the shot don't mention it. It's probably a subjective reaction to their dislike of Americans. Anyway, just sweat it out tonight, and you'll feel fine in the morning."

I was enormously grateful to learn this, and returned to my room, where I kept a careful check on my temperature. For the next couple of hours it rose gradually, reaching a peak of 102.5 about 4 A.M., and then, as Michel had predicted, it subsided gradually until, just as the first daylight filtered through my mosquito netting, it hit ninety-nine, and I fell asleep. When Michel rapped on my door at seven o'clock, a final check revealed that my temperature was perfectly normal. I felt a cold shower might not be wise after the fever, but I did manage to shave myself with soap and cold water.

At breakfast, which consisted of bananas and flying fish, Michel seemed amused about something. "Confess to me," he said, a twinkle in his eye. "You miss the hot water—am I right?"

"Not really," I said, "It's just a little rough shaving."

"Aha!" he said. "I suspected it. No one told you: Down here it is always wise to bring an electric razor. But you must have a variable transformer for different currents, and a set of foreign plugs for different-sized sockets."

"I know all about that," I said. "But I prefer soap and water, hot or cold."

Since we would not be there for the big midday French meal, the inn's proprietor fixed us a picnic-lunch basket of bread, goat cheese, and bananas. (Rates were on the American plan and included meals.) Then he took us by boat across the bay to Fort-de-France. He and Michel sat up in the bow, beneath a canopy, and chatted, and I was left in the stern, where I was free to command a clear view of the mountains of Martinique and to feel the invigorating touch of the salt spray.

In town, we had no trouble renting a car, a Ford Prefect, and Michel turned out to be quite a confident driver. The only difficulty came when we got off the main drag and onto a road that, especially on steep inclines, became a mere gully of gravel. Then the car was apt to founder, and the only solution was for me to get out and push, which I did, successfully, six or seven times. But at one unusually steep impasse this did not work. The wheels would do nothing but spin. As I bent over to get a firmer grip on the rear bumper and gave a mighty heave, my glasses fell off and were swept into the vortex of a spinning tire. For an instant, I was afraid that they might have been ground up in the gravel, but it turned out that only one lens was crushed and the frame itself was intact, enabling me to still see twenty-twenty with my right eye. Michel was afraid the glass of the crushed lens might have damaged the tire, but a thorough inspection showed that this was not so. We agreed that the insertion of something adhesive between the rear tires and the gravel might help, and as we poked about the roadside, gathering bits of driftwood and decayed coconut shells, we observed a huge dark fellow in an adjacent field loading sugar cane onto the back of a burro. When Michel explained our predicament to him, the fellow agreed, for a few ranes, to give us a hand.

From the start, the fellow, whose name was something like Merry Bell, had a condescending attitude, and I did not like him. Anyway, as he and I took our respective stations at each end of the rear bumper. Michel, back in the driver's seat, gave the car the gas. Again the tires would do nothing, but spin and spout blue smoke. I had the feeling that Merry Bell and I were not pushing quite in unison, and after several strenuous efforts I glanced at him and saw, through my right eye, that, instead of pushing uphill at the bumper, he was pulling it downhill. "What the hell are you doing?" I yelled, and, to circumvent the language barrier, grabbed Merry Bell's arms to illustrate for him the proper pushing procedure. He backed away quickly and retaliated with a thrust of his elbow, which caught me square in the midriff. At this point, I lost all touch with reality and, summoning up all my remaining might, swung a savage right hook at him. Fortunately, it missed. I lost my balance and collapsed in the dust.

"What is happening back there?" asked Michel.

Merry Bell began to yell in a strange patois that I don't think even Michel understood.

"He was pulling on the car the wrong way," I said. "Then he hit me in the gut. He probably thought he'd get a bigger tip if the car was hard to move."

"Get hold of yourself," said Michel. "You Americans think everybody in the world is out to take your money. These natives are just a quiet, easygoing people. He probably doesn't understand what the problem is."

Michel went over it with him again, and, pointing at me, said, "*Ça ne fait rien. Ça n'est qu'un Americain avec une bonett cassèe.*"

Merry Bell grinned at this, and under Michel's instructions managed to get the car onto firm ground.

When we were under way again, I apologized to Michel for the irrational outburst. "It's probably because I didn't get enough sleep last night," I said. "It makes me grumpy—ever since I was a kid."

"You should learn to control yourself," he said. "There's enough anti-American feeling in the Caribbean already without you starting trouble."

To soothe my nerves, I ate some goat cheese, and the mishap was forgotten when we spotted two Martinique girls on the road and offered them a lift. They were beautiful and friendly, and seemed interested, rather than annoyed, to learn that I was an American. I felt awkward, though, because of a certain mechanical difficulty that arose in addition to the language barrier. The girls were in the back seat, and because only my right eye had the benefit of a lens, I had to execute a complete pivot in my seat in order to see them distinctly. But I was not going to let this handicap in me conversationally, and from time to time would pivot about and inquire, *"comment s'appelle cet arbre-là?"*

"Quel arbe? Quel arbe?" they would exclaim, looking out the window with great concern. But the tree in question would already have been passed.

Still, we did get together on the name of a quiescent volcano on the horizon, and by the time the girls got out I was feeling encouraged. Michel tried to persuade them to come along farther with us, but they said they had to get home to do the washing. Although I thought the whole affair had gone off pretty well. Michel seemed irritated. "The next time that happens, let me handle it," he said.

I found that it strained my left eye to look through the lensless frame, and since I could find nothing with which to cover the opening and keeping one eye shut and the other open was also a strain, I decided to keep them both shut. Michel would give me a nudge every so often when we passed same form of particular interest, such as a banana plantation. All in all, although by the end of the day I was grateful to have seen something of the real Martinique, I resolved on the next island, St. Lucia, to return to meditation.

That night, I browsed through the St. Lucia chapter in *Escape to the West Indies,* and although I was still adamant about not wasting time on typical tourist attractions, I came across a passage of unusual interest. It said:

It [St. Lucia] has a drive-in volcano where an automobile can come within one hundred feet of the steaming, sulphurous rocks and boiling springs....Walk into the center of the gray, smoking, crater-like area, taking care not to burn your feet in one of the hot pools. To be on the inside of a volcano looking out is an amazing experience. Around you are hissing jets of steam and beyond the steam stand the high red immortelle trees that cover the hills along the lip of the crater. The experience is like a sudden safe descent into one of Dante's visions of the Infernó.

Picking up a guide at Soufriere is no problem: the guide is more likely to pick you up. He will lead you, after your inner view of the crater to the once-famous hot baths located directly above the crater entrance. These baths were built by Louis XVI for the health and comfort of the French garrison on the island. Now the stone troughs are discolored by age and rarely used, but your guide will lead you through a thicket and then to an ancient wooden enclosure. Inside are tub with hot water running through them. If you want a bath— and it is an exhilarating experience—the guide will clean out the tub, plug up the opening, and stand guard at the door while you luxuriate in one of the few natural hot baths now available in the entire Lesser Antilles.

This sounded quite pleasant, and when I reached St. Lucia I hoped to find a hotel near the drive-in volcano. But it wasn't that easy. I was anxious to get my glasses fixed, and there was no optician in the vicinity of the volcano. (I'd neglected to bring an extra pair of glasses with me, but from previous mishaps, I knew the prescription number by heart.) Michel had heard of a hotel in the interior that cost less than two dollars a day, including meals, but I decided to stay at a more expensive inn, near an optician, just for one night. Then, once my glasses were fixed, I could join him.

At my inn, which was so new it did not have a name yet, Jack, the proprietor, seemed confused and apologetic, but I assured him it would not bother me that things were a bit primitive, and he agreed to rent me a room for twelve dollars a day, on a trial basis. He went on to explain that he was not a real hotel proprietor but a schoolteacher from Nottingham, England; whose sister, Nellie, owned the inn. He had agreed to come to St. Lucia for a few weeks during his summer vacation, while his sister went home. "We thought the exchange might do us both good," he said. "And Nellie was exhausted from the ordeal of getting the inn built. There's a serious labor problem in St. Lucia. No one wants to work. For a while, I even had to iron the sheets myself."

He gave me a couple of sheets and some mosquito getting, and escorted me to my room, which turned out to have a curtain instead of a door. "Nellie thought it would discourage promiscuity among the guests," Jack explained.

It occurred to me that curtained bedroom might have just the reverse effect, but, as there were the other guests at the inn, this problem seemed, for the time being, academic. After making the bed, I took a walk to the beach, about a mile away. The shore was deserted, and when I collapsed in my towel in the sun I began to recapture that inner serenity I had not felt since Antigua. In fact, I fell asleep, and on waking I found that the skin of my chest and legs had turned a bright pink. The color darkened during dinner, and by bedtime I also had a little gastric acidity, for the flying fish were not as good as those I had eaten on Antigua.

I was not surprised, therefore, to awake screaming a couple of hours later. I was having another nightmare. I clutched under the pillow, looking for my glasses—or, rather, glass—and flicked on the light. At this juncture, the curtains of my room parted and Jack came in carrying a large highball glass. He looked strange and dishevelled and I guessed that my screaming had awakened him.

"Hi there, Jack," I said. "Sorry if I woke you. Everything's O.K. Just one of those damn nightmares of mine."

"So it's starting to happen to you, too," he said, sipping.

"What?" I asked.

"The nightmares. The darkness. The horror," he said.

"Nightmares?" I said. "Oh, they're nothing, really. Had them ever since I was a kid. Indigestion or something."

"Don't be fooled," he said. "At first, I thought it was just indigestion, the tropical food or something, but I know otherwise now. Mind awfully if I join you for a minute?"

Actually, I did mind. Lying there under the mosquito netting and the bare bulb, with my sunburn and indigestion, I wasn't much in the mood for sociability, but I saw no tactful way out of it. "O.K." I said. "Sit down and have one drink. Then I ought to get some solid shuteye. I'm supposed to take a little jaunt round your island tomorrow."

"My island?" exclaimed Jack, collapsing into a chair. "For God's sake, don't call it my island." He blinked and rolled his head back. "I guess you can see now why I don't drink during the day."

"Why is that?" I said.

"Because I know what would happen if I did," he said. "My hold on reality is already pretty tenuous. Look, why don't you take a tip from me and get out while you still can?"

"Out of the inn?" I said.

"No, no," he replied. "Out of St. Lucia. Out of the islands. Back to civilization, where you came from."

"But I can't," I said. "It's my vacation. I only get two weeks. I'm just down here to relax and think things over."

"My very words!" said Jack. "Exactly what I thought when I came, six weeks ago. God, it seems years, and I'm only just thirty. Would you believe it? Everyone thinks I'm about forty."

I assured him that he looked no older than thirty, and, realizing that the fellow was rather depressed, I suggested that maybe the responsibilities of the hotel were getting him down. "St. Lucia's supposed to be a beautiful island," I said. "Maybe if you got out a little more and saw some of the sights it would cheer you up."

"No, no," he said. "It's all a sham. All that tinsel on the surface only accentuates the darkness underneath. There's some kind of evil here. You feel it in the heat—a sensual, evil void. Sloth and drunkenness are only the first symptoms. You know what I think? I think Nellie plans to stay in England and leave me here to rot."

I suggested that even if Nellie should not return he could go back to England on his own.

"I suppose so," he said. "But I'm sick of England and teaching English. The cultural vacuum back there is as bad as the moral vacuum here. What I'd really like to do is to go to New York, but I hear it's hard to get work there, especially in the literary line, unless you've got contacts."

I would have preferred to avoid a literary conversation, but Jack was beginning to perk up a little. "Actually, I've got quite a bit of verse," he said. "Almost enough for a first volume. It's pretty wild stuff, but I understand that's the vogue today, especially in America."

I asked him if he'd like to recite a couple of his poems, after which, I said, I should really get some shuteye. He agreed to recite. His poems were not too wild, and I remember one that started:

Just give me a northern grave
When the long time comes...

My interest seemed to inspire Jack, who recited with sonorous gusto, and when he finally staggered out he seemed more hopeful.

The next day, after getting my glasses fixed I returned to bed, applying salves to my sunburn, and reading some more of *Escape to the West Indies*. I saw no sign of Jack, though I heard his typewriter going, but late in the afternoon Michel dropped by. I inquired how he had been spending his time.

"I have been by car throughout the whole interior," he said. "This is exactly what I've been looking for. There are sections of this island where no white man has ever been. True, the natives lack something—that French charm and friendliness—but in every other respect St. Lucia is superior even to Martinique. Such hills! Such genuine wildness! And the French influence is strong here, even in the names of the flowers—the bougainvillaea, the immortelle, the flamboyant. And then, of course, there are the hibiscus, the anthurium, the poinsettia."

"I suppose, then," I said, "that you will be staying around here awhile?"

"Oh, no," he replied. "What would be the possible point of that? It is just what I mean. Now that I have found the real island of my dreams, there is no need to go further. I guess I am a true traveller— what Baudelaire calls *les vrais voyageurs*. Are you familiar with those lines: '*Mais les vrais voyageurs sont ceux-là seuls qui partent pour partir*.'...No, now that I have discovered St. Lucia, I need go no further. In fact, I think I'll fly back to New York tomorrow and save up the rest of my vacation. That way I'll have a whole month next year. What about you?"

"I don't know," I said. "But where I work they're cracking down on guys who hoard up their vacations. Anyway, I'm too deep in this thing to pull out now."

"Well, I hope you find what you're looking for," Michel said. "I'll give you a call sometime, back in New York."

"Better than that," I said. "Let me call you."

And we agreed to have lunch together sometime.

Though I didn't mention it to Michel, I had decided that day on a rather desperate measure. The fact was that, in addition to my sinus trouble and sunburn, I had acquired other maladies, which I feared would require medical attention. Since Jack knew of no doctors on St. Lucia except "voodoo" Unattractive tourist trap though it was, it would undoubtedly have some legitimate doctors available. In any case, I didn't feel up to rowing, or even being towed to Pigeon Island, and the St. Lucia airport informed me that I could charter a helicopter to Pigeon Island direct from Barbados.

I was afraid that any arrival in Barbados as a semi-invalid might make me unpopular, but I found that the cash in the Royal Hotel, a spot remembered by my cabdriver, did not resent me or my nationality. In fact, she arranged to have a doctor call on me after I was settled. My room was directly over the Caribbean, which was surprising, for it seemed a tradition in the West Indies to keep the hotels well inland. When the doctor, a kindly West Indian arrived, he gave me a complete physical examination. It turned out that I had pseudo-dysentery and a fungus infection of the throat in addition to my sinus trouble and sunburn, but he said that my high blood pressure and nervous tension were probably due to some deeper cause. "You seem to be fighting something," he said.

I told him of my sojourns on Antigua, Martinique, and St. Lucia, and of my hopes of eventually reaching Pigeon Island. He looked at me severely. "It's out of the question for you to travel any more in your condition," he said.

As the implications of this pronouncement sank in, I slowly rose in bed. "No more travelling?" I said. "But I've only got a week's vacation left. I can't just lie here in Barbados. I've got to get to Pigeon Island."

"Can't be helped," he said, laying a restraining hand on my shoulder. "Right now, you need several days of complete rest in bed."

He prescribed an assortment of sleeping pills and tranquillizers, and suggested I move to an air-conditioned room on the other side of the hotel. "The damp salt air is bad for your throat," he explained. "The air-conditioning dehumidifies the air. Besides, the sound of that surf pounding all night on the shore can get on your nerves."

Once this move was effected, my humiliation was complete, and, lying in bed, inhaling the cool, dehumidified air, lulled into a bogus sense of serenity by the gentle hum of the air-conditioner, I resolved to regard the rest of my vacation with a kind of stoic fatalism.

Three days later, the doctor pronounced me cured, so I rose and headed into the bar. There I ran into a pharmaceutical salesman from Texas who seemed to be buying everybody drinks. He bought me one, and I asked him how business was going. "Fantastic!" he said, and mentioned that eighty-six and a half per cent of his gross sales consisted of sleeping pills and tranquillizers.

"For the tourists?" I asked.

"No, no. For the natives," he said. "They're all nervous wrecks. Don't ask me why. Some say it's because they're getting Americanized—cultural conflicts and all that. Anyway, they gobble up Miltowns like they were peanuts. What a racket!"

He seemed a pleasant fellow, and I asked him if he'd join me for lunch at the hotel. "Lunch, yes," he said. "This place, no. In my book, the food they dish out around here—flying fish and all that jazz—is strictly for the birds. But I tell you what. We'll make lunch on me. I know a great place up the beach that imports fresh steaks from the States. Strictly porterhouse. I got a little Thunderbird outside. Let's drink up, take a spin around, and see if we can't connect with a couple of gals someplace."

We did just that, and things worked out quite well. In fact, I found a kind of transcendent relief in the recognition that my vacation was a complete failure. Since I only had three days left, there wasn't much I *could* do but lie around on the beach acquiring a typical tourist tan or explore the little ocean-front clubs and bars, dancing with girls who were strictly on vacation. I even decided, my last night, that Barbados might be a good place to visit—sometime when I'm not on vacation, that is. Who knows? That way, even Bermuda might not be so bad. Riding around on that little motor bicycle was kind of fun, too.

In 1934, just as Europe crept to the brink of disaster,
London socialite Barbara Greene horrified her friends
by announcing she was off to Africa. She would
accompany her cousin, the esteemed writer Graham
Greene, on what would turn out to be an epic trek
through Liberia. Her travel notes, full of humor
and startling insights, apply the optic of a gossip
columnist to what is usually described through the
ethnographer's lens. The resulting vision of escape
from (over) civilization produces a liberating sense
of vertigo: the totally unfamiliar familiarized so that
at once reassured and titillated, one experiences
perfect peace.

from *too late to turn back*

BARBARA GREENE

it all happened after a wedding. "Why don't you come to Liberia with me?" I was asked by my cousin Graham, and, having just had a glass or two of champagne, it seemed a remarkably easy thing to do. I agreed at once. It sounded fun. Liberia, wherever it was, had a jaunty sound about it. Liberia! The more I said it to myself the more I liked it. Life was good and very cheerful. Yes, of course I would go to Liberia. All difficulties vanished in a surprising and slightly disconcerting way. I found out that Liberia was a black republic on the West Coast of Africa. I heard that its rulers were immoral and not to be trusted in any way. I was told that a trek through the hinterland was dangerous and extremely unhealthy. I read that it was one of the few parts of the world that was still unexplored. After a while my sense of elation vanished into thin air. I love my creature comforts; I had no real wish for adventure in the wilds, but apparently it was written in the stars that I should go, and by the time I had found out what I had let myself in for it was too late to turn back. It was all made so easy for me. I was told exactly what to take, and I even found on my arrival in Liberia that I had brought more or less the right things. There were a few mistakes of course. By someone whom I considered a good authority I was told to walk in riding-boots because of snakes. It sounded a little hot and uncomfortable, but who was I to judge of these things? So with a slightly doubtful mind I packed them with my other things. That, however, was but a slight mistake and only worth mentioning as it meant that I had to have shorts made in a great hurry in Freetown at the last minute. These shorts were of strange shape, very full and very brief, that somehow managed to look like a ballet skirt. I am tall and hefty and later, as we got tired towards the end of our trip, these shorts were to get so much on my cousin's nerves that he was ready to scream every time he saw them.

My camping equipment, my food, my ticket, everything was procured for me and I found myself with plenty of leisure to sit back and read. *The British Encyclopedia*, the League of Nations Report—which was far from comforting—and any other book or journal about Liberia that I could lay my hands on.

One of the few things that I had to do for myself was to get my visa from the Liberian Consulate in London. This was not so easy as might be thought. As I could not find where the Consulate was from the telephone book, I approached Thos. Cook. After a long wait I was given an address in the City. The numbers in what must surely be the most deserted street in London had apparently all been changed, for the number I was looking for was now a church. It was all very difficult, but I said to myself: "Don't give up. Things will be more difficult than this in the jungle." And so, with new life in me, I eventually managed to track down the Consul in his lair. It was a strange office, small, dirty, and very untidy. A meal was obviously just over, for dirty plates were lying everywhere about the room. The waste-paper basket was full of them. I had brought a friend with me, a Dutchman, and I began to feel glad that I was not alone, for I was not welcomed very warmly. Perhaps I had disturbed their afternoon sleep, or perhaps they were not used to visitors, for they did not seem to know what to do with me. There were two dark young men, and they spoke with a strong accent. "Liberians," I thought. "Pale kinds of half-castes." And if I had not been getting a little tired of sitting there doing nothing I would have got excited at the thought. They could not understand what I wanted, or that one should want to go to Liberia at all. I explained again. I waited. Then one of the young men spoke to the other in another language. To my great astonishment my companion joined in the conversation. They were all Dutchmen. After that we suddenly found ourselves the best of friends. I paid my guinea, and I got my visa, a large red seal stuck into my passport.

After that there was nothing to do except say good-bye. My friends were inclined to be sentimental, for they found it more exciting to believe that I would never return. They had been reading up about Liberia and, rather like myself I am afraid, were inclined to believe in the most lurid reports. So I wept a little, and boasted a lot, and went to a great many farewell parties, and tried very hard to look like an explorer as I left London in a thick mackintosh and a "sensible" hat. And gradually that sinking feeling left me and I was left full of the most glorious excitement. My strength became as the strength of ten. I could have faced a hundred angry tribes, or coped quite easily with a love-sick chief. I went over in my mind all the stories I had heard of Liberia and still, with a child-like *naïveté* believing in them all, imagined myself forever facing danger with a smile.

Now that I am back I can hardly recall all that I was told. Certainly cannibals figured largely, and slavery. Death by the most horrible diseases, and rape, appeared to be such everyday occur-rences out there that they seemed hardly worth mentioning. They were just some of the things that one took for granted, more or less. We had been told that there were few wild animals, which certainly eased our anxiety a little bit as neither of us could be called experi-enced shots. Apart from other things there was also the danger of getting off the track and losing our way. The possibility of starving seemed to me fairly remote. It struck me that we were taking an enormous amount of food. Somehow tins of things look so much more than they really are, as we found to our regret later on.

So we spent our time on board our little cargo boat—named most suitably *The David Livingstone*—thinking of dangers, and learn-ing the jargon of the West Coast of Africa from our five fellow-passengers. We drank "coasters" and ate heavy meals in the stuffy lit-tle dining-room. I foolishly slept a great deal instead of, wisely, doing exercises to harden my feet. The days passed slowly but happily. The sunsets were flamboyant as if painted for a second-rate musical com-edy, but the nights were warm and starlit, and somehow exciting as only tropical nights can be.

We called at a few ports, but they made little impression on me. I remember that I had never before seen Madeira in the rain. Then, somewhere else, I remember drinking sweet white wine in the blaz-ing sun, surrounded by glowing bougainvillea. A day or two later I remember the big black eyes fringed by artificial eyelashes, the lumpy figures, and the dirty yellow curls of the Spanish prostitutes in some night club we got to at three o'clock in the morning. The place was filthy. Someone was playing a guitar badly, and someone else was singing shrilly out of tune. A madman, drunk, and with curiously twitching limbs, was walking round the room from table to table, screaming out all kinds of threats.

After a while our excitement grew. There had been an outbreak of yellow fever on the coast and we found port after port closed to us. "Of course," I thought. "The White Man's Grave. That's what they call this part of the world at home. How very pleasant."

We stopped outside the ports. From a distance the little towns looked green and peaceful. At one of these places we left behind us the only other woman passenger, a frightened, repressed little woman who had never before left Liverpool. With a scared face she said good-bye to us and went to join a husband she had not seen since her honeymoon. She was off to start a new life in a continent which she felt in her little provincial soul she would never understand, and where yellow-fever and perhaps death were waiting to give her a welcome.

•

By five o'clock the village was astir. The darkness gradually changed into a misty grey light, and the rats scuttled away into their hiding-places. The night had seemed endless. Although I had always been told that the rat population of London was as great as the human population, I had never before seen one in my life. They are dirty creatures, and though no doubt there have been times when a tamed rat has been a solace and a joy to some poor prisoner shut away and forgotten for life, it is not an animal one would befriend from choice. My disgust of rats had been strengthened perhaps on the voyage out, for I had been reading *Four Frightened People* during the long days on board. The story came back to my mind vividly as I sat up in bed. There is a realistic description of a rat running along a passage. Suddenly it tumbles over and lies quite still. It is dead. The dreadful realisation gradually awakes in the mind of the onlooker that bubonic plague has broken out on board.

I had read in the British Government Blue Book a list of diseases that flourish in the interior of Liberia. I went over them in my mind. Malaria, elephantiasis, yaws, hook-worm, smallpox, dysentery. Did it also mention plague? I racked my brains and tried to see the print before my eyes. I remembered the rats of Monrovia were mentioned. Yes. And, of course, it also said that no steps were taken against plague, that nothing was organised to prevent it spreading and that there was no medical supervision whatsoever of boats touching the Liberian coast. I listened to the rats rushing round my hut, and remembered that plague is carried by rats.

I spent the whole night sitting up in bed frankly terrified. My hands moved round the edge of my bed, continuously tucking in my mosquito-net. I had a fearful idea that if the rats were hungry they might bite through the net, and start nibbling my toes. One of the nuns at Bolahun had most vividly described to us how she had woken up one night to find a rat on her face. A singularly unpleasant experience. In the darkness of the night my imagination ran riot. I wondered how many there were round me. But I need not have been so scared. The rats were fat and well fed, and apart from the noise they made, they left me in peace. For two or three nights they upset me and after that I grew so used to them that I ceased to notice them, and they bothered me no more.

It is strange, and perhaps rather horrible, how quickly we adapt ourselves to our surroundings. My life in England had been laid in pleasant places. All my life I had been used to well-cooked food and beautiful clothes, a lovely house filled with people who smoothed out for me as far as possible the rough patches on my road through life. I was taken care of and spoilt both by my family and my friends, and the little, dull, tiresome everyday household things were automatically done for me. I had liked to find my evening clothes spread out for me ready pressed on my bed, my bath ready for me, and then to come down to a dinner lit by candle-light. Beauty, comfort, and a good deal of luxury had been part of my life. I was used to it, and I knew that when I returned to England it would immediately become part of my life again. In Liberia I was surrounded by rats, disease, dirt, and foul smells, and yet in a very few days I had sunk to that level and did not mind at all.

We never had enough boiled water to wash really properly. Our clothes were never clean. The bristles of my hair-brush were eaten away entirely by the rats in this dirty village. It was my own fault, for I had left the brush out of my suit-case, but it meant that there was nothing I could do except throw it away; and so for the next two months—till I reached England—I did not brush my hair again. It got stiff with dust and stood out round my head like a halo.

Graham looked rather unshaved. It was not long before he gave up all attempt at shaving and tried to grow a beard. It did not get along very fast, and he never really passed the untidy beach-comber stage. My face was burnt and brown, and the dust was so rubbed into it that it took me literally weeks when I got to England to get it to look normal again. I kept my nails short, but they got broken round the edges. I was quite certainly not a thing of beauty, a joy for ever. But it did not worry me. It was all part of the existence we were leading and seemed to be perfectly natural.

We dressed, and while I was dressing I tried to see where the swarm of rats could now be hiding. But they were completely invisible. It was necessary to be careful not to put one's foot on the ground unless one had very thick soles to one's shoes. Nasty little jiggers would worm their way under one's toe-nails and happily make their home there. Though it was quite easy to have them cut out, and not particularly painful, it became tiresome if one did not notice it at once and started off on the day's trek, for the jigger would grow and send little pin-pricks of burning pain through one's foot. But however careful we were, they would creep into our feet somehow, and we soon got used to calling for the boy to come and cut them out.

I went out into the sunlight. The village was even dirtier than we had realised the night before. The tumbled-down huts were huddled together, so that there was hardly any space between them. The whitewash round the base had long ago peeled off, so that they looked grey and down-at-heel. A hideous woman walked round scraping up goat dung with her hands, on one of which there was an open sore. Goats, cows with their ribs sticking up under their thin flesh in unsightly lumps, chickens and unhealthy dogs were wandering around. The smell was sickening, and as there was a slight breeze the filthy dust blew into our eyes and throats.

Our carriers were making no attempt to get our things packed up. They were sitting about in the dust languidly and lazily. During the night they had spread themselves through the village, sleeping in whichever hut had room for extra inhabitants, for even in this village the spirit of hospitality was very great. The headman was walking about in his usual dreamy fashion. In his right hand he carried a rattle that he always had with him, and which he would shake rhythmically. He walked among the men, smiling his pleasant, vague smile, good-natured, charming, and utterly inefficient.

The name of the village was Duogobmai, and my cousin asked how far it was to Nicoboozu, which was one of the villages we were aiming at. The cry we were to hear so many times throughout our journey from our carriers rose up to heaven firmly and loudly that morning. "Too far. Too far."

"We can't stay here," we said. "It's disgusting. How far is it to the next village?"

"Too far. Too far." And the carriers sat firmly on the ground and refused to budge.

We could not blame them. The trek the day before had been very hard, and we knew that they deserved a rest. Amadu's feet were sore, and though they healed much faster, that morning they looked nearly as bad as mine. But he did not complain. The boys had been told in Freetown to look after us and their loyalty was as firm as the rock of ages. In all circumstances they upheld us against the carriers. Our word was law. They bowed their heads, and obeyed.

In spite of the dirt, I was secretly rather glad when my cousin decided that we would have to spend a day resting before going on. I had not looked forward to a long march and sat for some time in my hut bathing my feet in Epsom salts dissolved in warm water. After that we sat on our chairs in front of the hut and got out our books. As a child I had often had to play a complicated game which involved answering a great many questions. I was never very interested in the game, for it seemed to me that the questions were too academic, and too useless for everyday life. But one of the questions was, I remember, "If you had to spend the rest of your life on a desert island, what two books would you take, and why?" One of my cousins once slightly enlivened the game with a small flash of wit by answering, "Lamb and Bacon." But in my answers I never rose to anything higher than the heavily obvious. My time had been wasted, I had apparently learnt absolutely nothing from the game. So far as I remember, no one ever suggested Saki or Somerset Maugham. But nevertheless I think the choice was not entirely foolish, for though they interested me they demanded no great concentration from a tired brain. But they certainly had their limitations. One read through them too quickly. It would have been better to have taken some more ambitious book my mind could have struggled with while I was still fresh, and to have been able to keep the short stories for later. But I had no other books with me. Graham was soon deep in the *Anatomy of Melancholy*. I had already read right through the stories of Saki and Somerset Maugham, and now bored and listlessly I started again at the beginning.

The villagers crowded round us. They pinched my arms to see what my white skin felt like. Their great staring eyes watched every movement. They gaped at me as I wrote in my diary, as I bent to tie up my shoe lace, or when the dust in my throat made me choke. And they rose as one man when the demands of nature made me wish to disappear into the bush alone for a moment. It was a long path that led down into the forest, but they followed, silent and curious. I turned round and said irritably: "Shoo! Go away!" and waved my arms. They stared, and the children crept closer. I called my cousin to bring his camera. He stood and guarded my way while I dashed into the bush. The children watched him lifting up the little black box, and then, screaming, they ran away.

My eyes left my book. I had read several pages without taking in a single word of what I was reading. I had not, after all, come all this way to read short stories several times over. There was surely something in this wretched village that could amuse or distract me; something that was not entirely repellent.

Our cook was preparing some fish that he had managed to get hold of somehow for our lunch. He sat in the road absorbed in his work, like a priest preparing a sacrifice. The expression on his face was intent and uplifted. The expression on his face was intent and uplifted. He was not disturbed by the scraggy, unhealthy dogs which came up and sniffed at the fish, but nonchalantly put out his hand and pushed them away. Neither did he mind the skinny chickens scratching in the dust, or the goats that bumped up against him and got in his way. All round him the dust was blowing in little clouds through the village. We could not help fearing that this peculiarly unpleasant sight might spoil our appetites for the food he was preparing with such care, so we asked him to move somewhere where we could not see him. Seriously he collected his things together and shuffled off in his long white robes, a little stream of goats and dogs following him.

Our carriers enjoyed the village, for they had nothing to do all day and the chief had given them good food. I envied them their ability of being entirely idle without boredom. They could sit, leaning against the sides of the huts for hours, doing nothing, saying nothing and, I am convinced, thinking nothing. They were contented, for they lived in the moment, and just then they had everything they wanted—the burning sun on their skins, enough to eat and plenty of companionship. And they also had the monkey to keep them amused. It sat all day on Mark's head, and hissed and spat when Laminah came near it with his irritating tricks. Its little blood-shot eyes glimmered with hate, and Mark would take it off his head for a few moments and pet it and give it a banana to eat.

It seemed a long day, for nothing happened. From time to time we moved our chairs a little bit, for the sun was blinding and we tried to keep in the shade. As we moved, all our audience moved too. Graham gave a very old man a cigarette. He spluttered and choked, and the tears rolled down his cheeks as he tried to smoke it, and then he passed it on. A wave of life passed over the group round us as long as the cigarette lasted, and then died down like a puff of wind on a summer's day. It was very hot, and I had not yet got used to the smell of black bodies.

The chief came and sat near us, and his eyes glistened greedily as he saw the whisky bottle. My cousin, remembering the food he had given the carriers, gave him a drink as a sign of gratitude. The chief tossed it off, and in less than a second he was blind drunk. He got up unsteadily, and muttering and dribbling he tottered round the village. We saw him rolling off to his hut, and we were not sorry to see the last of him. He was a nasty, depraved old man, with a crafty, mean face, and obviously at some time must have known civilisation of the coast. There was nothing simple and unspoilt about this village. It was twisted and bad. There was an atmosphere of decay everywhere. One could feel it, see it, and smell it. Even the children were like horrid old men, and their wicked little faces grinned at us. I felt that if we stayed in this village much longer we, too, would deteriorate and go bad, the atmosphere of degeneration was so strong. It was all round us and touched us closely. It lay in the air we breathed and in the food we eat. How this loathsome unhealthiness had crept in I do not know, but I could only suppose that it had come up somehow from the semi-civilisation of the coast. I kept looking at Graham to see if I could see any change beginning in him, for I could not understand how we could escape being contaminated. I thought I might see that shameful, shameless look creep into his eyes. I half expected his face to alter, and his body to become diseased and horrible like those around us. The unlovely nakedness pressing so close to me filled me with repulsion. It disgusted me. There was no beauty, no freshness, in the village anywhere.

Night came at last. We ate our supper in front of the gaping crowds, and drank whisky. We would like to have entered a state of sweet forgetfulness, to feel the sharp edges blurred. It would be pleasant if, for the rest of the evening, we could lose this sense of quivering disgust at the sore bodies around us—if we could rise above them or, at any rate, feel sympathy for them. But the whisky seemed to have no effect on us at all. We drank again, and thought of our friends in London, and wondered what they were doing, and where they were. I began to get that feeling of being outside my own body, and I watched from afar those two little white creatures in the heart of Liberia among the dirt and filth. Two small white puppets, pulled by strings out of their usual course, and dragged hither and thither into incongruous situations. Two white dolls sitting stiffly on absurd green canvas chairs, drinking whisky, and wondering where the strings would pull them to next. So useless, so ineffective—just paper dolls who would soon pass on and leave the rotting village to decay and die.

The hours crawled by, and at last it was late enough to go to bed. It was another sleepless, fearful night among the rats. I lay awake, but desperately tired, and longed for the grey light of the dawn to come creeping into my hut.

We left Duogobmai next morning as early as possible, and walked away from it with no regrets in our hearts. It was a beautiful morning, although it soon got very hot, and the walk was pleasant. Graham raced on ahead as usual, but I sauntered. The men were in a good mood and sang their strange songs without stopping. We walked through thick forest, but the track was easy, and the way was much shorter than I had imagined it would be. We could have walked only eight or nine miles when we arrived at Nicoboozu, and I felt quite fresh as I walked into the village.

Nicoboozu was a charming place and beautifully clean. The huts were far apart from one another, and the spaces in between were swept. All through the village we could hear the sounds of laughter and gaiety. We were in the heart of the Buzie country, which is supposed to be the only artistic tribe of Liberia, although until we came to this village we had seen no signs of their culture. Here everything was beautiful. The bases of the huts were painted with strange designs. The village blacksmith made rings and bracelets out of old Napoleon coins which were still to be found in French Guinea, and which were brought over into Liberia by the wandering tribe, the Mandingos. The women also wore beautiful little ornaments in their fuzzy black hair. There were men busy weaving cloth on their primitive looms. The patterns were simple, effective, and unselfconscious. They wove the material in long strips, securing one end with a heavy stone, which they moved farther and farther from the loom as they went on weaving. The people, artistic by nature, were incapable of making ugly things. The spearheads and swords were most delicately carved.

It was impossible not to feel happy. Our one grumbling porter had left us, and we had got one in his place who loved to sing. It was agony to him to keep silent. He was a member of the Buzie tribe, and all the time his voice could be heard lifted up in weird, monotonous songs.

The village was a wonderful contrast from Duogobmai. We were welcomed enthusiastically by the men and women. They flocked round us, merry and high-spirited, chattering as madly as birds at dawn. The women felt the material of my shorts, rubbing it between their fingers like women at a bargain sale. The men stood round smiling. With very few exceptions did the men of the country ever look upon me with special interest as a woman. To them I was just some white creature, strange and curious perhaps, but not in the least sexually exciting. I could have wandered round by myself with perfect safety.

In a way, I suppose, my cousin and I were a kind of circus to the natives, an unexpected amusement brought suddenly into their lives for a day or two. On those occasions when I had a hut to myself at night I had no fear at all that my slumbers might be disturbed by the Don Juan of the village. The first time, I confess, I had wondered whether I should have the revolver within reach, but as I occasionally walk or do odd things in my sleep, I thought on the whole it might be better kept under lock and key in the money-box. But I quickly realised that my appeal was non-existent, and though in any other circumstances my pride might have been hurt, in Liberia I could but feel profoundly thankful!

The village girls crowded into my hut with me and watched with great interest while I changed my shirt and washed. I did not mind their being there. They were charming, and smiled at me so excitedly and shyly. When I washed myself they could not understand what the soap was, but loved the way it made the water fluffy. They dipped the tips of their fingers into it when I had finished, and then gazed at the bubbles as they gradually disappeared. I broke off a small corner of the soap and gave them a piece, and it was passed round eagerly from hand to hand, till one of them tried to eat it. They stroked my arms, not rudely and inquisitively as they had done it at the last village, but gently, which I learnt later was a sign of approval. Although we could exchange no word, we laughed together and felt friendly and happy.

The women had their breasts, and sometimes the whole of their bodies down to the waist, cut in strange patterns during their time in bush school. Some of the very young girls in this village were quite lovely; they held their heads high and moved gracefully. But disease soon ravaged their bodies. The older women looked gaunt and withered, and unattractive in their nakedness. But in spite of the sores and the unhealthiness there was a freshness in the village, a cleanliness of spirit, and a charm that came straight from the heart. Their manners were good and dignified. The women realised at once when I no longer wanted to have them near me, and gracefully they withdrew and left me alone. Somehow we came very near to understanding one another, and I felt I was among people I liked.

I went out and wandered round the village. It was similar to all other villages. It was set on a clearing on the top of the hill, and down below I could see the river. In the centre of the village there was the usual palaver-house, a hut with open sides, where any kind of meetings and discussions could be held. The blacksmith was working in his smithy. I did not at that time know how important a man the blacksmith was—more important than the chief himself—but I noticed that the men and women gathered round his fire for a chat and a gossip.

A curious smell spread through the whole village. It was unlike anything I had ever smelt in Europe. It was heavy and nauseating. I had noticed it already sometimes on our trip, but it was only at Nicoboozu that I learnt that it was the food for our men that smelt in this unappetising way.

The chief roused himself from his slumbers and asked us to come and inspect it. There were eight enormous bowls of rice covered with an evil-smelling, bright yellow sauce, with odd lumps of meat or fish thrown on the top. It was a most revolting sight, but our men's eyes brightened. It was their one meal of the day. In our ignorance at first we occasionally allowed them to eat in the mornings, before we started on the day's march. We soon learnt that those invariably were bad days. The men were not used to two meals a day, and it made them lazy and ill-tempered. That night they were delighted with what they received. "Plenty fine chop," said Mark greedily, as he elbowed himself into a place by one of the bowls. The men crouched over their food, hollowed out their right hands into a kind of spoon, mixed up the food in the bowl, and stuffed their mouths full. There was no talking or laughing while they ate. It was a very serious business. Hurriedly they crammed themselves up with food, chewed it quickly and stuffed it down, and then, satiated, they got up slowly; cheerful and good-natured.

Graham and I had our supper. It was one of our happiest evenings together—one of the last times when we could talk completely naturally to one another, without wondering whether anything we said could possibly hurt the other in any way. So soon after that we had to give up discussing subjects on which we held different points of view. It sounds unbelievably childish now, but in our weariness we got easily impatient with arguments. My tiredness made my brain work even more slowly than it usually does, and I would grope unsuccessfully for the words I needed. Sometimes as I was in the very middle of saying something my strength would give out and I would murmur weakly, "I expect you're right, really," which must have irritated my cousin profoundly. Graham, on the other hand, would sometimes become rather obstinate, hanging on to some small, unimportant point like a dog to a bone. But we never quarrelled, not once. We knew so well that it was the ghastly damp heat that was lowering our vitality, and we would smile at one another and think, "We won't talk about that again." Politics was the first thing to go. I sometimes heard myself expressing the most extraordinary ideas, professing the strangest beliefs. Words would come out of my mouth which had nothing to do with my own thoughts. I would listen to the tired voice, and think, "What an odd thing to say." Sometimes what I was saying would sound so dull that I could hardly bear to hear it myself, and I would lose interest in the middle of a sentence. So many unfinished sentences; so many words; sounds trailing away into nothingness and floating off into the hot, moist air. One subject after another would be put away, left on one side, marked carefully, "Not wanted during voyage," till gradually practically nothing remained on the last day or two of our trip except the enthralling subject of food. By that time, of course, it was the one thing above all others that really interested us, and we found that we did not irritate each other by longing for different kinds of food. But those days were still to come. In Nicoboozu we did not even guess that they would ever come. We were feeling so well, and not yet tired, and our minds were fresh. Both of us were enchanted with the village, happy and completely under the spell of the African night.

Rather messily with our hands we squeezed out some limes, added a little whisky and pretended that we were drinking ice-cold cocktails. We lingered over our meal. Our cook had made us an enormous omelette, opened a tin of something for our second course, and with a lack of imagination that was unusual for him, he made another large omelette, which, however, he called a pancake. Amadu, Laminah, and Mark served us with the greatest dignity and care, as if we were dining at some important function in London. The food that they placed before us might have been the most rare, the most exotic dishes. My shorts felt shorter than ever. An evening gown and orchids would have fitted better with their manner.

We ate in front of our hut, and as we were eating, the daylight disappeared with tropical suddenness, and night fell. It was a warm night, but not too hot. A small moon appeared in the sky, and the little white huts shone in the silver light around us. An unreal light, rather theatrical. I began quite suddenly to feel the overwhelming magic of Africa. Its strange charm crept over me. Like a drug it gets into the brain and sends it to sleep, so that nothing remains alive but the senses. The warmth flows into one's limbs, the music of the harps into the soul, the timelessness into the spirit, and the rest is perfect well-being and a tremendous peace. I wanted to hang on to the minute. It was one of those moments in life when one is stand- ing on tiptoe, afraid to move or breathe for fear one might break the spell; one of those precious times when one feels, "I am perfect- ly happy." I was conscious of it as I was sitting there in the dark. At that moment I wanted nothing more, nothing different in any way.

barbara greene   271

The women were walking through the village carrying glowing wood from the smithy with which to light the fires they always had in their huts during the night, and gradually through the door of every hut could be seen little leaping flames. All round us were the sounds of tinkling harps. Our carriers were sitting together laughing and contented, drinking palm wine.

There was a breathless moment of hesitation in the air, as if time for once was standing still so that we might absorb the moment; to give us this one chance to fill ourselves to the utmost with peace and beauty.

A few women came and danced in front of us. They were led by a hideous old hag, who cackled as she twisted and shook her withered body to the rhythm of the rattles. It was, to our ideas, an ugly dance, and even the youngest of the women could not succeed in looking graceful as she stuck out her behind and kicked out her legs. But they were merry and gay. They danced in a small circle, with their fingers held out straight, and slapped their thighs in time to the music. Their movements were awkward and jerky, but they laughed and, as they danced, they called out jokes to each other.

After that there was more dancing. The moon goes to the heads of the natives like strong wine. All night they danced. The men began and the women moved to one side and watched. One could feel the excitement. Sometimes they let out strange little shouts. They stamped their feet and clapped their bodies with their hands. Even the children feel the strong influence of the moon, and the little naked piccaninnies were hopping madly round between the houses. Later, as the moon waned, we saw less and less dancing, but that night they were drunk with it.

I would like to linger over this evening, but there is nothing more one can say. Nothing happened. There was no sense of anticlimax. It was something perfect in itself. There was a moon and a native village, dancing, and naked black babies laughing. There were two white people watching and having their arms stroked from time to time. There was friendliness, and gaiety that came straight from the heart. And, wonder of wonders, there was a hut that night with no rats!

The scientist, poet, and lover fill us with envy. So voracious and absolute is their absorption in the object of their passion—intellectual, artistic, amatory—that it leaves no foothold for the claims of that distracting life that ordinarily splinters our days into a thousand meek annoyances, quick fixes, and petty disappointments. They, the lucky ones, are capable of the ultimate escape—they have tapped into a source of ecstasy and enchantment that makes the very thought of escape ludicrous. Vladimir Nabokov, an esteemed lepidopterist with a genius for language (to reverse the usual priority of his vocations) beguiles us to follow him through the magic door of his lepidopteric passion into a realm where the lover, the poet, and the scientist merge into one. And where chasing after a butterfly is the next best thing to nirvana.

from *speak, memory*

VLADIMIR NABOKOV

1

on a summer morning, in the legendary Russia of my boyhood, my first glance upon awakening was for the chink between the white inner shutters. If it disclosed a watery pallor, one had better not open them at all, and so be spared the sight of a sullen day sitting for its picture in a puddle. How resentfully one would deduce, from a line of dull light, the leaden sky, the sodden sand, the gruel-like mess of broken brown blossoms under the lilacs—and that flat, fallow leaf (the first casualty of the season) pasted upon a wet garden bench!

But if the chink was a long glint of dewy brilliancy, then I made haste to have the window yield its treasure. With one blow, the room would be cleft into light and shade. The foliage of birches moving in the sun had the translucent green tone of grapes, and in contrast to this there was the dark velvet of fir trees against a blue of extraordinary intensity, the like of which I rediscovered only many years later, in the montane zone of Colorado.

From the age of seven, everything I felt in connection with a rectangle of framed sunlight was dominated by a single passion. If my first glance of the morning was for the sun, my first thought was for the butterflies it would engender. The original event had been banal enough. On the honeysuckle, overhanging the carved back of a bench just opposite the main entrance, my guiding angel (whose wings, except for the absence of a Florentine limbus, resemble those of Fra Angelico's Gabriel) pointed out to me a rare visitor, a splendid, pale-yellow creature with black blotches, blue crenels, and a cinnabar eyespot above each chrome-rimmed black tail. As it probed the inclined flower from which it hung, its powdery body slightly bent, it kept restlessly jerking its great wings, and my desire for it was one of the most intense I have ever experienced. Agile Ustin, our town-house janitor, who for a comic reason (explained elsewhere) happened to be that summer in the country with us, somehow managed to catch it in my cap, after which it was transferred, cap and all, to a wardrobe, where domestic naphthalene was fondly expected by Mademoiselle to kill it overnight. On the following morning, however, when she unlocked the wardrobe to take something out, my Swallowtail, with a mighty rustle, flew into her face, then made for the open window, and presently was but a golden fleck dipping and dodging and soaring eastward, over timber and tundra, to Vologda, Viatka and Perm, and beyond the gaunt Ural range to Yakutsk and Verkhne Kolymsk, and from Verkhne Kolymsk, where it lost a tail, to the fair Island of St. Lawrence, and across Alaska to Dawson, and southward along the Rocky Mountains—to be finally overtaken and captured, after a forty-year race, on an immigrant dandelion under an endemic aspen near Boulder. In a letter from Mr. Brune to Mr. Rawlins, June 14, 1735, in the Bodleian collection, he states that one Mr. Vernon followed a butterfly nine miles before he could catch him (*The Recreative Review or Eccentricities of Literature and Life*, Vol. 1, p.144, London, 1821).

Soon after the wardrobe affair I found a spectacular moth, marooned in a corner of a vestibule window, and my mother dispatched it with ether. In later years, I used many killing agents, but the least contact with the initial stuff would always cause the porch of the past to light up and attract that blundering beauty. Once, as a grown man, I was under ether during appendectomy, and with the vividness of a decalcomania picture I saw my own self in a sailor suit mounting a freshly emerged Emperor moth under the guidance of a Chinese lady who I knew was my mother. It was all there, brilliantly reproduced in my dream, while my own vitals were being exposed: the soaking, ice-cold absorbent cotton pressed to the insect's lemurian head; the subsiding spasms of its body; the satisfying crackle produced by the pin penetrating the hard crust of its thorax; the careful insertion of the point of the pin in the cork-bottomed groove of the spreading board; the symmetrical adjustment of the thick, strong-veined wings under neatly affixed strips of semitransparent paper.

2

I must have been eight when, in a storeroom of our country house, among all kinds of dusty objects, I discovered some wonderful books acquired in the days when my mother's mother had been interested in natural science and had had a famous university professor of zoology (Shimkevich) give private lessons to her daughter. Some of these books were mere curios, such as the four huge brown folios of Albertus Seba's work (*Locupletissimi Rerum Naturalium Thesauri Accurata Descriptio...*), printed in Amsterdam around 1750. On their coarse-grained pages I found woodcuts of serpents and butterflies and embryos. The fetus of an Ethiopian female child hanging by the neck in a glass jar used to give me a nasty shock every time I came across it; nor did I much care for the stuffed hydra on plate CII, with its seven lion-toothed turtleheads on seven serpentine necks and its strange, bloated body which bore buttonlike tubercules along the sides and ended in a knotted tail.

Other books I found in that attic, among herbariums full of alpine columbines, and blue palemoniums, and Jove's campions, and orange-red lilies, and other Davos flowers, came closer to my subject. I took in my arms and carried downstairs glorious loads of fantastically attractive volumes: Maria Sibylla Merian's (1647–1717) lovely plates of Surinam insects, and Esper's noble *Die Schmetterlinge* (Erlangen, 1777), and Boisduval's *Icones Historiques de Lépidoptères Nouveaux ou Peu Connus* (Paris, begun in 1832). Still more exciting were the products of the latter half of the century—Newman's *Natural History of British Butterflies and Moths*, Hofmann's *Die Gross-Schmetterlinge Europas*, the Grand Duke Nikolay Mihailovich's *Mémoires* on Asiatic lepidoptera (with incomparably beautiful figures painted by Kavrigin, Rybakov, Lang), Scudder's stupendous work on the *Butterflies of New England*.

Retrospectively, the summer of 1905, though quite vivid in many ways, is not animated yet by a single bit of quick flutter or colored fluff around or across the walks with the village schoolmaster: the Swallowtail of June, 1906, was still in the larval stage on a roadside umbellifer; but in the course of that month I became acquainted with a score or so of common things, and Mademoiselle was already referring to a certain forest road that culminated in a marshy meadow full of Small Pearl-bordered Fritillaries (thus called in my first unforgettable and unfadingly magical little manual, Richard South's *The Butterflies of the British Isles* which had just come out at the time) as *le chemin des papillons bruns.* The following year I became aware that many of our butterflies and moths did not occur in England or Central Europe, and more complete atlases helped me to determine them. A severe illness (pneumonia, with fever up to 41° centigrade), in the beginning of 1907, mysteriously abolished the rather monstrous gift of numbers that had made of me a child prodigy during a few months (today I cannot multiply 13 by 17 without pencil and paper; I can add them up, though, in a trice, the teeth of the three fitting in neatly); but the butterflies survived. My mother accumulated a library and a museum around my bed, and the longing to describe a new species completely replaced that of discovering a new prime number. A trip to Biarritz, in August 1907, added new wonders (though not as lucid and numerous as they were to be in 1909). By 1908, I had gained absolute control over the European lepidoptera as known to Hofmann. By 1910, I had dreamed my way through the first volumes of Seitz's prodigious picture book *Die Gross-Schmetterlinge der Erde*, had purchased a number of rarities recently described, and was voraciously reading entomological periodicals, especially English and Russian ones. Great upheavals were taking place in the development of systematics. Since the middle of the century, Continental lepidopterology had been, on the whole, a simple and stable affair, smoothly run by the Germans. Its high priest, Dr. Staudinger, was also the head of the largest firm of insect dealers. Even now, half a century after his death, German lepidopterists have not quite managed to shake off the hypnotic spell occasioned by his authority. He was still alive when his school began to lose ground as a scientific force in the world. While he and his followers stuck to specific and generic names sanctioned by long usage and were content to classify butterflies by characters visible to the naked eye, English-speaking authors were introducing nomenclatorial changes as a result of a strict application of the law of priority and taxonomic changes based on the microscopic study of organs. The Germans did their best to ignore the new trends and continued to cherish the philately-like side of entomology. Their solicitude for the "average collector who should not be made to dissect" is comparable to the way nervous publishers of popular novels pamper the "average reader"—who should not be made to think.

There was another more general change, which coincided with my ardent adolescent interest in butterflies and moths. The Victorian and Staudingerian kind of species, hermetic and homogeneous, with sundry (alpine, polar, insular, etc.) "varieties" affixed to it from the outside, as it were, like incidental appendages, was replaced by a new, multiform and fluid kind of species, organically *consisting* of geographical races or subspecies. The evolutional aspects of the case were thus brought out more clearly, by means of more flexible methods of classification, and further links between butterflies and the central problems of nature were provided by biological investigations.

The mysteries of mimicry had a special attraction for me. Its phenomena showed an artistic perfection usually associated with man-wrought things. Consider the imitation of oozing poison by bubblelike macules on a wing (complete with pseudo-refraction) or by glossy yellow knobs on a chrysalis ("Don't eat me—I have already been squashed, sampled and rejected"). Consider the tricks of an acrobatic caterpillar (of the Lobster Moth) which in infancy looks like bird's dung, but after molting develops scrabbly hymenopteroid appendages and baroque characteristics, allowing the extraordinary fellow to play two parts at once (like the actor in Oriental shows who *becomes* a pair of intertwisted wrestlers): that of a writhing larva and that of a big ant seemingly harrowing it. When a certain moth resembles a certain wasp in shape and color, it also walks and moves its antennae in a waspish, unmothlike manner. When a butterfly has to look like a leaf, not only are all the details of a leaf beautifully rendered but markings mimicking grub-bored holes are generously thrown in. "Natural selection," in the Darwinian sense, could not explain the miraculous coincidence of imitative aspect and imitative behavior, nor could one appeal to the theory of "the struggle for life" when a protective device was carried to a point of mimetic subtlety, exuberance, and luxury far in excess of a predator's power of appreciation. I discovered in nature the nonutilitarian delights that I sought in art. Both were a form of magic, both were a game of intricate enchantment and deception.

3

I have hunted butterflies in various climes and disguises: as a pretty boy in knickerbockers and sailor cap; as a lanky cosmopolitan expatriate in flannel bags and beret; as a fat hatless old man in shorts. Most of my cabinets have shared the fate of our Vyra house. Those in our town house and the small addendum I left in the Yalta Museum have been destroyed, no doubt, by carpet beetles and other pests. A collection of South European stuff that I started in exile vanished in Paris during World War Two. All my American captures from 1940 to 1960 (several thousands of specimens including great rarities and types) are in the Mus. of Comp. Zoology, the Am. Nat. Hist. Mus., and the Cornell Univ. Mus. of Entomology, where they are safer than they would be in Tomsk or Atomsk. Incredibly happy memories, quite comparable, in fact, to those of my Russian boyhood, are associated with my research work at the MCZ, Cambridge, Mass. (1941–1948). No less happy have been the many collecting trips taken almost every summer, during twenty years, through most of the states of my adopted country.

In Jackson Hole and in the Grand Canyon, on the mountain slopes above Telluride, Colo., and on a celebrated pine barren near Albany, N.Y., dwell, and will dwell, in generations more numerous than editions, the butterflies I have described as new. Several of my finds have been dealt with by other workers; some have been named after me. One of these, Nabokov's Pug (*Eupithecia nabokovi* McDunnough), which I boxed one night in 1943 on a picture window of James Laughlin's Alta Lodge in Utah, fits most philosophically into the thematic spiral that began in a wood on the Oredezh around 1910—or perhaps even earlier, on that Nova Zemblan river a century and a half ago.

Few things indeed have I known in the way of emotion or appetite, ambition or achievement, that could surpass in richness and strength the excitement of entomological exploration. From the very first it had a great many intertwinkling facets. One of them was the acute desire to be alone, since any companion, no matter how quiet, interfered with the concentrated enjoyment of my mania. Its gratification admitted of no compromise or exception. Already when I was ten, tutors and governesses knew that the morning was mine and cautiously kept away.

In this connection, I remember the visit of a schoolmate, a boy of whom I was very fond and with whom I had excellent fun. He arrived one summer night—in 1913, I think—from a town some twenty-five miles away. His father had recently perished in an accident, the family was ruined and the stouthearted lad, not being able to afford the price of a railway ticket, had bicycled all those miles to spend a few days with me.

On the morning following his arrival, I did everything I could to get out of the house for my morning hike without his knowing where I had gone. Breakfastless, with hysterical haste, I gathered my net, pill boxes, killing jar, and escaped through the window. Once in the forest, I was safe; but still I walked on, my calves quaking, my eyes full of scalding tears, the whole of me twitching with shame and self-disgust, as I visualized my poor friend, with his long pale face and black tie, moping in the hot garden—patting the panting dogs for want of something better to do, and trying hard to justify my absence to himself.

Let me look at my demon objectively. With the exception of my parents, no one really understood my obsession, and it was many years before I met a fellow sufferer. One of the first things I learned was not to depend on others for the growth of my collection. One summer afternoon, in 1911, Mademoiselle came into my room, book in hand, started to say she wanted to show me how wittily Rousseau denounced zoology (in favor of botany), and by then was too far gone in the gravitational process of lowering her bulk into an armchair to be stopped by my howl of anguish: on that seat I had happened to leave a glass-lidded cabinet tray with long, lovely series of the Large White. Her first reaction was one of stung vanity: her weight, surely, could not be accused of damaging what in fact it had demolished; her second was to console me: *Allons donc, ce ne sont que des papillons de potager!*—which only made matters worse. A Sicilian pair recently purchased from Staudinger had been crushed and bruised. A huge Biarritz example was utterly mangled. Smashed, too, were some of my choicest local captures. Of these, an aberration resembling the Canarian race of the species might have been mended with a few drops of glue; but a precious gynandromorph, left side male, right side female, whose abdomen could not be traced and whose wings had come off, was lost forever: one might reattach the wings but one could not prove that all four belonged to that headless thorax on its bent pin. Next morning, with an air of great mystery, poor Mademoiselle set off for St. Petersburg and came back in the evening bringing me ("something better than your cabbage butterflies") a banal Urania moth mounted on plaster. "How you hugged me, how you danced with joy!" she exclaimed ten years later in the course of inventing a brand-new past.

Our country doctor, with whom I had left the pupae of a rare moth when I went on a journey abroad, wrote me that everything had hatched finely; but in reality a mouse had got at the precious pupae, and upon my return the deceitful old man produced some common Tortoiseshell butterflies, which, I presume, he had hurriedly caught in his garden and popped into the breeding cage as plausible substitutes (so *he* thought). Better than he, was an enthusiastic kitchen boy who would sometimes borrow my equipment and come back two hours later in triumph with a bagful of seething invertebrate life and several additional items. Loosening the mouth of the net which he had tied up with a string, he would pour out his cornucopian spoil—a mass of grasshoppers, some sand, the two parts of a mushroom he had thriftily plucked on the way home, more grasshoppers, more sand, and one battered Small White.

In the works of major Russian poets I can discover only two lepidopteral images of genuinely sensuous quality: Bunin's impeccable evocation of what is certainly a Tortoiseshell:

> And there will fly into the room
> A colored butterfly in silk
> To flutter, rustle and pit-pat
> On the blue ceiling...

and Fet's "Butterfly" soliloquizing:

> Whence have I come and whither am I hasting
> Do not inquire;
> Now on a graceful flower I have settled
> And now respire.

In French poetry one is struck by Musset's well-known lines (in *Le Saule*):

> Le phalène doré dans sa course légère
> Traverse les prés embaumés

which is an absolutely exact description of the crepuscular flight of the male of the geometrid called in England the Orange moth; and there is Fargue's fascinatingly apt phrase (in *Les Quatres Journées*) about a garden which, at nightfall, *se glace de bleu comme l'aile du grand Sylvain* (the Poplar Admirable). And among the very few genuine lepidopterological images in English poetry, my favorite is Browning's

> On our other side is the straight-up rock;
> And a path is kept 'twixt the gorge and it
> By boulder-stones where lichens mock
> The marks on a moth, and small ferns fit
> Their teeth to the polished block
>
>   ("By the Fire-side")

It is astounding how little the ordinary person notices butterflies. "None," calmly replied that sturdy Swiss hiker with Camus in his rucksack when purposely asked by me for the benefit of my incredulous companion if he had seen any butterflies while descending the trail where, a moment before, you and I had been delighting in swarms of them. It is also true that when I call up the image of a particular path remembered in minute detail but pertaining to a summer before that of 1906, preceding, that is, the date on my first locality label, and never revisited, I fail to make out one wing, one wingbeat, one azure flash, one moth-gemmed flower, as if an evil spell had been cast on the Adriatic coast making all its "leps" (as the slangier among us say) invisible. Exactly thus an entomologist may feel some day when plodding beside a jubilant, and already helmetless botanist amid the hideous flora of a parallel planet, with not a single insect in sight; and thus (in odd proof of the odd fact that whenever possible the scenery of our infancy is used by an economically minded producer as a ready-made setting for our adult dreams) the seaside hilltop of a certain recurrent nightmare of mine, whereinto I smuggle a collapsible net from my waking state, is gay with thyme and melilot, but incomprehensibly devoid of all the butterflies that should be there.

I also found out very soon that a "lepist" indulging in his quiet quest was apt to provoke strange reactions in other creatures. How often, when a picnic had been arranged, and I would be self-consciously trying to get my humble implements unnoticed into the tar-smelling charabanc (a tar preparation was used to keep flies away from the horses) or the tea-smelling Opel convertible (benzine forty years ago smelled that way), some cousin or aunt of mine would remark: "Must you *really* take that net with you? Can't you enjoy yourself like a normal boy? Don't you think you are spoiling everybody's pleasure?" Near a sign NACH BODENLAUBE, at Bad Kissingen, Bavaria, just as I was about to join for a long walk my father and majestic old Muromtsev (who, four years before, in 1906, had been President of the first Russian Parliament), the latter turned his marble head toward me, a vulnerable boy of eleven, and said with his famous solemnity: "come with us by all means, but do not chase butterflies, child. It spoils the rhythm of the walk." On a path above the Black Sea, in the Crimea, among shrubs in waxy bloom, in March 1918, a bow-legged Bolshevik sentry attempted to arrest me for signaling (with my net, he said) to a British warship. In the summer of 1929, every time I walked through a village in the Eastern Pyrenees, and happened to look back, I would see in my wake the villagers frozen in the various attitudes my passage had caught them in, as if I were Sodom and they Lot's wife. A decade later, in the Maritime Alps, I once noticed the grass undulate in a serpentine way behind me because a fat rural policeman was wriggling after me on his belly to find out if I were not trapping songbirds. America has shown even more of this morbid interest in my retiary activities than other countries have—perhaps because I was in my forties when I came there to live, and the older the man, the queerer he looks with a butterfly net in his hand. Stern farmers have drawn my attention to NO FISHING signs; from cars passing me on the highway have come wild howls of derision; sleepy dogs, though unmindful of the worst bum, have perked up and come at me, snarling; tiny tots have pointed me out to their puzzled mamas; broad-minded vacationists have asked me whether I was catching bugs for bait; and one morning on a wasteland, lit by tall yuccas in bloom, near Santa Fe, a big black mare followed me for more than a mile.

4

When, having shaken off all pursuers, I took the rough, red road that ran from our Vyra house toward field and forest, the animation and luster of the day seemed like a tremor of sympathy around me.

Very fresh, very dark Arran Browns, which emerged only every second year (conveniently, retrospection has fallen here into line), flitted among the firs or revealed their red markings and checkered fringes as they sunned themselves on the roadside bracken. Hopping above the grass, a diminutive Ringlet called Hero dodged my net. Several moths, too, were flying—gaudy sun lovers that sail from flower to flower like painted flies, or male insomniacs in search of hidden females, such as that rust-colored Oak Eggar hurtling across the shrubbery. I noticed (one of the major mysteries of my childhood) a soft pale green wing caught in a spider's web (by then I knew what it was part of a Large Emerald). The tremendous larva of the Goat Moth, ostentatiously segmented, flat-headed, flesh-colored and glossily flushed, a strange creature "as naked as a worm" to use a French comparison, crossed my path in frantic search for a place to pupate (the awful pressure of metamorphosis, the aura of a disgraceful fit in a public place). On the bark of that birch tree, the stout one near the park wicket, I had found last spring a dark aberration of Sievers' Carmelite (just another gray moth to the reader). In the ditch, under the bridgelet, a bright-yellow Silvius Skipper hobnobbed with a dragonfly (just a blue libellula to me). From a flower head two male Coppers rose to a tremendous height, fighting all the way up—and then, after a while, came the downward flash of one of them returning to his thistle. These were familiar insects, but at any moment something better might cause me to stop with a quick intake of breath. I remember one day when I warily brought my net closer and closer to an uncommon Hairstreak that had daintily settled on a sprig. I could clearly see the white W on its chocolate-brown underside. Its wings were closed and the inferior ones were rubbing against each other in a curious circular motion—possibly producing some small, blithe crepitation pitched too high for a human ear to catch. I had long wanted that particular species, and, when near enough, I struck. You have heard champion tennis players moan after muffing an easy shot. You may have seen the face of the world-famous grandmaster Wilhelm Edmundson when, during a simultaneous display in a Minsk café, he lost his rook, by an absurd oversight, to the local amateur and pediatrician, Dr. Schach, who eventually won. But that day nobody (except my older self) could see me shake out a piece of twig from an otherwise empty net and stare at a hole in the tarlatan.

5

Near the intersection of two carriage roads (one, well-kept, running north-south in between our "old" and "new" parks, and the other, muddy and rutty, leading, if you turned west, to Batovo) at a spot where aspens crowded on both sides of a dip, I would be sure to find in the third week of June great blue-black nymphalids striped with pure white, gliding and wheeling low above the rich clay which matched the tint of their undersides when they settled and closed their wings. Those were the dung-loving males of what the old Aurelians used to call the Poplar Admirable, or, more exactly, they belonged to its Bucovinan subspecies. As a boy of nine, not knowing that race, I noticed how much our North Russian specimens differed from the Central European form figured in Hofmann, and rashly wrote to Kuznetsov, one of the greatest Russian, or indeed world, lepidopterists of all time, naming my new subspecies *"Limenitis populi rossica."* A long month later he returned my description and aquarelle of *"rossica* Nabokov" with only two words scribbled on the back of my letter: *"bucovinensis* Hormuzaki." How I hated Hormuzaki! And how hurt I was when in one of Kuznetsov's later papers I found a gruff reference to "schoolboys who keep naming minute varieties of the Poplar Nymph!" Undaunted, however, by the *populi* flop, I "discovered" the following year a "new" moth. That summer I had been collecting assiduously on moonless nights, in a glade of the park, by spreading a bedsheet, over the grass and its annoyed glow worms, and casting upon it the light of an acytelene lamp (which, six years later, was to shine on Tamara). Into that arena of radiance, moths would come drifting out of the solid blackness around me, and it was in that manner, upon that magic sheet, that I took a beautiful *Plusia* (now *Phytometra*) which, as I saw at once, differed from its closest ally by its mauve-and-maroon (instead of golden-brown) fore wings, and narrower bractea mark and was not recognizably figured in any of my books. I sent its description and picture to Richard South, for publication in *The Entomologist.* He did not know it either, but with the utmost kindness checked it in the British Museum collection—and found it had been described long ago as *Plusia excelsa* by Kretschmar. I received the sad news, which was most sympathetically worded ("...should be congratulated for obtaining...very rare Volgan thing...admirable figure...") with the utmost stoicism; but many years later, by a pretty fluke (I know I should not point out these plums to people), I got even with the first discoverer of *my* moth by giving his own name to a blind man in a novel.

Let me also evoke the hawkmoths, the jets of my boyhood! Colors would die a long death on June evenings. The lilac shrubs in full bloom before which I stood, net in hand, displayed clusters of a fluffy gray in the dusk—the ghost of purple. A moist young moon hung above the mist of a neighboring meadow. In many a garden have I stood thus in later years—in Athens, Antibes, Atlanta—but never have I waited with such a keen desire as before those darkening lilacs. And suddenly it would come, the low buzz passing from flower to flower, the vibrational halo around the streamlined body of an olive and pink Hummingbird moth poised in the air above the corolla into which it had dipped its long tongue. Its handsome black larva (resembling a diminutive cobra when it puffed out its ocellated front segments) could be found on dank willow herb two months later. Thus every hour and season had its delights. And, finally, on cold, or even frosty, autumn nights, one could sugar for moths by painting tree trunks with a mixture of molasses, beer, and rum. Through the gusty blackness, one's lantern would illumine the stickily glistening furrows of the bark and two or three large moths upon it imbibing the sweets, their nervous wings half open butterfly fashion, the lower ones exhibiting their incredible crimson silk from beneath the lichen-gray primaries. *"Catocala adultera!"* I would triumphantly shriek in the direction of the lighted windows of the house as I stumbled home to show my captures to my father.

6

The "English" park that separated our house from the hayfields was an extensive and elaborate affair with labyrinthine paths, Turgenevian benches, and imported oaks among the endemic firs and birches. The struggle that had gone on since my grandfather's time to keep the park from reverting to the wild state always fell short of complete success. No gardener could cope with the hillocks of frizzly black earth that the pink hands of moles kept heaping on the tidy sand of the main walk. Weeds and fungi, and ridgelike tree roots crossed and recrossed the sun-flecked trails. Bears had been eliminated in the eighties, but an occasional moose still visited the grounds. On a picturesque boulder, a little mountain ash and a still smaller aspen had climbed, holding hands, like two clumsy, shy children. Other, more elusive trespassers—lost picnickers or merry villagers—would drive our hoary gamekeeper Ivan crazy by scrawling ribald words on the benches and gates. The disintegrating process continues still, in a different sense, for when, nowadays, I attempt to follow in memory the winding paths from one given point to another, I notice with alarm that there are many gaps, due to oblivion or ignorance, akin to the terra-incognita blanks map makers of old used to call "sleeping beauties."

Beyond the park, there were fields, with a continuous shimmer of butterfly wings over a shimmer of flowers—daisies, bluebells, scabious, and others—which now rapidly pass by me in a kind of colored haze like those lovely, lush meadows, never to be explored, that one sees from the diner on a transcontinental journey. At the end of this grassy wonderland, the forest rose like a wall. There I roamed, scanning the tree trunks (the enchanted, the silent part of a tree) for certain tiny moths, called Pugs in England—delicate little creatures that cling in the daytime to speckled surfaces, with which their flat wings and turned-up abdomens blend. There, at the bottom of that sea of sunshot greenery, I slowly spun round the great boles. Nothing in the world would have seemed sweeter to me than to be able to add, by a stroke of luck, some remarkable new species to the long list of Pugs already named by others. And my pied imagination, ostensibly, and almost grotesquely, groveling to my desire (but all the time, in ghostly conspiracies behind the scenes, coolly planning the most distant events of my destiny), kept providing me with hallucinatory samples of small print: "...the only specimen so far known..." "...the only specimen known of *Eupithecia petropolitanata* was taken by a Russian schoolboy..." "...by a young Russian collector..." "...by myself in the Government of St. Petersburg, Tsarskoe Selo District, in 1910...1911...1912...1913..." And then, thirty years later, that blessed black night in the Wasatch Range.

At first—when I was, say, eight or nine—I seldom roamed farther than the fields and woods between Vyra and Batovo. Later, when aiming at a particular spot half-a-dozen miles or more distant, I would use a bicycle to get there with my net strapped to the frame;

but not many forest paths were passable on wheels; it was possible to ride there on horseback, of course, but, because of our ferocious Russian tabanids, one could not leave a horse haltered in a wood for any length of time: my spirited bay almost climbed up the tree it was tied to one day trying to elude them: big fellows with watered-silk eyes and tiger bodies, and gray little runts with an even more painful proboscis, but much more sluggish: to dispatch two or three of these dingy tipplers with one crush of the gloved hand as they glued themselves to the neck of my mount afforded me a wonderful empathic relief (which a dipterist might not appreciate). Anyway, on my butterfly hunts I always preferred hiking to any other form of locomotion (except, naturally, a flying seat gliding leisurely over the plant mats and rocks of an unexplored mountain, or hovering just above the flowery roof of a rain forest); for when you walk, especially in a region you have studied well, there is an exquisite pleasure in departing from one's itinerary to visit, here and there by the wayside, this glade, that glen, this or that combination of soil and flora—to drop in, as it were, on a familiar butterfly in his particular habitat, in order to see if he has emerged, and if so, how he is doing.

There came a July day—around 1910, I suppose—when I felt the urge to explore the vast marshland beyond the Oredezh. After skirting the river for three or four miles, I found a rickety footbridge. While crossing over, I could see the huts of a hamlet on my left, apple trees, rows of tawny pine logs lying on a green bank, and the bright patches made on the turf by the scattered clothes of peasant girls, who, stark naked in shallow water, romped and yelled, heeding me as little as if I were the discarnate carrier of my present reminiscences.

On the other side of the river, a dense crowd of small, bright blue male butterflies that had been tippling on the rich, trampled mud and cow dung through which I trudged rose all together into the spangled air and settled again as soon as I had passed.

After making my way through some pine groves and alder scrub I came to the bog. No sooner had my ear caught the hum of diptera around me, the guttural cry of a snipe overhead, the gulping sound of the morass under my foot, than I knew I would find here quite special arctic butterflies, whose pictures, or, still better, nonillustrated descriptions I had worshiped for several seasons. And the next moment I was among them. Over the small shrubs of bog bilberry with fruit of a dim, dreamy blue, over the brown eye of stagnant water, over moss and mire, over the flower spikes of the fragrant bog orchid (the *nochnaya fialka* of Russian poets), a dusky little Fritillary bearing the name of a Norse goddess passed in low, skimming flight. Pretty Cordigera, a gemlike moth, buzzed all over its uliginose food plant. I pursued rose-margined Sulphurs, gray-marbled Satyrs. Unmindful of the mosquitoes that furred my forearms, I stooped with a grunt of delight to snuff out the life of some silver-studded lepidopteron throbbing in the folds of my net. Through the smells of the bog, I caught the subtle perfume of butterfly wings on my fingers, a perfume which varies with the species—vanilla, or lemon, or musk, or a musty, sweetish odor difficult to define. Still unsated, I pressed forward. At last I saw I had come to the end of the marsh. The rising ground beyond was a paradise of lupines, columbines, and pent-stemons. Mariposa lilies bloomed under Ponderosa pines. In the distance, fleeting cloud shadows dappled the dull green of slopes above timber line, and the gray and white of Longs Peak.

I confess I do not believe in time. I like to fold my magic carpet, after use, in such a way as to superimpose one part of the pattern upon another. Let visitors trip. And the highest enjoyment of time-lessness—in a landscape selected at random—is when I stand among rare butterflies and their food plants. This is ecstasy, and behind the ecstasy is something else, which is hard to explain. It is like a momentary vacuum into which rushes all that I love. A sense of oneness with sun and stone. A thrill of gratitude to whom it may concern—to the contrapuntal genius of human fate or to tender ghosts humoring a lucky mortal.

Some of the very best escapes sneak up on us
unawares, seemingly unbidden. Accidental deviations
from a well-laid plan, they start, innocently enough, in
momentary inattention or a sudden lapse of
judgment. Call them gifts of fate or jumbo-sized
Freudian slips, but, whatever name they go by, these
uncharted course changes invariably launch us, much
to our subsequently endless gratitude and glee, into
worlds we would otherwise lack the nerve to enter.
Packed off to the Sorbonne in 1926, Joseph
Wechsberg is derailed from his practical studies into
the demi-monde of Parisian soubrettes, gigolos,
hawkers, and street performers: in short, into the
bohemia of Utrillo, Degas, Balzac, and Baudelaire—
teeming with the erotic and gustatory delights that
to this day are synonymous with the magical
word "Paris."

the first time i saw paris

JOSEPH WECHSBERG

Paris, reine du monde,
Paris, jeune et blonde…
—Song of Paris

i saw paris for the first time on a crisp, sunny morning in the autumn of 1926. I had gone there to study at the Sorbonne. My family was dissatisfied with the progress of my education in Vienna, where I had neglected to acquire an extensive knowledge in economics though I had become an expert at grand opera. They said that a semester or two at the Sorbonne would "round out" my education. They were worried because I had shown too much interest in music, writing, and other "breadless" arts.

"You must study law, finance, and economics," an old aunt said to me. "Think of the future of our bank!" The poor woman was bedridden with a chronic heart ailment, and her children didn't dare tell her that the family bank existed no longer.

I created a crisis when I declared, at my grandmother's seventieth birthday party, that I was going to play the violin—for money. The family was shocked. A nineteen-year-old boy doesn't know what he wants to do, they were saying; he is told by his uncles and aunts, who know best. My mother started to cry. Then Uncle Siegfried, my brother's and my legal guardian, came up with the idea of the Sorbonne.

"Let him go to Paris," he said. "A few months there will make him forget all that nonsense about playing the fiddle."

Uncle Siegfried owned a prosperous general store in Přívoz, a suburb of Ostrava on the banks of the Oder. The store was crammed with textiles, sauerkraut, stockings, pickles in large barrels, hardware, spices, open canvas bags filled with coffee, rice, barley, dried peas, dried lentils, fishing gear, smoked herring, meats, mouse traps, cheeses, sticks of sausages hanging from the walls, candles and holy pictures, chocolate and flypaper. A wave of naphthalin, cinnamon, and bay leaf fused with the fragrance of toilet water and smoked herring, the smell of Pilsen beer, imported Jamaica rum, and the slivovitz that Uncle Siegfried and his clerks produced in the back room.

Uncle Siegfried was widely respected in the neighborhood for the quality of his slivovitz and for his generous credit policy. "If you wait long enough, you don't have to pay him back," his customers used to say. He was a powerful man with a large, black mustache and no hair on his head, which was always covered. In winter he wore a cap, in summer a Panama hat. Like the management of the State Railroads, Uncle Siegfried recognized only two seasons, winter and summer, irrespective of temperatures. Winter began on November 1, summer on May 1.

He ran his retailing empire from behind an old-fashioned cash register, where he received visitors, extended credit, handed candy to small boys, and, made phone calls to the Odéon Cinema, which he ran as a profitable sideline. Uncle Siegfried looked upon himself as a patron of the arts. Playing the fiddle was all right, he used to say—*after* working hours.

I arrived in Paris at the Gare de l'Est and told the taxidriver to take me to Montparnasse, on the Left Bank, where the Sorbonne and other institutions of higher learning are located, but he misunderstood my pronunciation of "Montparnasse" and took me to Montmartre instead. I knew nothing about Montmartre. I watched the meter click ahead with alarming speed, and when it jumped to nine francs I told the driver to stop, gave him ten francs, took my bag, and got out.

I found myself in the middle of a large square. The blue-white signs said PLACE PIGALLE. It seemed a nice, quiet neighborhood. I knew nothing of Paris, but to me, that autumn morning at half past eight, Place Pigalle looked like a typical Paris square.

Yes, I decided, this was the place to live. In a dark, narrow side street I found a small, dreary hotel, with broken windowpanes and a shield: RÉGENCE HÔTEL. The place appealed to me: it seemed run down and would probably be inexpensive. My funds were small and inelastic. Uncle Siegfried, mindful of the temptations that might beset a young man in Paris, had decided that I would be given a fixed amount of money for the entire trip. The length of my stay would depend on the strength of my moral principles. If I threw my money away on loose women and wine, I would be back soon. If I stretched my money, through thrift and asceticism, I could stay longer. Thus, Uncle Siegfried reasoned, Paris would teach me a lesson in morality and in the virtue of thrift.

The tiny, narrow entrance smelled of cheap perfume and of absinthe. There was no lobby. Behind a ramshackle desk sat a fat, middle-aged lady wearing a stained silk dressing-gown that was bursting along the seams. So was the lady. She was reading a paperbound novel and dunking a *croissant* into a glass of red wine. She didn't look at me when I came in.

I said I wanted a room. Without interrupting her reading, she reached over her shoulder and took a key from one of the nails on the key-board behind her.

"*C'est pour un moment?*" she asked.

I said no, for a whole month.

She looked up, for the first time, and stared fixedly behind me as though she expected to see someone else.

"*Mais vous êtes seul!*" she said. Her mouth fell open, revealing a depressing job of French dentistry.

Her behavior was odd, but I'd read odd stories about the French. "Of course I'm alone," I said. "Now, how about the room?"

She lifted her fat forearms to heaven in a gesture of bewilderment, sighed deeply, took the key, and came out from behind the desk. The Régence Hôtel seemed to dispense with such luxuries as bellboys, receptionists, porters, elevators, telephones, palm trees, or room service. The *patronne* (I soon found out that she was the owner) ran the hotel herself with the help of François and Madeleine, a decrepit couple.

We walked up on the winding stairway. Halfway between two floors the *patronne* showed me the *cabinet*, which was built into the round wall, like a secret chamber. It was very quiet in the hotel, just what I wanted. I've always been a light sleeper. The *patronne* walked down a corridor and opened a room. On the floor was a heap of stockings, high-heeled shoes, dainty underthings, a dress, a hat, and the handbag of a lady who seemed to have shed her things on the spot, and in a hurry.

Then I saw the lady. She was in bed. Asleep. Her dark locks covered one side of her face, but the other was not unattractive. She wore no nightshirt.

The *patronne* gave an angry shrug, saying: *"Ça, alors!"* closed the door, and went on. The next room presented a Toulouse-Lautrec sort of still life of overturned bottles, filled ashtrays, half-filled glasses, and an empty, unmade bed.

"Excusez," the *patronne* said, to no one in particular, since the room was empty. She hastily closed the door and mumbled something. French people were certainly peculiar. The *patronne* didn't speak the academic French that I had learned in school. She would swallow the endings of most words. I decided that the French didn't speak good French.

The next room was unoccupied. It contained a washbasin behind a Japanese screen, a clothes-hanger by the door, a light-bulb dangling from a piece of string, and a very large bed. There was no closet. I asked how much the room was by the month. After much silent counting and lip-moving, the *patronne* quoted a price that was well within the limits of my budget. I was delighted. At the door she turned around and gave me what seemed to be a last glance of motherly affection.

"Listen, *mon petit*," she said, "are you sure you really want to stay in here?"

I nodded. She gave a sigh. She said this room had no key, but that I could bolt it from the inside.

"I'm always downstairs," she said. "When I have my dinner, François will be at the desk."

She went out, shaking her head and muttering in despair. I thought she was a character straight out of Balzac. My acquaintance with Frenchwomen was based solely on the works of Flaubert and Balzac.

I was tried after sitting up all night on the train. I hung up my suit, washed—the water was ice-cold—and went to bed. The bed was very comfortable.

When I woke up, it was dark outside. Every six seconds there was lightning, followed by no thunder. I got up and looked out. The lightning was caused by a neon sign across the street saying: LE PARADIS. From the street came the distorted sounds of voices, cars, whistles, shouts, and two hurdy-gurdies playing simultaneously *Auprès de ma blonde* and *Ain't She Sweet?* A drunk's voice shouted: *"Ta gueule!"*

Inside the hotel there seemed to be a lot of animation. People were laughing in the corridors, and I heard the clinking of glasses. Twice somebody tried to get into my room. I shaved—the water was piping hot now—dressed, and left the room. Downstairs two girls stood in front of the *patronne's* desk. The *patronne* was still reading her paper-bound book, which, I saw, was the memoirs of the Marquis de Sade.

"Bonsoir, chéri," said the older of the two girls. She had curls all over and wore a very tight skirt of a shiny material. She was spreading clouds of the cheap perfume that I'd smelled here in the morning. I said *bonsoir.*

"Qu'il est mignon!" said the other girl. She was from Bordeaux. She must have been around when they discovered that 1899 would be an exceptional vintage in the Médoc.

"So you're the fellow who took the room for the whole month?" the curled girl said. Both exploded into coloratura laughter.

"Girls, *alors, alors!*" said the *patronne.*

"We're going to have fun with him," said Miss Vintage Bordeaux.

"Yes, *the whole month!*" the other one cried. That killed them. The curled one laughed so hard that she dropped her purse. I bent down and picked it up for her.

The door was opened and a girl and a man came in. The girl greeted everybody like an old friend, and the *patronne* said: "The twenty-three, Yvonne, as usual." The man behind her seemed embarrassed.

"That's *him!*" Miss Vintage Bordeaux said to the new girl, pointing at me.

"Oh!" she said, and gave me a respectful glance. Then she turned toward her escort and said: "Come on, *chéri,*" and they went upstairs.

I left the hotel. I knew the facts of life in Paris; I had been told by my worldly-wise friends that almost every Parisian hotel would let you have a room for a few hours, or a fraction thereof. In fact, a number of rooms on the lower floors were set aside for the pursuit of sinful happiness, I'd been told, but from the third floor up the guests were eminently respectable. My room was on the third floor.

At the corner I stood still and gasped. The blue-white signs still said "PLACE PIGALLE," but the square didn't seem to be the one I had seen in the morning. It was past ten P.M. All the shops were open and brightly lighted. On the sidewalk in front of the Café Le Paradis, an all-girl orchestra on a platform was playing *Singing in the Rain.* In the middle of the boulevard de Clichy several painters had put up their oils and watercolors under the trees. Near the Moulin Rouge a merry-go-round made shrieking noises. There was a cacophony of jazz music, organ-grinders, automobiles tooting their horns, policemen using their whistles, sightseeing Cook's buses ("Paris by Night") using *their* horns, and passers-by using their lungs. It was worse than Times Square on New Year's Eve. Men in need of a shave edged up to me, speaking French and Arabic, offering "genuine Tabriz rugs," dirty postcards, Moroccan leather goods, their younger sisters, and a whitish powder that looked like, but wasn't, sugar. The peddlers hastily departed when two policemen approached. The police, I noticed, walked in pairs here.

I became aware of the persistent gnawing in my stomach. I hadn't eaten for over twenty-four hours. There was a restaurant next to Le Paradis, but the prices on the menu, which was displayed in a picture frame next to the entrance, ruled the place out for my budget. There were other restaurants, equally expensive. Most of them had dim lights. As you entered, the first thing you saw was a table with an arrangement of expensive fruit in a basket. The entrance was guarded by a couple of middleweights, wearing tuxedos. Once in a while a few dazed foreigners would stop to look at the fruit arrangement on the table, and before they could say "Crêpes Suzette," the middleweight tuxedos had bounced them in.

After a while I discovered a delicatessen that seemed to be a hangout of taxi-drivers, night-club musicians, girls of small if any virtue, and artists from the near-by Cirque Médrano. I ordered a *bock*—a wineglass filled with beer—and a French sandwich, a paper-thin slice of ham between two large slices of French bread.

It was almost two A.M. when I got back to the Place Pigalle. The noise was worse than before. A second merry-go-round on the boulevard was doing good business. Below the window of my room a street trio—violin, accordion, and drums—was playing *Mon Paris.* A thin, transparent-looking girl with big, haunting eyes and deep-red, heart-shaped lips sang the chorus in a shrill, somewhat guttural voice. After each chorus she would step among the listeners who formed a circle around the band to sell the sheet music of *Mon Paris*, for one franc a copy. Afterward the audience would join her and the orchestra in another chorus.

There was cheerful confusion in the narrow street crowded with cops, drunks, girls, flower-venders, tourists, more girls, peddlers, and *maqueraux*—"mackerels," as the French call their gigolos. In front of the Régence Hôtel, Miss Vintage Bordeaux stood with a silky-haired *maquereau*. He had polished fingernails and a tight-fitting jacket. She wanted to introduce me to him, but I escaped into the hotel and ran up the stairway. In my room I bolted the door from the inside.

I went to bed but I couldn't sleep. In the room next to me a man and a woman argued about the lousy sum of twenty francs. Downstairs the band was playing *Les Fraises et les Framboises*, and the girl's voice sang the chorus with a haunting ring. All night long doors were banged and people kept coming and going; glasses were broken and bells rang; once there seemed to be a fight among the girls in front of the hotel, and I heard police whistles. Dawn came reluctantly to the Place Pigalle, the neon sign LE PARADIS stopped blinking, and I fell into exhausted sleep.

I woke up at noon, tired and miserable. I went down and told the *patronne* I couldn't sleep in her hotel and would have to leave. She understood my reasons but refused to refund my money. She talked darkly about laws and the *règlement*, and about two *brigadiers* who were her good friends.

As I didn't know then that in Paris a *brigadier* is not a general officer, but a cop on the beat, I dropped the subject of money. I was stuck. The next night I slept a little better, and the following week I slept like a log. The trick was to stay up with the local populace and go to sleep with them, at dawn. Once in a while everybody would be roused when the cops raided Le Paradis and arrested the dope-peddlers, but thereafter all would be quiet for a few days.

After a few weeks I became acquainted in the *quartier*. I found a *prix-fixe* restaurant in a quiet side street less than a hundred yards and more than a hundred years from Place Pigalle. The restaurant had a tiled floor, sprinkled with sawdust. There were small tables for four, covered with large sheets of white paper. When a guest had finished his meal, the waiter would write the *addition* on the paper, roll the paper with the bread crumbs together, and take it away. The next guest was given a fresh sheet of paper. The place was always crowded with little girls from the near-by department stores, pale clerks, and minor officials from the *Mairie* of the 18th Arrondissement whose faces had taken on the dusty, parchment-colored hue of their files.

There were no tourists with guidebooks, not even Frenchmen from the *provinces*. The guests of the restaurants never went to Place Pigalle after nightfall. One man lived right behind the Moulin Rouge music hall, but he had never been inside. They discussed Place Pigalle with clinical detachment, the way brokers discuss shares, and actors their makeup. "Pigalle," they agreed, was a *formidable affair*, a sound business venture. If the silly foreigners wouldn't spend their money here, all the *Montmartrois* would have to pay higher taxes. "Pigalle," was all right as long as it created prosperity.

There was no fancy fruit arrangement on a table inside the entrance of the Prix-Fixe, no tuxedoed middleweight waiting to bounce you in. The proprietor himself would stand there, and after you'd come to his place twice, he would shake hands with you, and you belonged. It was customary to shake hands with the waiter, too—but not with the guests at your table, no matter how well you knew them.

My waiter was Gaston, an old, asthmatic man who suffered from rheumatism. On days when the weather was about to change, he was ill-tempered and disinclined to listen to the guest's order. Instead he would bring the guest what he himself liked to eat. But his taste was excellent and usually he made a better choice than I should have done.

The Prix-Fixe was a good place to round out one's education. I learned that it was all right to read *L'Intransigeant* while you ate the hors-d'œuvre, but not afterward. The hors-d'œuvre—*thon à l'huile, œuf dur mayonnaise,* or a slice of *pâté Maison* served on a lonely salad leaf—could be handled with the right hand while the left held the newspaper. After the hors-d'œuvre, you would place the paper under your seat and were supposed to converse with the neighbors at your table about local problems of the *arrondissement.* Listening to the quiet voices, you wouldn't have known that there existed Paris, or France, or Europe, or the rest of the world.

It was a nice place. I didn't know then that there existed restaurants in Paris like Lapérouse, L'Escargot, or La Tour d'Argent, where the *couvert* cost as much as the entire menu here. I'm sure that my Prix-Fixe never made the Club des Cent or *Parmi les Meilleures Tables de France*, but at the age of nineteen the enthusiasm of the heart is stronger than the fastidiousness of the palate. The omelet was light and fluffy, the *bœuf à la bourguignonne* delicious and aromatic, and the tender, small *bifteck* garnished with a heap of fresh watercress.

There were two menus, at 7:50 and at 10 francs, including the *couvert*, a small bottle of wine or a big bottle of *bière de Strasbourg*, and bread *à discretion*. (Four pieces of bread were permissible, I learned; to take more was considered indiscreet.) The smaller menu offered hors-d'œuvre, entrée, one vegetable, dessert, or cheese. On holidays I threw my money away recklessly and feasted on the ten-franc menu, which included a fish course.

The menu was written in violet ink and was as difficult to read as a French railroad schedule. The specialties of the day, like de-luxe trains, were marked in red ink. The specialties were "homely" dishes, *cassoulet toulousain, haricot de mouton, blanquette de veau à l'ancienne*, or a *petite marmite*. Since Gaston liked those dishes, I had them frequently. Gaston said that the best thing one can say about a restaurant is that it's "almost like home." There were no *suprêmes d'écrevisses au champagne* on the menu, no *escalopes de foie gras à la Talleyrand*, or *crêpes Suzette*. But the *tripes* were marvelous.

I learned many things at the Prix-Fixe. You would place one end of the napkin inside your shirt collar. You would wipe your plate with a piece of bread until it was clean. Each course, even potatoes and vegetables, was served on a special plate, but you always used the same fork and knife. If you forgot and accidentally left your fork and knife on the used plate, Gaston would gently lift them up and place fork and knife on the paper sheet.

I often admired Gaston's virtuosity. He could carry three small wine bottles by their necks between forefinger and middle finger of his right hand, while his forearm was loaded with three plates; his left hand would swing a filled bread basket. When he wasn't carrying plates, he would cut long sticks of French bread into small pieces with the cutting machine. He always kept the baskets well filled.

Young couples would hold hands while they ate a delicious *raie au beurre noir* or a *vol-au-vent*. Between bites of food they would exchange passionate kisses. No one sitting near pretended to notice, but everybody looked pleased, and there was a glow of happiness about the place. Gaston beamed. He used to say that love enhanced digestion. Sometimes a girl who had exchanged kisses with a man one day would come with another man the next day and kiss him just as passionately. Infatuations were short-lived, but they were violent. It was a very romantic Prix-Fixe.

Most of the customers lived in the small, steep side streets off the boulevard de Clichy, or up on the Butte Montmartre, the hill district north of Place Pigalle, which is crowned by Sacré-Cœur church and *les lieux ou souffle l'ésprit*, as Barrès once said. They had savings books with the nearest branch of the Crédit Lyonnais; their idea of a wild Saturday night spree was to go to a neighborhood cinema to see the latest exploits of Arsène Lupin, Master Detective, and afterward to sip a *chocolat* at Dupont (*"Chez Dupont Tout Est Bon"*). On Sunday afternoon they would venture out as far as the Grands Boulevards or the Champs-Élysées to take a look at the shop windows and have a *bock* on a café terrace. The Champs-Élysées, being actually located on the Right Bank, was considered neutral territory. Beyond, there was no man's land.

The inhabitants of the Butte Montmartre didn't recognize the rest of Paris, or of France. The Left Bank was like an unknown foreign country for which you needed visas and special permits. You had no business going there except on legitimate errands, such as to borrow money or to visit the grave of Baudelaire at Montparnasse Cemetery. The inhabitants of Montmartre were enthusiastic cemetery-goers. I spent many an afternoon at Montmartre Cemetery, visiting the graves of Heinrich Heine, Henri Murger, and Hector Berlioz. Several times in the course of my conversations at the Prix-Fixe I told my table companions that I had come to Paris to study at the Sorbonne. They thought I was joking and burst out laughing. I stopped talking about the Sorbonne and decided to round out my education, informally and alfresco, on the streets and squares of Montmartre.

The faculty had prominent experts in specialized fields of knowledge. My art instructors were the sidewalk painters. Some of them had been drinking-and-arguing companions of Utrillo, Utter, Suzanne Valadon, Friesz, and Raoul Dufy in the days when no one wanted their paintings. Now they were arguing *about* Utrillo and

joseph wechsberg   **301**

Dufy, and they would never agree. Often such arguments would last all night long. In the early dawn we would walk up to Montmartre Cemetery. At the grave of Mme Récamier we would stop and one member of the faculty, a leading anti-Utrilloist, would impersonate a grief-stricken Chateaubriand delivering the funeral sermon for Mme Récamier. He was a moving speaker, and at the end of his sermon everybody was crying. To refresh ourselves, we would proceed to the Moulin de la Galette for a couple of *bocks* before going to bed, between seven and eight in the morning.

My economics teachers were the sidewalk peddlers from North Africa. I learned a great many things from them that had never been taught at Vienna's College for World Trade. I learned which French department produced "genuine Tabriz" rugs (Bouches-du-Rhône), the difference between Moroccan art work in Fez and Meknès (Fez was best for copper work, Meknès for silver and leather), or how to make sure that profits from dope-peddling surpass occasional losses (choose a location guarded by older *brigadiers* who can't run as fast as you do).

I had become acquainted with the members of the trio who performed nightly in the street in front of the Régence Hôtel. Théophile, the drummer, was a scholarly-looking fellow with the face of a thoughtful airedale. His family lived in a respected neighborhood near the Porte d'Italie; his father, a patriotic, parochial, parsimonious *petit bourgeois*, was head bookkeeper at the Société Générale. In the daytime Théophile worked there as junior bookkeeper, but he said he wasn't interested in his daytime career. His vocation was *le jazz*, hot or cold. He was in love with Claudia, the transparent girl singer, and they were engaged to be married. It was a shock for me, for I had become infatuated with the girl's haunting voice.

Théophile's family didn't object to his nocturnal activities. He said it would never occur to them to "travel"—*voyager*, he called it—to Place Pigalle, fifteen minutes by Métro from the Porte d'Italie.

"They might as well go to Papeete, Tahiti," he said, and laughed.

"But don't you have an uncle who doesn't like music?" I asked him enviously.

He gave me a blank stare. He didn't know what I was talking about.

Théophile's burning ambition was to become a regular *chef d'orchestre* and run his own band. It would have five members, he said. Around Pigalle, the *chef d'orchestre* is supposed to supply the music, and Théophile had already built up a substantial repertory of Salbert's Music Arrangements for Small Orchestra. He owned three stands and the percussion instruments and drums on which he performed. He promised to give me a *cachet*—a temporary job—as violinist as soon as he could set up his *affaire*. A cousin of his mother owned a country inn with a garden and dance hall in Saint-Rémy-les-Chevreuse, half an hour by train from the Gare Montparnasse. The cousin, a patron of the arts, was willing to give "Théophile et Son Orchestre" a start, provided it would cost him nothing. Théophile figured out, with the help of two itinerant math teachers from North Africa, that a dancing crowd of two hundred, paying two francs a person, would enable him to pay each of us thirty francs for the afternoon, and the cost of transportation besides. The cousin would throw in supper gratis.

It sounded too good to be true, but one Sunday afternoon we actually rode out on the train from the Gare Montparnasse. There were five of us: Théophile and Claudia, a saxophone-player, a pianist, and myself. Everybody was uncomfortably silent as we entered Left Bank territory after crossing the Seine and proceeded through enemy-infested boulevards to the railroad station. Théophile carried the drums, and Claudia carried the music. She looked lovelier, more haunting than ever.

Théophile et Son Orchestre were a great success at the cousin's inn, but I wasn't. I'd been raised musically on Bach, Brahms, and Beethoven, and now I had to dish out *Strawberries and Raspberries* and *Mon Paris*. My foxtrots were too fast and my *java* sounded like a Mozart minuet. I was glad when it was all over and the orchestra was having supper in the big kitchen with the cousin and his relatives: onion soup, thick slices of garlicky *gigot rôti* with *pommes lyonnaises*, salad, cheese, a good Beaujolais. It was a great day. Everybody had too much Beaujolais and was singing. I had earned thirty francs and had been invited by a French family, a rare distinction for a foreigner in France.

A few weeks later I ran into a former classmate from my home town who had also come to Paris to round out his education at the Sorbonne. He went there every day at eight in the morning, and listened to many lectures: *"Le Consulat et l'Empire," "Les Trésors de la Renaissance," "La Poésie en 1852," "Camées et émaux."* He knew a lot about *"L'Histoire de la musique en France,"* but he had never heard of *"Théophile et Son Orchestre"* and was shocked when I told him of Saint-Rémy-les-Chevreuse. He had been to the Montparnasse Cemetery but had missed the graves of Baudelaire and Maupassant. He knew no native Parisian. He had been twice on the Eiffel Tower, and spoke an academic and, to me, completely unintelligible French.

He took me to his favorite restaurant. The menu featured goulash *à la hongroise* and *Wiener Schnitzel*. An anemic girl from Scotland looked shocked when I wiped my plate clean with a piece of bread. The proprietor was from Bucharest and shook hands with no one. Afterward my classmate took me to the Rotonde and showed me the American expatriates. The evening was a total loss. At ten P.M. sneaked away on the Nord-Sud subway. I was lonely and homesick for Montmartre.

It was good to get back to Pigalle. The racket of the hurdy-gurdies, whistles, shouting people, and tooting horns was like the ticking of an old grandfather clock in a quiet living-room. I was back where I belonged. I didn't tell my friends where I had spent the evening. I was ashamed.

I might have stayed in Montmartre indefinitely if Uncle Siegfried hadn't come to Paris one night on the late train. He had gone on business to Switzerland, to buy Lindt chocolates and Emmental cheese, and had promised my mother to look me up. He went straight to the Régence Hôtel. When I came there at two in the morning, as was my habit, I found my uncle sitting at a sidewalk table next to the all-girl orchestra of the Café Le Paradis. I noticed that Uncle Siegfried, ordinarily a strong man—he had been decorated with the Austrian Army's gold *Tapferkeitsmedaille* for bravery in the First World War—looked pale and shaken.

I sat down next to him on the terrace. That, it turned out, was a mistake. Several of my North African economics teachers came by and tried to sell my uncle genuine Tabriz rugs from the Bouches-du-Rhône department, and one, Mohammed ben Ali, sat down beside us, offered my uncle his young sister and the white stuff that looked like, but wasn't, sugar, and told me that he'd just won a three-hundred-meter race against an aging *brigadier*.

Then Théophile and Claudia dropped in. Claudia kissed me on the cheek and Théophile paid me thirty francs for last Sunday's work. My uncle wanted to know what the money was for. I told him proudly about my job with Théophile et Son Orchestre. My uncle said nothing, but his face took on the hue of moldy herring. Miss Vintage Bordeaux ambled by, stopping at our table, giving me a kiss on the cheek, and asking: *"Ça va, chéri?"* She winked at my uncle and said there was nothing she would deny a friend of a friend of mine, and then she gave *him* an affectionate kiss on the cheek and pulled up a chair.

Uncle Siegfried shouted: *"Garçon!"*, paid, and made a humiliating scene on the café terrace, in front of my friends and teachers. He shouted that I was a rotter, giving a bad name to my family, and that he was going to take me to the Left Bank *right now!* My friends and teachers listened on in horrified silence.

That very night Uncle Siegfried moved me out of the Régence Hôtel and installed me in a drab, dull pension near the Sorbonne. It belonged to a former *lycée* teacher from Grenoble who had coffee for breakfast and read the collected works of La Rochefoucauld. Visitors had to be announced at the desk. There was a bed check at midnight. The roomers were dull, rich boys from Switzerland and Indo-China who pretended to be gifted and broke. They would get up at seven-thirty in the morning, and spent all day long at the Sorbonne.

I was miserable in Montparnasse. In the evening I would sneak off for a few hours to Place Pigalle. But it wasn't the same any more. My friends and teachers began to suspect me of being a Left Bank spy. Miss Vintage Bordeaux no longer kissed my cheek, Théophile hired another violinist, and one night Mohammed ben Ali offered me his white stuff, as though I were a tourist. I was no longer welcome in Montmartre and stopped going there. A few weeks later I left Paris and went back home.

In the hands of Sylvia Townsend Warner, a perfectly
pedestrian occurrence—the escape of a caged bird—
turns into a subtle metaphor for the "escape" of an
ordinary event from its habitual and totally
unremarkable context, that, in its turn, stimulates
wonderful, figural flights of fancy. For Warner, nothing
impoverishes our experience of life as much as the
proliferation of restrictions and habits that mechanize
our progress from birth to death. Which is why,
sometimes, losing one's bearings is the most direct
way of finding one's way to the vibrant core of the
imagination. In "A View of Exmoor," Warner takes us
on a hilarious "outing" that, recounted with refined
craftmanship and an impeccable sense of timing,
leaves us with a renewed appreciation for the
importance of being eccentric. As evanescent as a
bubble, "A View of Exmoor" buoys the spirits.

a view of exmoor

SYLVIA TOWNSEND WARNER

from bath, where Mr. Finch was taking the waters, the Finches travelled by car into Devonshire to attend the wedding of Mrs. Finch's niece, Arminella Blount. This was in 1936, when weddings could be garish. The Finches made a very creditable family contribution—Mrs. Finch in green moire, Cordelia and Clara in their bridesmaids" dresses copied from the Gainsborough portrait of an earlier Arminella Blount in the Character of Flora, Mr. Finch in, as his wife said, his black-and-gray. Arden Finch in an Eton suit would have looked like any normal twelve-year-old boy in an Eton suit if measles had not left him preternaturally thin, pale, and owl-eyed.

All these fine feathers, plus two top hats, an Indian shawl to wrap around Arden in case it turned cold, and a picnic basket in case anyone felt hungry, made the car seem unusually full during the drive to Devonshire. On the return journey it was even fuller, because the Finches were bringing back Arminella's piping bullfinch and the music box that was needed to continue its education, as well as the bridesmaids' bouquets. It was borne in on Mr. Finch that other travellers along the main road were noticing his car and its contents more than they needed to, and this impression was confirmed when the passengers in two successive charabancs cheered and waved. Mr. Finch, the soul of consideration, turned in to a side road to spare his wife and daughters the embarrassment of these public acclamations.

"'Pember and South Pigworthy,'" Mrs. Finch read aloud from a signpost. "The doctor who took out my tonsils was called Pember. It's so nice to find a name one knows."

Mr. Finch replied that he was taking an alternative way home.

After a while, he stopped and looked for his road map, but couldn't find it. He drove on.

"Father," said Cordelia a little later, "we've been through this village before. Don't you think we had better ask?"

"Is *that* all it is?" said Mrs. Finch. "What a relief. I thought I was having one of those mysterious delusions when one half of my brain mislays the other half."

Mr. Finch continued to drive on. Arden, who had discovered that the bars of the bird cage gave out notes of varying pitch when he plucked them, was carrying out a systematic test with a view to being able to play "Rule Britannia." Cordelia and Clara and their mother discussed the wedding.

Suddenly, Mrs. Finch exclaimed, "Oh, Henry! Stop, stop! There's such a beautiful view of Exmoor!"

Ten-foot hedges rose on either side of the lane they were in, the lane went steeply uphill, and Mr. Finch had hoped that he had put any views of Exmoor safely behind him. But with unusual mildness he stopped and backed the car till it was even with a gate. Beyond the gate was a falling meadow, a pillowy middle distance of woodland, and beyond that, pure and cold and unimpassioned, the silhouette of the moor.

"Why not," Mr. Finch said, taking the good the gods provided, "why not stop and picnic?" It occurred to him that once the car was emptied, the road map might come to light.

The Finches sat down in the meadow and ate cucumber sandwiches. Arden wore the Indian shawl; the bullfinch in its cage was brought out of the car to have a little fresh air. Gazing at the view, Mrs. Finch said that looking at Exmoor always reminded her of her Aunt Harriet's inexplicable boots.

"What boots, Mother?" Cordelia asked.

"She saw them on Exmoor," Mrs. Finch said. "She and Uncle Lionel both saw them; they were children at the time. They were picking whortleberries—such a disappointing fruit! All these folk art fruits are much overrated. And nobody's ever been able to account for them."

"But why should they have to be accounted for?" Clara asked. "Were they sticking out of a bog?"

"They were in a cab."

"Your Aunt Harriet—" Mr. Finch began. For some reason, it

angered him to hear of boots being in a cab while he was still in doubt as to whether the map was in the car.

"Of course," Mrs. Finch went on, "in those days cabs were everywhere. But not on Exmoor, where there were no roads. It was a perfectly ordinary cab, one of the kind that open in hot weather. The driver was on the box, and the horse was waving its tail to keep the flies off. They looked as if they had been there quite a long time."

"Days and days?" Arden asked.

"I'm afraid not, dear. Decomposition had not set in. But as if they had been there long enough to get resigned to it. An hour or so."

"But how could Aunt Harriet tell how long—"

"In those days, children were very different—nice and inhibited," Mrs. Finch said. "So Aunt Harriet and Uncle Lionel observed the cab from a distance and walked on. Presently, they saw two figures— a man and a woman. The man was very pale and sulky, and the woman was rating him and crying her eyes out, but the most remarkable thing of all, even more remarkable than the cab, was that the woman wasn't wearing a hat. In those days, no self-respecting woman could stir out without a hat. And on the ground was a pair of boots. While Harriet and Lionel were trying to get a little nearer without seeming inquisitive, the woman snatched up the boots and ran back to the cab. She ran right past the children; she was crying so bitterly she didn't even notice them. She jumped into the cab, threw the boots onto the opposite seat, the driver whipped up his horse, and the cab went bumping and jolting away over the moor. As for the man, he walked off looking like murder. So what do you make of that?"

"Well, I suppose they'd been wading, and then they quarrelled, and she drove away with his boots as a revenge," said Clara.

"He was wearing boots," said Mrs. Finch.

"Perhaps they were eloping," Clara said, "and the boots were part of their luggage that he'd forgotten to pack, like Father, and she changed her mind in time."

"Speed is essential to an elopement, and so is secrecy. To drive over Exmoor in an open cab would be inconsistent with either," said Mr. Finch.

"Perhaps the cab lost its way in a moor mist," contributed Arden. "Listen! I can do almost all the first line of 'Rule Britannia' now."

"But, Clara, why need it be an elopement?" Cordelia asked.

"Perhaps she was just a devoted wife who found a note from her husband saying he had lost his memory or committed a crime or something and was going out of her life, and she seized up a spare pair of boots, leaped hatless into a cab, and tracked him across Exmoor, to make sure he had a dry pair to change into. And when Harriet and Lionel saw them, he had just turned on with a brutal oath."

"If she had been such a devoted wife, she wouldn't have taken the boots away again," Clara said.

"Yes she would. It was the breaking point," Cordelia said. "Actually, though. I don't believe she was married to him at all. I think it was an assignation and she'd taken her husband's boots with her as a blind."

"Then why did she take them out of the cab?" inquired Clara. "And why didn't she wear a hat, like Mother said? No, Cordelia! I think your theory is artistically all right. It looks the boots straight in the face. But I've got a better one. I think they spent a guilty night together and, being a forgetful man, he put his boots out to be cleaned and in the morning she was hopelessly compromised, so she snatched up the boots and drove after him to give him a piece of her mind."

"Yes, but he was wearing boots already," Cordelia said.

"He would have had several pairs. At that date, a libertine would have had hundreds of boots, wouldn't he, Mother?"

"He might not have taken them with him wherever he went, dear," said Mrs. Finch.

Mr. Finch said, "You have both rushed off on an assumption. Because the lady drove way in the cab, you both assume that she arrived in it. Women always jump to conclusions. Why shouldn't the cab have brought the man? If she was hatless, she might have been an escaped lunatic and the man a keeper from the asylum, who came in search of her."

"Why did he bring a pair of boots," said Mr. Finch firmly.

"He can't have been much of a lunatic-keeper if he let her get away with his cab," Clara said.

"I did not say he was a lunatic-keeper, Clara," said Mr. Finch. "I was merely trying to point out to you and your sister that in cases like this one must examine the evidence from all sides."

"Perhaps the cabdriver was a lunatic," said Arden. "Perhaps that's why he drove them onto Exmoor. Perhaps they were *his* boots, and the man and the woman were arguing as to which of them was to pay his fare. Perhaps—"

Interrupted by his father and both his sisters, all speaking at once, Arden returned to his rendering of "Rule Britannia." Mrs. Finch removed some crumbs and a few caterpillars from her green moire lap and looked at the view of Exmoor. Suddenly, a glissando passage on the bird cage was broken by a light twang, a flutter of wings, a cry from Arden. The cage door had flipped open and the bullfinch had flown out. Everybody said "Oh!" and grabbed at it. The bullfinch flew to the gate, balanced there, flirted its tail, and flew on into the lane.

It flew in a surprised, incompetent way, making short flights, hurling itself from side to side of the lane. But though Cordelia and Clara leaped after it, trying to catch it in their broad-brimmed hats, and though Arden only just missed it by overbalancing on a bough, thereby falling out of the tree and making his nose bleed, and though Mr. Finch walked after it, holding up the bird cage and crying "Sweet, Sweet, Sweet" in a falsetto voice that trembled with feeling, the bullfinch remained and, with a little practice, flew better and better.

"Stop, all of you!" said Mrs. Finch, who had been attending to Arden, wiping her bloodstained hand son the grass. "You'll frighten it. Henry, do leave off saying "Sweet—you'll only strain yourself. What we need is the music box. If it hears the music box, it will be reminded of its home and remember it's a tame bullfinch. Arden, dear, please keep your shawl on and look for some groundsel, if you aren't too weak from loss of blood."

The music box weighed about fifty pounds., it was contained in an ebony case that looked lie a baby's coffin, and at every movement it emitted reproachful chords. On one side, it had a handle; on the other side, the handle had fallen off, and by the time the Finches had got the box out of the car, they were flushed and breathless. His groans mingling with the reproachful chords, Mr. Finch staggered up the lane in pursuit of the bullfinch, with the music box in his arms. Mrs. Finch walked beside him, tenderly entreating him to be careful, for if anything happened to it, it would break Arminella's heart. Blithesome and cumberless, like the bird of the wilderness, the bullfinch flitted on ahead.

"I am not carrying this thing a step further," said Mr. Finch, setting down the music box at the side of the lane. "Since you insist, Elinor, I will sit here and play it. The rest of you can walk on and turn the bird somehow and drive it back till the music reminds it of home."

Clara said, "I expect we shall go on for miles."

Seeing his family vanish around a bend in the lane, Mr. Finch found himself nursing a hope that Clara's expectation might be granted. He was devoted to music boxes. He sat down beside it and read the list of its repertory, which was written in a copperplate hand inside the lid: *Là Ci Darem la Mano; The Harp That Once Through Tara's Halls; The Prayer from "Moïse"; The Copenhagen Waltz*. A very pleasant choice for an interval of repose, well-earned repose, in this leafy seclusion. He ran his finger over the prickled cylinder, he blew away a little dust, he wound the box up. Unfortunately, there were a great many midges, the inherent pest of leafy seclusions. He paused to light a cigar. Then he set off the music box. It chirruped through three and a half tunes and stopped, as music boxes do. Behind him, a voice said somewhat diffidently, "I say. Can I be any help?"

Glancing from the corner of his eye, Mr. Finch saw a young man whose bare ruined legs and rucksack suggested that he was on a walking tour.

"No, thank you," Mr. Finch said. Dismissingly, he rewound the music box and set it going again.

Around the bend of the lane came two replicas, in rather bad condition, of Gainsborough's well-known portrait of Arminella Blount in the Character of Flora, a cadaverous small boy draped in a bloodstained Indian shawl, and a middle-aged lady dressed in the height of fashion who carried a bird cage. Once again, Mr. Finch was forced to admit the fact that the instant his family escaped from his supervision they somehow managed to make themselves conspicuous. Tripping nervously to the strains of "The Copenhagen Waltz," the young man on a walking tour skirted around them and hurried on.

"We've got it!" cried Mrs. Finch, brandishing the bird cage.

"Why the deuce couldn't you *explain* to that young man?" asked Mr. Finch. "Elinor, why couldn't you explain?"

"But why should I?" Mrs. Finch asked. "He looked so hot and careworn, and I expect he only gets a fortnight's holiday all the year through. Why should I spoil it for him? Why shouldn't he have something to look back on in his old age?"

The infirmity and disenfranchisement of old age brings with it profound alienation, and, in extreme cases, paranoia. Sometimes the physical feebleness, the disorientation, the overwhelming, almost global sense of loss that comes from the gradual erosion of faculties and friendships, seems worse than death itself. Eavesdropping on the dementia of an elderly widow, Isaac Bashevis Singer ventures into the tenebrous psychic realm of death-in-life that is the grim destiny of the aged, urban recluse. But, even here, in the soul's final, bleak entrapment in the body, Singer manages to show, despair is not inescapable. For, however unlikely a form it might take, grace clears a path to understanding and joy.

the key

ISAAC BASHEVIS SINGER

at about three o'clock in the afternoon, Bessie Popkin began to prepare to go down to the street. Going out was connected with many difficulties, especially on a hot summer day: first, forcing her fat body into a corset, squeezing her swollen feet into shoes, and combing her hair, which Bessie dyed at home and which grew wild and was streaked in all colors—yellow, black, gray, red; then making sure that while she was out her neighbors would not break into her apartment and steal linen, clothes, documents, or just disarrange things and make them disappear.

Besides human tormentors, Bessie suffered from demons, imps, Evil Powers. She hid her eyeglasses in the night table and found them in a slipper. She placed her bottle of hair dye in the medicine chest; days later she discovered it under the pillow. Once, she left a pot of borscht in the refrigerator, but the Unseen took it from there and after long searching Bessie came upon it in her clothes closet. On its surface was a thick layer of fat that gave off the smell of rancid tallow.

What she went through, how many tricks were played on her and how much she had to wrangle in order not to perish or fall into insanity, only God knew. She had given up the telephone because racketeers and degenerates called her day and night, trying to get secrets out of her. The Puerto Rican milkman once tried to rape her. The errand boy from the grocery store attempted to burn her belongings with a cigarette. To evict her from the rent-controlled apartment where she had lived for thirty-five years, the company and the superintendent infested her rooms with rats, mice, cockroaches.

Bessie had long ago realized that no means were adequate against those determined to be spiteful—not the metal door, the special lock, her letters to the police, the mayor, the FBI, and even the president in Washington. But while one breathed one had to eat. It all took time: checking the windows, the gas vents, securing the drawers. Her paper money she kept in volumes of the encyclopedia, in back copies of the *National Geographic*, and in Sam Popkin's old ledgers. Her stocks and bonds Bessie had hidden among the logs in the fireplace, which was never used, as well as under the seats of the easy chairs. Her jewels she had sewn into the mattress. There was a time when Bessie had safe-deposit boxes at the bank, but she long ago convinced herself that the guards there had passkeys.

At about five o'clock, Bessie was ready to go out. She gave a last look at herself in the mirror—small, broad, with a narrow forehead, a flat nose, and eyes slanting and half-closed, like a Chinaman's. Her chin sprouted a little white beard. She wore a faded dress in a flowered print, a misshapen straw hat trimmed with wooden cherries and grapes, and shabby shoes. Before she left, she made a final inspection of the three rooms and the kitchen. Everywhere there were clothes, shoes, and piles of letters that Bessie had not opened. Her husband, Sam Popkin, who had died almost twenty years ago, had liquidated his real-estate business before his death, because he was about to retire to Florida. He left her stocks, bonds, and a number of passbooks from savings banks, as well as some mortgages. To this day, firms wrote to Bessie, sent her reports, checks. The Internal Revenue Service claimed taxes from her. Every few weeks she received announcements from a funeral company that sold plots in an "airy cemetery." In former years, Bessie used to answer letters, deposit her checks, keep track of her income and expenses. Lately she had neglected it all. She even stopped buying the newspaper and reading the financial section.

In the corridor, Bessie tucked cards with signs on them that only she could recognize between the door and the door frame. The keyhole she stuffed with putty. What else could she do—a widow without children, relatives, or friends? There was a time when the neighbors used to open their doors, look out, and laugh at her exaggerated care; others teased her. That had long passed. Bessie spoke to no one. She didn't see well, either. The glasses she had worn for years were of no use. To go to an eye doctor and be fitted for new ones was too much of an effort. Everything was difficult—even entering and leaving the elevator, whose door always closed with a slam.

Bessie seldom went farther than two blocks from her building. The street between Broadway and Riverside Drive became noisier and filthier from day to day. Hordes of urchins ran around half-naked. Dark men with curly hair and wild eyes quarreled in Spanish with little women whose bellies were always swollen in pregnancy. They talked back in rattling voices. Dogs barked, cats meowed. Fires broke out and fire engines, ambulances, and police cars drove up. On Broadway, the old groceries had been replaced by supermarkets, where food must be picked out and put in a wagon and one had to stand in line before the cashier.

God in Heaven, since Sam died, New York, America—perhaps the whole world—was falling apart. All the decent people had left the neighborhood and it was overrun by a mob of thieves, robbers, whores. Three times Bessie's pocketbook had been stolen. When she reported it to the police, they just laughed. Every time one crossed the street, one risked one's life. Bessie took a step and stopped. Someone had advised her to use a cane, but she was far from considering herself an old woman or a cripple. Every few weeks she painted her nails red. At times, when the rheumatism left her in peace, she took clothes she used to wear from the closets, tried them on, and studied herself in the mirror.

Opening the door of the supermarket was impossible. She had to wait till someone held it for her. The supermarket itself was a place that only the Devil could have invented. The lamps burned with a glaring light. People pushing wagons were likely to knock down anyone in their path. The shelves were either too high or too low. The noise was deafening, and the contrast between the heat outside and the freezing temperature inside! It was a miracle that she didn't get pneumonia. More than anything else, Bessie was tortured by indecision. She picked up each item with a trembling hand and read the label. This was not the greed of youth but the uncertainty of age. According to Bessie's figuring, today's shopping should not have taken longer than three-quarters of an hour, but two hours passed and Bessie was still not finished. When she finally brought the wagon to the cashier, it occurred to her that she had forgotten the box of oatmeal. She went back and a woman took her place in line. Later, when she paid, there was new trouble. Bessie had put the bill in the right side of her bag, but it was not there. After long rummaging, she found it in a small change purse on the opposite side. Yes, who could believe that such things were possible? If she told someone, he would think she was ready for the madhouse.

When Bessie went into the supermarket, the day was still bright; now it was drawing to a close. The sun, yellow and golden, was sinking toward the Hudson, to the hazy hills of New Jersey. The buildings on Broadway radiated the heat they had absorbed. From under gratings where the subway trains rumbled, evil-smelling fumes arose. Bessie held the heavy bag of food in one hand, and in the other she grasped her pocketbook tightly. Never had Broadway seemed to her so wild, so dirty. It stank of softened asphalt, gasoline, rotten fruit, the excrement of dogs. On the sidewalk, among torn newspapers and the butts of cigarettes, pigeons hopped about. It was difficult to understand how these creatures avoided being stepped on in the crush of passers-by. From the blazing sky a golden dust was falling. Before a storefront hung with artificial grass, men in sweated shirts poured papaya juice and pineapple juice into themselves with haste, as if trying to extinguish a fire that consumed their insides. Above their heads hung coconuts carved in the shapes of Indians. On a side street, black and white children had opened a hydrant and were splashing naked in the gutter. In the midst of that heat wave, a truck with microphones drove around blaring out shrill songs and deafening blasts about a candidate for political office. From the rear of a truck, a girl with hair that stood up like wires threw out leaflets.

It was all beyond Bessie's strength—crossing the street, waiting for the elevator, and then getting out on the fifth floor before the door slammed. Bessie put the groceries down at the threshold and searched for her keys. She used her nail file to dig the putty out of the keyhole. She put in the key and turned it. But woe, the key broke. Only the handle remained in her hand. Bessie fully grasped the catastrophe. The other people in the building had copies of their keys hanging in the superintendent's apartment, but she trusted no one—some time ago, she had ordered a new combination lock, which she was sure no master key could open. She had a duplicate key somewhere in a drawer, but with her she carried only this one. "Well, this is the end," Bessie said aloud.

There was nobody to turn to for help. The neighbors were her blood enemies. The super only waited for her downfall. Bessie's throat was so constricted that she could not even cry. She looked around, expecting to see the fiend who had delivered this latest blow. Bessie had long since made peace with death, but to die on the steps or in the streets was too harsh. And who knows how long such agony could last? She began to ponder. Was there still open somewhere a store where they fitted keys? Even if there were, what could the locksmith copy from? He would have to come up here with his tools. For that, one needed a mechanic associated with the firm which produced these special locks. If at least she had money with her. But she never carried more than she needed to spend. The cashier in the supermarket had given her back only some twenty-odd cents. "O dear Momma, I don't want to live anymore!" Bessie spoke Yiddish, amazed that she suddenly reverted to that half-forgotten tongue.

After many hesitations, Bessie decided to go back down to the street. Perhaps a hardware store or one of those tiny shops that specialize in keys was still open. She remembered that there used to be such a key stand in the neighborhood. After all, other people's keys must get broken. But what should she do with the food? It was too heavy to carry with her. There was no choice. She would have to leave the bag at the door. "They steal anyhow," Bessie said to herself. Who knows, perhaps the neighbors intentionally manipulated her lock so that she would not be able to enter the apartment while they robbed her or vandalized her belongings.

Before Bessie went down to the street, she put her ear to the door.

She heard nothing except a murmur that never stopped, the cause and origin of which Bessie could not figure out. Sometimes it ticked like a clock; other times it buzzed, or groaned—an entity imprisoned in the walls or the water pipes. In her mind Bessie said goodbye to the food, which should have been in the refrigerator, not standing here in the heat. The butter would melt, the milk would turn sour. "It's a punishment! I am cursed, cursed," Bessie muttered. A neighbor was about to go down in the elevator and Bessie signaled to him to hold the door for her. Perhaps he was one of the thieves. He might try to hold her up, assault her. The elevator went down and the man opened the door for her. She wanted to thank him, but remained silent. Why thank her enemies? These were all sly tricks.

When Bessie stepped out into the street, night had fallen. The gutter was flooded with water. The streetlamps were reflected in the black pool as in a lake. Again there was a fire in the neighborhood. She heard the wailing of a siren, the clang of fire engines. Her shoes were wet. She came out on Broadway, and the heat slapped her like a sheet of tin. She had difficulty seeing in daytime; at night she was almost blind. There was light in the stores, but what they displayed Bessie could not make out. Passers-by bumped into her, and Bessie regretted that she didn't have a cane. Nevertheless, she began to walk along, close to the windows. She passed a drugstore, a bakery; a shop of rugs, a funeral parlor, but nowhere was there a sign of a hardware store. Bessie continued on her way. Her strength was ebbing, but she was determined not to give up. What should a person do when her key was broken off—die? Perhaps apply to the police. There might be some institution that took care of such cases. But where?

There must have been an accident. The sidewalk was crowded with spectators. Police cars and an ambulance blocked the street. Someone sprayed the asphalt with a hose, probably cleaning away the blood. It occurred to Bessie that the eyes of the onlookers gleamed with an uncanny satisfaction. They enjoy other people's misfortunes, she thought. It is their only comfort in this miserable city. No, she wouldn't find anybody to help her.

She had come to a church. A few steps led to the closed door, which was protected by an overhang and darkened by shadows. Bessie was barely able to sit down. Her knees wobbled. Her shoes had begun to pinch in the toes and above the heels. A bone in her corset broke and cut into her flesh. "Well, all the Powers of Evil are upon me tonight." Hunger mixed with nausea gnawed at her. An acid fluid came up to her mouth. "Father in Heaven, it's my end." She remembered the Yiddish proverb "If one lives without a reckoning, one dies without confession." She had even neglected to write her will.

Bessie must have dozed off, because when she opened her eyes there was a late-night stillness, the street half-empty and darkened. Store windows were no longer lit. The heat had evaporated and she felt chilly under her dress. For a moment she thought that her pocketbook had been stolen, but it lay on a step below her, where it had probably slipped. Bessie tried to stretch out her hand for it; her arm was numb. Her head, which rested against the wall, felt as heavy as a stone. Her legs had become wooden. Her ears seemed to be filled with water. She lifted one of her eyelids and saw the moon. It hovered low in the sky over a flat roof, and near it twinkled a greenish star. Bessie gaped. She had almost forgotten that there was a sky, a moon, stars. Years had passed and she never looked up—always down. Her windows were hung with draperies so that the spies across the street could not see her. Well, if there was a sky, perhaps there was also a God, angels, Paradise. Where else did the souls of her parents rest? And where was Sam now? She, Bessie, had abandoned all her duties. She never visited Sam's grave in the cemetery. She didn't even light a candle on the anniversary of his death. She was so steeped in wrangling with the lower powers that she did not remember the higher ones. For the first time in years, Bessie felt the need to recite a prayer. The Almighty would have mercy on her even though she did not deserve it. Father and Mother might intercede for her on high. Some Hebrew words hung on the tip of her tongue, but she could not recall them. Then she remembered. "Hear, O Israel." But what followed? "God forgive me," Bessie said. "I deserve everything that falls on me."

It became even quieter and cooler. Traffic lights changed from red to green, but a car rarely passed. From somewhere a Negro appeared. He staggered. He stopped not far from Bessie and turned his eyes to her. Then he walked on. Bessie knew that her bag was full of important documents, but for the first time she did not care about her property. Sam had left a fortune; it all had gone for naught. She continued to save for her old age as if she were still young. "How old am I?" Bessie asked herself. "What have I accomplished in all these years? Why didn't I go somewhere, enjoy my money, help somebody?" Something in her laughed. "I was possessed, completely not myself. How else can it be explained?" Bessie was astounded. She felt as if she had awakened from a long sleep. The broken key had opened a door in her brain that had shut when Sam died.

The moon had shifted to the other side of the roof—unusually large, red, its face obliterated. It was almost cold now. Bessie shivered. She realized that she could easily get pneumonia, but the fear of death was gone, along with her fear of being homeless. Fresh breezes drifted from the Hudson River. New stars appeared in the sky. A black cat approached from the other side of the street. For a while, it stood on the edge of the sidewalk and its green eyes looked straight at Bessie. Then slowly and cautiously it drew near. For years Bessie had hated all animals—dogs, cats, pigeons, even sparrows. They carried sicknesses. They made everything filthy. Bessie believed that there was a demon in every cat. She especially dreaded an encounter with a black cat, which was always an omen of evil. But now Bessie felt love for this creature that had no home, no possessions, no doors or keys, and lived on God's bounty. Before the cat neared Bessie, it smelled her bag. Then it began to rub its back on her leg, lifting up its tail and meowing. The poor thing is hungry. I wish I could give her something. How can one hate a creature like this, Bessie wondered. O Mother of mine, I was bewitched, bewitched. I'll begin a new life. A treacherous thought ran through her mind: perhaps remarry?

The night did not pass without adventure. Once, Bessie saw a white butterfly in the air. It hovered for a while over a parked car and then took off. Bessie knew it was a soul of a newborn baby, since real butterflies do not fly after dark. Another time, she wakened to see a ball of fire, a kind of lit-up soap bubble, soar from one roof to another and sink behind it. She was aware that what she saw was the spirit of someone who had just died.

Bessie had fallen asleep. She woke up with a start. It was daybreak. From the side of Central Park the sun rose. Bessie could not see it from here, but on Broadway the sky became pink and reddish. On the building to the left, flames kindled in the windows; the panes ran and blinked like the portholes of a ship. A pigeon landed nearby. It hopped on its little red feet and pecked into something that might have been a dirty piece of stale bread or dried mud. Bessie was baffled. How do these birds live? Where do they sleep at night? And how can they survive the rains, the cold, the snow? I will go home, Bessie decided. People will not leave me in the streets.

Getting up was a torment. Her body seemed glued to the step on which she sat. Her back ached and her legs tingled. Nevertheless, she began to walk slowly toward home. She inhaled the moist morning air. It smelled of grass and coffee. She was no longer alone. From the side streets men and women emerged. They were going to work. They bought newspapers at the stand and went down into the subway. They were silent and strangely peaceful, as if they, too, had gone through a night of soul-searching and come out of it cleansed. When do they get up if they are already on their way to work now, Bessie marveled. No, not all in this neighborhood were gangsters and murderers. One young man even nodded good morning to Bessie. She tried to smile at him, realizing she had forgotten that feminine gesture she knew so well in her youth; it was almost the first lesson her mother had taught her.

She reached her building, and outside stood the Irish super, her deadly enemy. He was talking to the garbage collectors. He was a giant of a man, with a short nose, a long upper lip, sunken cheeks, and a pointed chin. His yellow hair covered a bald spot. He gave Bessie a startled look. "What's the matter, Grandma?"

Stuttering, Bessie told him what had happened to her. She showed him the handle of the key she had clutched in her hand all night.

"Mother of God!" he called out.

"What shall I do?" Bessie asked.

"I will open your door."

"But you don't have a passkey."

"We have to be able to open all doors in case of fire."

The super disappeared into his own apartment for a few minutes, then he came out with some tools and a bunch of keys on a large ring. He went up in the elevator with Bessie. The bag of food still stood on the threshold, but it looked depleted. The super busied himself at the lock. He asked, "What are these cards?"

Bessie did not answer.

"Why didn't you come to me and tell me what happened? To be roaming around all night at your age—my God!" As he poked with his tools, a door opened and a little woman in a housecoat and slippers, her hair bleached and done up in curlers, came out. She said, "What happened to you? Every time I opened the door, I saw this bag. I took out your butter and milk and put them in my refrigerator."

Bessie could barely restrain her tears. "O my good people," she said. "I didn't know that..."

The super pulled out the other half of Bessie's key. He worked a little longer. He turned a key and the door opened. The cards fell down. He entered the hallway with Bessie and she sensed the musty odor of an apartment that has not been lived in for a long time. The super said, "Next time, if something like this happens call me. That's what I'm here for."

Bessie wanted to give him a tip, but her hands were too weak to open her bag. The neighbor woman brought in the milk and butter. Bessie went into her bedroom and lay down on the bed. There was a pressure on her breast and she felt like vomiting. Something heavy vibrated up from her feet to her chest. Bessie listened to it without alarm, only curious about the whims of the body; the super and the neighbor talked, and Bessie could not make out what they were saying. The same thing had happened to her over thirty years ago when she had been given anesthesia in the hospital before an operation— the doctor and the nurse were talking but their voices seemed to come from far away and in a strange language.

Soon there was silence, and Sam appeared. It was neither day nor night—a strange twilight. In her dream, Bessie knew that Sam was dead but that in some clandestine way he had managed to get away from the grave and visit her. He was feeble and embarrassed. He could not speak. They wandered through a space without a sky, without earth, a tunnel full of debris—the wreckage of a nameless structure—a corridor dark and winding, yet somehow familiar. They came to a region where two mountains met, and the passage between shone like sunset or sunrise. They stood there hesitating and even a little ashamed. It was like that night of their honeymoon when they went to Ellenville in the Catskills and were let by the hotel owner into their bridal suite. She heard the same words he had said to them then, in the same voice and intonation: "You don't need no key here. Just enter—and *mazel tov*."

*The impulse to escape—a pogrom, persecution,
extermination—is embedded in the DNA of Jewish
culture. So deeply does it reach into the soul, that
even in those spells when prejudice goes dormant,
that ancient, itinerant gene manifests itself as an itch
to draw away from the tight circle of community—
even one thrown up as a bulwark against intolerance
and hostility. Dan Jacobson, the child of Jewish
immigrants to South Africa, shows how being Jewish
developed an almost instinctive, tropic sympathy with
members of other unjustly treated and despised racial
groups. In their aimless caperings about town, the old
Jew and the young Zulu—as unlikely a pair as Don
Quixote and Sancho Panza—find their own brands of
respite from the particular depredations to which each
is in thrall.*

the zulu and the zeide

DAN JACOBSON

old man grossman was worse than a nuisance. He was a source of constant anxiety and irritation; he was a menace to himself and to the passing motorists into whose path he would step, to the children in the streets whose games he would break up, sending them flying, to the householders who at night would approach him with clubs in their hands, fearing him a burglar; he was a butt and a jest to the African servants who would tease him on street corners.

It was impossible to keep him in the house. He would take any opportunity to slip out—a door left open meant that he was on the streets, a window unlatched was a challenge to his agility, a walk in the park was as much a game of hide-and-seek as a walk. The old man's health was good, physically; he was quite spry, and he could walk far, and he could jump and duck if he had to. And all his physical activity was put to only one purpose: to running away. It was a passion for freedom that the old man might have been said to have, could anyone have seen what joy there could have been for him in wandering aimlessly about the streets, in sitting footsore on pavements, in entering other people's homes, in stumbling behind advertisement hoardings across undeveloped building plots, in toiling up the stairs of fifteen-storey blocks of flats in which he had no business, in being brought home by large young policemen who winked at Harry Grossman, the old man's son, as they gently hauled his father out of their flying-squad cars.

"He's always been like this," Harry would say, when people asked him about his father. And when they smiled and said: "Always?" Harry would say, "Always. I know what I'm talking about. He's my father, and I know what he's like. He gave my mother enough grey hairs before her time. All he knew was to run away."

Harry's reward would come when the visitors would say: "Well, at least you're being as dutiful to him as anyone can be."

It was a reward that Harry always refused. "Dutiful? What can you do? There's nothing else you can do." Harry Grossman knew that there was nothing else he could do. Dutifulness had been his habit of life: it had had to be, having the sort of father he had, and the strain of duty had made him abrupt and begrudging: he even carried his thick, powerful shoulders curved inwards, to keep what he had to himself. He was a thick-set, bunch-faced man, with large bones, and short, jabbing gestures; he was in the prime of life, and he would point at the father from whom he had inherited his strength, and on whom the largeness of bone showed now only as so much extra leanness that the clothing had to cover, and say: "You see him? Do you know what he once did? My poor mother saved enough money to send him from the old country to South Africa; she bought clothes for him, and a ticket, and she sent him to her brother, who was already here. He was going to make enough money to bring me out, and my mother and my brother, all of us. But on the boat from Bremen to London he met some other Jews who were going to South America, and they said to him: 'Why are you going to South Africa? It's a wild country, the savages will eat you. Come to South America and you'll make a fortune.' So in London he exchanges his ticket. And we don't hear from him for six months. Six months later he gets a friend to write to my mother asking her please to send him enough money to pay for his ticket back to the old country—he's dying in Argentina, the Spaniards are killing him, he says, and he must come home. So my mother borrows from her brother to bring him back again. Instead of a fortune he brought her a new debt, and that was all."

But Harry was dutiful, how dutiful his friends had reason to see again when they would urge him to try sending the old man to a home for the aged. "No," Harry would reply, his features moving heavily and reluctantly to a frown, a pout, as he showed how little the suggestion appealed to him. "I don't like the idea. Maybe one day when he needs medical attention all the time I'll fell differently about it, but not now, not now. He wouldn't like it, he'd be unhappy. We'll look after him as long as we can. It's a job. It's something you've got to do."

More eagerly Harry would go back to a recital of the old man's past. "He couldn't even pay for his own passage out. I had to pay the loan back. We came out together—my mother wouldn't let him go by himself again, and I had to pay off her brother who advanced the money for us. I was a boy—what was I?—sixteen, seventeen, but I paid for his passage, and my own, and my own, and my mother's and then my brother's. It took me a long time, let me tell you. And then my troubles with him weren't over." Harry even reproached his father for his myopia; he could clearly enough remember his chagrin when shortly after their arrival in South Africa, after it had become clear that Harry would be able to make his way in the world and be a support to the whole family, the old man—who at that time had not really been so old—had suddenly, almost dramatically, grown so short-sighted that he had been almost blind without the glasses that Harry had had to buy for him. And Harry could remember too how he had then made a practice of losing the glasses or breaking them with the greatest frequency, until it had been made clear to him that he was no longer expected to do any work. "He doesn't do that any more. When he wants to run away now he sees to it that he's wearing his glasses. That's how he's always been. Sometimes he recognizes me, at other times, when he doesn't want to, he just doesn't know who I am."

What Harry said about his father sometimes failing to recognize him was true. Sometimes the old man would call out to his son, when he would see him at he end of a passage, "Who are you?" Or he would come upon Harry in a room and demand of him, "What do you want in my house?"

"Your house?" Harry would say, when he felt like teasing the old man. "Your house?"

"Out of my house!" the old man would shout back.

"Your house? Do you call this your house?" Harry would reply, smiling at the old man's fury.

Harry was the only one in the house who talked to the old man, and then he didn't so much talk to him, as talk of him to others. Harry's wife was a dim and silent woman, crowded out by her husband and the large-boned sons like himself that she had borne him, and she would gladly have seen the old man in an old-age home. But her husband had said no, so she put up with the old man, though for herself she could see no possible better end for him than a period of residence in a home for aged Jews which she had once visited, and which had impressed her most favourably with its glass and yellow brick, the noiseless rubber tiles in its corridors, its secluded grassed grounds, and the uniforms worn by the attendants to the establishment. But she put up with the old man; she did not talk to him. The grandchildren had nothing to do with their grandfather—they were busy at school, playing rugby and cricket, they could hardly speak Yiddish, and they were embarrassed by him in front of their friends; and when the grandfather did take any notice of them it was only to call them Boers and *goyim* and *shkotzim* in sudden quavering rages which did not disturb them at all.

The house itself—a big single-storeyed place of brick, with a corrugated iron roof above and a wide stoep all round—Harry Grossman had bought years before, and in the continual rebuilding the suburb was undergoing it was beginning to look old-fashioned. But it was solid and prosperous, and withindoors curiously masculine in appearance, like the house of a widower. The furniture was of the heaviest African woods, dark, and built to last, the passages were lined with bare linoleum, and the few pictures on the walls, big brown and grey mezzotints in heavy frames, had not been looked at for years. The servants were both men, large ignored Zulus who did their work and kept up the brown gleam of the furniture.

It was from his house that old man Grossman tried to escape. He fled through the doors and the windows and out into the wide sunlit streets of the town in Africa, where the blocks of flats were encroaching upon the single-storeyed houses behind their gardens. And in these streets he wandered.

It was Johannes, one of the Zulu servants, who suggested a way of dealing with old man Grossman. He brought to the house one afternoon Paulus, whom he described as his "brother." Harry Grossman knew enough to know that "brother" in this context could mean anything from the son of one's mother to a friend from a neighbouring *kraal*, but by the speech that Johannes made on Paulus's behalf he might indeed have been the latter's brother. Johannes had to speak for Paulus, for Paulus knew no English. Paulus was a "raw boy," as raw as a boy could possibly come. He was a muscular, moustached and bearded African, with pendulous ear-lobes showing the slits in which the tribal plugs had once hung; and on his feet he wore sandals the soles of which were cut from old motor-car tyres, the thongs from red inner tubing. He wore neither hat nor socks, but he did have a pair of khaki shorts which were too small for him, and a shirt without any buttons: buttons would in any case have been of no use for the shirt could never have closed over his chest. He swelled magnificently out of his clothing, and above there was a head carried well back, so that his beard, which had been trained to grow in two sharp points from his chin, bristled ferociously forward under his melancholy and almost mandarin-like moustache. When he smiled, as he did once or twice during Johannes's speech, he showed his white, even teeth, but for the most part he stood looking rather shyly to the side of Harry Grossman's head, with his hands behind his back and his bare knees bent a little forward, as if to show how little he was asserting himself, no matter what his "brother" might have been saying about him.

His expression did not change when Harry said that it seemed hopeless, that Paulus was too raw, and Johannes explained what the baas had just said. He nodded agreement when Johannes explained to him that the baas said that it was a pity that he knew no English. But whenever Harry looked at him, he smiled, not ingratiatingly, but simply smiling above his beard, as though saying: "Try me." Then he looked grave again as Johannes expatiated on his virtues. Johannes pleaded for his "brother." He said that the baas knew that he, Johannes, was a good boy. Would he, then, recommend to the baas a boy who was not a good boy too? The baas could see for himself, Johannes said, that Paulus was not one of these town boys, these street loafers: he was a good boy, come straight from the *kraal*. He was not a thief or a drinker. He was strong, he was a hard worker, he was clean, and he could be as gentle as a woman. If he, Johannes, were not telling the truth about all these things, then he deserved to be chased away. If Paulus failed in any single respect, then he, Johannes, would voluntarily leave the service of the baas, because he had said untrue things to the baas. But if the baas believed him, and gave Paulus his chance, then he, Johannes, would teach Paulus all the things of the house and the garden, so that Paulus would be useful to the baas in ways other than the particular task for which he was asking the baas to hire him. And, rather daringly, Johannes said that it did not matter so much if Paulus knew no English, because the old baas, the *oubaas*, knew no English either.

It was as something in the nature of a joke—almost a joke against his father—that Harry Grossman gave Paulus his chance. For Paulus was given his chance. He was given a room in the servants' quarters in the back yard, into which he brought a tin trunk painted red and black, a roll of blankets, and a guitar with a picture of a cowboy on the back. He was given a houseboy's outfit of blue denim blouse and shorts, with red piping round the edges, into which he fitted, with his beard and physique, like a king in exile in some pantomime. He was given his food three times a day, after the white people had eaten, a bar of soap every week, cast-off clothing at odd intervals, and the sum of one pound five shillings per week, five shillings of which he took, the rest being left at his request, with the baas, as savings. He had a free afternoon once a week, and he was allowed to entertain not more than two friends at any one time in his room. And in all the particulars that Johannes had enumerated, Johannes was proved reliable. Paulus was not one of these town boys, these street loafers. He did not steal or drink, he was clean and he was honest and hard-working. And he could be gentle as a woman.

It took Paulus some time to settle down to his job; he had to conquer not only his own shyness and strangeness in the new house filled with strange people—let alone the city, which, since taking occupation of his room, he had hardly dared to enter—but also the hostility of old man Grossman, who took immediate fright at Paulus and redoubled his efforts to get away from the house upon Paulus's entry into it. As it happened, the first result of this persistence on the part of the old man was that Paulus was able to get the measure of the job, for he came to it with a willingness of spirit that the old man could not vanquish, but could only teach. Paulus had been given no instructions, he had merely been told to see that the old man did not get himself into trouble, and after a few days of bewilderment Paulus found his way. He simply went along with the old man.

At first he did so cautiously, following the old man at a distance, for he knew the other had no trust in him. But later he was able to follow the old man openly; still later he was able to walk side by side with him, and the old man did not try to escape from him. When old man Grossman went out, Paulus went too, and there was no longer any need for the doors and windows to be watched, or the police to be telephoned. The young bearded Zulu and the old bearded Jew from Lithuania walked together in the streets of the town that was strange to them both; together they looked over the fences of the large gardens and into the shining foyers of the blocks of flats; together they stood on the pavements of the main arterial roads and watched the cars and trucks rush between the tall buildings; together they walked in the small, sandy parks, and when the old man was tired Paulus saw to it that he sat on a bench and rested. They could not sit on the bench together, for only whites were allowed to sit on the benches, but Paulus would squat on the ground at the old man's feet and wait until he judged the old man had rested long enough, before moving on again. Together they stared into the windows of the suburban shops, and though neither of them could read the signs outside the shops, the advertisements on billboards, the traffic signs at the side of the road, Paulus learned to wait for the traffic lights to change from red to green before crossing a street, and together they stared at the Coca-cola girls and the advertisements for beer and the cinema posters. On a piece of cardboard which Paulus carried in the pocket of his blouse Harry had had one of his sons print the old man's name and address, and whenever Paulus was uncertain of the way home, he would approach an African or a friendly-looking white man and show him the card, and try his best to follow the instructions, or at least the gesticulations which were all of the answers of the white men that meant anything to him. But there were enough Africans to be found, usually, who were more sophisticated than himself, and though they teased him for his "rawness" and for holding the sort of job he had, they helped him too. And neither Paulus nor old man Grossman were aware that when they crossed a street hand-in-hand, as they sometimes did when the traffic was particularly heavy, there were white men who averted their eyes from the sight of this degradation, which could come upon a white man when he was old and senile and dependent.

Paulus knew only Zulu, the old man knew only Yiddish, so there was no language in which they could talk to one another. But they talked all the same: they both explained, commented and complained to each other of the things they saw around them, and often they agreed with one another, smiling and nodding their heads and explaining again with their hands what each happened to be talking about. They both seemed to believe that they were talking about the same things, and often they undoubtedly were, when they lifted their heads sharply to see an aeroplane cross the blue sky between two buildings, or when they reached the top of a steep road and turned to look back the way they had come, and saw below them the clean impervious towers of the city thrust nakedly against the sky in brand-new piles of concrete and glass and face-brick. Then down they would go again, among the houses and the gardens where the beneficent climate encouraged both palms and oak trees to grow indiscriminately among each other—as they did in the garden of the house to which, in the evenings, Paulus and old man Grossman would eventually return.

In and about the house Paulus soon became as indispensable to the old man as he was on their expeditions out of it. Paulus dressed him and bathed him and trimmed his beard, and when the old man woke distressed in the middle of the night it would be for Paulus that he would call—"*Der schwarzer*," he would shout (for he never learned Paulus's name), "*vo's der schwarzer*"—and Paulus would change his sheets and pyjamas and put him back to bed again. "Baas *Zeide*," Paulus called the old man, picking up the Yiddish word for grandfather from the children of the house.

And that was something that Harry Grossman told everyone of. For Harry persisted in regarding the arrangement as a kind of joke, and the more the arrangement succeeded the more determinedly did he try to spread the joke, so that it should be a joke not only against his father but a joke against Paulus too. It had been a joke that his father should be looked after by a raw Zulu: it was going to be a joke that the Zulu was successful at it. "Baas *Zeide!* That's what *der schwarz-er* calls him—have you ever heard the like of it? And you should see the two of them, walking about in the streets hand-in-hand like two schoolgirls. Two clever ones, *der schwarzer* and my father going for a promenade, and between them I tell you you wouldn't be able to find out what day of the week or what time of day it is."

And when people said, "Still that Paulus seems a very good boy," Harry would reply:

"Why shouldn't he be? With all his knowledge, are there so many better jobs that he'd be able to find? He keeps the old man happy— very good, very nice, but don't forget that that's what he's paid to do. What does he know any better to do, a simple kaffir from the *kraal*? He knows he's got a good job, and he'd be a fool if he threw it away. Do you think," Harry would say, and this too would insistently be part of the joke, "if I had nothing else to do with my time I wouldn't be able to make the old man happy?" Harry would look about his sitting-room, where the floorboards bore the weight of his furniture, or when they sat on the stoep he would measure with his glance the spacious garden aloof from the street beyond the hedge.

"I've got other things to do. And I had other things to do, plenty of them, all my life, and not only for myself." What these things were that he had had to do all his life would send him back to his joke. "No, I think the old man has just found his level in *der schwarzer*— and I don't think *der schwarzer* could cope with anything else."

Harry teased the old man to his face too, about his "black friend," and he would ask his father what he would do if Paulus went away; once he jokingly threatened to send the Zulu away. But the old man didn't believe the threat, for Paulus was in the house when the threat was made, and the old man simply left his son and went straight to Paulus's room, and sat there with Paulus for security. Harry did not follow him: he would never have gone into any of his servants' rooms least of all that of Paulus. For though he made a joke of him to others, to Paulus himself Harry always spoke gruffly, unjokingly, with no patience. On that day he had merely shouted after the old man, "Another time he won't be there."

Yet it was strange to see how Harry Grossman would always be drawn to the room in which he knew his father and Paulus to be. Night after night he came into the old man's bedroom when Paulus was dressing or undressing the old man; almost as often Harry stood in the steamy, untidy bathroom when the old man was being bathed. At these times he hardly spoke, he offered no explanation of his presence: he stood dourly and silently in the room, in his customary powerful and begrudging stance, with one hand clasping the wrist of the other and both supporting his waist, and he watched Paulus at work. The backs of Paulus's hands were smooth and black and hairless, they were paler on the palms and at the finger-nails, and they worked deftly about the body of the old man, who was submissive under the ministrations of the other. At first Paulus had sometimes smiled at Harry while he worked, with his straightforward, even smile in which there was no invitation to a complicity in patronage, but rather an encouragement to Harry to draw forward. But after the first few evenings of this work that Harry had watched, Paulus no longer smiled at his master. And while he worked Paulus could not restrain himself, even under Harry's stare, from talking in a soft, continuous flow of Zulu, to encourage the old man and to exhort him to be helpful and to express his pleasure in how well the work was going. When Paulus would at last wipe the gleaming soap-flakes from his dark hands he would sometimes, when the old man was tired, stoop low and with a laugh pick up the old man and carry him easily down the passage to his bedroom. Harry would follow; he would stand in the passage and watch the burdened, barefooted Zulu until the door of his father's room closed behind them both.

Only once did Harry wait on such an evening for Paulus to reappear from his father's room. Paulus had already come out, had passed him in the narrow passage, and had already subduedly said: "Good night, baas," before Harry called suddenly:

"Hey! Wait!"

"Baas," Paulus said, turning his head. Then he came quickly to Harry. "Baas," he said again, puzzled and anxious to know why his baas, who so rarely spoke to him, should suddenly have called him like this, at the end of the day, when his work was over.

Harry waited again before speaking, waited long enough for Paulus to say: "Baas?" once more, and to move a little closer, and to lift his head for a moment before letting it drop respectfully down.

"The *oubaas* was tired tonight," Harry said. "Where did you take him? What did you do with him?"

"Baas?" Paulus said quickly. Harry's tone was so brusque that the smile Paulus gave asked for no more than a moment's remission of the other's anger.

But Harry went on loudly: "You heard what I said. What did you do with him that he looked so tired?"

"Baas—I—" Paulus was flustered, and his hands beat in the air for a moment, but with care, so that he would not touch his baas. "Please baas." He brought both hands to his mouth, closing it forcibly. He flung his hands away. "Johannes," he said with relief, and he had already taken the first step down the passage to call his interpreter.

"No!" Harry called. "You mean you don't understand what I say? I know you don't," Harry shouted, though in fact he had forgotten until Paulus had reminded him. The sight of Paulus's startled, puzzled, and guilty face before him filled him with a lust to see this man, this nurse with the face and the figure of a warrior, look more startled, puzzled, and guilty yet; and Harry knew that it could so easily be done, it could be done simply by talking to him in the language he could not understand. "You're a fool," Harry said. "You're like a child. You understand nothing, and it's just as well for you that you need nothing. You'll always be where you are, running to do what the white baas tells you to do. Look how you stand! Do you think I understood English when I came here?" Harry said, and then with contempt, using one of the few Zulu words he knew: "*Hamba*! Go! Do you think I want to see you?"

"*Au* baas!" Paulus exclaimed in distress. He could not remonstrate; he could only open his hands in a gesture to show that he knew neither the words Harry used, nor in what he had been remiss that Harry should have spoken in such angry tones to him. But Harry gestured him away, and had the satisfaction of seeing Paulus shuffle off like a schoolboy.

Harry was the only person who knew that he and his father had quarrelled shortly before the accident that ended the old man's life took place; this was something that Harry was to keep secret for the rest of this life.

Late in the afternoon they quarrelled, after Harry had come back from the shop out of which he made his living. Harry came back to find his father wandering about the house, shouting for *der schwarzer*, and his wife complaining that she had already told the old man at least five times that *der schwarzer* was not in the house: it was Paulus' afternoon off.

Harry went to his father, and when his father came eagerly to him, he too told the old man, "*Der schwarzer's* not here." So the old man, with Harry following, turned away and continued going from room to room, peering in through the doors. "*Der schwarzer's* not here," Harry said. "What do you want him for?"

Still the old man ignored him. He went down the passage towards the bedrooms. "What do you want him for?" Harry called after him.

The old man went into every bedroom, still shouting for *der schwarzer*. Only when he was in his own bare bedroom did he look at Harry. "Where's *der schwarzer*?" he asked.

"I've told you ten times I don't know where he is. What do you want him for?"

"I want *der schwarzer*."

"I know you want him. But he isn't here."

"I want *der schwarzer*."

"Do you think I haven't heard you? He isn't here."

"Bring him to me," the old man said.

"I can't bring him to you. I don't know where he is." Then Harry steadied himself against his own anger. He said quietly: "Tell me what you want. I'll do it for you. I'm here, I can do what *der schwarz-er* can do for you."

"Where's *der schwarzer?*"

"I've told you he isn't here," Harry shouted, the angrier for his previous moment's patience. "Why don't you tell me what you want? What's the matter with me—can't you tell me what you want?"

"I want *der schwarzer.*"

"Please," Harry said. He threw out his arms towards his father, but the gesture was abrupt, almost as though he were thrusting his father away from him. "Why can't you ask it of me? You can ask me—haven't I done enough for you already? Do you want to go for a walk?—I'll take you for a walk. What do you want? Do you want—do you want—?" Harry could not think what his father might want. "I'll do it," he said. "You don't need *der schwarzer.*"

Then Harry saw that his father was weeping. The old man was standing up and weeping, with his eyes hidden behind the thick glasses that he had to wear: his glasses and his beard made his face a mask of age, as though time had left him nothing but the frame of his body on which the clothing could hang, and this mask of his face above. But Harry knew when the old man was weeping—he had seen him crying too often before, when they had found him at the end of a street after he had wandered away, or even, years earlier, when he had lost another of the miserable jobs that seemed to be the only one he could find in a country in which his son had, later, been able to run a good business, drive a large car, own a big house.

"Father," Harry asked, "what have I done? Do you think I've sent *der schwarzer* away?" Harry saw his father turn away, between the narrow bed and the narrow wardrobe. "He's coming—" Harry said, but he could not look at his father's back, he could not look at his father's hollowed neck, on which the hairs that Paulus had clipped glistened above the pale brown discolorations of age—Harry could not look at the neck turned stiffly away from him while he had to try to promise the return of the Zulu. Harry dropped his hands and walked out of the room.

No one knew how the old man managed to get out of the house and through the front gate without having been seen. But he did manage it, and in the road he was struck down. Only a man on a bicycle struck him down, but it was enough, and he died a few days later in the hospital.

Harry's wife wept, even the grandsons wept; Paulus wept. Harry himself was stony, and his bunched, protuberant features were immovable; they seemed locked upon the bones of his face. A few days after the funeral he called Paulus and Johannes into the kitchen and said to Johannes: "Tell him he must go. His work is finished."

Johannes translated for Paulus, and then, after Paulus had spoken, he turned to Harry. "He says, yes baas." Paulus kept his eyes on the ground; he did not look up even when Harry looked directly at him, and Harry knew that this was not out of fear or shyness, but out of courtesy for his master's grief—which was what they could not but be talking of, when they talked of his work.

"Here's his pay." Harry thrust a few notes towards Paulus, who took them in his cupped hands, and retreated.

Harry waited for them to go, but Paulus stayed in the room, and consulted with Johannes in a low voice. Johannes turned to his master. "He says, baas, that the baas still has his savings."

Harry had forgotten about Paulus's savings. He told Johannes that he had forgotten, and that he did not have enough money at the moment, but would bring the money the next day. Johannes translated and Paulus nodded gratefully. Both he and Johannes were subdued by the death there had been in the house.

And Harry's dealings with Paulus were over. He took what was to have been his last look at Paulus, but this look stirred him again against the Zulu. As harshly as he told Paulus that he had to go, so now, implacably, seeing Paulus in the mockery and simplicity of his houseboy's clothing, to feed his anger to the very end Harry said: "Ask him what he's been saving for. What's he going to do with the fortune he's made?"

Johannes spoke to Paulus and came back with a reply. "He says, baas, that he is saving to bring his wife and children from Zululand to Johannesburg. He is saving, baas," Johannes said, for Harry had not seemed to understand, "to bring his family to this town also."

The two Zulus were bewildered to know why it should have been at that moment that Harry Grossman's clenched, fist-like features should suddenly seem to have fallen from one another, nor why he should have stared with such guilt and despair at Paulus, while he cried, "What else could I have done? I did my best," before the first tears came.

Drugs, sex, and rock 'n' roll ruled supreme as the
escape hatches of the "turn on, tune in, drop out"
adepts of the 1960s. At the same time that Jimmy
Hendrix, Cat Stevens, and the Rolling Stones took
their quest for this 3-D nirvana-of-the-senses to
Morocco, the intensely reclusive, cerebral Elias Canetti
joined a film crew in Marrakesh during the last years
of French rule. Not surprisingly, the sixty-two-year-old
philosopher-aphorist did not drop acid. Instead, his
route to spiritual liberation ran through the intellect
and the ear. Beguiled by the haunting sounds of the
souk, Canetti came to understand the human voice as
the pure expression of the self escaping from the
limitations of the body. In this profoundly moving and
beautiful meditation from his "Record of a Visit,"
Canetti looks at language and probes its capacity to
define us as human, and thereby, to lock us,
unalterably, in the condition of being human.

from *the voices of marrakesh*

ELIAS CANETTI

The cries of the blind

here i am, trying to give an account of something, and as
soon as I pause I realize that I have not yet said anything at all. A
marvellously luminous, viscid substance is left behind in me, defying
words. Is it the language I did not understand there, and that must
now gradually find its translation in me? There were incidents,
images, sounds, the meaning of which is only now emerging; that
words neither recorded nor edited; that are beyond words, deeper
and more equivocal than words.

A dream: a man who unlearns the world's languages until
nowhere on earth does he understand what people are saying.

What is there in language? What does it conceal? What does it rob
one of? During the weeks I spent in Morocco I made no attempt to
acquire either Arabic or any of the Berber languages. I wanted to
lose none of the force of those foreign-sounding cries. I wanted
sounds to affect me as much as lay in their power, unmitigated by
deficient and artificial knowledge on my part. I had not read a thing
about the country. Its customs were as unknown to me as its people.
The little that one picks up in the course of one's life about every
country and every people fell away in the first few hours.

But the word "Allah" remained; there was no getting round that.
With it I was equipped for that part of my experience that was most
ubiquitous and insistent, and most persistent: the blind. Travelling,
one accepts everything; indignation stays at home. One looks, one
listens, one is roused to enthusiasm by the most dreadful things
because they are new. Good travellers are heartless.

Last year, approaching Vienna after a fifteen-year absence, I passed through *Blindenmarkt*—in English "Blind Market," as one might say "Slave Market"—a place whose existence I had never previously suspected. The name struck me like a whiplash, and it has stayed with me since. This year, arriving in Marrakesh, I suddenly found myself among the blind. There were hundreds of them, more than one could count, most of them beggars. A group of them, sometimes eight, sometimes ten, stood close together in a row in the market, and their hoarse, endlessly repeated chant was audible a long way off. I stood in front of them, as still as they were, and was never quite sure whether they sensed my presence. Each man held out a wooden alms dish, and when someone tossed something in the proffered coin passed from hand to hand, each man feeling it, each man testing it, before one of them, whose office it was, finally put it into a pouch. They *felt* together, just as they murmured and called together.

All the blind offer one the name of God, and by giving alms one can acquire a claim on him. They begin with God, they end with God, they repeat God's name ten thousand times a day. All their cries contain a declension of his name, but the call they have once settled on always remains the same. The calls are acoustical arabesques around God, but how much more impressive than optical ones. Some rely on his name alone and cry nothing else. There is a terrible defiance in this; God seemed to me like a wall that they were always storming in the same place. I believe those beggars keep themselves alive more by their formulas than by the yield of their begging.

Repetition of the same cry characterizes the crier. You commit him to memory, you know him, from now on he is there; and he is there in a sharply defined capacity: in his cry. You will learn no more from him; he shields himself, his cry being also his border. In this one place he is precisely what he cries, no more, no less: a beggar, blind. But the cry is also a multiplication; the rapid, regular repetition makes of him a group. There is a peculiar energy of asking in it; he is asking on behalf of many and collecting for them all. "Consider all beggars! Consider all beggars! God will bless you for every beggar you give to."

It is said that the poor will enter paradise five hundred years before the rich. By giving alms you buy a bit of paradise from the poor. When someone has died you follow on foot, with or without trilling mourners, swiftly to the grave, in order that the dead shall soon achieve bliss. *"Blind men sing the creed."*

Back from Morocco, I once sat down with eyes closed and legs crossed in a corner of my room and tried to say "Alláh! Alláh! Alláh!" over and over again for half an hour at the right speed and volume. I tried to imagine myself going on saying it for a whole day and a large part of the night; taking a short sleep and then beginning again; doing the same thing for days and weeks, months and years; growing old and older and living like that, and clinging tenaciously to that life; flying into a fury if something disturbed me in that life; wanting nothing else, sticking to it utterly.

I understood the seduction there is in a life that reduces everything to the simplest kind of repetition. How much or how little variety was there in the activities of the craftsmen I had watched at work in their little booths? In the haggling of the merchant? In the steps of the dancer? In the countless cups of peppermint tea that all the visitors here take? How much variety is there in money? How much in hunger?

I understood what those blind beggars really are: the saints of repetition. Most of what for us still eludes repetition is eradicated from their lives. There is the spot where they squat or stand. There is the unchanging cry. There is the limited number of coins they can hope for. Three or four different denominations. There are the givers, of course, who are different, but blind men do not see them, and their way of expressing their thanks makes sure that the givers too are all made the same.

The unseen

At twilight I went to the great square in the middle of the city, and what I sought there were not its colour and bustle, those I was familiar with, I sought a small, brown bundle on the ground consisting not even of a voice but of a single sound. This was a deep, long-drawn-out, buzzing "e-e-e-e-e-e-e-e-." It did not diminish, it did not increase, it just went on and on; beneath all the thousands of calls and cries in the square it was always audible. It was the most unchanging sound in the Djema el Fna, remaining the same all evening and from evening to evening.

While still a long way off I was already listening for it. A restlessness drove me there that I cannot satisfactorily explain. I would have gone to the square in any case, there was so much there to attract me; nor did I ever doubt I would find it each time, with all that went with it. Only for this voice, reduced to a single sound, did I feel something akin to fear. It was at the very edge of the living; the life that engendered it consisted of nothing but that sound. Listening greedily, anxiously, I invariably reached a point in my walk, in exactly the same place, where I suddenly became aware of it like the buzzing of an insect:

"e-e-e-e-e-e-e-"

I felt a mysterious calm spread through my body, and whereas my steps had been hesitant and uncertain hitherto I now, all of a sudden, made determinedly for the sound. I knew where it came from. I knew the small, brown bundle on the ground, of which I had never seen anything more than a piece of dark, coarse cloth. I had never seen the mouth from which the "e-e-e-e-e-e-" issued; nor the eye; nor the cheek; nor any part of the face. I could not have said whether it was the face of a blind man or whether it could see. The brown, soiled cloth was pulled right down over the head like a hood, concealing everything. The creature—as it must have been—squatted on the ground, its back arched under the material. There was not much of the creature there, it seemed slight and feeble, that was all one could conjecture. I had no idea how tall it was because I had never seen it standing. What there was of it on the ground kept so low that one would have stumbled over it quite unsuspectingly, had the sound ever stopped. I never saw it come, I never saw it go; I do not know whether it was brought and put down there or whether it walked there by itself.

The place it had chosen was by no means sheltered. It was the most open part of the square and there was an incessant coming and going on all sides of the little brown heap. On busy evenings it disappeared completely behind people's legs, and although I knew exactly where it was and could always hear the voice I had difficulty in finding it. But then the people dispersed, and it was still in its place when all around it, far and wide, the square was empty. Then it lay there in the darkness like an old and very dirty garment that someone had wanted to get rid of and had surreptitiously dropped in the midst of all the people where no one would notice. Now, however, the people had dispersed and only the bundle lay there. I never waited until it got up or was fetched. I slunk away in the darkness with a choking feeling of helplessness and pride.

The helplessness was in regard to myself. I sensed that I would never do anything to discover the bundle's secret. I had a dread of its shape; and since I could give it no other I left it lying there on the ground. When I was getting close I took care not to bump into it, as if I might hurt or endanger it. It was there every evening, and every evening my heart stood still when I first distinguished the sound, and it stood still again when I caught sight of the bundle. How it got there and how it got away again were matters more sacred to me than my own movements. I never spied on it and I do not know where it disappeared to for the rest of the night and the following day. It was something apart, and perhaps it saw itself as such. I was sometimes tempted to touch the brown hood very lightly with one finger—the creature was bound to notice, and perhaps it had a second sound with which it would have responded. But this temptation always succumbed swiftly to my helplessness.

I have said that another feeling choked me as I slunk away: pride. I was proud of the bundle because it was alive. What it thought to itself as it breathed down there, far below other people, I shall never know. The meaning of its call remained as obscure to me as its whole existence: but it was alive, and every day at the same time, there it was. I never saw it pick up the coins that people threw it; they did not throw many, there were never more than two or three coins lying there. Perhaps it had no arms with which to reach for the coins. Perhaps it had no tongue with which to form the "l" of "Allah" and to it the name of God was abbreviated to "e-e-e-e-e." But it was alive, and with a diligence and persistence that were unparalleled it uttered its one sound, uttered it hour after hour, until it was the only sound in the whole enormous square, the sound that outlived all others.

The pieces in this collection were taken from the editions listed below.

Amen, Grover. "Escape." Originally appeared in *The New Yorker*, April 20, 1963.

Babel, Isaac. *Collected Stories*. New York: Penguin Books, 1998.

Brodkey, Harold. *Stories in an Almost Classical Mode*. New York: Knopf, 1988.

Bunin, Ivan. *The Gentleman from San Francisco*. New York: Knopf, 1934.

Canetti, Elias. *The Voices of Marrakesh*. New York: Continuum Publishers, 1981.

Chabon, Michael. *The Amazing Adventures of Kavalier & Clay*. New York: Random House, 2000.

Churchill, Winston. *Young Winston's Wars: The Original Dispatches of Winston S. Churchill*. New York: Viking Press, 1972.

Finkel, Michael. "Desperate Passage." Originally appeared in *The New York Times Magazine*, June 18, 2000.

Ginzburg, Eugenia Semyonovna (trans. Paul Stevenson, Max Hayward). *Journey into the Whirlwind*. New York: Harcourt Brace & Company, 1967.

Greene, Barbara. *Too Late to Turn Back*. New York: Viking Press, 1981.

Larsen, Nella. *An Intimation of Things Distant: The Collected Fiction of Nella Larsen*. New York: Anchor Books, 1992.

Lawrence, D.H. *The Complete Short Stories Vol. III*. New York: Viking Books, 1961.

Litvinoff, Emanuel (editor). *The Penguin Book of Jewish Short Stories*. New York: Penguin Books, 1979. (For "The Zulu and the Zeide" by Dan Jacobson.)

Nabokov, Vladimir. *Speak, Memory*. New York: Putnam Books, 1966.

Parsons, Elizabeth. "The Nightingale Sings." From *55 Short Stories from The New Yorker*. New York: Simon & Schuster, 1949.

Saunders, George. "The Barber's Unhappiness." Originally appeared in *The New Yorker*, December 20, 1999.

Schickler, David. "Jamaica." Originally appeared in *The New Yorker*, January 7, 2002.

Updike, John (editor). *The Best American Short Stories of the Century.* New York: Houghton Mifflin Company, 1999. (For "The Things They Carried" by Tim O'Brien and "The Key" by Isaac Bashevis Singer.)

Updike, John. *The Afterlife and Other Stories.* New York: Knopf, 1994.

Warner, Sylvia Townsend. "A View of Exmoor." From *55 Short Stories from The New Yorker.* New York: Simon & Schuster, 1949.

acknowledgments

Escapade

As escapes, stories have always been our favorite alternatives to escapades. For one, they're everywhere: in books, in overheard conversations, even on the backs of milk cartons. For another, they get us into a lot less trouble than playing hooky from work. The idea for this collection materialized on the sun-warmed deck of our beach cottage, in the company of friends—raconteurs all—who, inspired by a glass of wine and a hefty dose of conviviality, gilded the lily of escape with their own favorite tales.

To Karen Brooks, Lynn Nesmith, Bill LeBlond, Adair Lara, and, especially, to Matthew Lore, our muse and extraordinary guide—our heartfelt thanks! To Richard Pine, our visionary agent, who, though not with us in person, but in spirit that autumn afternoon, we raise a toast of gratitude. We thank Christopher DiLascia for sharing his poem "Escape"; Tanya Supina for reading all the stories; and, above all, Bianca Lencek-Bosker, for always having an opinion.

For their suggestions and responses, we owe a big debt of gratitude to Zhenya Bershtein, Paul Bragdon, Susan Fillin-Yeh, Catherine Glass, Louise Hornby, Christian Hubert, Roger Porter, Jud Rosengrant, Ellen Stauder, Peter Steinberger, Monica Wesolowska, and Celeste Wesson.

For help with logistics, we gratefully acknowledge Oriana Walker, Ryan Stuewe, Olga Kopaigorodskaia, and Lois Hobbs, as well as the staffs at Reed College Library, Multnomah County Public Library, and Powell's Books.

No one is more deserving of our appreciation than the production staff: Shawneric Hachey, for being the virtuoso of permissions; Sue McCloskey, for being always on target, always on track; Pauline Neuwirth, for her elegant, light touch with book design; Mittie Hellmich, for her ecstatically escapist photographs; and Howard Grossman for coming through with a cover that says it all. And, yes, to the authors of the stories: "Thanks." We couldn't have done it without you.

Grover Amen wrote for *The New Yorker* and published a collection of poems, *F Train Ramble*.

Isaac Babel (1894–1940) was born in the Jewish ghetto of Odessa, Ukraine. A short story writer and playwright who was a correspondent with the Red Army forces of Semyon Budyonny during the Russian civil war, Babel's fame is based on his stories of the Jews in Odessa and his novel *Red Cavalry*. In 1940, he was tried and convicted of espionage and shot in a Siberian prison camp on Stalin's orders. His charges were posthumously cleared in 1954. He was the first major Russian Jewish writer to write in Russian.

Harold Brodkey (1930–1996) was born in Staunton, Illinois, grew up in Missouri, and was graduated from Harvard College. In 1954 his first story appeared in *The New Yorker*, where his work continued to appear for many years. His books included *First Love and Other Sorrows, Stories in an Almost Classical Mode, The Runaway Soul*, and *This Wild Darkness*.

Ivan Bunin (1870–1953) was born in Voronezh, Russia. A poet, short story writer, translator, and novelist, he wrote about the decay of Russian nobility and of peasant life, and in 1933 was the first Russian to receive the Nobel Prize for Literature. Bunin emigrated to France in 1920 and was condemned by the Russian government as a traitor. He died impoverished in exile in the South of France in 1953.

Elias Canetti (1905–1994) was awarded the Nobel Prize in Literature in 1981. His writings include a novel, *Auto-da-Fé*, and three volumes of memoirs, *The Tongue Set Free, The Torch in My Ear*, and *The Play of the Eyes*.

Michael Chabon is the author of two collections of stories, *A Model World* and *Werewolves in Their Youth*, and three novels, *The Mysteries of Pittsburgh, Wonder Boys*, and *The Amazing Adventures of Kavalier & Clay*, for which he won the Pulitzer Prize. He lives with his family in northern California.

Winston Churchill (1874–1965) was Britain's most celebrated statesman, military leader, and strategist. He is the author of several books, including *The History of the English Speaking People,* which earned him the Nobel Prize for Literature in 1953.

Michael Finkel is a contributing writer to *The New York Times Magazine* and *National Geographic Adventure* and is the author of *Alpine Circus.*

Eugenia Semyonova Ginzburg (1896–1980), history professor at the University of Kazan, was arrested in 1937, during the Stalin purges, on trumped-up charges of "participation in a Trotskyist terrorist group." Separated from her two young sons and husband, she spent two years in solitary confinement in the infamous Butyrki Prison in Moscow and another eighteen years in hard labor camps and exile. Her two-volume autobiography, translated as *Journey into the Whirlwind* and *Within the Whirlwind,* is a moving record of the disenchantment and rebirth of a once-loyal member of the Communist Party, and of the despair and suffering of a wife and mother. It was never published openly in the Soviet Union.

Barbara Greene was born in 1907 on a coffee plantation in Brazil, matured in London, and, at twenty-seven, set off for Liberia with her cousin Graham Greene, whom she surpassed in better surviving the travails of travel in Africa— and in writing about them. In the late 1930s, she settled in Germany, marrying Count Rudolph Strachwitz and encouraged him in his conspiratorial work against Hitler. *Too Far to Turn Back: Barbara and Graham Greene in Liberia* is her best-known book.

Dan Jacobson was born in Johannesburg to Jewish Lithuanian parents. He has worked as a teacher in London, a journalist in South Africa and has also spent some time on a kibbutz in Israel. He moved to England in 1958 where he pursued an academic career, starting as a lecturer at University College London and becoming Emeritus Professor in 1994.

Nella Larsen (1891–1964) was the author of two novels and several short stories. She received a Guggenheim fellowship to write a third novel in 1930 but, unable to find a publisher for it, she disappeared from the literary scene and worked as a nurse until her death.

D.H. Lawrence (1885–1930) was an English novelist and poet ranked among the most influential and controversial literary figures of the twentieth century. In his more than forty books, including *Lady Chatterley's Lover, The Rainbow,* and *Women in Love,* he celebrated his vision of the natural, whole human being, opposing the artificiality of modern industrial society with its dehumanization of life and love.

Vladimir Nabokov (1899–1977) was born in St. Petersburg, Russia. His family fled to Germany in 1919, during the Bolshevik Revolution. He studied French and Russian at Trinity College in Cambridge, then lived in Berlin and Paris, where he launched his literary career. In 1940 he moved to the United States and achieved renown as a novelist, poet, critic, and translator. He taught literature at Wellesley, Stanford, Cornell, and Harvard. In 1961 he moved to

Montreux, Switzerland, where he died in 1977.

Tim O'Brien graduated in 1968 from Macalester College in St. Paul. He served as a foot soldier in Vietnam from 1969 to 1970, after which he pursued graduate studies in Government at Harvard University, then later worked as a national affairs reporter for the *Washington Post*. He now lives in Massachusetts.

Elizabeth Parsons was born in Hartford, Connecticut, and lived and worked at various periods of her life in and near Boston and in Maine. Her stories appeared in *The New Yorker, Harper's Bazaar,* and several other magazines. "The Nightingales Sing" appeared in her first book, *An Afternoon.*

George Saunders's stories have appeared in *The New Yorker, Story*, and *Harper's*, and have received three National Magazine Awards and appeared three times in the O. Henry Awards collections. He teaches in the Creative Writing Program at Syracuse University.

David Schickler is a graduate of the Columbia M.F.A. program. His stories have appeared in *The New Yorker, Tin House,* and *Zoetrope.* He lives in New York.

Isaac Bashevis Singer (1904–1991) was the author of many novels, short stories, children's books, and three memoirs. He won the Nobel Prize for Literature in 1978.

John Updike, born in 1932 in Shillington, Pennsylvania, is the author of more than fifty books, including collections of short stories, poems, and criticisms. His novels have won the Pulitzer Prize (twice), the National Book Award, the National Book Critics Circle Award, the Rosenthal Award, and the Howells Medal. His most recent books include *Gertrude and Claudius* and *More Matter.*

Sylvia Townsend Warner (1893–1978) was a poet, short story writer, frequent *New Yorker* contributor, and novelist, as well as an authority on early English music. She lived for many years with her companion, Valentine Ackland, in a house in the country in Dorset, England. Her many books include *Mr. Fortune's Maggot, The Corner that Held Them,* and *Kingdoms of Elfin.*

Joseph Wechsberg was born in Czechoslovakia in 1907. After working as a translator, he published his first essay for *The New Yorker* in 1948. The author of twenty-seven books, Wechsberg died in Vienna in 1983.

about the editors

Lena Lenček and Gideon Bosker specialize in popular culture and have co-written or edited more than twelve books, including *The Beach: The History of Paradise on Earth,* a *New York Times* Notable Book for 1998, *Beach: Stories by the Sand and Sea,* and, *Sail Away: Stories of Escaping to Sea.* Lenček is a professor of Russian and the humanities at Reed College, and Bosker, a physician, is an assistant clinical professor of medicine at Yale University School of Medicine. They live in Portland, Oregon.

4975